Alexa crossed t

He had just unzipped a giant suitcase—black, of course—and draped a clump of black, button down shirts on the bed. Some looked to be made of cotton, others of a silkier material.

"Are you color blind?" she wanted to know.

He glanced up. "You're here to help me unpack?"

"Of course not!" Alexa felt embarrassed, but didn't retreat. "We need to hash out rules so we can live in peace."

He pulled out a pile of black pants. Some jeans, some slacks.

"Would you stop that?" she demanded. "I'm trying to have a serious conversation."

"I can't unpack at the same time?"

Alexa gritted her teeth. "I have no desire to see any of your black...unmentionables."

An actual smile curled his lips, and he stopped pulling items from his suitcase. "Then wait in the sitting area. I'll be five minutes."

Alexa narrowed her eyes. She didn't want to stay here, but she didn't want to retreat, either. And she wanted to assert her rules first—before the bodyguard had a chance to make a power grab. "I'll make it snappy," she said, averting her eyes as he pulled smaller black items from the suitcase and tucked them in the dresser. "I have one rule. You leave me alone, and I'll leave you alone."

"Fine." Jamison pulled a thick book from the bottomless suitcase and placed it on the bedside table. What was that? *War and Peace*? Certainly appropriate for their living situation.

"Well then," Alexa said, pleased. "I'll leave you to sort your outfits by color. I'm never sure—does black silk go with black cotton?" With this saucy comment, which likely sailed right over his unfashionable head, she turned to leave.

"I have a rule."

Alexa turned back. She should have known her triumph had been too easy.

"You don't leave this apartment without me."

Also by Jennette Green

The Commander's Desire
Murder by Nightmare
(a novelette)

Her Reluctant ***Bodyguard***

Jennette Green

Diamond Press

This is a work of fiction. Names, characters, places, and incidents either are the product of the author's imagination or are used fictitiously, and any resemblance to actual persons, living or dead, business establishments, events, or locales is entirely coincidental.

HER RELUCTANT BODYGUARD

A Diamond Press book / published in arrangement with the author

Copyright © 2010 by Jennette Green
Cover design by Rae Monet

All rights reserved.

This book, or parts thereof, may not be reproduced in any form without permission, except in the case of brief quotations embodied in critical articles or reviews. The scanning, uploading, and distribution of this book via the Internet or any other means without the permission of the publisher is illegal and punishable by law. Please purchase only authorized electronic editions, and do not participate in or encourage piracy of copyrighted materials. Your support of the author's rights is appreciated.

All Scripture quotations, unless otherwise indicated, are taken from the Holy Bible, NEW INTERNATIONAL VERSION®. Copyright © 1973, 1978, 1984 by Biblica, Inc. All rights reserved worldwide. Used by permission. NEW INTERNATIONAL VERSION® and NIV® are registered trademarks of Biblica, Inc.

Scripture quotations marked "NKJV™" are taken from the New King James Version®. Copyright © 1982 by Thomas Nelson, Inc. Used by permission. All rights reserved.

ISBN: 978-0-9844044-0-7

Library of Congress Control Number: 2010927923
Library of Congress Subject Headings:
Man-woman relationships—Fiction
Love stories
Bodyguards—Fiction
Inspirational fiction
Suspense fiction
Europe—Fiction

Diamond Press
3400 Pegasus Drive
P.O. Box 80043
Bakersfield CA 93380-0043
www.diamondpresspublishing.com

Published in the United States of America.

*"I sought the LORD, and He answered me;
He delivered me from all my fears."*
Psalm 34:4

CHAPTER ONE

IT CAN'T BE. Not possibly! Alexa peered through a doorway, trying to catch a better glimpse of the man on the *Today Show* set. He perched on a stool, opposite the pixie-faced co-host of the show. The object of her speculation wore a steel gray suit that emphasized his lean elegance.

This was no good. He faced away from her. Silently, Alexa skulked across the set, hoping no one would notice her. Unfortunately, a broad-shouldered, muscular man in black came toward her, but she struggled to ignore him. He was so short that she could easily see over him in her three-inch heels. She sidled sideways, wanting to get a better look.

It *was* Colin Radcliffe, international pop star! Alexa's heart fluttered. She loved his songs, and the sound of his voice. And to think, he was being interviewed on the same day she was.

"Ma'am." The low voice commanded her attention, but she didn't want to listen. What if she pretended not to hear? After all, just *one* more step and she would be able to see Colin's face clearly. Impulsively, she edged closer.

The man in black closed within four feet of her. Now the sheer physical force of his presence stopped her. In fact, she fought an overwhelming desire to retreat. He would let her get no closer to the star. Disappointment arose. She had just wanted to look. After all, she wasn't a salivating, rabid fan. Or was she?

Now a man with 'Security' written across his jacket appeared from her left, grabbing her attention. "Miss," he whispered. "We're taping. Wait over there." He pointed.

"I'm so sorry." Embarrassed, Alexa quickly obeyed. Obviously, she had breached a security code. What had she been thinking? Her impulsive nature had again taken her down the wrong path.

Colin's interview quickly ended. With sorrow, she watched him disappear from the set. Her dreams of accidentally bumping into him and maybe getting his autograph disappeared in smoke.

"Ma'am. Your turn." A young man beckoned to her.

She was led to a couch, and a man took the place of the pixyish woman. Heart thundering, Alexa smoothed her pencil slim skirt and fiddled with her cross necklace, making sure the clasp wasn't halfway down her throat. A technician tucked Alexa's auburn hair behind one shoulder.

"Just relax," he advised her. "It'll be over in a flash."

Alexa's mouth went dry, facing the black eyes of the cameras. She had been interviewed on national television three times, and this would be the last. Her book tour was almost complete, about which she had mixed feelings. Her fifteen minutes of fame were almost over. *What next,* a small part of her wondered. *Is this it? At twenty-nine, the peak of my career—my life?*

It was a strange thing to wonder when she was about to go on national television, and maybe push her fame out to sixteen minutes. A red light glowed on the camera.

"Good morning..." began the co-host, and perspiration dampened Alexa's skin. She was on live television. Millions of eyes were watching her. *Her.* But viewers were interested in Priscilla's life, she reminded herself. Not hers. She drew a calming breath.

"Miss Kaplan, I understand your biography is based on your childhood friendship with legendary chef, Priscilla Blake."

"Yes. Priscilla and I became best friends in kindergarten...." A faint tremor seized her hands, as was usual whenever she was in front of any group of people—let alone millions—but it didn't show up in her voice, thank goodness.

The man smoothly led her through the list of questions about Priscilla's problems with dyslexia and her refusal to concentrate in school. An unhappy, unsettled home life hadn't helped matters. In fact, although Alexa didn't mention it to the interviewer, it was the common bond that had knit Alexa and Priscilla together from the start. It was also one of the reasons why their friendship had survived each of their difficult high school years.

Alexa delved into the familiar, publicly known part of the story. Her friend's life had down-spiraled in high school when she had become addicted to drugs. By her senior year, most of Priscilla's old friends and teachers had abandoned her; all except for Alexa and their home economics teacher, who had discovered Priscilla's discerning palate and aptitude for creating outlandish, delicious entrées.

Halfway through recounting Priscilla's unlikely rise to fame by winning a reality cooking show, Alexa remembered to smile at the glowing camera. She even remembered an anecdote her publicist had advised her to include. When the co-anchorman chuckled, a warm glow filled her.

"Ms. Blake has become legendary, and in no small part due to your humorous, sensitive portrayal of her as a struggling teen. I suspect your friendship played a pivotal role in her life." Before Alexa could reply, the co-host finished up, "It's a story of winning over all odds. Something we all want to do. Thank you, Miss Kaplan."

Alexa smiled. "Thank you."

At the first opportunity, she left the set, feeling relieved it was over.

"Excellent interview." The cultured English voice came from her left.

Alexa whirled. "Colin Radcliffe! I...I thought you'd gone," she stammered. She blinked, and would have pinched herself, too, if she didn't think it would look ridiculous. "I just *love* your songs."

Now, how simpering had that sounded? She flushed. "I mean, it's an honor to meet you. I'm Alexa Kaplan."

"I know. I just listened to your interview."

"You did?" She felt flattered. "Thank you."

His blue eyes sparkled down at her and Alexa's heart skipped. He was much better looking in person than on the cover of a CD. His blond hair was perfectly cut, accenting the sharp, almost gaunt angles of his face. And he was at least six foot two.

"You're tall!" Then she warmed at his grin. "I mean, I've met a lot of male celebrities on this book tour. Most are surprisingly short." At almost five foot ten, it was a thing she noticed. "They look like a bunch of munchkins."

Munchkins? Why did her mouth have to outrun her brain now, of all times?

He laughed at her outrageous comment. "You have a thing against short men?"

"No. Of course not," she said, feeling even more uncomfortable with her thoughtless words. Plenty of short men were running around. In fact, one stood just behind Colin, standing solidly beside a linebacker with blond hair. Both were unassuming. In fact, she would have overlooked them both, if not for guilt for her prejudicial comment. This particular short man might be five foot six. Maybe five foot seven if he stretched. If one discounted his square, uncompromising jaw, he looked a cross between a popular germophobe on cable and a dark-haired elf she had just seen in an old movie, and he wore all black.

In fact, was this the man who had warned her away from the set?

Uncomfortably, she stared at him, wondering. She had never actually looked at his face. He returned her stare, his dark eyes cool and unfriendly. It must be the same man. The powerful, warning vibe she had felt before smoldered now, tightly leashed.

A little unnerved, she glanced sideways. The first man stood, shoulder to arm, beside the gigantic man with spiky blond hair. That one was certainly tall—maybe even six foot six—but she wasn't necessarily attracted to men with tree trunks for legs and shoulders the size of Texas, either. What a pair!

"They are perfectly *nice*," she said now in a low voice to Colin. "It's just..."

"You don't date them."

"Well, no," she agreed, and shut her mouth. Colin did not need to know her long—unnaturally so, according to her sister—list of criteria she used to narrow down dating material. Number one was the men she dated had to be at least six foot one, so she could wear heels if she wanted to. Maybe that was terribly superficial, but she didn't like the idea of towering over a man. This pop star, however, was perfect. At least six foot two. She flushed then, at her thoughts.

He chuckled. "Do I pass?"

Her face warmed still more. "All I meant..."

"I'm teasing." His mouth still quirked at the corners. "How about lunch?"

"Lunch? With you?" She momentarily felt lightheaded, as if she had stood up too soon and all of the blood had drained from her head. *Don't swoon,* she told herself. *You're not a teeny bopper with a silly crush.* "Of course. I'd love to. But it's not even nine o'clock."

"Where are you staying?"

"The Michelangelo. It's a few blocks from here."

"I know where it is. I've got another interview now, but I'll pick you up at twelve-thirty at your hotel."

"Great. Fabulous."

He grinned. "Cheerio, then."

Alexa stared after him, transfixed by a mixture of wonder and disbelief. Had her favorite pop star truly just asked her to lunch? This time she did pinch herself. It smarted.

❈ ❈ ❈ ❈ ❈

Alexa paced the luxurious lobby of the Michelangelo at 12:20 P.M. She loved the warm ambience of the elegant hotel. The soft, warm orange and gold colors made her feel welcome, and so had all of the staff, even though she sensed the hotel was geared to a pricier clientele than she. She had found it on an internet special.

Alexa still was barely able to believe that Colin Radcliffe had asked her on a lunch date. Why had he? More importantly—would he truly come?

A black Lincoln town car pulled to a stop outside and the hotel doorman let in a black-uniformed chauffeur. "Alexa Kaplan?"

He had come.

"Yes." Heart thumping faster, she followed him through the double set of doors into New York's chilly March afternoon. He opened the back door and there was Colin.

Pulse beating rapidly, she slid in next to him. "Hi," she said with a grin.

"Hi, yourself. I'm relieved you didn't stand me up."

"You're joking, right? I was afraid you would forget *me*."

"Not a chance."

"Take us to the Serafina," he told the driver.

The short distance to the restaurant was accomplished slowly. The driver drove aggressively, but repeatedly slowed and swerved for weaving bicycles and brash pedestrians crossing against the light.

"I'm glad I'm not driving," Alexa murmured.

Colin smiled at her. His eyes were as bright blue as before. She couldn't get over their clear color. Periwinkle, she decided.

Colin said, "New York is a remarkable city. I love the energy. Is this your first visit?"

"Yes. I've seen as much as I could. I'm leaving tomorrow." They slipped out of the car at the Italian restaurant. "I saw the

U.N. building and Times Square, of course, and the Statue of Liberty."

Inside, the waiter ushered them to a table at the back of the restaurant. Alexa sat with her back to a wooden casing against the wall, while Colin sat across from her. On the white wall to her right, beyond a low wooden barrier and another set of tables, flickered a silent, black and white movie. Italian, by the look of it.

"Cool!" she said. "What a neat idea."

When Colin smiled, his charm seemed to reach out and envelop her. It made her want to smile, too. He asked, "Do you understand Italian?"

"No. Just French, and not much of that."

"Have you ever been to Europe?"

"No, but I'd love to go. Maybe with all of the royalties from my book," she suggested brightly. "Are you from London?"

He nodded. "Born and bred." He smiled again, and with fascination, Alexa noted the tiny lines radiating from his eyes, and the dimple in his cheek. He laughed a lot. That was a good sign. "The food here is delicious. I always try to stop by when I'm in New York."

Alexa perused the menu. Choosing would be difficult, for Italian food was her favorite. Not only that, it was difficult to concentrate. Just sitting here with Colin was so exciting. Her gaze kept dancing from Colin to the flickering images on the adjacent wall.

And then she saw them. The two men from the television studio. The tall man and the short one—Mutt and Jeff, like the old comic strip characters. Had they somehow followed Colin? Were *they* the rabid fans?

Apprehension sped up her pulse. The suspicious duo sat at a small table pushed flush with the movie wall. Both had a perfect view of her table. Of Colin. In fact, both kept glancing at the famous pop star.

Lifting her menu, she hissed, "I think we've been followed."

"What?" Colin frowned.

"Over there. Two o'clock." The star turned openly, but she continued to furtively peer over her menu. With a smile, he turned back. "That's Mart and Jamison."

"Who are they?" She sent them another suspicious glance. The blond one gave her a faint smile, but the dark-haired one did not. In fact, he radiated antagonism.

"My bodyguards," he said simply, as if this were a normal occurrence. Well, of course it was, for him.

"I see. Then I won't worry that they keep staring at you."

"They're staring at you."

"Me? Why?" Feeling ill at ease, she took a sip of water.

"They're ensuring you're not a threat to me."

She choked on a laugh, and water unfortunately spurted from her mouth. "You're joking."

"No." Another look at the bodyguards proved they weren't laughing, either. The dark one's bad attitude seemed to have soured the blond one's mood, for both now stared at her with cool, unfriendly expressions. Maybe the short one had heard her thoughtless munchkin comment. She felt another tug of remorse for her insensitive words. Maybe that's why he seemed to dislike her already. That, and because she hadn't listened to his warning to get off the set.

She flirted with the idea of apologizing. No. It might be best to forget the whole incident. Especially if he hadn't heard her inappropriate comment in the first place.

Instead, she lowered her menu and sent the bodyguards a friendly smile. Neither responded, although the blond one looked down at his bread plate, as if uncomfortable. The black-haired one returned her stare, unblinking.

"I'm sure they do a good job," she said, returning her attention to Colin.

"They're the best in the business."

The waiter took their order, and then Colin said, "I have to confess to an ulterior motive for asking you to lunch."

"Really?" What could a legendary pop star possibly want from her?

"I'm planning to write an autobiography. A publisher's been pressuring my agent about it."

"I thought you had a tour coming up in Europe." She had learned that by eavesdropping on his television segment. "Do you have time to write an autobiography?"

"No. That's why I need you."

"Me?" Facts clicked together. Surprised, she said, "You want me to ghostwrite your autobiography?"

"Would you be interested?" His quizzical smile looked surprisingly self-deprecating.

How could he even wonder?

"I'd be honored! But," she added quickly, "I'd have to run it by my agent. Also, I'd want my name on the cover. Your name plus 'with Alexa Kaplan.' I need the publishing credits. Shared royalties, too."

"Your name on the cover, plus royalties. Done."

"Don't you think you'd better read my book first? See if you like my writing style?"

His mouth curved up into a slow, heart-stopping smile. "I like your style already, Alexa."

She blushed. Sometimes she hated the fair skin that accompanied her shoulder length, straight copper hair. It did have unusual, natural blond highlights, thanks to her willowy Scandinavian mother, and she didn't freckle, which was a nice blessing from her burly Austrian father, as were her blue-green eyes, but her face and skin always showed every nuance of her emotions.

Colin studied her for a moment, and then said diffidently, "Why did you go into writing, Alexa? You must know you're an incredibly beautiful woman. Have you ever been asked to model?"

Another faint flush warmed her face. "A top modeling agent approached me when I was sixteen." It was a fact few people knew. "But that's not where I wanted to go with my life." In truth, the offer to model had scared her. She had been quiet and shy back then, and didn't like attention on her outward appearance. She wanted people to like who she was on the inside.

"So you decided to write." She detected genuine interest in Colin's question.

"Yes. In college, I majored in English." Actually, she had felt more secure with her nose in a book than carousing with her friends. The loud, partying male types were too boisterous for her, anyway. They possessed an unpredictable rawness that inexplicably unnerved her. When she had become a Christian, the partying ceased to be an issue. Which was certainly fine with her. Then she got to meet an entirely new type of man.

"Anyone special in your life right now?"

Alexa wondered why he could possibly want to know. He couldn't be interested in her, could he? Her heart skipped at the thought. *Stop it,* she told herself. Of course he wasn't. "No." But it came out sounding like a question.

"If I ask you to write the book, it'll take up weeks of your time. Possibly even pull you away from home for a while."

"I have no attachments. Except to my sister and parents, of course. And I work for my brother-in-law—he publishes a magazine. I might be able to take a leave of absence."

"All right, then. It's settled."

Alexa didn't see how anything could possibly be settled. She withdrew her business card from her purse. "If you decide you want to hire me, give me a call."

"I will." He flashed a grin. "I look forward to it."

He was too charming for his own good, Alexa decided. But his smiles made her heart flutter, and she hoped he would call her. In the meantime, she would enjoy this lunch with him.

She found Colin to be wry, funny, and actually sweet from time to time. Of course, she didn't know him well enough to know if it was all an act, but she enjoyed talking with him very much.

What if he really *was* all he appeared to be? Could he possibly be the Prince Charming she had dreamed of since she was an adolescent?

At the tender age of fourteen, she had set up strict criteria for a qualifying husband. These still held. Besides the height requirement, she preferred that he have blond hair, blue eyes, and be nice looking. Colin met each of them.

The other half of her criteria included intangible necessities, and some had been added later—like he had to be a Christian. Was Colin? A sense of humor was a bonus, too. She also wanted a refined and even-tempered man. Absolutely no raw, aggressive types for her. Also, her ideal man had to be honest, with high integrity. Both were important in order for her to respect him. She needed a man she could look up to. But more than anything else, she wanted a man she could talk to—someone who loved her for who she was on the inside.

The remainder of the lunch went all too quickly, and when Alexa placed her napkin on the table, she realized she had been laughing too hard at everything Colin said. Just like one of his lovesick fans. But she couldn't seem to help herself.

They drove back to the Michelangelo, and when the driver opened her door, Colin pressed a kiss to her cheek. Thrills raced up her spine. She did not take liberties and kiss him back, for she felt the unfriendly eyes of his bodyguards in the car behind them.

"Thank you for a wonderful lunch."

"I'll call you soon," he promised.

Her steps seemed to float into the hotel. Would he truly call her?

What would it be like, spending quality time with such a charming, interesting man? She would certainly get to know him well if she ghostwrote his book. Alexa imagined spending candlelit evenings together, laughing over anecdotes of his life.

By that evening, however, when she snuggled into bed, Alexa's more pragmatic side had taken over. Would Colin truly call her? He was a celebrity, after all. Normal people rarely followed through on half of their promises. What were the chances a famous man would? Especially with the tour coming up, all of the publicity to handle, groupies hounding him...

She didn't expect to hear from him. Not really.

❄ ❄ ❄ ❄ ❄

Three weeks later

At her desk, Alexa quickly scarfed down a tuna sandwich and carrot sticks. Ted wanted the magazine copy proofed by three o'clock.

Betty buzzed her. "Call on line three." As usual, she neglected to name the caller.

Alexa rapidly chewed through her carrot and picked up the phone. "Yes?" she said, gulping the last prickly morsels. "Alexa here."

She heard a faint sound, which might have been a laugh. "Colin Radcliffe. How are you, Alexa?"

"Colin!" For a moment, she was speechless. "I didn't think...I mean, hello!"

Now she heard a chuckle for sure. "Have you given more thought to writing my autobiography?"

"Well, yes. Of course! That is, if you're asking me." Alexa realized she sounded like a breathless teenager again.

"I am. Will you?"

"Yes," she exclaimed, and then mentally slapped herself. "I mean, I would be happy to do it," she said in a calmer tone. "Of course, my agent will need to look over the details first."

He laughed again. The husky, deep sound thrilled her. "Great. My lawyer will call you. First, though, I want to make you aware of two problems. The publisher wants a rough draft ready in six weeks. And I'm going on tour next week."

Mentally, Alexa scrambled. She had an endless list of commitments over the next month and a half. Most could be rescheduled with artful finagling. The others...well, she'd need to train her assistant to take more of the load.

"I could probably write a rough draft in six weeks," she agreed slowly. "But you're going on tour? How would we meet so I could ask you questions? I suppose I could call you." Alexa frowned. She would rather speak with him in person in order to get a true sense of the man. Then she could write an accurate portrayal of his life and personality.

"Come with me on the tour," he said in her ear.

"What?" Alexa jerked to her feet, not sure if she had heard right. Her rolling chair zipped into the printer table behind her.

"Come with me to Europe. You'll have a blast."

"Come to Europe? With you?" She really must stop repeating everything he said. What would he think of her creative abilities, let alone the state of her mushy mind? "That sounds wonderful. A dream, really, but expensive. I'm not sure..."

"Tab's on me. You'll stay with me, travel with me."

Alexa wasn't sure that she liked the sound of this, but didn't parrot his words. They zinged around in her brain, though. "I'm not sure that's a good idea."

"Why not? People travel with me all the time."

"Well, fine. But you're not expecting...fringe benefits, are you?" Then she bit her tongue. Had she actually blurted those words to a pop star? However, as a Christian, she had strict morals she lived by. And living with a rock star promised all sorts of not-so-unforeseen temptations and complications.

He chuckled in her ear. "I wouldn't say 'no' to fringe benefits. But no. You'd have your own rooms. No strings. Just a working relationship. Unless you want that to change."

She cleared her throat. "I won't. I want that clear from the start." Silence from the other end of the line. "Would you rather hire someone else?"

"No, I don't." He sounded puzzled. "But I thought we connected. If I'm mistaken, I apologize."

"No. Well, yes. I mean, yes, I find you attractive." What an understatement. "But I'm a Christian. I don't...you know, do the casual sex thing." Mortification burned her cheeks and she was glad he wasn't there to see. "I mean," she hastily backpedaled, "not that you'd want to do such a thing with me. I just want everything clear from the get-go." She waited anxiously, worried that he wouldn't be able to respect her feelings. That he'd laugh and think she was an uptight prude.

Colin did laugh, but she thought she detected relief in it. "You're a funny girl. Refreshing. I like that. Ground rules are set, then. Do you want to come?"

"Of course I want to come." What she wanted was to find a table and dance on it!

"My lawyer will contact you with the details. Go ahead and give him the number of your agent. Way it's looking now, we'll hook up in London."

"Sounds fabulous. Thank you so much!"

"Later." He clicked off.

Hugging her arms to herself, Alexa twirled in a silly, dreamy circle. Could this truly be real? She would get to know her favorite singer, write a guaranteed bestseller, and travel Europe for six weeks. If she didn't know she was awake, or how much it hurt, she would pinch herself again. Her sister would never believe this.

❋ ❋ ❋ ❋ ❋

"Are you sure you want to do this?" Beth sat on her suitcase while Alexa tried to zip it shut.

"It won't zip!" she moaned.

"What did you pack?"

"Everything. And I can't put the saline solution for my contacts in my carry-on. My toothpaste, either. I hate those terrorists. They're making flying a nightmare." Alexa frowned at the suitcase.

"How many pairs of shoes did you pack?" her sister wanted to know.

Alexa counted in her head. "Nine? Tennis shoes, two pairs of flats, and six high heels."

"*Six* pairs of high heels?"

"What can I say? Shoes are my weakness. Especially heels."

Beth surveyed Alexa's baggage. "Put a few pairs in your carry-on."

Alexa rolled her eyes. "Like that would go over well with the airlines."

"Then leave a few here. Or bring another suitcase."

"I can't do that. I'll barely manage toodling around the airport with my carry-on, laptop computer, and dragging my suitcase behind me. How would I manage two suitcases?"

"Colin Radcliffe's a rich guy. Surely he'll send someone to pick you up."

"Well, yes."

"Go for it, then. Plus, what about souvenirs? You'll need a whole suitcase just to pack those. You know Timmy and Annie are expecting presents when you get back."

"And you." She smiled at her sister.

"I wouldn't mind some Swiss chocolate. You are going to Switzerland, aren't you?"

"Yes. London, then Paris, Spain, Italy, and Switzerland." Colin's lawyer had faxed her the itinerary yesterday. The tickets to London were already tucked into her purse. Alexa couldn't believe she was going to Europe. Really, it all seemed like a fairy tale come true.

She threw items from her overstuffed suitcase into a smaller, matching case. Both zipped shut. "Good!" Alexa flopped backward onto the bed, beside her sister. "Thanks for coming over to help, Beth."

"I wouldn't miss it. It's just like we used to fantasize when we were kids. I envy you."

"You don't. You love Ted and the kids."

"I do. But adventure... I probably won't get much of that. You'll have to live it for me. And write every week—or call. I know how terrible you are at writing."

"Except for books," Alexa agreed with a smile.

They lay there in silence, staring at the ceiling. Miniature flecks of rainbow light sparkled across it. Alexa had exchanged her standard bedroom light fixture for a miniature crystal chandelier. Not practical or cost effective, but she loved it.

"What's he like?" Beth asked. She sounded serious now.

"Don't worry. He's great."

"Does he know you're a Christian?"

"Yes. I even told him I wouldn't have sex with him."

"You didn't!" Her sister sounded scandalized.

"I want everything out front. You know how I am."

"Yes, I do. You're the picture of tact."

"I need to learn more about that from you," she admitted. "But I do try."

"He's certainly handsome."

"Even more so in person. And he's charming and funny. And tall, too."

Beth giggled. "Over six-one, I take it."

"Oh, yes. And he's got the most gorgeous blue eyes. You know blue is my favorite color. And thick blond hair." She sighed.

"You sound twelve."

"I feel twelve. I'm scared about that. I feel like this is all a fairy tale, and I'll wake up next in the dungeon. It can't possibly be this good, can it? Not real life? I must be missing something. Or something will go wrong. It's inevitable."

"I can't believe this is you talking, Miss Optimistic. You always believe the best about everything."

On her elbow, Alexa turned to her sister with a frown. "What if I'm wrong? What if this turns into a nightmare?"

"I can't imagine how," her sister said dryly. "But if it does, fly home. Have you signed a contract?"

"Yes. I've agreed to deliver a rough draft of seventy thousand words in six weeks. And I gave them your name and address as one of my references. I hope that's okay. I think they're doing a major background check on me."

"I'm sure they are. And yes, that's fine." Beth frowned. "I don't know much about writing, but it sounds like you've got your work cut out for you."

"I can do it. As long as I get lots of quality time with Colin to ask questions."

Beth giggled. "Mmhm. Like questions are all you're interested in."

Alexa lightly punched her sister's arm. "What do you know?"

"I know you're going to have a great time." Her sister sounded serious again. "Remember, you can call me anytime. You never have to be alone. And God is with you, too."

"I know. I'm glad about that."

"I've never heard you sound so insecure."

"I always feel insecure. When I go out, I check to see if I've buttoned my blouse right, or if I've washed the toothpaste off the corner of my mouth. I'm insecure in a lot of ways." She knew it was probably a result of their shared, difficult childhood, but Alexa would rather not think about that on the eve of her wonderful adventure. She sat up, and so did Beth.

"You're one of the strongest people I know," her sister said. "Just be careful. Colin's world is not yours and he's not the guy next door. Make sure you find a man who loves you, for you. Not for your looks. A man who will support you in everything you do. Wacky as it may be sometimes."

"Thanks, sis." Impulsively, she hugged Beth. "I don't know what I'd do without you."

"Just be careful," her sister said. "It's been a long time since you've actually let a guy into your heart." She pulled back. "Call me when you get there. I can't wait to hear what London's like."

"I will." Alexa's imagination took flight then, leaving her dark worries behind like so many shadowed rain clouds. All she saw were bright days, filled with sunshine and adventure. Thrilling days, to do what she loved best—writing—and getting to know a sensational man.

She had been silly to think anything would go wrong. Everything would be perfect.

CHAPTER TWO

Rain dripped down in the gathering gloom of dusk outside of Heathrow Airport in London. Not an auspicious start to her fairy tale adventure, Alexa decided. She stood in the baggage claim area with her carry-on bag and laptop case slung over her shoulders. At her feet rested her mammoth suitcase and its smaller twin. She had stood here for twenty minutes already, cranking her neck to and fro, searching for the driver who was supposed to pick her up.

She had seen uniformed men with caps carrying cardboard signs, all right. But they had picked up clumps of Japanese businessmen. Worry was beginning to eat at her. What if Colin had forgotten about her? He was a busy star. Surely things slipped through the cracks. Apparently, she was one of them.

Of course, Colin wouldn't come to pick her up himself. That would be crazy, even though she would love it. His adoring fans would mob him.

Alexa shoved her suitcases into a clump and walked toward the sliding doors. They swooshed open, letting in a rush of cold damp. She shivered. Not exactly welcoming. And she didn't see anyone pacing back and forth outside, looking for her, either.

She stepped inside again, shivering. Maybe she should take out her coat, for when the driver did come. She would need it out in that wet.

Alexa went down on her knees and tugged open the zipper to her largest suitcase. When she lifted the top, her jaw dropped. "*Oh, no!*"

Her cosmetics case was open, her clothes were wadded into wrinkled blobs, but worst of all, two of the saline bottles for her contacts had popped open during the flight. All of her clothes were damp—especially her woolen trench coat, which she had laid so carefully on top, in preparation for just such weather as this. In fact, she realized, pawing through the disorganized mess, the coat was soaked.

"I can't believe this!" she wailed softly. Obviously, her bag had been targeted for inspection. No doubt because of all the liquid-filled bottles she had packed, full of saline solution for her contacts.

"Someone's going to pay!" she muttered, ordering her aching eyes not to leak. "Or I'll know why."

"You're blaming the airline for your terrible packing job?" The deep, faintly melodic voice spoke behind her. Its speaker sounded foreign. Maybe Italian.

She spun on her knees, in outrage glaring up at the rude interloper. Then her mouth gaped open. It was Colin's dark-haired bodyguard. The one who had reminded her of an elf.

The *nerve* of the man.

"It's you!" Rising to her feet, she took uncharitable satisfaction in towering over him in her high heels. "Are you Mutt, or Jeff?" she inquired frostily.

His lips tightened. "I'm here to drive you." He wore a black windbreaker and black jeans. They matched his black hair, black eyes, and black attitude, she decided.

"It's about time." She couldn't believe her own rude words. "I've been waiting a half an hour." An exaggeration. "And my coat is wet," she said inconsequentially. Now she noticed that her suitcase was wide open, its messy contents displayed to the world—including her lacy pieces of underwear. Mortified, she pounced on it, and zipped it closed. Guilt for her annoyed comments prickled; unfortunately, too late.

"It's raining," the bodyguard said tersely, flicking a disapproving glance at her thin blouse.

More irritation surged, but she struggled to ignore it. "I don't need a coat. Let's go." She hefted up her carry-on and laptop, grabbed the carry strap of her mammoth suitcase, and started walking. It was an unruly suitcase, as she knew from experience, and so she tried to be extra careful. If she tugged too hard to the left or to the right, it would tip over.

Alexa marched out the door and down the little incline. The suitcase raced after her. She jerked it to the right at the last minute, so it wouldn't hit her legs, and it flopped over.

"Drat." Her face burned. Awkwardly, she bent to right it. Her shoulder bag flopped forward, banging her arms. The laptop hit the ground. She growled behind her teeth.

She saw the bodyguard's black legs standing unhelpfully a distance away. Her smaller suitcase was in his hand. No delicate pull straps for him. Well. Hair disheveled, she straightened, all to rights again. Now it occurred to her that she didn't know where they were going.

She gave him a cool stare. "Lead on, then."

Expressionlessly, he moved in front of her. She carefully followed him down the sidewalk and around hurrying people. Her suitcase fell over two more times, and her cotton blouse was thoroughly damp by the time a crowd of people suddenly rushed out another set of sliding doors. She jerked to a halt and the dratted suitcase spilled over again. Tears were close, now. This was no fairy tale!

What was she doing here, in a foreign airport, with a surly man? With wrinkled, ruined clothes. She was soaking wet, her suitcase wouldn't behave, and that jerk wouldn't stop to help her.

Not that she would, if she had been him, Alexa admitted. She had been terribly rude. But then again, so had he.

And where was he? Panic surged. The people were gone and she had righted her suitcase again, but the bodyguard had disappeared. Alexa bit her lip, hoping the pain would keep the tears at bay.

"I'll take that." He was at her elbow, bending to unstrap the silly leash from the suitcase. He plucked it from her hand, lifted the case as if it weighed nothing, and deposited it in the back of a large black car. She knew little about cars, but this one looked expensive.

Alexa hurried and slid into the backseat. Thankfully, heat blasted inside the car, for she was thoroughly chilled. He slammed the door, getting in on the passenger's side—no, driver's side, here in England. Rain glistened in his wavy hair. He looked at her in the rearview mirror. "Royalty, are you?"

"What is that supposed to mean?"

"You expect me to be your chauffeur?"

"Well, aren't you?" she retorted outrageously, peeved still further.

The hard eyes looked disgusted. "Please yourself."

Alexa sat in silence while her "chauffeur" drove. She felt like a naughty child who had been disciplined. She didn't like the feeling. And she didn't like the thought of him looking down his nose at her, either. She hated anyone thinking badly of her.

But he had started it!

She crossed her arms and stared out the window. She noticed now that her blouse was wet enough that she could see her bra through it. Great! She hugged her arms tighter against herself.

They drove in silence through the black, wet streets. He drove the car fast and well. At least he was a competent driver.

At last they turned into a quiet neighborhood with large homes and towering trees. A gate barred the entrance to one of these houses. They stopped and a uniformed guard allowed them through. Then they slid over the black pavement to a detached garage. The car purred inside, and then the engine went silent. Equally silently, its driver exited and unloaded her suitcases from the back.

Alexa felt very uncomfortable by now. The silence and guilt for her biting words at the airport made her feel awful.

She edged out of the car, gripping her smaller bags. Why couldn't she learn to be tactful, like her sister?

The bodyguard had both suitcases in hand and he headed over the grass for the house. She hurried after him, mentally despising her high heels that tripped over every little grass clump and hole. Rain poured down on her head, soaking her further, and she shivered, freezing cold. Her hair fell in wet, stringy clumps about her face. Vainly, she hoped Colin wouldn't greet her. At least not immediately. She must look like a drowned rat.

The bodyguard opened a side door and she hurried in after him, eager for dry warmth. They entered a kitchen, painted a warm yellow, with cream colored cupboards and granite countertops. The refrigerator, stove, and microwave were stainless steel, and up-to-the-minute in function and design. Alexa imagined microwaving a cup of tea.

But no rest for the weary. The bodyguard led her up a narrow staircase, turned right, and then nudged open a door with his foot. She followed him into a lovely room with thick white rugs on the floor, an ivory and lace covered bed with a canopy, wallpaper strewn with yellow roses, and warm, dark wood furniture. It felt open and spacious, and smelled super—like orange blossoms.

Alexa smiled, lowering her bags to the floor. "It's beautiful!" she breathed.

"Are you finished with my services?" The bodyguard's tone sounded deferential, but he stood with his legs slightly apart and hands behind his back. It came off as hostile.

Alexa kicked off the infernal high heels and made a decision. "I think we've started out on the wrong foot. I'm Alexa." She started to put out her hand, but then realized her blouse was now see-through. Embarrassed, she crossed her arms again.

No friendliness entered the black eyes. "Jamison."

He wasn't making this easy. She bit her lip. "I was rude. I'm sorry."

"Apology accepted." He headed for the door.

"Wait! Aren't you going to apologize to me?"
"For what?"
"For your sarcastic comments at the airport."
"I would, if they mattered to you. But they don't."
"Excuse me?" Without thinking, Alexa put her hands on her hips and glared.
"Sorry...Alexa. But you're a type. I've got you nailed down." His gaze didn't even flicker in the direction of her now visible bra.
"Type? Nailed down?" She didn't like the sound of this.
"You're a beautiful woman, Alexa. You know it and you use it to get what you want. I'll be watching you."
Incensed, she said the first rash thing that came to her mind. "And you know what they say about short men; they overcompensate to cover up their deficits." Alexa didn't know the quote. She was just making it up. And very unChristian it was, she realized, too late. Her mouth! "I'm so *sorry*..."
But he turned without a word and was gone. The only indication of his anger was the sharp click of the door latch as it closed.
Alexa stared at the door. Now what had she done? Not only had she attacked his height, but she had insinuated he might have other deficits, too. What had gotten into her? How could she possibly say such terrible things to that man?
But he wasn't exactly Mr. Sweetness and Light, either, she reminded herself. Not that that excused her behavior in the *least*.
Alexa wanted to call her sister. She wanted to burst into tears. This trip was not turning out anything like she had hoped. Not if that irksome bodyguard was about to become a permanent fixture in her life. She would avoid him. She would do everything in her power to steer clear of him. And if she couldn't; well, she would take the high road, no matter how hard that might be. In fact, from now on, she would treat him with faultless courtesy.
That man would not be the end to her fairy tale.

✳ ✳ ✳ ✳ ✳

A private bath was attached to Alexa's room, and filled with fluffy white towels and luscious smelling toiletries. She felt much better after a shower and change of clothes. Now she was ready to see Colin—if he was here tonight.

A timid knock sounded on the door. "Miss?"

Alexa hurried for the door, relieved someone had come for her. She was hungry, and didn't know if she should go out and wander the halls looking for the dining room, or wait for someone to fetch her. It felt awkward to be in a foreign country in a stranger's house. She didn't know what was expected of her, and she had already made one enemy. She didn't want to make more.

She flung the door open wide. "Yes?"

The portly, comfortable woman on the other side jumped a bit, her eyes round. A white cap was pinned to her head, and she wore a uniform. "Mr. Colin has asked that you join him for supper."

"How lovely. Thank you for coming to get me. Let me slip on my shoes." She quickly did so—flats, this time—and hurried after the woman. "I'm Alexa." She was anxious to make at least one friend in this house. Besides Colin, of course.

"I'm Mrs. Stroud, the housekeeper." The woman cast her a nervous smile and led the way down the hall—in a different direction from the one Jamison had brought her, Alexa noted. This direction ended in a wide balcony overlooking a sweeping, curved staircase. A massive chandelier sparkled overhead, shooting brilliant lights everywhere.

"It's beautiful," Alexa breathed. She loved chandeliers. Hence the one in her bedroom back home. Feeling like she was in a dream, she floated down the staircase after Mrs. Stroud. She felt like a princess about to enter the ball. Her imagination conjured up a sparkling array of guests below—including a few of Colin's famous friends, of course—and black-suited waiters swooping about carrying platters of champagne to the guests.

Perhaps dancing would take place over there, between the marble columns...

"This way." Mrs. Stroud smiled. "You look enraptured, you do, miss."

Alexa couldn't say it looked just like a fairy tale. She was an adult, after all. "It's lovely," she sighed instead.

"Mr. Colin will be pleased you like it," the woman said comfortably, and ushered her into a room lined with books and plush green velvet chairs.

"Thank you, Mrs. Stroud." Alexa and the other woman exchanged a smile, and the door closed quietly behind her.

Colin had been sitting in front of a roaring fire. Now he stood. "Alexa! How good to see you."

She tried to walk sedately to Colin. It was difficult. With his warm grin, it seemed natural to hurry over. It was nice to at last feel so welcome.

He took her hand and kissed it. "You are as beautiful as I remember. More so."

She blushed. "Thank you."

He turned to a table with a decanter and two cut crystal glasses. "A drink?"

"A soda, if you have it."

He smiled over one shoulder. "Of course. How was your trip?"

With a rueful laugh, Alexa gave him the short, funny version of her wrangled suitcase. "Everything is fine now."

He handed her the soda and urged her to join him in front of the warm fire. Alexa hadn't realized how cold her hands were until she leaned forward, holding them to the heat. She glanced at her host, noticing everything about him. Her heart thrummed. He had neat, strong looking hands, intensely blue eyes, and thick blond hair. The sharp angles of his face relaxed when he smiled at her.

She said, "Your home is lovely. Thank you for letting me stay here."

"Thank *you* for agreeing to write my autobiography. I hope you won't find it too boring."

She laughed. "I doubt that."

"The first concert of our tour is tomorrow night. I'd like for you to come. Of course, you'll have a backstage pass."

Her lips parted. "I'd love that."

"Good. I thought you might enjoy it. And it will be good background for the book."

"That will be perfect. I'll also need to do research for the book. Do you have an hour free tomorrow morning?"

"I can carve out a few minutes. And I've got reams of newspaper clippings all in scrapbooks. My mother collected them. Photo albums, too."

"Terrific." Alexa sipped her drink and hoped she could ask Colin all of the questions she needed to in those few minutes tomorrow. Of course, she could ask a few questions tonight, too, to get started.

"Let me give you an idea of the schedule," Colin said. "We'll be in London through the end of this week, and then we'll head to Paris. I'd like to leave the photo albums and earliest scrapbooks here."

"I see I'll have my work cut out for me." She smiled.

"Enough work chat," Colin said. "I'd like to learn more about you."

Laughing, Alexa answered his many interested questions. She was flattered that he wanted to know so much about her. "But my life is boring compared to yours."

"Nothing about you is boring, Alexa." His eyes twinkled. "That's why I asked you to come."

"That, and the book, right?" she asked dryly.

He chuckled and she relaxed. He really did like her. He seemed to enjoy her sense of humor. And he was very down-to-earth. Not at all what she had thought a superstar would be like.

They ate supper together; two people at a long, empty table. The food was delicious, but Alexa felt funny sitting at the austere, highly polished table while people flitted in and out, bringing food and clearing away used dishes. She counted five different people serving just Colin and herself. It all felt very strange.

She forked up the last of her dessert—a delicious trifle. "Where does everyone else eat?"

"In the kitchen, and Mart and Jamison grab a bite when they can. Sometimes they eat with me, if I don't have guests."

"Oh."

"You're frowning." He frowned a little, too, as if her opinion mattered to him. "You think I don't let Jamison and Mart associate with guests? Actually, they work then. They're always on guard, but most of all when other people are in the house."

"Where are they now, then?"

"Mart's out in the hall. Jamison's in the control room. They're the best." He flicked a thumb up and threw a grin toward the ceiling. Alexa followed his gaze and saw a small, almost invisible dark lens buried there. "I wanted to eat alone with you tonight."

"Thank you." Uncomfortably aware now that the prickly Jamison's eyes were watching her, she pressed her napkin to her mouth, and then lowered it again to her lap.

"I assume all went well when Jamison picked you up at the airport?" Colin said, sipping his wine.

Alexa cast a glance at the ceiling camera. "Uh...fine."

"Jamison's a man of few words. But he's got a heart of gold."

"Mmhm," she said noncommittally. "I didn't know Jamison was an Italian name."

"It's not. His father is Italian, and he grew up in Italy, except for summers in America. His mother is Italian American. She liked the name Jamison. And Jethro—you know, from the *Beverly Hillbillies*?"

This inexplicably struck Alexa's funny bone. Regrettably, she snorted in an unladylike manner. "His name is Jamison Jethro?"

"Jamison Jethro Constanzo."

She lowered her head so Jamison couldn't see her smile. "I see," she said in a strangled voice.

Colin grinned. "I think he'll kill me for telling you that."

"Maybe he wasn't listening. I certainly won't tell him. We don't exactly get along." Then she bit her lip. Maybe she shouldn't have said that. "I mean..."

"I understand." His blue eyes looked sharp and considering. "I'll keep that in mind." Colin changed the subject and spoke about the upcoming tour. It sounded like fun, although it came as a surprise they wouldn't be staying in hotels. Alexa would get her own small apartment in each building where Colin would stay.

"Your flats are complete with a kitchen and all the necessities," her host assured her. "Top of luxury. Perfect for your living and working comfort." Apparently, he owned a penthouse in Paris. Alexa's apartment would be a few floors down, and it was owned by a friend of his. In addition, he had arranged for prime accommodations in all of the other destinations, as well.

"They're top-of-the-line flats," he explained. "They offer daily maid service, laundry, and a gym. I prefer flats over hotels, for security is tighter. They cater only to a select clientele. On the other hand, my band likes the hotel nightlife." He shrugged. "Whatever suits. I hope the accommodations are to your liking, Alexa."

"I'm sure they'll be wonderful," she said. "Thank you so much. You'll probably think I'm silly, but this all seems like a fairy tale to me." Embarrassment warmed her cheeks then, for she remembered the testy bodyguard was listening in on their conversation. Probably that vapid comment had him laughing up his sleeve.

Colin, however, appeared pleased. "I'm flattered you think so." He lifted his wine glass. "To the tour."

She clinked her soda glass against it. "To your tour. And our book." She smiled at Prince Charming. Surely all would be smooth sailing from now on. She dismissed the niggling unease about the too short meeting tomorrow. Soon she would schedule a longer one to gather all of the necessary information. No need to worry.

❋ ❋ ❋ ❋ ❋

The next morning, after a quick breakfast of tea and toast, which Mrs. Stroud had thoughtfully delivered, a knock sounded on Alexa's bedroom door. Her heart leaped. Maybe it was Colin, coming to collect her for their meeting.

Alexa hurried in her stockinged feet to fling open the door. When she looked up, expecting to see Colin's face, she saw nothing but empty air. Her gaze dropped several inches before encountering black hair. "Oh. It's you." Hope was replaced by discomfort. She had hoped, perhaps unrealistically, not to see him again.

Jamison's black gaze was equally unfriendly. "Colin wants you." He turned abruptly and headed down the hall.

Did he expect her to follow him like a puppy?

Alexa scowled and shut the door. If so, he had another think coming.

Failure one for her good resolutions. However, in her own defense, she wasn't prepared yet. She slipped on new high heels that matched her warm-toned, caramel pantsuit, and rubbed a sheer gloss on her lips. There. Now she was ready. Never mind she didn't know where to meet Colin. She could ask someone—but certainly not that disagreeable bodyguard.

A hard rap came at the door. She opened it and looked down. With her heels on, Jamison barely reached her nose level. "Yes?" she inquired.

His black eyes looked hard, and lips thinned. "If your majesty is ready, follow me."

"How kind of you to offer," she retorted, trotting fast in his wake. More unfortunate, impulsive words sped off her tongue. "Civility goes a long way. Or don't they teach you manners in bodyguarding school?"

He turned so fast that she almost smacked into him. Luckily, she careened into the wall instead. It all happened so fast that she spun on one spiky heel and twisted on the other.

A terrible cracking sound rent the air, and then she abruptly lost three inches in height.

She stared in horror. Her new strappy sandals! "Now see what you've done!" she accused.

"Want me to break off the other one, too?" he suggested unrepentantly. "Then you'll have a matched set."

Alexa gasped. "You obnoxious man!"

"Good thing I'm not looking for kudos from you, then."

"What's with the American slang? I thought you were Italian!"

His dark eyes flashed, but he did not reply.

"I need to change my shoes," she informed him. "Why don't you just tell me where to go?"

His eyebrows climbed.

Alexa flushed when she realized the double meaning of her words. "I *mean* tell me how to get to Colin's office—or wherever I'm going."

Jamison glanced at his black watch. "Be quick. Colin's only got half an hour."

Clearly, the recalcitrant bodyguard intended to wait for her. Oh, goody. Alexa slipped off her dead shoes and sadly placed them in the back of her closet. They had cost a hundred dollars. Maybe when she got home she would get them repaired. For now, her tan heels would have to make do.

Actually, Alexa realized it was a good thing she had returned to the room, for she had forgotten her notepad and digital recorder during her initial conflagration with Jamison. Fully prepared this time, she exited her room. The bodyguard waited for her, just as she had feared. Remorse over her snappish comments warred with irritation with him. No matter how hard it might be, she had to try to take the high road.

With a disapproving curl to his lip, he asked, "How many pairs of heels did you pack, anyway?"

"Feeling intimidated?" she asked sweetly, unable to help herself.

He took off down the hall with his back to her. "No. But I wonder what deficiencies you're trying to cover."

Alexa gasped in outrage, and her good resolutions again deserted her. "You rude man! Does Colin know you treat his guests this way?"

Jamison turned suddenly, and she skidded to a halt. "Stop doing that!" she complained.

His level black gaze held hers, looking ominous. "Are you threatening me?"

Alexa refused to back down, and stared down her nose at him. "He deserves to know, especially if you're this rude to everyone."

"You get that prize." He started walking again.

"Oh! Well, aren't I lucky?"

"Why don't you tell him?" Jamison suggested. "Then Mart will have to deal with you. Poor guy."

"Just draw me a floor plan of the house. Then I won't need either of you," she retorted.

Jamison gestured toward an open door. "Colin's study."

Alexa had barely noticed descending the grand staircase, for she had been so busy sniping at Jamison. "Thank you," she said stiffly. "Your help—and company—left much to be desired."

Jamison disconcertingly leaned closer. "Ditto."

She rolled her eyes just as Colin emerged. The star kissed her cheek. "Alexa, love, you look beautiful this morning."

"Thank you."

Jamison turned on his heel, but not before Alexa spotted the sneer curling his lip. She longed to zing him with another attack, but didn't want to appear childish to Colin. With a narrowed gaze, she watched the bodyguard stroll away, doubtless to find fresh prey. She trembled a little—both from the encounter and from her own appalling inability to resist Jamison's provocative comments. What had gotten into her? And why had he taken such an immediate dislike to her?

"Sleep well?" Colin inquired, ushering her into a dark paneled room, lined with books.

"Yes," she assured him.

Two other people occupied the room. A stocky, muscular man with blondish gray hair razored into a buzz cut caught her attention first. It was hard to ignore him. His hard, aggressive stance reminded her of a pit bull, and he hovered near the door, as if eager to escape.

"Alexa, I'd like you to meet my manager, Paddy Ferguson."

"It's nice to meet you," she said.

A silver, half moon scar bracketed one side of the manager's mouth, and his eyes were like pale green chips of ice. Those hard orbs sized her up, as if assessing her worth to both Colin and the tour. With an abrupt, dismissive turn of his shoulders, he addressed Colin. "We're almost sold out in Paris. Barcelona, Rome, and Zurich are at half-capacity or less."

Colin's lips twisted. "It's the economy. This down slump is hitting everyone in the pocketbook."

"I'll get those numbers up. Don't worry about it." Lifting a brusque hand in farewell, he left.

Colin's wry smile remained. "That's Paddy. He's not a schmoozer—except when he absolutely has to be. But he's the best brain in the business. I'm lucky to have him."

"He seems determined."

"He is. Nothing gets in Paddy's way. If it does, he runs it over." Colin chuckled. "The tour will be a complete success. I have no doubt about that."

Alexa's attention turned to the other occupant of the room. A woman with a perky cap of blond hair sat on a chair beside Colin's desk. She shot Alexa a quick frown. Then Alexa wondered if she had imagined it, because the next instant the petite woman affixed a wide smile upon her face.

"Alexa, I'd like you to meet Eve, my secretary. Eve, Alexa. As I told you, she's going to write my autobiography."

Eve said, "Pleased to meet you. I'm sure we will be working closely together. Colin is busy most of the time." Her accent—or lack thereof—placed her as an American.

"Yes." Colin turned down his perfectly cut mouth. "If you have questions, ask Eve. She knows everything about me. How long have you been with me, Eve? Five years?"

"Seven." Eve's gray eyes smiled at Alexa, but a flash of something—perhaps fear, or malice—flared in them.

Eve's demeanor made Alexa feel uncomfortable. In addition, her unease from last night intensified. So, Colin was a busy man. She should have expected that. Fine. Then she would make the most of each meeting that she could finagle with him. But one thing had already become clear; she would prefer to spend as little time as possible with Eve.

"Now." Colin turned to a pile of stacked albums. Perhaps fifteen, Alexa guessed. "Start with these. The photo albums are labeled, and you might find events you want to discuss in the book. Note those and ask me later. The scrapbooks are pretty self-explanatory, righto?"

Colin seemed edgy, and soon explained it. "I have an appointment in a few minutes. Do you have any questions, or would you like to start with the albums?"

Alexa flipped on her digital recorder. "Give me a quick idea of the message you'd like to convey with the book. Something you want your fans to take away from reading it."

Crossing his arms, Colin fingered his chin. "That's a tough one. I want people to know I come from the working class. My da was a plumber, my mum a house cleaner. I'm a chap like any other. I want the book to be an inspiration and encouragement to others, especially kids, to pursue their dreams."

Alexa smiled. "I like it." She asked a few more questions, and then Colin had to leave. He said a house man would carry the albums to her room.

Eve lingered behind as Alexa selected two albums to bring upstairs now. "Anything I can help you with?" Eve's words were cordial, but her tone sounded cold.

Alexa wondered about the other woman's attitude. Did she think Alexa was interloping on her turf? "Are you a writer, too?" she asked cautiously.

"Oh, heavens no!" Eve laughed sharply. "Why would you ask?"

"You don't like me." Alexa rued her habitual lack of tact. "What I mean is, have I done something to upset you?"

"Of course not." Eve pressed her lips together. "We've only just met."

"I don't intend to cause trouble. I hope you know that."

"I know Colin is very taken with you. However, if you step out of bounds and hurt him, you'll answer to me." With that menacing statement, the secretary swept from the room.

Alexa stared after her. Eve obviously felt protective of Colin. Because he was her employer? Or because she possessed deeper feelings for him? Alexa decided then and there that she would be a fool to get on Eve's bad side. Eve appeared quiet and meek with Colin, but underneath, she might well be a cat with claws. It remained to be seen whether the cat would attack.

When Alexa returned to her room, she found a detailed map of the house, hand drawn in precise, bold lines, under her door. Clearly, Jamison had drawn it and delivered it. It irritated her, because he most certainly hadn't done it to be helpful. It was his means to get rid of a nuisance. Her.

Alexa found herself wasting several minutes thinking up sarcastic words of thanks for the bodyguard. If he had shown up, she would have delivered them, too, with much relish.

Thankfully, he didn't. Wasn't it about time she behaved like a civilized adult with him?

Alexa settled down to sort through the various albums that Colin had leant her. The job would take every spare minute this week. Hopefully, she would find an afternoon to explore London. After all, she had never been there before, and may never return again after this trip.

Alexa threw herself into the work by writing notes and piecing together the beginning of an outline on her computer. She wanted to get as much done as possible now, for she would have to stop work early this evening. Tonight was the concert. She couldn't wait. What would it be like to arrive at the concert on the arm of a rock star?

✵ ✵ ✵ ✵ ✵

That night, just as she had dreamed, Alexa rode with Colin to the concert. She had never been in a limousine before, and reverently touched the soft, white leather seats. Even more amazing, she could stretch out her long legs. Plenty of room. She even spied a mini-refrigerator. Doubtless for celebrating after the concert.

The limo purred to stop outside the private entrance to the concert stadium. The driver came around and opened the door, and then Colin took her hand and helped her out. "Come on, love."

As soon as Alexa slid outside, cameras flashed. Several television cameras pointed their way, and female fans screamed from the sidelines, waving banners.

"Now you'll be famous, too," Colin joked with a grin. He waved and blew kisses to his fans as he strolled toward the entrance. Alexa's heart jumped and skittered. She was at her favorite star's concert. And he was holding her hand! She had to remind herself to keep breathing. It was hard. Part of her felt just like those teenagers screaming on the sidelines.

Inside, Colin instructed her to get a backstage pass from an assistant, and then he peeled off toward the dressing rooms. Alexa draped the purple pass, attached to a purple cord, around her neck.

"Come with me." Mart, the blond linebacker, appeared by her side. "Colin asked me to show you around." A Texas drawl flavored his words.

"You're American."

Sea green eyes grinned down at her. "Born and bred."

Mart pointed out the lounge where she would go at the end of the concert. "The groupies hang out over there," he drawled, pointing to a different room. "I imagine you'll want to steer clear of them."

"Maybe not," Alexa said. "I've never experienced the groupie subculture before."

Mart raised a brow. "It's a spectacle. Mostly women dressed in skimpy clothes, throwing themselves at Colin. Culture is not in their vocabulary."

"All the same." Alexa smiled. "I'll need to observe it for the book." As the tour progressed, she realized that while Mart may look like a stereotypical jock, he was funny and sharp. She laughed repeatedly at his dry comments. She was glad that she had told Colin about her problem with Jamison. At least she wasn't saddled with him tonight.

After a bit, Colin came out dressed in hip-hugging leather pants, a white shirt unbuttoned midway down his chest, and a leather vest. His hair was mussed and spiky. He headed for the far side of the stage, where he engaged in a long, intense conversation with Paddy.

Mart needed to speak to another guard for a moment, so Alexa sat on a couch and watched the bustle. She was amazed by all of the equipment backstage. Setup for the concerts must take an incredible amount of time. People rushed to and fro, completing the last minute jobs before the show began.

Colin was too busy to speak to her, but Alexa didn't expect anything different. She spied Jamison talking to the other guards. He gestured with relaxed authority toward different spots on stage, obviously giving them instructions. Was he the head of Colin's security? Even Mart listened to his friend for a few minutes before returning to Alexa's side.

"Show's about to start." Mart escorted Alexa to her seat near the stage. "Have fun," he grinned. "Come backstage at the end."

The concert started with a flash of sparkling white lights, and then Colin appeared, dead center of the stage, and women screamed long and loud and jumped up and down. Alexa gave a short scream, too, and then felt embarrassed. But she couldn't swallow her silly grin as she stood with the other fans. She realized then that she would probably have to stand for the rest of the concert--at least, if she wanted to see anything.

Blue, strobing lights flashed across the stage, and the drummer rolled the drums. More screams pierced the air.

Then, with a flash of the guitar, Colin played the first, vibrating note of his most famous song. Alexa found herself clasping her hands, waiting for the next note. His arm whirled through the air, and the concert screamed to life.

Alexa swayed with the others and joined in the familiar choruses. Excitement charged through her, electrified by Colin's performance. He knew just how to keep the crowd in the palm of his hand. Alexa loved every one of his songs, but especially the few, softly crooned love ballads. She could not get over the fact that she was *here*, watching her favorite star sing! And she was actually staying at his house. It seemed, once again, like an incredible fairy tale come true.

By the time the concert ended, Alexa's emotions were charged so high that she felt like one of his groupies. She fought her way backstage, where a harried looking security guard checked passes, letting people through one at a time. Alexa immediately saw the "groupie" area. Colin stood there, greeting fans with a handshake and a high watt smile, while Jamison and Mart stolidly flanked him.

Most fans were women, as Mart had said. Many wanted autographs, and behaved in a normal fashion. Others pressed kisses to his cheeks. One fainted. Alexa was embarrassed for her female species. Never mind that part of her wanted to run and get his autograph, too. She managed to control herself—barely. Colin still vibrated with an electric energy that sucked the fans to him like a magnet. He had been blessed by the gifts of both charisma and musical genius.

Alexa decided to retreat to the lounge before she embarrassed herself. The next hour or more whirled by. Members of the band introduced themselves. Some had long hair, a few were pencil thin with tattoos, but all were courteous and friendly.

Mart appeared at her side. "Colin's going out with the band. Do you want to come, or go home?"

Alexa felt wired, but she wasn't a partying type of girl. Especially when Colin was the main person she would know.

He'd be too busy to spend much time with her. "Home," she said. "I've got to work in the morning."

Mart led her out to a small fleet of black cars. He spoke through a window to a driver, and then opened the door for her. "He'll see you home."

"Thanks, Mart." Alexa leaned back in the plush seat and tried to relax. It was impossible. She felt like dancing.

❈ ❈ ❈ ❈ ❈

Back at Colin's house, Alexa still floated on an emotional high, replaying the concert in her head. The magic in the air! The beautiful, crooning love songs lilting from Colin's perfect tenor! The memories still trembled along her heart strings, thrilling her. It seemed like Colin's soul came through in his music. His voice was strong, yet tender.

She sighed, chin in her hand, and stared at her blank computer screen. Alexa wanted to write down all of her impressions while they were still fresh. So she would do it— and censor nary a one. She could edit out her star-struck awe later.

Alexa typed like crazy for three hours. By the end of that time, her neck ached and her watch said two o'clock. If she didn't suspect most of her ravings were silly tripe, her book would be ten pages closer to completion.

When she stretched, Alexa realized that she still wore her evening clothes. Heels and all. With a grimace, she kicked them off. Until now, she hadn't noticed how the straps dug into her ankles.

Alexa was afraid to look at what she had written. Probably it was all silly fluff. But since it was out of her system, now she could write the concrete details of the concert. Like who was backstage, the mood of the crowd, the size of the stadium; things like that.

She needed a cup of tea. Then she could settle down and have a good work session. Colin wouldn't be available tomorrow morning, so she could sleep in a little, and then get back to work on the albums.

Pleased with the good start she had made—possible fluff and all—Alexa slipped down the narrow staircase in her nyloned feet. She knew the kitchen was this way, since Jamison had brought her upstairs that first night through the bowels of the house. Not through the grand front entrance, of course.

Voices filtered up the stairs from the kitchen and she halted, surprised she wasn't the only one awake.

"Alexa's hot," Mart said. "And smart. Colin's got himself a live one this time."

Alexa's cheeks warmed. They were talking about her. She felt both embarrassed and uncomfortable. She didn't think of herself as beautiful, although many others had told her so. Colin—and Jamison—included. Although the latter, hardly in a complimentary way.

Jamison said, "'Hot' means trouble. Colin had better watch out."

"Awful *hot* under the collar, bud," Mart said. "She's got you worked up."

"She's trouble," Jamison said darkly.

"But beautiful. Admit it, man."

"Yes, she's beautiful, but..."

At that moment, Alexa tumbled off the bottom stair. She had been leaning too far forward, straining to hear their conversation. She didn't even know why it enthralled her so.

Embarrassed to be caught eavesdropping, she sailed immediately into the room. Mart sat at the table, sipping a soft drink. Cheeks hot with chagrin, she glared at Jamison, who leaned against the nearest counter.

"You're doomed to disappointment if you're attracted to me," she told him. Of course, she knew he wasn't, but as usual with him, her foolish tongue sped ahead of her better sense.

Jamison took a quick breath and glanced at the ceiling, as if questioning God why he had to be tortured by the likes of her. "Nothing better to do than eavesdrop?"

"I came for tea. I didn't expect to find you here discussing me behind my back." With that verbal shot, she glided to the sink like a regal princess. Luckily, she saw a mug hanging on the rack so she didn't have to fumble through a cupboard.

Then Alexa realized that Mart might take her comments personally, too. Dismay arose. Quickly, she struggled to find tactful words to patch things up with Mart. With a bang, they came—in her sister's voice in her head.

"Although I appreciate you saying nice things about me." She twinkled a smile at Mart, who grinned back. She ignored Jamison altogether, ran water in a cup, and then deposited it in the microwave.

"For the record," Jamison's voice held a rough edge now, "just because I said you're beautiful doesn't mean I'm attracted to you. First, I'd have to be attracted to Amazons. And I'm not."

With narrowed eyes, she surveyed the man across the room. "No, of course not. Which I'm extremely grateful for, by the way. I'd hate to hurt your fragile ego." More retaliatory words came, which she knew her tactful sister would not approve of, but they rolled out anyway. "Small men like you have to find tiny, weak women you can dominate. That's the only way you can convince yourself that you're terribly big and strong and powerful. And when I say *small* I don't mean *short*." She lifted her eyebrows for emphasis.

"Ouch, man," Mart said from the table. He covered a smile by lifting the glass to his lips.

Jamison's dark eyes gleamed; controlled, as she was beginning to suspect he always was, but furious. He said nothing, though, and just watched her. She began to feel uncomfortable. Had she said too much? Of course she had. In fact, she had been horribly rude! *Why* couldn't she control her tongue with Jamison?

But he had just insulted her!

Thankfully, the microwave buzzed, so she turned and pulled out her sizzling hot mug. Now, if only she knew where they kept the tea...

She opened the cupboards nearest her, but found nothing but dishware. She still felt Jamison's gaze prickling into her, and she felt uncomfortable and self-conscious. Further testiness bubbled in her, but she struggled to suppress it. That rude man. He brought out the worst in her, and she didn't like it. Not at all. If she was smart, she wouldn't say another word to him.

Where was the tea? Exasperated and embarrassed, she sent a prayer heavenward. *Please help me, God!* And she meant for more than help finding the tea. Swallowing her pride, she turned to Mart. "Do you know where the tea is?"

"Don't drink the stuff." He flicked a finger toward his friend. "Jamison does, though."

Alexa would sooner drink plain scalding water than ask that particular man for any favors. But would she appear intimidated by his stare if she didn't speak to him? How could he gain the upper hand by saying nothing at all? Frustrated, she turned her gaze to him. Never in her life had she met a more profoundly annoying man. "Where would the tea be?" she inquired, icing her tone with sugar.

By way of an answer, he moved toward her. Her uncomfortable feeling rose. Why couldn't he just tell her?

She wouldn't move, though. He wouldn't scare her off. He came very close. Only a foot away now. His wavy black hair came to her eye level. She rued the fact that she had left her heels upstairs. Then he'd be at chin level!

Now he went on tiptoe, facing her, and disconcertingly, his dark gaze came level with hers. Up close, a potent virility radiated from him, and her skin prickled. The desire to retreat overwhelmed her. She smelled the clean scent of soap and a spicy aftershave. He was leaning toward her! What was he doing?

Alexa's eyes widened in alarm, and she gasped in a quick breath. Then she realized he had opened a cupboard overhead and plucked down a box from the top shelf.

"Tea, princess."

She snatched it from him, accidentally grazing his rough fingers. A shock went through her at the contact. Fueled by hate—no, she couldn't hate him. That wouldn't be right. Strong dislike, then. That was it. "Thank you," she said through her teeth. "You are so kind."

"At your service." She didn't miss the sarcastic tone. Or the fact he had just called her "princess." He really thought she was haughty and high and mighty. He had inquired if she had thought she was royalty in the car at the airport. And then, when she had inadvertently let it slip in his hearing that she felt like she was living in a fairy tale...well, he must have connected all of the dots. Hence, his not so flattering coronation of her as "princess."

She ignored him as he moved away, and focused completely upon fixing her tea—and keeping her mouth shut. She had made enough inflammatory remarks for one night. She really did need to call her sister for tips on tact. And she needed to pray for help, too.

The two men muttered behind her, and when she had finished concocting her tea, she discovered only Mart remained in the room.

She smiled at him. "Goodnight, Mart. I had a wonderful time at the concert."

An odd light sparkled in his eyes. "Me, too." He hesitated. "Alexa, don't chew up my buddy and spit him out. He's a good guy, with a heart as big as Texas."

"I have yet to see that side of him. But I'll try to control myself," she agreed. "Sometimes my mouth runs away with me. I hope I haven't made you into an enemy, too."

"Naw." With a grin, the blond-haired giant leaned back in his chair. "I think you're going to make this tour interesting."

"I hope you mean that in a good way."

"We'll see." The chair dropped to the floor again. "We'll see."

CHAPTER THREE

WEDNESDAY MORNING Alexa awoke early, like she normally did at home, and decided it was time to resume her exercise program, and her daily devotional, too. Usually, she ran the stairs in her apartment complex and did a few other exercises inside her living room, as she didn't have time to go to a gym. And now, since she would spend the next six weeks slaving over her computer, she figured she had better get some exercise.

So Alexa crept through the quiet house at 5:30 A.M., ran up and down the stairs to the kitchen, and then retired to her room to complete her workout. Luckily, she encountered no one. Afterward, she spent time reading the Bible, which she sorely needed to do. Her behavior lately—especially with Jamison—left much to be desired. Afterward, she enjoyed a chat over tea and toast with Mrs. Stroud in the kitchen. The housekeeper was a warm and cheerful woman, and Alexa liked her very much.

Alexa spent the rest of the day poring through the neatly labeled photo albums. Colin had been a cute little boy with white blond hair. Little surprise there. What did surprise her were the numerous pictures of him with dirt on his face, multiple bandages, and even a cast at age ten. Evidently, he had been quite the adventurer. She made careful note of the questions to ask Colin when she saw him next.

It wasn't at dinner that night. Mrs. Stroud informed her that Colin was out with friends. Alexa asked to eat in the kitchen with the rest of the staff, since she didn't want to eat alone at the long table, like Mrs. Stroud had originally intended.

That meant she ate with Jamison and Mart. Thankfully, Jamison said little, and disappeared soon.

Before bed, she called Beth for the first time. With the eight hour time difference, it was two o'clock in the afternoon in California.

"I saw you on TV this morning!" Beth immediately squealed.

"You what?" Alexa gasped.

"Haven't you seen yourself on the telly?"

"I don't have time to watch TV. What do you mean? What did you see?"

"On the morning news show they mentioned Colin's tour. Anyway, they showed a clip of Colin near his black limo, and there you were beside him!"

Alexa couldn't say anything for a minute, for she was so shocked. Then, "I hope you recorded it."

"I didn't know you'd be on it, silly. But I'm recording the entertainment shows tonight, just in case they show it."

Alexa still couldn't believe it. "Did they mention my name, too?"

"Yes. They said you're his newest lady love."

Alexa giggled. "That's ridiculous. You know how they like to make things up."

"So how is my famous sister doing? What's London like?"

"Fabulous." Alexa sighed, and quickly brought her sister up to date. She left out the squabbles with Jamison, however. They weren't worth mentioning. "And Colin is so sweet. He doesn't seem like a star at all. He's funny, self-deprecating, and down to earth."

"Sounds like you're in love."

Alexa heard the criticism in her sister's voice. "You sound like Scrooge, Beth." She was hurt, and also experienced a little prick to her fairy tale bubble. Thankfully, it didn't pop. "Aren't you happy for me?"

"Of course I am. But everything I've read about Colin says he's a player. Be careful, Alexa."

"I'm almost thirty, Beth."

"Yes, but you're not exactly wise to the ways of the world, are you? Don't forget what happened with Paul. You haven't let yourself get close to a man since college. I'm afraid you're ripe for a big fall. And Colin seems perfect, doesn't he? Handsome, charming...does he meet all of your criteria, Alexa?"

"So far, every one," she admitted.

A silence elapsed. "Be careful."

"I will." The conversation turned to other matters, and then they said goodbye. It had been good to talk to her sister, but truthfully, Alexa hadn't liked her warnings about Colin.

Was Colin a player? Or was he the sweet, genuine man she had begun to know? Until she found out, Alexa would be careful. Beth's warning had been unnecessary, however. Alexa already knew that learning to trust a man enough to give him her heart again would be difficult. She could not bear another broken heart.

❈ ❈ ❈ ❈ ❈

The next few days flew by. Alexa took a black cab to the Underground—or the "tube," as Londoners called it—on Thursday morning. Finally, a clear, blue sky day. Perfect for sightseeing. The tube confused her for a few minutes, until she realized that trains ran at different levels. She read the signs, and then rode the steep escalator down to the level she needed, and rode the tube into the heart of London. There, she found the red, double-decker bus hop-on hop-off tour to sightsee London.

Alexa made it to Buckingham Palace minutes before eleven-thirty in the morning and managed to spy the changing of the guard, and next visited Piccadilly Circus and took a picture, along with the other tourists, of the statue dubbed "Eros." She was amused to learn that "Eros" was not supposed to be the god of love at all, but rather the "Angel of Christian Charity." Afterward, she walked to Trafalgar Square.

For lunch, she stopped and had a sandwich with a "rocket," which she was surprised to learn meant a green salad with dressing. She spent some time trying to find a public restroom—surprisingly difficult to find—and then hopped a bus to see Westminster Abbey, and rode by Hyde Park. Then she just rode the bus, seeing as much as she could see. The time galloped by too fast. She wanted to take the river tour, but it would take two hours. No time to shop for souvenirs for Annie and Timmy, either. Maybe she could return later in the week and shop at Selfridges before leaving for Paris.

The book took every scrap of time from late Thursday afternoon on, for she had to finish wading through the six photo albums Colin's mother had neatly compiled. So many pictures! So many potential stories for the book.

Alexa had already written pages of notes and possible questions for Colin, but she hadn't seen him since the concert. He was never home, not even for meals. Thursday night she ran across him just before he left the house.

"Colin!" she called after him.

He looked harried. "I'm off now, love."

"We need to make an appointment to discuss the book."

"Talk to Eve, then—wait. I gave her a few days holiday. How about this—we'll have lunch on Sunday." With a cheery wave, he disappeared through the door.

Alexa frowned. Not promising at all.

At least Jamison stayed out of her hair. Every time she spied his black clad form, he kept to the background, a quiet, unassuming presence. His silent pretence didn't fool her for one second, however. She knew very well that underneath it all simmered raw, carefully controlled aggression. Jamison kept a watchful eye on everyone in the house, including her. And he strolled the outside perimeter, too.

Friday morning, while running the stairs in the early peace of the morning, she almost barreled into him. Alexa was on her way up, and Jamison on his way down.

Black flashed in the corner of her eye, and when Jamison flipped sideways, pressing his back to the wall, she staggered in the other direction. His sleeve brushed her bare arm and she glared at him, breathing hard. "Can't you watch where you're going?" Once again, her tongue ran without thinking, and she felt a sting of remorse. What was wrong with her? If she couldn't watch her tongue, how would they ever get along?

His black gaze swept down her body, clad in a large T-shirt and tight lycra pants. She had pulled her hair into a pony tail, and Alexa knew perspiration glistened on her face. But the bodyguard chose to comment on none of those things.

"So, you do own normal shoes."

"Heels are normal," she corrected him. "Tennis shoes are for exercising."

His eyes looked hard. "Do you often run through the house before anyone's awake?"

Alexa gasped at his not so subtle accusation. "I'm not running *through* the house, in case you're blind. I'm running the stairs. For exercise," she clarified.

"Stay out of Colin's wing."

Alexa glared. "I'm not a stalker! Or is that what you think?"

"Stay on your side of the house. I'll be watching to make sure you do."

"Fine. Waste your time. I'm not running again until next Monday. Five-thirty, in case you want to synchronize watches." She bared her teeth in a fake smile and sprinted to her room. That insufferable man! Fury and indignation fueled the rest of her workout.

After that encounter, Alexa felt Jamison's eyes upon her on more than one occasion. No doubt he was still suspicious of her, and would report any unauthorized behavior to Colin.

He was entirely too distrustful, but why? Of course, that was his job. But he had disliked her on sight. Why? Had he overheard her comment about short men back in New York, and taken umbrage with that? Alexa frowned. Well, whatever. She just wanted to steer clear of Mr. Sunshine.

❋ ❋ ❋ ❋ ❋

Alexa's fingers flew over the keyboard on Saturday morning. Only two days left in London. She had woken up at five o'clock this morning so she could finish work early today. It was overcast outside, but she wanted to spend this afternoon shopping for souvenirs for her family. Hopefully, it wouldn't rain.

She had just finished a quick lunch, and was almost done with the last photo album.

A knock came at her door. "Come in," she called.

Mrs. Stroud poked her head inside. "Letter for you, miss."

"Thank you." Alexa accepted it and closed the door after the housekeeper. She turned it over in her hand. Who knew her address in London?

No one. She hadn't given it to anyone, since she would only be here one week. The envelope showed no return address.

With curiosity, Alexa opened it. A photo of Colin and herself standing beside a limousine confronted her, pasted on a ruled sheet of paper. The photo had been cut from a tabloid, if the caption, "Colin's American beauty" was any indication. Below the photo, words cut from newsprint were pasted unevenly across the page. The message screamed larger than the tiny words themselves.

> *Die.*
> *Colin isn't yours.*
> *Go home, Alexa Kaplan.*

Alexa dropped the paper as if it were stained with acid.

The flimsy sheet fluttered in a soft, sweeping nose dive to the floor. How could something so insubstantial turn her world upside down? The black hatred had jumped at her from the page. A living, corrosive force.

What should she do with it?

Show Colin. Surely he would know what to do. Didn't stars deal with crazed stalkers all the time? She needed his experience, and his comfort, too.

Alexa had watched enough detective shows to know that she shouldn't touch the note again. She might smudge the sender's prints. If he'd left any. She grabbed a tissue and snared the note, but didn't worry about taking care with the envelope. The entire postal service had likely handled it, so any prints would be useless. She fairly flew downstairs to Colin's study.

The door stood half open, so she knocked and poked her head inside. It was dark. No Colin. Wasn't he ever home?

Alexa felt even more distraught. She wanted to tell someone about the note *now*. Maybe she should leave Colin a message, so he could contact her when he got back.

Good idea. She hurried to his broad wooden desk. The only light in the room filtered in through the partially drawn tapestry drapes. She found pencil and paper and quickly scribbled a note, all the while feeling uncomfortable to be in his private office, uninvited.

There. She placed it in the middle of his desk. A bright light flashed on overhead. Alexa gasped, hand flying to her mouth, tissue wrapped note and all.

Jamison advanced into the room. "What are you doing in here?"

Alexa recovered her breath, but her heart still pounded. Guilt was part of it. She crossed her arms, tucking the note out of sight. "What does it look like? I need to see Colin."

Jamison strolled closer, his movements controlled and menacing. In full bodyguard mode, Alexa realized—and *she* was the threat.

But what about the threat to her? Protectively, she folded the note more tightly and slipped it between her arm and torso. She did the same with the envelope, on the other side. "I need to see Colin," she repeated.

The bodyguard had closed within three feet of her now, and her skin prickled. His gaze flickered to her crossed arms. "Give it to me."

"Excuse me?" She pretended ignorance.

The black eyes looked like obsidian. "Now."

"It's none of your business."

"Now it is. You're trespassing."

Alexa felt frustrated, and tears hovered alarmingly near the surface. Her fear of the note, coupled with the antagonistic aggression of the bodyguard, made her want to run and hide. But of course, she did neither. She lifted her chin. "Get Colin. I'll give it to him."

"Doesn't work that way, princess." In one swift movement, his hand shot out and slipped under her arm, which was pressed close to her side. His fingers felt hard and businesslike as he plucked the note from her grasp.

She gasped and jerked back. "How dare you touch me!" Tears burned in earnest, then, at the presumptuous violation.

"I warned you, princess." How Alexa hated that caustic nickname! The bodyguard said, "What is this? A love note?" Contempt hardened his eyes.

"Not hardly! And keep your prints off it," she gritted.

With care, Jamison unfolded the note and swiftly scanned it. No expression registered on his face, but he read it again. "Where did you get this?" The black eyes remained just as hard, just as suspicious.

"I didn't cut and paste it, if that's what you're thinking. It came in the mail today."

"Where's the envelope?"

Unwillingly, Alexa extended it to the bodyguard. He scanned both sides.

"Satisfied?" Alexa wanted to know. "I thought Colin could help me. Has he dealt with this before?"

"He gets frequent threats."

"Do his guests?"

"No."

"So now what do I do?" she demanded.

"Nothing. I'll talk to Colin." Jamison turned away. "Don't leave the house."

"I'm under house arrest?" Alexa could not believe her ears. "I don't think so. I'm going into London this afternoon."

"Now you're not." He disappeared through the door.

Alexa's mouth gaped, and then snapped shut. The nerve of that smug, obnoxious man! And she suspected he had extracted some sort of perverse delight in telling her what to do, too.

As if she would obey him.

Her fear of the note was now swamped by rebellious ire at the highhanded bodyguard. She wasn't a child. And he certainly had no authority over her. And she had worked so hard this morning so she could go out today. Jamison Jethro Constanzo would not stop her. After all, she had shopping to do.

Upstairs, Alexa turned off the computer and prepared for her outing. She called a black cab to meet her at the entrance gate. A little fear returned when she thought about the note, but she told herself to ignore it. It was only a note. Weren't threatening note writers—and crank callers—mostly gutless cowards? They lusted for the power to intimidate and frighten others, but did so from a safe distance; hidden behind unknown return addresses and blocked caller ids.

No one would come after her. And she refused to be intimidated by a malicious person, anyway. When would she ever return to London? At the end of the tour she would return for a few days, but who knew if the book would be finished by then, or if she would have a chance to shop?

Mind made up, Alexa hurried downstairs and out the front door. Happily, Jamison was nowhere to be seen. The guard let her out the front gate with a cheery smile and a wave, even. Pleased, Alexa climbed into the cab and didn't look back.

Alexa thoroughly enjoyed her afternoon, and was glad the overcast clouds held back their rain. She found a Paddington bear for Timmy and a princess doll for Annie while she shopped in Selfridges and the shopping district around it. Good thing she had brought the extra suitcase. Alexa even found two magnets for her refrigerator back home. One of London Bridge—which she still hadn't seen yet—and one of Buckingham Palace.

The afternoon was an unqualified success. Only one moment of alarm came when she hurried along the wide, busy sidewalk, hugging the edge, near the boulevard. She had spied a café and wanted to have high tea there, like the proper English did.

A swell of people going in the opposite direction pushed into her, and then Alexa felt a hard shove at her shoulder. She teetered precariously on her high heels, and then pitched into the street, right in the path of an oncoming lorry.

Terror surged, and the next moment passed in slow motion. Not sure how she managed it, Alexa landed on her toe and twisted, lunging back toward the sidewalk. She landed on her knees, safely, just as the truck roared by.

Shaking, she wobbled upright. No one paid any attention to her. She had dropped the bags, and now searched for them. One had been kicked near a post and she found the other in the street. Sadly, Paddington's bag had tire tracks over it, and the bear's legs looked unnaturally flat. Added to all that, she spotted two huge runs in her nylons, and her knees looked black with grime. Still, it could have been worse.

All the same, Alexa trembled and her teeth chattered as she crossed the street to the café. The feeling of being out of control in that one moment—vulnerable and unable to protect herself—had terrified her. She had felt like an adolescent again, unable to control her world as it had careened toward disaster.

Alexa had tea, with paper thin sandwiches and fairy cakes, but found herself still trembling during the meal. She wanted to return to Colin's—to the comfort of somewhere familiar and safe.

Soon after the quick tea, a taxi dropped her off in front of Colin's gate. Gathering her battered bags together, Alexa tapped on the guard's door.

It was a different guard. He peered at her, his eyebrows aloof. "Yes, miss?"

"I'm Alexa Kaplan. I'm staying here as Colin's guest."

"Very good, miss. I'll call the house."

After a lengthy phone conference, the gate opened. With relief, Alexa hurried to the front door.

Unfortunately, the first person she saw inside was Jamison. No doubt he had been alerted to her return by the gate security guard.

"Enjoy your afternoon?" His deep, melodious Italian voice was deceptively mild, for it was hard to miss the black thundercloud of his brow.

Alexa chose to ignore it. "Why, yes. How nice of you to ask."

"Come with me."

Alexa lifted the dirty shopping bags. "Thanks. But I think I'll run these upstairs, first."

Jamison stared at them and then, disconcertingly, at her knees, bared by the gigantic rips in her nylons. "What happened to you?"

"I tripped off the sidewalk," she said airily.

He looked down further. "I see your heels survived."

"Disappointed?"

The black gaze returned to her face. "Come with me."

"I need to change." Alexa headed for the stairs.

"Now." He didn't raise his voice, but the controlled force behind that single word made Alexa pause.

"Make it easy on yourself, Alexa. Swallow your pride and come with me."

"Why?" she demanded.

"Colin wants to see you."

"Well, okay then." Alexa had no problem coming if Colin wanted to see her—too bad about her filthy nylons, though. But everything within her rebelled at obeying the bodyguard. He knew this. She could tell it by his flashing dark eyes and the tension radiating from his body.

She sailed by him. "Colin's study?" she inquired over her shoulder.

The bodyguard did not reply. Instead, a hard hand on her elbow forced her to stop. Affronted, she glared at him. "Get your hand off me."

"You were lucky today, princess," he said in a low voice. "You think that note was a joke?"

"No." She wrenched her arm free. "But I also know I won't let some sicko—or a mini Mussolini—dictate my life."

A muscle twitched in his jaw. "You are acting like a child, Alexa. Today you were easy prey for a kidnapper...or a killer." The Italian accent suddenly seemed more pronounced and threatening. Like a character from the *Godfather*.

Alexa tried to ignore the chill that raced over her skin. "The note was a hoax."

"Really? You said you tripped today. Did you? Or were you pushed?"

Unexpected fear sliced through her. The incident flashed back through her mind. "It was crowded. Someone accidentally knocked me into the street." She looked away, biting her lip, remembering the horror of the moment. "In front of a truck," she added in a thin voice.

He drew in a harsh breath.

"It was an accident," she insisted.

"Maybe. Maybe not."

"Doesn't Colin get these notes all of the time? How often does someone actually try to attack him?"

"More often than you'd think. He got a note like yours today."

"He did?" Another chill went through her. "What did it say?"

He hesitated, as if weighing the wisdom of sharing that particular piece of information with her. "To send you home."

"That would please you, wouldn't it?" she accused. But inside, she was frightened and upset. What if Colin did send her home? Then again, maybe he should, if her presence endangered him. But what about the book?

Jamison said harshly, "If you had been killed today, it would have eaten Colin up. He'd feel responsible, because you're under his protection."

Alexa glanced at Colin's closed study door.

"Look at me," Jamison urged, and reluctantly, she did so. "Your rebellious shot at me could have cost you your life. Was the shopping worth it?"

Alexa glared, trying to ignore the prickles of guilt mixing with the fear. "It wasn't about you," she informed him. *Liar,* she told herself. This man got under her skin like a splinter.

"No?" He sounded like he didn't believe her. "You're a grown woman, Alexa. Next time you want to run off like a child, use your common sense."

His words burned, mostly because they were true. Maybe she had acted like a child, defiantly running off like that. However, she would never admit that to the bodyguard. He was entirely too full of himself. And on top of that, why was she letting his take on the accident scare her? Who was he to say the incident in London had been an attack? How could he possibly know? In fact, the more she thought about it, the more ridiculous it seemed.

She sent him a cool glance. "Is Colin in his study?"

"Yes."

His black, censorious gaze held hers, making her temper surge. However, she merely said, "Thank you," and stalked with as much pride as possible to Colin's door, mangled shopping bags swinging.

"Come in," Colin answered to her knock.

Unfortunately, Jamison followed her inside.

Colin sat at his desk, but his head snapped up when he saw her. His worried frown cleared. "Alexa!" He stood and greeted her with outstretched hands. Feeling embarrassed, she dropped the bags and squeezed his hands in return.

"I'm sorry I worried you," she said. "I guess I didn't take the threat seriously enough."

"I'm relieved you're all right."

"I told her about the threat you received," Jamison said.

Colin turned his attention to Alexa. "So you understand I'm taking both threats seriously."

"Tell him what happened in the city," Jamison interfered again.

"*Nothing* happened." Alexa frowned, but refused to look at the bodyguard. "It was crowded and someone pushed me, that's all."

"Into the street, in front of a truck," Jamison finished.

"Alexa." Colin's blue eyes darkened with concern.

"It was an accident, not an attack."

Colin shook his head. "All the same, I need to take protective measures."

Concern arose. "Do you want me to go home?"

"No, of course not. But I am worried about you, so I'm going to assign Jamison as your bodyguard."

Jamison. Her bodyguard? Alexa's mouth opened in horror.

Jamison watched her, his face impassive, all the while standing in his usual bodyguard stance; his shoulders straight, black clad legs apart, and hands clasped in front of his compact body.

"No," she breathed.

"Jamison is the best." Colin frowned, seeming to misunderstand. "You'll be safe with him. Here in London you're safe in my house, but if you go out, Jamison will need to go with you."

"But..." Alexa wanted to ask why Mart couldn't be assigned to her, and then realized how ungrateful that would sound. Colin was being chivalrous, and trying to protect her. "Thank you," she said stiffly. "But I'm sure I won't require his services."

"Are you sure? We're leaving Monday, so tomorrow is our last day here."

"Tomorrow's Sunday?" Alexa had momentarily lost track of time. "I did want to go to church." Surely Jamison wouldn't want to accompany her. The very thought made her want to smile.

Colin smiled. "Jamison?"

The bodyguard growled, "You can come to my church."

Taken aback, Alexa looked from Jamison to Colin. Jamison attended church? Then again, maybe he realized he needed forgiveness for his black soul. Who was she to stand in the way of his eternal salvation?

"Fine," she said. "What time?"

"Meet me downstairs at ten o'clock."

"It's a date," she said cheekily, and to her delight, the bodyguard stiffened. Probably repulsed, she decided with satisfaction. She turned to Colin. "Thank you for taking care of me. By the way, I finished with all of the photo albums this morning. Are we still on for tomorrow? I've got lots of questions for you."

"Absolutely. I've been looking forward to our lunch." The blue eyes sparkled at her, and she twinkled back.

"Perfect," she said.

❋ ❋ ❋ ❋ ❋

The next morning the trip to church was accomplished in silence, which was just fine with Alexa. After the pastor greeted Alexa, he shook Jamison's hand and called him by name, which surprised her. As did the smile the bodyguard gave him. It certainly lightened his features! But it settled back into unfriendly lines when he looked at her.

"Up there," he said.

Alexa slid into a pew, and Jamison slid in beside her. However, a good three feet separated them. Alexa didn't know whether to be pleased or annoyed. Definitely pleased, she decided.

She felt it was up to her to be the bigger person and try to be civil. It was high time, anyway. God couldn't be too pleased with her recent behavior. "It's beautiful in here," she commented. "I love the stained glass windows."

"Huh," he grunted.

Alexa frowned at him as he continued to read the bulletin, apparently intent on ignoring her. "Why aren't you speaking to me today?"

He flicked her an unfriendly glance. "We get along best when we don't speak."

Alexa felt annoyed, although she couldn't fault his logic. She also felt oddly hurt, which made no sense at all. Fine, she told herself. Let him be rude. It only reflected on his character, not hers. Thankfully, the music started soon, so she didn't have long to feel uncomfortable with the silence between them.

Alexa loved to sing, and was glad to recognize several of the hymns and praise songs. To her surprise, the bodyguard beside her sang each song in a low, pleasing baritone. Clearly, he knew the songs well.

Could he possibly be a Christian?

Alexa found this hard to believe. However, who was she to judge? Her behavior lately had been far from exemplary. Only God knew Jamison's dark heart.

In the quiet, reflective prayer time, Alexa asked forgiveness for her own sins. And she wondered again why it was so hard to curb her tongue around Jamison. He was obnoxious, yes, but something else about him disturbed her.

During the last moments of prayer, quiet truth opened up in her heart. Jamison reminded her of the partying men she had met in college. Not that she could ever imagine Jamison uncoiling enough to party. No. But like those aggressive, confident men, he wasn't predictable or tame. He unnerved her. Even so, it was no excuse to beat him off with sarcastic words.

She enjoyed the sermon. Perhaps appropriately, the topic focused on dealing with one's enemies.

The pastor advised, "'Fear of man will prove to be a snare, but whoever trusts in the LORD is kept safe. And remember Psalm twenty-three, also. 'Even though I walk through the valley of the shadow of death, I will fear no evil, for you are with me...'"

A shiver slid through Alexa, for his words reminded her of the threatening note and her near death experience in the city.

Toward the end of the sermon, new verses nipped at her conscience, too. Like loving one's enemies and praying for them. She slid a glance at Jamison. Maybe he wasn't exactly her enemy, and she certainly couldn't imagine liking him, let alone loving him. But she could pray for him—and she could try to treat him with more kindness. *Lord help me.*

❈ ❈ ❈ ❈ ❈

Alexa brought her digital recorder to lunch, along with her notebook of questions and a photo album. So far, she had found it impossible to schedule time with Colin, except for this lunch. Frequent meetings kept him out of the house. She had seen him for a few seconds here and there over the last few days, but that was it. On those rare occasions, she had been able to ask him a few questions, but hadn't been fully prepared to take advantage of those moments. Now she realized she had to be ready at all times.

In fact, Alexa was beginning to suspect Colin balked at the idea of actually sitting down and working on the book. Colin appeared to be a free-spirited sort of a man. He was outgoing and charming, but he wasn't much of a planner. That was Eve.

Alexa discovered the secretary was already seated at the table with Colin when she arrived for lunch. She was ridiculously disappointed—not to mention apprehensive—to see Eve. So far, she had managed to avoid Colin's mercurial secretary.

"Alexa." Colin stood and greeted her with a kiss on the cheek. Eve glanced away, taking a sip of water while this transpired. Alexa didn't feel comfortable enough to kiss Colin back, but she gave him a quick hug and found her seat. Colin sat at the head of the table, with Alexa and Eve on either side of him.

Alexa lifted her recorder. "Be prepared to be taped, Colin. You're a hard man to pin down, so I've got to take advantage of every opportunity."

Eve eyed the recorder with suspicion. "You can't record our private conversation."

Colin chuckled, and dimples appeared in his sharply angular face. He smiled warmly at Alexa. "Alexa's got my number, as they say in America. It's okay with me."

"I'll warn you before I turn it on," Alexa promised.

French onion soup came first, served in a china bowl so thin Alexa could see her fingers through it. She knew, because she surreptitiously experimented. She ate carefully, needless to say. Each time her silver spoon clanked against the bowl she flinched, afraid it would shatter. After that, they ate beef Wellington, and then a warm bread pudding.

During the meal, encouraged by Alexa's questions about pictures in the album, Colin serenaded them with stories from his youth. He laughed at the picture of him and a huge shaggy dog, both covered in mud.

"Ah, yes. I remember that time. Mutt and I got into a great many scrapes. That time, I'd heard that mud baths were supposed to be cleansing. My mum said so. She always talked of visiting a spa when she had saved up enough. I didn't see why she had to pay for a spa when we had plenty of mud in the lot next door. I decided I'd give her a mud bath for her birthday. But I experimented first on Mutt and me, just to make sure we'd come up smelling like daisies."

Alexa choked with laughter. "And did you?"

"Let's just say me mum didn't get a mud bath for her birthday. Or ever."

Even the serious secretary cracked a smile. All during the meal she had repeatedly glanced between Colin and Alexa, as if searching for a place to find fault. It made Alexa feel uncomfortable.

The meal drew to a close. Colin dabbed his mouth and put his napkin on the table. "Sorry I've got to run, but I have a meeting with Paddy in an hour. Have you got enough material for the book, Alexa?"

"Enough for a few days. But I've got more questions I need answered. You want me to leave the photo albums here, right?"

"Correct. Eve can answer your questions." He grinned at the secretary, and she blossomed into a smile at his attention. A faint blush stained her cheeks. "Eve knows everything about me."

With a smile, Alexa attempted to joke, "You must be his number one fan, Eve."

"That would be my mum," Colin said with a rueful grin. "Cheers, you two. I'll see you both tomorrow morning. We'll leave for Heathrow at nine sharp."

"Okay." Alexa smiled after Colin, and then directed it to Eve. "I appreciate you helping me with the photos."

"You'll have to give me back all of the albums and scrapbooks tonight."

Alexa frowned. "But Colin said I could bring the scrapbooks I hadn't finished."

"I'll be in charge of them. We can't have any getting lost."

"Do you think I would lose them?"

Eve had the grace to look a little embarrassed. "Maybe not on purpose."

"I'll keep the one I'm working on and give you the others," Alexa compromised. "I'll work on it while we travel to Paris."

Eve's eyes narrowed. "Fine," she said shortly. "But be careful with it. They can't be replaced."

Goodness, she was prickly. Alexa searched for a safe topic, and remembered the earliest scrapbooks she had already read through. "Did his mother make all of the scrapbooks?"

"Most. I made the latest ones."

Alexa smiled, still striving to be friendly. "I'll bet that's something you didn't find in your job description."

"Colin didn't ask me. I just do it."

Somehow, that struck Alexa as a bit odd. "That's nice of you."

Eve shrugged. "Now ask your questions. I have work to do."

Clearly, Eve did not want to be friends, and frankly, Alexa was tired of trying. She asked questions, received succinct replies in response, and then Alexa retreated to her room to begin transcribing the recording.

Clearly, the secretary saw her as some sort of a threat and had made up her mind to dislike Alexa. Fine. It wasn't necessary to be friends. But it was too bad someone that close to Colin didn't like her. She hoped Eve's critical attitude didn't warp Colin's view of her. And she hoped Colin would be easier to interview while on the tour. Otherwise, writing this book could prove to be extremely difficult.

CHAPTER FOUR

The next morning, they flew to Paris in Colin's private jet. Alexa knew the band equipment would arrive via trucks on the slower ferry across the English Channel.

April in Paris! Alexa had dreamed of visiting ever since taking French in high school.

Driving out of the airport, she rode in the front seat of Colin's car, next to the driver, Hathaway. He was a balding man, and the silent sort. The cars carrying the band members and the bodyguards followed behind them.

Overhead, the sky was a deep, clear blue, and a faint breeze ruffled the tree leaves. In the distance, she glimpsed the Eiffel tower, and as they pulled into the heart of the city, the car crept along with the slow afternoon traffic toward their destination.

Alexa drank in everything. Hurrying people, cafés with striped awnings; the entire air of Paris sizzled with a new kind of energy—unique from New York or London, or any other large city she had visited. Even better, she soon learned that their apartment building was within walking distance of the Eiffel Tower. How perfect!

"Here we are," Hathaway said, stopping before a massive, stone-fronted building with narrow, arched windows. It was seven stories high. Ornately carved, double wooden doors hinted at the luxury within. "I'll check you and the gov in at the office. Wait here."

A few minutes later, the driver emerged with a liveried doorman and they packed the bags from two cars onto trolleys. Apparently, the band would travel to their hotel later. Hathaway handed Colin several packets of keys.

Alexa wondered how much to tip the doorman, and then realized she didn't have any euros. Now he would think she was a rude American. Great.

"Hathaway will see to the bags," Colin spoke up. "Everyone else come to the penthouse. I've ordered in food and drinks. Let's celebrate the start of our road tour!"

Well, good. Now Alexa didn't have to worry about tipping the doorman. And she would get to see a penthouse for the first time in her life. What could be better? Quickly, she packed the scrapbook and laptop she had used on the plane into her half-empty case and put it on a trolley, so she wouldn't have to lug them to Colin's penthouse.

She followed Colin and the others into the elevator and rode to the top of the building. Polished mirrors lined the elevator walls, and Alexa found them disconcerting, for everywhere she looked were people, people, and more reflected people.

As a nod to arriving in one of the most fashion conscious cities in the world, today Alexa wore gold sparkly heels, a crisp linen skirt, and a golden silky blouse over an ivory camisole. Jamison wore black, as usual, and stood silently ahead of her.

Colin opened the double doors to his flat, and a burst of sunshine and shimmering chandeliers met Alexa's eyes. Exquisite vases and paintings decorated every available space. The sitting area came first, followed by a bar and kitchen. Long, narrow windows skirted by exterior black railings punctuated the length of the large apartment, affording a glorious view of Paris and a park. Alexa slipped over to investigate. The breath caught in her throat. The Eiffel Tower appeared close enough to touch.

"Champagne, everyone?" Colin called. "Or soft drinks. Choose your poison."

Everyone collected drinks and snacks from the platters of cheeses and fruit on the counters.

Alexa realized she was starving, and heaped her napkin high. Jamison brushed by. "Hungry?" he muttered.

She frowned, but managed to control her tongue.

"Hear, hear." Colin raised his champagne flute. "To the tour! As you know, we're scheduled for four performances in each city, with a day's rest before and after. I figure that's about a week at each stop. I expect everyone to work hard, and play harder. Cheers!"

"Cheers," chorused the others. Alexa sipped her cola while the others drank champagne.

The party hummed after that. Alexa mingled, speaking to the band members she had met at the concert, and meeting still others. Mart laughed loudly, and ribbed a couple of the guys near him. She noticed that even Jamison smiled and talked with everyone. What a surprise that a cordial side to his personality existed! The bodyguard drank a clear, fizzy liquid. Not champagne like most everyone else. That was Jamison, always controlled and watchful. Always kept his wits about him and his head on straight.

"Alexa." Colin nudged her arm and his warm grin made Alexa melt. He truly did like her. No matter the warnings from her sister, Alexa felt deep in her heart that Colin was a genuine guy who wanted to be liked for himself, just like everyone else. And she definitely liked him. How could she not? He was the perfect man, and fit every one of her criteria—except she still wasn't sure if he was a Christian.

"Hey," she grinned back. "Great party. And I love your penthouse. What a fabulous view."

"I'm glad you like it. I'll invite you to dinner one night. I'll order in and we'll enjoy the view together." His blue eyes sparkled.

Alexa took a quick sip of cola. He was flirting with her! She smiled as steadily as she could. "I'd like that." But she also knew Colin and his hectic schedule. He meant well, but he'd be terribly busy the entire time in Paris. Not to mention, he'd perform four of those nights.

"Colin." Paddy's brusque voice interrupted their conversation. "I've got the latest numbers."

When Alexa would have stepped back to give them privacy, Colin's quick touch detained her. "Is Paris sold out?"

"Not yet. And numbers in Barcelona and Rome aren't moving."

"I trust you, Paddy." Colin clapped the burly man on the back. "You're the man to get things rolling. Have you got a plan?"

Paddy shot Alexa a curt, dismissive look. Clearly, he didn't think she should be privy to their conversation. "Yes."

"I knew it. Sign me up for more interviews, if needed."

"Right." With a forceful turn to his shoulders, Paddy headed for the bar.

"Forgive Paddy," Colin said. "The concerts aren't filling up as he'd like. He takes it personally."

Maybe the manager took it too personally. Alexa eyed him across the room. Bottled up frustration rolled from Paddy in palpable, aggressive waves. He seemed primed to explode if anyone crossed his path.

The old memory of shattering pottery echoed through Alexa's skull, and she abruptly shivered.

Colin frowned. "Alexa? Are you all right?"

"What? Oh...yes." The past was done, and long ago resolved. Wasn't it? Then why had that upsetting memory flashed? With an effort, Alexa focused into the present. "If the concerts don't fill up, will you cancel the tour?"

Colin laughed easily. "No, love. We've sold enough tickets to cover our expenses. And I couldn't disappoint the fans. We've nothing to worry about." He smiled. "Paddy is a profit hound. As he should be. It's his job. Plus, his contract guarantees his percentage of the profit goes up with a full house."

Alexa relaxed. "So he has incentive to make sure it's sold out."

"It works out to everyone's advantage." Colin smiled. "I have no doubt Paddy will pull a miracle from his hat. It won't be the first time." His grin faded. "Unfortunately, I need to talk to you about something more serious. Jamison, old boy." He got the bodyguard's attention as he passed by, and then addressed them both. "Jamison knows, but you don't, Alexa. We've received more threats on both of our lives. Specific threats."

Alarm arose. "What do you mean?"

"I don't want to scare you, but the authorities agree we need to take the threats seriously. The note sender is threatening that she—or he or they—is following us, and unless you go home now, she'll kill us both." He frowned. "She's ordered me to stop seeing you."

Alexa's face warmed. "But we're not...dating."

"This person is crazy. Facts don't matter. Besides, she understands what could happen between us."

"Maybe I should go home. I don't want to put your life in danger."

"Are you frightened?"

Was she? "Not really. I mean, it all seems so bizarre, like a hoax. Maybe that's all it is."

"We can't take that chance. If you want to stay and finish writing the book, I'd like you to. But it's your choice."

"I want to finish the book. I won't let a disturbed person scare me off."

"Good." Colin smiled. "I hoped you'd say that. Here's the thing. While you're touring with me, I want you protected. And that means all the time. You're not safe anywhere, not even in your apartment."

"I'm not?"

"You're not. Security is good here, but it's not enough to satisfy me. That's why I've taken the liberty of switching you over to a flat with a large sitting room and kitchen."

She was confused. "You did? Why?"

"You'll be spending most of your time there, and I want you to be comfortable. Also, the flat includes two bedrooms.

All together, it provides plenty of room for you and your protection to live together comfortably."

"Protection? Live together?" Alexa wasn't liking the sound of this. Beside her, Jamison stiffened. "What protection do you mean?"

"Jamison, if you're up for it, I'd like you to guard Alexa twenty-four/seven."

Jamison's jaw dropped, but then his teeth snapped together. He gave a short nod.

Alexa, however, was overcome with horror. "Jamison would live with me?" she cried out. "Colin, no! I mean, I appreciate your willingness to protect me, but... Jamison and I do not get along. Haven't you noticed?" It was high time to return that fact to Colin's attention.

Amusement sparkled. "Under the circumstances, it's the best choice I can make. And don't worry about Jamison. He's a monk."

Alexa slid a glance at the bodyguard. She wasn't sure if she believed that. But she did believe that he was very self-controlled at all times.

Colin gave his bodyguard a grin. "Although I'm not sure why. Plenty of female fans go for him."

Jamison's shoulders shifted, as if uncomfortable.

Alexa shot Jamison another glance. They did? She gave him a fleeting, albeit unwilling appraisal. His dark brows were straight, and his eyes intensely black. Besides a strong, uncompromisingly stubborn cast to his jaw and a small bump on his nose, which indicated it might have been broken once, his features were well-formed, she reluctantly admitted. In fact, he might even be considered handsome—if one wanted to look at him that way. Which she did not. Just as she did not want to be saddled with his presence for the entire tour.

A feeling of doom overtook her, and she grasped for straws...for freedom from this undeserved prison sentence. "Don't you need him to guard you?"

"I have Mart, and I've hired another guard for me, plus others to police the concerts. I'll be fine."

With a sick feeling in the pit of her stomach, Alexa glanced at Jamison. His dark eyes regarded her steadily. He wasn't afraid to be chained to her. In fact, was that a dare in the black depths? Instantly, she stiffened her spine. "I mean," she said stiffly, "it will be fine. But not pleasant." The understatement of all time!

"Good," Colin smiled. "Your luggage is already in your rooms. Here are your keys." He pulled them from his pocket and dropped one into each of their hands. He lifted his glass. "Cheers." And then he strolled away.

Alexa gasped, unable to help herself, and glared at Jamison. "You'd better stay out of my space."

"Want me to buy tape and mark it down the middle of the flat?"

Alexa curled her lip. "You are so childish. I just meant, you stay in your space, and I'll stay in mine."

He put down his glass. "How about we go check out our quarters?"

It was a challenge. Alexa finished her cola and did the same. "Fine. Let's get the rules hashed out right now."

In silence, they rode down the elevator to the second floor. They walked side by side down the empty hall. Alexa felt extremely uncomfortable with him by her side. She could not believe that she would be forced to live with this man.

Jamison stepped in front of her to open the door.

"Excuse me, but do you have to be rude?" Alexa said. "I was here first."

He sent her an annoyed look. "I need to check the flat to make sure it's safe. It's my job."

She crossed her arms. "Oh. Well, go to it, then."

He turned unexpectedly and all at once he was too close, for she had crowded behind him, eager for a first peep into the room. Alarmed, she staggered back so fast her heel snagged on the carpet. Only his strong hand on her wrist stopped her flailing descent to the floor.

He hauled her upright and pulled her within inches of him. Like in the kitchen late that one night, his potent masculinity accosted her, accelerating her pulse. The black gaze bored into hers. "Let's get something straight right now, princess. I am not your servant. Don't treat me like one."

She twisted her wrist, breaking his hold. An old judo self-defense move. Alexa struggled to regain her pride. "Touchy, aren't you? Is that your short complex coming through again?"

"Do you want to start an argument right now?"

"Well, I don't want you to carry me across the threshold, if that's what you're asking," she returned sarcastically.

He set his jaw. "Come in when I call you."

Of course, Alexa did no such thing. The instant he disappeared through the door, she slipped in behind him. She gasped at the sparkles of gold and shimmering cut glass dangling from a chandelier overhead. Colin had certainly spared no expense for this apartment. Or did it belong to one of his friends, too? Another pop star, perhaps, or an actress? No personal photos were displayed.

Before her were a couch and armchair covered in striped sateen in muted rust, gold, and green shades. The predominant colors in the room were gold and light green. The coffee table looked to be mahogany, and a giant television covered the wall just to the right of the front door.

Beyond the sitting room was a kitchen, complete with a large window overlooking the city, as well as cabinets, stove, sink, and a small refrigerator. A gleaming dining table was situated to the left, near a door into which Jamison had disappeared. Alexa guessed it was one of the bedrooms. She spotted a matching door on her right.

She prowled through the large, airy room, gently touching vases painted in fine oriental designs, as Jamison crossed to check the other bedroom. In the kitchen, she was pleased to discover that the refrigerator and freezer were full, including frozen pizzas, frozen dinners, and various drinks. Chips, along with canned and boxed goodies, filled the shelves.

"Look at this!" she breathed.

"What?"

She felt Jamison's presence behind her, but forgot to be annoyed with him in the wonder of her discovery. "Look at all the food!"

"Hungry already?" he wanted to know.

Alexa rolled her eyes. She said with exaggerated patience, "Is this normal? Does Colin always stock his flats with food?"

"Yes." Jamison opened the refrigerator to investigate. "Doesn't look like we'll starve."

Unease slid through Alexa at the "we" reference. "Do you mean to say we'll eat here together?"

"Unless you can afford to go out every night. I can't." He pulled a bottled water from the refrigerator.

"Hmph." Alexa didn't know what to say to this. Next, she investigated the bedrooms, and discovered each had an attached bath. Her luggage had been placed in the room to the right of the front door as she had come in. She returned to the living area. Jamison was nowhere to be seen.

So she crossed to poke her head into his room. He had just unzipped a giant suitcase—black, of course—and draped a clump of black, button down shirts on the bed. Some looked to be made of cotton, others of a silkier material.

"Are you color blind?" she wanted to know.

He glanced up. "You're here to help me unpack?"

"Of course not!" Alexa felt embarrassed, but didn't retreat. "We need to hash out rules so we can live in peace."

He pulled out a pile of black pants. Some jeans, some slacks.

"Would you stop that?" she demanded. "I'm trying to have a serious conversation."

"I can't unpack at the same time?"

Alexa gritted her teeth. "I have no desire to see any of your black...unmentionables."

An actual smile curled his lips, and he stopped pulling items from his suitcase. "Then wait in the sitting area. I'll be five minutes."

Alexa narrowed her eyes. She didn't want to stay here, but she didn't want to retreat, either. And she wanted to assert her rules first—before the bodyguard had a chance to make a power grab. "I'll make it snappy," she said, averting her eyes as he pulled smaller black items from the suitcase and tucked them in the dresser. "I have one rule. You leave me alone, and I'll leave you alone."

"Fine." Jamison pulled a thick book from the bottomless suitcase and placed it on the bedside table. What was that? *War and Peace*? Certainly appropriate for their living situation.

"Well then," Alexa said, pleased. "I'll leave you to sort your outfits by color. I'm never sure—does black silk go with black cotton?" With this saucy comment, which likely sailed right over his unfashionable head, she turned to leave.

"I have a rule."

Alexa turned back. She should have known her triumph had been too easy.

"You don't leave this apartment without me."

Alexa fell silent for one long beat, absorbing the full, horrifying implications of his statement. "Excuse me? I'm supposed to be chained to you night and day?"

"That's what twenty-four/seven means." He flipped the suitcase shut. The rasp of the zipper sounded like machine gun fire in the suddenly silent room. "If you want to run the stairs, I go with you. If you want to shop, I go with you. If you want to sight-see, I go with you. Think of me as your shadow."

"Hence the black," she said sarcastically. But further words evaded her. A sick feeling dropped into the pit of her stomach. She and Jamison, joined at the hip for almost five weeks? They couldn't breathe the same air without fighting! Her fairy tale had officially transformed into a nightmare. She muttered, "We're going to kill each other."

"I promise I won't kill you, princess. It's not in my job description." How could he look so amused?

Alexa growled under her breath. "How about we don't speak? I think you had the right idea at church."

"Fine with me."

"Good." Alexa stalked to her room. How, oh *how* could she possibly make this situation work? Besides hiding out in her room all day?

As if she would. This was Paris! Alexa had dreamed of visiting ever since high school. Back then, she had envied her French Club friends who had been able to afford the trip to France during spring break of her senior year. Unfortunately, her parents had been going through an awful divorce then. They couldn't afford it. Now Alexa wanted to scour Paris. She wanted to visit every single café, historical landmark, tiny bookshop...well, maybe not *every* one. But at least she would carve out as much time as she could. After all, the book was her first priority.

Unfortunately, her bodyguard would go with her. This prospect darkened the allure of exploring the romantic city. Maybe Jamison would follow two steps behind her, so she wouldn't have see him. *No.* Mentally, she chastised herself for even thinking such a terrible thing. Wasn't she supposed to love her enemies? She wasn't doing a very good job.

"Rrrr." Alexa threw herself onto the wide, luxurious bed. She had arrived in paradise, but was chained to the hound of hell.

❈ ❈ ❈ ❈ ❈

After the brief moment of frustration, Alexa felt calmer. She unpacked, marveling at the lushness of her bedroom. She explored the bath, which included a huge, claw-footed tub, thick, soft white towels, and bottles of shampoo and lotion. She smeared the peach lotion on her hands. Yum. Sweet and fruity. She even discovered a miniature sewing kit. If only she knew how to sew, that would be helpful.

Just like in the main living room, the furniture in her room was made of ornate, curved wood and smooth, silky fabrics, accented in gold. When Alexa fleetingly forgot about the black knight in the scenario, she discovered that she still felt like a princess living in a fairy tale.

She frowned. But not the kind of princess Jamison had labeled her—haughty and snotty. What did he know? Furthermore, what did she care?

She did, because she didn't like anyone—even Jamison—thinking ill of her. Clearly, though, her attitude toward him left much to be desired. Why did she keep reverting to snappy, tart comebacks with him?

Because he was obnoxious!

Maybe that was part of the reason. Disturbingly, he burrowed under her skin like no one else ever had. But did that matter? Wasn't it time for her to act like the adult? Five weeks was a long time to wage war in a small apartment.

For long, silent moments, Alexa prayed for help with dealing with her exasperating bodyguard. Then she drew a fortifying breath and headed for the kitchen to retrieve a soda.

Like a shadow, Jamison melted from the kitchen to the living room and settled on the sofa. Good, he was following the rule. Her rule. Maybe at this rate they could actually cohabitate. As long as he stayed out of her space, all would be well. ...And as long as she controlled her unruly tongue, too.

Alexa spent the rest of the afternoon working on the manuscript. It would take at least three weeks to go through all of Colin's scrapbooks and add the most important, interesting bits to the book. She would have to wrest the remaining scrapbooks from Eve tomorrow. Not to mention setting up an appointment with Colin. She needed more stories from him.

How much time would Colin be able to spend with her? Her heart sped up, imagining the candlelit dinner he had promised in the penthouse. Well, had he actually promised candlelight? But an intimate dinner with Colin, looking out on the sparkling lights of Paris... How could it be anything but romantic?

Reality nipped in, then. If last week was any indication, she may not get as much time as she would like with Colin. Maybe not even the dinner. She would have to plan extra opportunities to get the material needed for the book. A side benefit would be enjoying his intoxicating company. Alexa sighed, and it sounded dreamy, even to her. But who cared? She was living a fantasy. Why not enjoy it?

At dinner time, Alexa smelled pizza baking. Her mouth watered. Had Jamison made enough to share? Or would she be expected to bake her own?

She slipped out to the kitchen. One-third of a pizza rested on the counter, fresh from the oven. More saliva dripped into her mouth. Obviously, Jamison had pulled it from the freezer and baked it.

She looked over her shoulder at the back of his black head, where he sat on the couch, watching the news.

"Umm." She cleared her throat. "Can I have some? Pizza, I mean."

"Suit yourself."

"Thank you." Alexa ignored his acerbic response and greedily pulled two thick slices onto a plate. One piece remained.

Where should she eat? She paused uncertainly. Not in her room. That seemed too antisocial, even for the rule. But at the same time, she didn't want to sit next to Jamison on the sofa, either. She elected for the table situated near the wall between the kitchen and sitting room areas.

Yummy! Cheesy with the works. Alexa inhaled her two pieces, and then returned to the counter for the last piece; unfortunately, at the same time Jamison arrived. He stopped a good distance from her.

Alexa could take the last piece. She read it in his deferential, but at the same time hostile, stance that he would let her. All the same, she lifted the piece and offered it to him, crust snared between her thumb and forefinger. The end drooped toward the floor. "Want it?"

"If you don't."

"We could share."

His black gaze traveled from her to the pizza. "You're going to lose it."

"Lose what?"

In one lightening lunge, he whipped his plate forward and caught the top half of the pizza, toppings and all, on his plate.

"Oops," Alexa said. "Good save."

"I'll take this half."

Alexa gaped. She was left with the crust, complete with a doughy textured, red dimpled top. "That's not fair."

"You offered half. I'm accepting." He returned to the living room.

Alexa stared after him, not believing her ears. The black-hearted devil! The selfish weasel. She had a good mind to snatch it away from him.

Her better half said it wouldn't bode well for their cohabitating relations. And what about her resolution to change her behavior?

Her evil half didn't care. She marched into the living room, naked crust and all, and snatched the delectable slab of cheesy goodness right out of his hands. He had been about to take a bite. His white teeth snapped shut and he stared up at her, startled.

"You pig!" she cried, ripping his half in half. "I won't let you get away with that." She tore her own crust in half and deposited half of each on his plate. Her hands were red and messy and greasy, but she didn't care. She slapped her two halves together and took a bite, glaring at him the whole while.

He deliberately wiped his hands on a paper napkin and stood, forcing her to back up. Much as her attitude had been in-his-face a moment ago, she didn't literally want to be in his face. Or anywhere near him, for that matter.

He stepped toward her, and she took another step back, chewing furiously. He took another step and she stumbled backward, off the lip of the area rug. "What are you doing?" she mumbled, mouth full.

"Uncomfortable, princess?" She felt the heat of his words.

She finally swallowed. "Don't pull any macho man attitude on me," she warned, glaring down at him. "I'm not scared of little people." Although Alexa instantly regretted the rude words, it was too late to retract them.

His dark eyes blackened, and leashed anger radiated. "Don't test me, princess."

"I'm sorry." She bit her lip. "But don't test *me*. You were rude and selfish. I don't have to stand for that."

Was that a glimmer of a smile? Couldn't be. "You're right."

Alexa was not sure how to respond to this turnaround.

He handed her his plate. "Take mine."

Her food had suddenly hit bottom, and she felt full now. "Thank you, but I don't want it. It's yours. Or are you afraid of getting my cooties?"

He smiled. It was the first one he had ever given her, and it did wonders for his face. The dark eyes lightened to brown, and laugh lines crinkled from the corners. "Cooties don't scare me." In fact, Alexa got the feeling nothing scared him.

She backed away with a mumbled, "Good." Alexa returned to the kitchen, where she searched for the trash bin. She found it under the sink.

"You're going to throw out perfectly good pizza?" he sounded incredulous, now, behind her.

"Do you want it?"

"Absolutely."

She scraped the mangled pizza from her plate into an unattractive clump on his. "There you go."

"Next time give me the extra slice."

She narrowed her eyes. Of course, the brief truce had been too good to last. More regrettable, impulsive words sped out. "You're obnoxious, did you know that? I thought bodyguards were supposed to be quiet and unassuming. You know, seen and not heard?"

"Don't count on it, princess." With that exertion of manly obnoxiousness, he returned to the couch. Alexa rolled her eyes to the heavens. Why had she been saddled with that recalcitrant man? If this latest confrontation was any indication, the days ahead would prove far from smooth, rule or no rule.

CHAPTER FIVE

THE NEXT MORNING, Alexa dialed the number for the penthouse and pressed the gold metal receiver to her ear.

"Colin Radcliff's office." Definitely Eve's frosty voice.

"Hi, Eve. It's Alexa. I need the other scrapbooks. When can I come get them?"

"Colin's out, so now would be fine. Bring the other scrapbook with you."

Alexa frowned. What did that mean—"Colin's out, so now would be fine"? Clearly, the secretary desired to keep Alexa and Colin apart. "I'll be there in a minute."

Gathering up the scrapbook, Alexa slipped out of her room and headed for the door. Mart sat on the couch, watching television. Somehow, the giant man looked totally out of place on the fancy furniture. Alexa slowed down. "Where's my favorite bodyguard?"

Mart cast her a grin. "You mean I'm not?"

She grinned back. "Actually, you are. But where's Jamison?"

"Working out in the gym downstairs. Colin is, too. So I get to baby-sit you."

"Would you come with me to the penthouse?"

He hefted his bulk up off the couch. "That's my job."

Upstairs, Eve peered suspiciously through the cracked door of the penthouse. This morning she wore fashionable, silver-rimmed glasses.

"It's just us," Mart rumbled. "Open up, kid."

Eve frowned and snatched the scrapbook from Alexa at the first opportunity. "The others are over there." She pointed.

Alexa was vaguely surprised that Eve didn't want to dole out the remaining seven scrapbooks, one at a time. But then again, that would mean more trips for Alexa to the penthouse. Apparently, Eve wanted to avoid that scenario at all costs.

Alexa still couldn't figure out why Eve was so possessive of Colin. Was it because she was fanatically devoted to her job, or because she was in love with her boss? Either way, she made Alexa feel uncomfortable. "I also need to set up an appointment with Colin."

"I can answer all of your questions."

"I'm sorry, but you can't. I need stories from Colin, told from his perspective."

Eve's lips pressed into a thin line. "Huffiness will get you nowhere. Colin is busy. If you want help, you'll have to come through me."

Mart spoke with a thread of laughter in his Texas drawl, "Ease up, Eve. Alexa's doing her job, just like you."

Eve sent Mart a freezing glance. "I don't tell you how to do your job, Martin. Don't tell me how to do mine."

Mart's eyebrows climbed. He lifted his arms in mock surrender. "Whoa, Nelly."

Eve turned her glare upon Alexa, apparently unaware she had just been likened to a horse. "Colin...is...*very*...busy," she enunciated. "Sometimes fans don't get that."

"I have a book to write, Eve. Either help me, or I'll go over your head and deal with Colin directly. But I won't stand here and be attacked."

Eve's eyes narrowed to feral slits. "Don't threaten me, hussy. I've seen plenty of your kind. All you want is to rip your claws into Colin and eat his heart out. Well, you'll have to go through me, first."

Was Eve serious? "I don't want to sink my claws into Colin. I want to write my book. I'm under contract, and I have less than five weeks left. Now, either help me, or give me Colin's cell phone number."

"I will not!" Eve gasped.

"Then Mart will, won't you, Mart?" Alexa turned to the huge bodyguard.

"Well..." He looked from one woman to the other, and then appealed to Eve, "Alexa can ask Colin for it. Maybe you should cooperate."

With one tight movement, Eve spun and marched for the desk. She flipped through a bound volume; apparently Colin's appointment book. "He has an opening Thursday at two o'clock."

That was halfway through their stay in Paris. Alexa would have to work on the scrapbooks in the meantime, and work up a general outline for Colin to approve. "Fine. Pencil me in for the whole hour."

Eve scratched in the book with short, angry strokes. "Done. Now leave."

This was ridiculous. Alexa felt things had gotten completely out of hand with the secretary. Doubtless she would need Eve's help in the future to make further appointments, or to ask questions. "Look," she said. "It's true I like Colin, but I have no intention of hurting him. In fact, I've already told him I'm not interested in a fling."

"What?" Eve crossed her arms, clearly disbelieving.

"It's true. Ask him."

"Don't tell me you're not interested in Colin. Every breathing woman on the planet is interested in Colin."

"That might be a stretch. But yes, I think he's attractive. Don't you?"

Eve flushed. "This is not about me."

"Isn't it? You're awfully protective of him. You must care for him very much."

Eve turned away. "He's my boss. It's my job to care for him."

"Then you want what's best for him," Alexa persisted.

"Of course."

"Then help him. We've both signed a contract with the publisher. He needs this book done on time just as much as I do."

The secretary gnawed her lip. "I'll speak to him," she said finally. "And if what you say is true, then of course I'll...help you, as much as possible." Obviously, the last had been forced out at great cost.

"Thank you. I appreciate your help, Eve." Beth would be so proud of her hard won, tactful words. Alexa turned to the bodyguard. "Mart, would you please help me carry these scrapbooks downstairs?"

"Be happy to. Later, Eve."

They left the thin secretary staring after them, sweater wrapped tightly around herself. Alexa actually felt sorry for the other woman. Clearly, she felt threatened and worried...and maybe even confused about the right thing to do for her boss. Hopefully, Colin would help her to see reason.

❋ ❋ ❋ ❋ ❋

Late that afternoon, the phone rang. Alexa snatched it up. "Hello?"

"Alexa, love. It's Colin." As if that crisp, British voice could belong to anyone else.

"Hi, Colin!" Why did she sound so breathless? She sounded like a ninny.

"Eve told me about our appointment on Thursday. Sounds perfect. But I'd also like to invite you to dinner on Sunday night. I thought I'd better strike before your social calendar is booked up."

"I don't exactly have a swinging life, Colin," Alexa laughed.

"I'm sure you could if you wanted to."

His compliment warmed her heart. "Thanks, but I'm more of a one man woman."

"Good." His pleased voice notched down. "I hope I am that man?"

Alexa laughed. "You are as far as the book is concerned. As far as anything else...we'll just have to see."

"I look forward to the discovery process."

Goodness, he was smooth! Her cheeks warmed and she was glad he wasn't there to witness it. She also didn't know how to reply. "Thank you," she mumbled.

He laughed softly. "Eight-thirty, then? At the penthouse, like I promised. I have an interview at six."

"Thank you, Colin. It sounds wonderful."

"All else is well, then?"

"The book is fine..."

"Terrific. Also, Alexa, while you're here, take time to visit the Musée du Louvre. It's one of my favorite sights in Paris. Jamison will take you."

"I will. I'm thinking I'll go tomorrow afternoon."

"Terrific. I've got to ring off, but I'll see you Thursday?"

Alexa smiled. "See you then. 'Bye."

She sighed with pleasure at the thought of spending time with Colin on Thursday, and then for dinner Sunday night in the penthouse. She put her chin in her hand and daydreamed about the upcoming romantic night.

❈ ❈ ❈ ❈ ❈

The next morning, Alexa awoke early and decided to resume her workout routine. Even better, Mart would accompany her—not Jamison.

So far, Jamison had been beautifully following the rule. In fact, all day yesterday he had appeared to take great pains to ignore her. Exactly what she wanted, she told herself. She didn't care that he clearly preferred not to speak to her.

Now, clad in her workout clothes, Alexa hurried into the living room. Mart, as she had hoped, sat kicked back on the sofa, watching television.

"Good morning!" she called cheerily. "I'm going to run the stairs. Want to come with me?"

"Guess I don't have much choice." Mart rolled to his feet.

In the stairwell Alexa took off, pounding up the stairs, one flight, then two. She heard Mart puffing behind her. Then she spun and headed back down.

On her apartment floor level, she spotted Jamison trotting upstairs. He wore a black T-shirt and black shorts, and carried a bag in one hand. Alexa caught the scent of fresh baked bread.

Mart panted, "Jamison, buddy, you assigned me a.m. duty on purpose, didn't you?"

Her bodyguard grinned. "You need a cardio workout, Mart."

"No, man. You take over. I'll take the food inside."

Jamison cast Alexa a glance. "Fine. But this is your only reprieve, friend. I still need to work out."

"Whatever, buddy. Just save me now."

Alexa frowned and sprinted back upstairs, not waiting for her clearly unwilling bodyguard to join her. She ran as hard and as fast as she could, but still, she heard his footsteps gaining on her. No panting, either, like Mart had done. No, just silent, swift footsteps.

She pushed herself to run up three flights, then four. Jamison was right on her heels when a sharp pain pierced her chest. She struggled not to gasp too loudly, and spun and headed back down. Jamison, to her chagrin, wasn't breathing hard at all, and dogged her heels all the way down. She struggled to ignore him, and thankfully regained her breath by the time she reached her own floor again.

Alexa ran the stairs three more times, and by then perspiration ran in rivulets between her breasts and she felt sticky and icky, and couldn't hide her sharp, panting breaths. She cast Jamison a quick glance. To her satisfaction, sweat darkened his shirt and shone on his brow. His muscular chest heaved a little, too.

Alexa threw him an impertinent grin. "Too much of a workout for you?"

He actually smiled. "Go easy on Mart. Run up and down one flight. Then he can watch you from the landing when he gets tired."

"Sure. I'm happy to do whatever I can to help Mart."

"But you won't make things easy on me, will you?"

She met the unwavering challenge in the dark gaze. "Not a chance. By the way, where did you get the bread?"

"A street not far from here. Rue Cler."

"Is it a market?" Alexa had been thinking of items she would like to buy to add to the kitchen goodies. Like muffins or fruit. Maybe more cheese.

"The street is an open-air market with shops, too."

"Hmm." She reached for the door handle to enter the hall.

His hand closed over hers. "I'll go first."

Alexa snatched her hand free of his disturbing warmth. "Aren't you courteous. Don't you know ladies are supposed to go first?"

"Chivalry has nothing to do with it. It's my job." He edged his shoulder between her and the open doorway and surveyed the hall. Then he stepped back and held the door open. "After you."

Alexa was positive she didn't imagine the sarcastic curl to his lips. She gave him a narrow-eyed look. "Your manners astound me."

"At least something about me astounds you."

"What is that supposed to mean?"

"It means, princess, I know I'm beneath your notice. And believe me, I like it that way."

"Well then, don't worry. You won't have to endure anymore of my praise." She shoved her key in the lock to their flat, eager to escape his presence. She knew he'd leave now to work out in the gym downstairs. Thank goodness.

"Later," she mumbled, slipping into the apartment.

As the door closed, he murmured, "Ciao, princess."

Alexa hurried to the kitchen to sample a pinch of the bread before resuming her workout. Pure ambrosia! She sighed. Unfortunately, it didn't soothe her disturbed nerves. Maybe two pieces with butter later would do it.

Or not, if Jamison had returned by then.

After exercising and a quick breakfast, Alexa worked hard for the remainder of the morning, transcribing her recording of Colin's stories, and then she began to skim through the remaining scrapbooks in order to flesh out her potential outline. She wanted to spend the afternoon exploring Paris. Then it occurred to her that she would need to notify Jamison, since he would need to accompany her.

Jamison sat on the couch munching chips when she exited from her room at 11:30 A.M. The maid was just leaving, and Alexa discovered that she had left more supplies, including milk, pizza, cheddar cheese, and vegetables. As Alexa prepared a tuna sandwich, she announced to the back of Jamison's head, "I'm going out this afternoon."

"Are you requesting my company?"

Alexa rolled her eyes. "Do I have a choice? I'm telling you, so you can prepare yourself."

"*Can* I prepare myself for an afternoon with you?"

"I can't wait to spend time with you, either," she said sweetly.

"Where to?"

"I want to check out that Rue Cler you told me about. And I'd like to go to the Eiffel Tower and the Louvre. Notre-Dame Cathedral, too, if we have time."

Jamison glanced at his watch. "We'd better leave soon, then."

Of course she knew that. Wisely, though, she curbed her tongue.

❋ ❋ ❋ ❋ ❋

Alexa decided to visit Rue Cler first. Luckily, it wasn't far. As they walked, she relished the perfect weather—clear blue skies, and a stiff breeze. It was a little chilly, but fine with her sweater on. After a few minutes, Jamison turned down a picturesque cobblestone street. No cars were allowed there. Little shops had newspapers, crates of fruits and vegetables, and other items on display outside. Alexa spied a wine shop, a *fromage* shop with wedges and cylinders of all sorts of delicious looking cheese, and a butcher's shop. Later, maybe she would come back and buy some Swiss cheese. She preferred it to the cheddar the maid had left.

The people shopping on the street looked like true Parisians—a man in shirtsleeves wore a beret, and several women carried cloth shopping bags. They spoke rapid French. It felt like an authentic neighborhood in old Paris. Alexa loved it.

She struggled to ignore Jamison, walking at her side; the only dark blot on her horizon. Why, oh *why* did Colin have to assign him as her bodyguard? Colin knew how well she got along with Mart. Wouldn't it have made more sense to pair her up with him? Mart would have been a far more enjoyable companion for her long anticipated tour of Paris, that was for sure.

Alexa negotiated the cobbles as best she could, but her high heels slipped and her ankles twisted every few steps. She couldn't wait to see the Louvre later, too. Colin had raved about it.

Thinking about Colin temporarily made her forget Jamison, walking by her side. Until he unfortunately spoke. "Why did you wear those ridiculous shoes?"

Alexa frowned. She had vowed to control her tongue today. "I like them. You hate them because they make you look shorter."

"Isn't that why you wear them?"

Alexa ignored this, mostly because it was true. She wasn't proud of the fact. But she did love high heels. She always had. Sweetly, she asked, "Is it hard on your ego to be shorter than the woman you're with?"

His only reaction was a tightened jaw. "You look like a fool tripping over the cobbles."

Alexa did not want to admit that he was right. "I'm fine, can't you see?" she said haughtily. She walked a little faster. "In fact, why don't you keep up?"

Suddenly, her heel skidded and she stumbled. *Pride goes before destruction*—wasn't that what Proverbs said? Chagrinned, she grabbed at his shoulder for support. It was surprisingly sturdy. In fact, she was shocked to discover the casual, button-down black shirt he wore concealed thick, hard muscles.

She flushed, and quickly removed her hand the moment she regained her balance. Then she told herself, *Of course he has muscles.* Wasn't he a bodyguard? He worked out every morning. What did she expect? It was just that he was usually so quiet and unassuming on duty. Like he wanted to melt into the background. And yet Alexa could never ignore him. The tightly leashed force of his personality always grabbed her attention, over and over again, like a red flag.

"Now will you admit it?" Was that a small smile? It was! He was laughing at her.

Alexa flushed hotter, hating that she blushed so easily. She scowled. "Come on. I see a shoe store." She had spotted one down a side street.

"Your wish is my command, princess."

"Would you *please* stop calling me that!"

With Jamison hovering against the wall inside the store, Alexa found a pair of flats that matched her outfit. She preferred not to wear flats with a skirt, but that couldn't be helped. What she really wished was that she had worn jeans and sneakers.

Why hadn't she? Because she felt fashion conscious in the city of Paris? Or because she got a perverse pleasure from towering over Jamison, like he had accused? Both, most likely, she reluctantly admitted. What was wrong with her? She had never behaved like this with anyone else in her entire life. It disturbed her. And yet Jamison seemed to enjoy—no, deliberately *encourage*—the prickly side of their relationship. Why? More importantly, why did she enjoy responding in kind?

As Alexa wiggled her toes in the shoes, she pondered the question for another minute. In grade school, she had enjoyed a light, joking relationship with Ben, an old friend of hers. Although the verbal fencing with Jamison was similar, it also felt far more complicated. Was it Jamison's way to keep her at arm's length? Or was it his complex, male way of saying he liked her—a little—even though he may not want to? This idea surprised her. In that case, what did that say about her, since she relished their adversarial banter, too?

Alexa closed her mind to the topic. She was getting too philosophical, and seeing more meaning in flats vs. high heels than need be.

At least these flats were made of soft, supple leather. They weren't likely to give her blisters from walking miles this afternoon. "I don't see why you can't let me sightsee alone," she said experimentally, wiggling her toes in the soft new shoes. "For all you know, the note writer is in London."

"He...or she...mentioned killing you in Paris."

Alexa gasped at his bald statement. Then she scoffed, "Please. Nothing's happened. We're letting some gutless coward intimidate us."

"The threats are real, Alexa. We can't take a chance."

"I'm sick of it."

"Me, being your bodyguard?" Amusement lurked at the corners of his mouth.

"Yes! He's making my life a misery...and yours, too," she added generously.

"I get paid whether I watch you or Colin."

Alexa just managed to keep from rolling her eyes. Their confrontations didn't irk him like they did her? That maddening possibility couldn't possibly be true. "I'm done." She quickly paid and left the store with her impractical heels in a bag.

"Want me to carry that?" Jamison inquired.

Alexa blinked, nonplussed. Was he actually trying to be civil? "Thank you, but no."

"Suit yourself."

As the early afternoon passed, and Alexa explored the wonders of Paris, she regretted not taking Jamison up on his offer. He didn't ask again. They took the bus to the Eiffel Tower next, but when Alexa saw the long line winding away from the ticket area, she elected not to waste time by waiting to ride up in the Tower elevator.

"You want to see Notre-Dame Cathedral?" Jamison asked as they walked away.

"Yes." Alexa consulted her guidebook. "But the Louvre is closer."

"The Cathedral won't take long to explore, especially if you don't take the tour. Then you can save the rest of the afternoon for the Louvre."

Alexa saw the wisdom of Jamison's reasoning, and for once neglected to argue with him. "Lead on."

"We agree on something?"

"Don't get used to it," she warned. "Shall we take a cab?"

With a small smile, he flagged a cab. Alexa wanted to make the most of every minute, and didn't want to waste time waiting for busses or the Metro. She insisted on paying for the cab, however. Unfortunately, it took more euros than she had planned. She had converted fifty dollars in travelers' checks into euros with the efficient apartment manager this morning, but now wished that she had exchanged more.

Notre-Dame Cathedral was beautiful. She loved how it was on a little island, surrounded by stone walls with ivy drooping over the sides. The tall spire of the church and the Gothic architecture of the cathedral were breathtaking. Inside, while they mixed with the throngs of other visitors, Alexa took in the soaring ceilings and the beautiful details of the architecture. She decided not to visit the tiny museum, since it was almost midafternoon and she still wanted to visit the Louvre.

They took another cab to the Louvre, which left Alexa with only a little money left. Enough to tour the famous museum, thankfully, according to the guide book. She preferred to pay cash, so she wouldn't rack up charges on her credit cards.

The first glimpse of the magnificent Musée du Louvre building took her breath away. The beautiful architecture, the enormous glass *Pyramide,* and the fountains outside; everything stunned her.

Jamison directed her to the underground shopping area, called the Carrousel du Louvre, on the west side of the museum. Alexa was struck silent by the huge, classy underground mall with its pale, pristine walls and shiny floors, and huge glass windows to the shops. And the inverted glass pyramid that hung from the ceiling! Alexa loved it all.

Then Jamison led her to an underground entrance to the Louvre museum on the eastern side of the pyramid. He explained that this line was shorter than the ones at other entrances. They bought tickets at the automatic ticket machines, and Alexa spent a few happy hours exploring the museum. She lingered over the 'Winged Victory,' the 'Mona Lisa,' which she had always wanted to see, the 'Venus de Milo,' and other paintings and sculptures. Unfortunately, she felt that she had only scratched the surface when a glance at her watch said it was already after six.

Next, they explored the Carrousel du Louvre and she selected souvenirs for her family. Now it was close to seven o'clock, and Alexa's throat felt as dry as dust. Her stomach rumbled, too. Her euros were gone, so she reluctantly passed the tempting "food court," even though the drinks on the menus called to her parched throat. She looked for a water fountain, but couldn't find one.

"You ready to head back?" Jamison asked.

Alexa swallowed with difficulty, and nodded.

Jamison eyed her for a moment, then said, "Come with me," and headed back toward a small café.

Wonderful, sweet bakery smells assailed her nose, and she spied cola on the menu. Should she order? Did they take credit cards? Probably not. Why hadn't she used her charge card for the Louvre fee? Then she would still have euros. Disappointment lodged in Alexa's throat, which burned with fire by now, amplified by the anticipation of drinking a cold beverage. She swallowed her sticky saliva.

"Merci," Jamison said, and accepted a bag and two drinks. The petite woman at the counter dimpled a grin at him.

Two drinks? Did he plan to drink them both himself? They sat at a free table and Alexa licked her lips as he unpacked two ham and cheese croissants onto paper napkins. Anticipation churned in her stomach, and she raised her eyes to him.

"Hungry?" he asked.

"Yes! Please."

Jamison pushed one of the napkins across the table and put a tall, moisture beaded cup next to it.

"For me?" she asked, barely able to believe it.

His lips curved up, just the tiniest bit. "Do you have any euros left?"

"No," she admitted, and hesitantly sipped from the straw. Pure, cold cola ambrosia slid down her throat, and she closed her eyes with a sigh of bliss. "Thank you."

His unreadable gaze rested on her for a second. "You're welcome, Alexa."

Their lovely moments of truce unfortunately only lasted until they had thrown out their trash and exited the Louvre complex and stood outside. The sun still hovered above the horizon.

Alexa consulted her map. Now that she had visited the Louvre, there was one last place she wanted to visit; a small bookshop recommended by her internet searches back home.

"It's seven-thirty," Jamison said. Was that a hint he wanted to quit sightseeing? Was he tired of touring with her? Ridiculously, the thought hurt.

"Go back to the flat, if you want."

His gaze hardened into unfriendly black again. "You try my patience, princess."

"Do you have a television show coming on now?" Alexa inquired sweetly. "A soap opera, perhaps?"

"I don't watch *soap operas*," he said through his teeth. "I watch soccer."

Again, her impulsive mouth had run away from her. And after he'd been so nice, too! What was wrong with her? "I'm sorry. Really." She did mean it. Alexa bit her lip. "Go home, if you'd like. I'll be fine, I promise. Right now, I'm going to a bookshop. It's supposed to be open until eight o'clock." She pointed. "It's five blocks that way."

Never mind it was located in the complete opposite direction from the flat. How many more opportunities would she have to explore Paris? All too few.

Silently, Jamison accompanied her hurrying steps to the bookstore. It was fifteen minutes until closing. He perused the bookshelves in the French section, she noticed, while she had to ask the dour-faced clerk where the English books were kept. Still, it was fun.

Alexa loved visiting old bookstores just like this one. It was long, cramped, and narrow, with high shelves of books. She sniffed, enjoying the musty smell of old paper. Who knew what treasures lurked on these shelves? Maybe even a first edition by Voltaire. She popped back to the French section and did find books by that author, but none looked like a first edition.

The precious minutes crept by while Alexa chose two books. Both were by English authors she had never read before. One was a mystery, and the other a love story.

Jamison wandered over while she stood in line. It was past closing time. They had already turned the sign in the door. "Do you think they take Visa, Alexa?"

"Doesn't everyone?" She glanced at the cash register, where merchants usually displayed the credit cards they accepted. This one was blank.

It was her turn. "Huit euros," said the man with a long face and goatee.

She waved her credit card. "Oui?"

"Non." The dour man did not look amused. "Euros."

Disappointment sank her spirits. Next time, she would exchange more money for euros. "Okay." She turned away, but Jamison plucked the books from her hand and plunked them down on the counter, along with his mystery novel by Dick Francis. In English. He peeled bills from his wallet and handed them to the clerk. With a disapproving look at Alexa, the clerk gave Jamison a receipt, then flipped a hand at her, shooing her clueless American self along.

It made Alexa feel foolish.

Outside, Jamison handed over her books.

"Thank you," she said stiffly. "I appreciate it. I'll pay you back."

"Not necessary." He headed in the direction of home.

"But I insist," she said, hurrying along beside him.

"Accept a gift, Alexa," he said shortly.

This answer disturbed her still more. How could she accept a gift when he clearly seemed annoyed with her? In the interest of peace, however, she mumbled, "Thank you."

"You're welcome."

After they hailed another cab—for which Jamison also had to pay—they accomplished the rest of the trip home in silence.

❋ ❋ ❋ ❋ ❋

Back at the apartment, Alexa dropped her bags and purse to the floor, exhausted.

Jamison looked at them. "You're not going to leave them there, are you?"

She had had no intention of doing so, but his words stirred up her disturbed, irritated feelings from the book shop. She retorted, "What if I do? You can pick them up. That's your job, isn't it?" Of course Alexa wasn't serious, but once again, her impulsive mouth outran her better sense.

He grabbed her wrist before she could head for her room. "Don't talk down to me. I'm not your servant."

"I can't help but talk down to you," she returned flippantly. His strong fingers felt calloused. Disturbed, she looked down and saw the shocking contrast between his tanned skin and her pale skin—and how unexpectedly large his hand looked, encircling her slender wrist. Her heart beat faster. "Let go."

"When you treat me with respect."

Alexa bit her lip, loath to do anything he demanded of her. But he wasn't going to release her—that much was clear. Steel hardened his impossibly dark eyes. And he stood too close.

"Fine," she said. "I'll pick up the stuff myself."

"We can stand here all night, princess."

Annoyance mounted. "I have work to do now," she told him. "Unhand me."

He retained his grip, and she glared. "What do you want from me?"

"An apology."

She sealed her lips, and would have crossed her arms, too, if her wrist was free. Maybe she had been obnoxious, indicating that he should pick up her mess. Okay, completely obnoxious. But she didn't want to back down to him. She didn't want to let him win!

"Take your time, princess. I'm comfortable."

Alexa was not. She didn't like him so close to her. Her flesh prickled and jumped, urging her to break free. "This is ridiculous!" she said. "Do you have power and control issues, or what?"

He leaned closer, so his warm breath fanned her chin. "Do you have an ounce of warmth in that cold heart of yours?"

Her heart pounded alarmingly fast. "I am not cold," she denied, tilting away from him. "Just prickly. And untactful."

"And rude."

She glared. "You bring out the best in me."

"Ditto, princess."

"You're in my space."

He smiled, then. "And you hate it."

Unwanted emotions jangled inside her, not the least of which was unreasoning panic. Something told her to escape, and now, before she lost more than her pride to him. For self-preservation purposes only, she forced the galling, humble words out of her lips. "I'm sorry, okay?"

To her relief, he released her. "Was that so hard?"

"Being civil to you is next to impossible. When are you going to leave?"

"Leave?"

She waved toward the door. "Leave. Go somewhere else. I have work to do." She would think and breathe a lot easier if he left the apartment.

"I'm on duty."

"Please. Who's going to break in here at dinner time?"

By way of an answer, he sat on the couch and propped his feet on the coffee table. He picked up a magazine.

"Fine," she said. "Be a pigheaded, paranoid, pp..."

"Pip squeak?" he supplied.

Alexa glared. "I didn't say that."

"You would have, if you'd thought of it first." He licked a finger and turned the page.

Alexa stalked into her room and shut the door none too gently behind her. Surely, she had been wrong before. Jamison didn't like her at all. What was more, she didn't like her behavior around him, either. She became a flippant pain in the neck, and she hated it. She needed to talk to Colin about changing bodyguards. Or getting rid of a bodyguard entirely. One wasn't necessary. Who would hurt her? Colin was sweet to be so concerned about her, but perhaps a little overprotective.

❈ ❈ ❈ ❈ ❈

After frowning at her computer and accomplishing nothing for ten long minutes, Alexa called Beth and exploded, "He's driving me crazy!"

"Who?"

"Jamison, that's who!"

"I thought you were with Colin. Who's this Jamison?"

"My bodyguard," Alexa wailed.

Silence came from the other end of the line. Beth said, "Back up. Tell me what's going on. Why do you need a bodyguard?"

Alexa filled her sister in on the latest developments, and the threats against Colin and herself.

Beth gasped. "Are you all right?"

"I'm fine. Except now I have to live with this guy twenty-four/seven!"

"Colin? Or Jamison?"

"Jamison! He's driving me crazy. I don't know what to do. Every time I talk to him I sound like I'm twelve. All we do is fight. And he's obnoxious, too," she added darkly. "Don't think it's just me."

"Tell me about this guy," her sister said calmly.

"He's Colin's best bodyguard. He's Italian. And obnoxious."

Her sister chuckled. "Does Colin know you don't get along?"

"Yes! That's why I was surprised he stuck me with Jamison. At least Mart—the other bodyguard—and I get along."

"Maybe that's why he set you up with Jamison."

Alexa frowned. "Come again?"

"If you're right, and Colin is attracted to you, doesn't it make sense that he'd assign you a bodyguard you can't stand? Then he wouldn't have to worry about being jealous. You know all those stories about people falling in love with their bodyguard."

It made sense, put in that light. "I guess you're right. But what do I do in the meantime? He disrupts my concentration when I hear him in the other room. I can't write!" She was being overdramatic here, but she did find it difficult to concentrate.

"Alexa, let me give you some advice."

"Finally! That's why I called you. Plus, to hear your voice," Alexa said hastily.

"You can't fool me, sis. Listen closely. T...A...C...T. Try it. Believe it or not, it works. The next time you want to steam off at him, count to ten, and imagine what I would say."

"Like you're so perfect," she muttered.

"Alexa."

Alexa imagined her sister tapping her foot in America. "Okay. You're right. I'll try."

"Is he cute?"

"Who?"

"Jamison."

Alexa's mouth gaped. "No! Did I mention he's short?"

"Come on, Alexa. Tell me the truth. What does he look like?"

"I don't know." Alexa scowled. "He's like five foot seven. He's got dark hair. It's wavy. And dark brown eyes. And he wears all black *all* the time. And he's mostly quiet and unassuming, except around me."

"Let's see, bodyguards usually work out. Anything else you want to tell me?"

"Beth! Why do you care? If you must know, yes, he's got a lot of muscles."

"I see." Was her sister chuckling at the other end?

"What?" Alexa demanded. Was her sister on her side or not?

Her sister's voice came, choked with mirth. "Be careful, Alexa. It sounds like you're in a dangerous situation there."

Alexa held the phone away from her and stared at it. What had gotten into her sister? She pressed it to her ear again and said sarcastically, "Are you done laughing at my problems?"

"Yes, I'm sorry. Tell me more about Colin. Is he everything you thought?"

Alexa sighed, dreamy now. "Yes. He is the sweetest, funniest guy. And so down-to-earth. I really like him, Beth. I know I'm here to write his book, but I can't help but wish..."

"Be careful, Alexa." This time, her sister's voice sounded serious. "He's charismatic. Women all over the world are in love with him."

"But they don't know him," Alexa pointed out. "I do—at least a little. And I like him a lot. I know he likes me, too."

"I hope it works out for you, sis," Beth said softly. "But be careful, okay? Don't leave your heart with a man in Europe. And certainly not with a man who won't give you his, too."

CHAPTER SIX

ALEXA THOUGHT LONG and hard about Beth's words about both Colin and Jamison. Her sister was right—she did need to be careful with Colin. She was still star-struck, and vulnerable to his possibly worldly ways.

As for Jamison, she would try tact. She really would. But it wouldn't be easy.

Noon the next day proved her first opportunity to face her nemesis. Mostly because he had been working out, as usual, while she exercised, and she had chatted with Mart while she ate breakfast. A very friendly conversation, by the way. It proved she wasn't totally inept when it came to maintaining a positive relationship with the opposite sex. After breakfast, she had hidden in her room and compiled more information into her computer from the voluminous scrapbooks Colin had leant her.

By lunchtime, her back ached and one eye twitched. Definitely time for a break. After shutting down the computer, she opened her door a crack and peeked into the living area. There was Jamison, restlessly prowling the length of the room.

His dark eyes immediately zeroed in on her. "Come on out. I don't bite."

Alexa flung open the door. "Like you'd dare." Oops! Hadn't she just promised to be civil? "I mean," she said sweetly, "did you miss me?" Oops again! She sucked in a frustrated breath. "I mean," she tried again, "did you have a splendid morning?"

He stared at her, possibly wondering if she had misplaced her mind. "I hope you don't write like you talk. Colin will be up a creek."

Outraged, she glared. Then she counted to ten. "Aren't you pleasant?" She was pleased with her even tone.

He frowned. "What's up with you, princess?"

Alexa gasped in another breath. This was so hard! "I'm trying to be civil," she explained. "Don't you know what that is?"

"Yes. But I'm surprised you do."

Biting her lip, Alexa marched into the kitchen. Unfortunately, he followed her. Jamison leaned against a nearby counter while she prepared a cheese sandwich.

"So, how's the writing coming?"

She flicked him a suspicious glance. "Fine."

"Going to meet your deadline?"

"I plan to. As long as I don't get a bunch of interruptions." She closed her lips.

"Am I interrupting you?"

"Of course not." She gave him a perfectly fake smile. "You are a wonderful living companion. You don't smoke, you don't chew, and you don't throw rowdy parties. What more could I ask?"

"Speak the truth, princess."

Would he never stop calling her that infernal, caustic name? Her temper bubbled, but she gulped a glass of water to otherwise engage her mouth. She wiped her lips. No reply was a good reply, she decided. Beth would be proud.

"You think I'm perfect now, is that it?" he had the gall to ask.

She bit her lip and glared.

"Come on, princess. You're about to blow a fuse."

"I am not!"

He crossed his arms and watched her.

"I am *trying* to make the best of this intolerable situation," she gritted.

"Living in a luxurious flat is intolerable?"

"Living with *you* is intolerable!" she spurted. "Everywhere I go, there you are. I try to write, and I hear you watching TV. I want to run the stairs, and there you are. It'd be different if we could get along, but we already know that's impossible!"

"It's not a cakewalk for me either, princess."

"Would you *please* stop calling me that!" In frustration, she slapped a palm to her forehead. "I told Beth this would be impossible."

"Who's Beth?"

"My sister. I told her all about you. She said I need to be more tactful, so we can get along."

His eyes narrowed, surprised. "You told her all about me?"

"Don't get a big head! I had to describe the situation to her."

"I see." He smiled a little. "You had to call across the Atlantic to get advice about me. Never had that happen before."

"Don't flatter yourself. If you weren't such a pain in the...patootie...I wouldn't have had to waste my money on a call in the first place!"

"You mean Colin's money."

"I used my cell phone."

"So you aren't all about the free ride."

"I'm about the book!" she said, outraged. "Why else would I torture myself, living here with you?"

"Because the perks are so good."

"What perks?"

"Being a star's number one love interest." The dark eyes pinned her, so she couldn't move.

Her cheeks flushed. "I am not. Colin and I are just friends." She looked away. Never mind if part of her wanted it to be more.

"You think that now. But it'll change."

"What do you mean by that?"

It was his turn to look away. "What Colin wants, Colin gets."

"I'm not sure what you're insinuating, but Colin is not going to *get* me."

"Whatever you say, princess. It's just my job to keep you safe."

Alexa got the feeling Jamison was keeping information from her. "What do you know about Colin that you're not telling me?"

He shrugged. "He's had a lot of women. Be careful."

"Like you care," she muttered. It was strange how his words echoed her sister's. Both warned her about the pop star. But her sister couldn't know how sweet he was inside. And Jamison was a man. What did he know about the finer emotions? Neanderthal that he was.

❋ ❋ ❋ ❋ ❋

After lunch, the phone rang and Alexa snatched it up. Hopefully it wasn't Colin, calling to cancel their appointment in half an hour.

A rush of French bombarded her ear. She heard something about a *lettre*. "Excusez moi?" she said. "Anglais, s'il vous plaît."

The man spoke slower, in thickly accented English, "Madam, you have a letter. Would you like it carried to your room?"

"Oui. Merci." Alexa hung up.

"Who was that?" Jamison asked. He sat on the back of the couch, arms crossed.

"The concierge. I've got a letter. They're delivering it upstairs."

"I'll check it first."

Alexa blinked. "Excuse me? Tampering with mail is a federal crime. At least it is in the United States."

A knock came at the door. That was fast. Alexa hustled over, but Jamison was closer. He opened it and received the letter, pressing a euro into the porter's hand.

Alexa reached his side just as the door closed. "Let me see it," she insisted. "It's addressed to me."

"Are you expecting mail?"

"No," she admitted.

"Exactly." He flipped over the letter, showing her typed name and flat number. No return address. "I'll open it," he said, heading toward his room.

"I can do it. I'm not scared," she insisted, following him. It irritated her that Jamison was in her space all the time—in her apartment, in her air, and now, reading her mail—even if it was a threatening note. She watched him pull open a dresser drawer.

"Maybe not, princess," Jamison said, snapping on latex gloves, "but you might smudge the prints."

He was right. Still, she didn't have to like his authoritarianism. She crossed her arms and watched him carefully slit open the envelope with a wicked looking pocket knife. Surely he hadn't been trained to use knives on people. The thought made her shiver.

"Scared?" he inquired.

"No. Well, maybe a little nervous." She didn't care to explain what she had really been thinking.

Jamison carefully withdrew a paper dotted with pasted words. Alexa circled around behind him, so she could read over his muscular shoulder.

> *You don't listen well, Alexa Kaplan.*
> *Enjoy the Paris sights*
> *Your lust for Colin has its price.*
> *Death.*

And then a cartoon of a skull and crossbones.

"He saw us sightseeing yesterday." A creepy feeling slid down her spine. How long had the person followed them? All day?

Jamison faced her. "Now do you think they're serious? Do you understand why you need me?"

Alexa bit her lip. "Of course I understand why I need you. I just don't want..." she cut her arm through the air in a short, jerky motion, "...any of this."

Compassion gentled his gaze. His hand closed around her arm. "Are you all right?"

"Yes. No." Alexa blinked. She was scared to death. Someone had typed her room number on that envelope. The person knew where she lived. All of a sudden, she was grateful Jamison was there, protecting her. "I'm fine. But I don't like people trying to scare me."

Jamison said nothing, but removed his steadying hand. She wished he hadn't.

She said bravely, "But he hasn't done anything yet, has he?"

"Besides stalk you?"

It didn't sound good, put that way. "I mean, no one's actually tried to hurt me."

"Not yet."

She glared. "Aren't you comforting?"

"Realistic, Alexa. I don't want you to write off the danger you're in."

She glanced at the note still in his hand. "No chance of that now, is there?"

"I need to bring this to Colin."

She moved away. "Perfect, because I'm meeting with him in ten minutes. I'll get my things and we can go together."

He waited near the front door, and opened it for her as she arrived. "Never thought this day would come, princess."

"What do you mean?" she inquired suspiciously.

"You, actually inviting me to go somewhere with you." She saw the amusement in his gaze, and suddenly knew he was trying to distract her from the fear she felt.

Alexa said, more softly than she ordinarily might, "You're preferable to the alternative."

He smiled slightly, not offended, she was glad to see.

❈ ❈ ❈ ❈ ❈

Colin, Jamison, and Mart conferenced about the threatening note while Alexa set the two scrapbooks, rough outline, her digital recorder, and her notebook on the coffee table in the penthouse. Finally Jamison left, flipping open his cell phone. Mart disappeared into an adjacent room to watch television. Thankfully, Eve was nowhere to be seen. Alexa wondered if she had mentioned their squabble on Tuesday to Colin.

Colin joined her on the sofa. He looked more serious than normal. "Sorry about that. I don't like the thought of you being frightened by that letter."

"I'm fine. Jamison's going to call the police?"

"Just a precautionary measure. They need to be alerted to the situation here, and at the concerts, too."

"Of course."

His gaze moved to the coffee table. "It looks like we're in for quite a work session." He laughed, but Alexa could tell the idea of sitting still and concentrating on the project intimidated him. Hence, his past invitations to join him for a meal at the same time they worked.

"It won't hurt," she assured him.

He laughed sharper, sounding self-conscious. "Do I look frightened?"

"I don't know a lot about you, Colin, but you're a doer. You'd rather be singing or running around meeting people than sit still."

"You've got my number for sure, Alexa." The blue gaze looked surprised, but approving.

"I'll try to make it easy on you. I've made a rough outline. I want to go through it with you and see if you want to add or delete anything. Then we'll go through those two scrapbooks and see if they jog any memories. I can add those to the outline as well."

He leaned forward and picked up the three page outline with his long fingers. He had piano fingers, much like her mother had always called hers. Of course, Colin actually could play the piano, whereas she could not. He also played the guitar. If only she could be so musically coordinated.

"After we've finished, will the outline be complete?" he wanted to know.

"Yes, for the most part. If you have time, I'd like you to look through the other scrapbooks later, to make sure we're not leaving out anything important. Also, I'd like to interview your band and your employees, too. I'd like to get their take on you and the music group."

"I like it." Colin relaxed against the couch and read the outline. A faint frown knit his brows.

The hour passed quickly. Colin asked sharp, concise questions, and helped cut the outline by half. "I'd like more stories," he said. "Less statistics."

Finally, the time drew to a close and Alexa was pleased by their efforts. "I'll expect more of those stories on Sunday," she said. "To give you fair warning, I'm bringing my recorder."

Colin laughed. "I'd expect nothing less."

"And I'll send you a new outline either tomorrow or Saturday."

"No hurry." Colin glanced at his watch. "The time flew." He sounded rueful. "I was hoping to learn more about you."

"Sunday," she promised with a grin, gathering her things together.

"Is everything else all right?" Colin sounded genuinely concerned, and Alexa's heart turned over. "I mean besides the note, which again I'm sorry about."

"It's not your fault."

"You wouldn't have received it if it wasn't for me."

This was true, but Alexa dismissed it with a shrug.

"Are you and Eve getting along?" he asked unexpectedly.

Alexa's mouth opened, and then closed. Had that woman already begun to poison Colin's mind against her? "Actually, no," she said. "Did Eve mention what happened on Tuesday?"

"A little. I'd like your take on it."

Alexa heaved a breath. Good heavens, Eve *had* started to spew slander. Her temper bubbled. Even though sometimes her mouth got her into trouble, this time she had been nothing but nice to the other woman. Even her sister would be proud of her. It was frustrating, to say the least. Whatever the case, now it was time for Alexa to get her swing into the game.

"Eve doesn't like me very much," she said evenly. "She thinks I plan to cut out your heart and eat it with a spoon."

Colin chuckled, and his shoulders relaxed. "Eve can be over-protective at times. Don't worry about her. She's harmless."

"Okay." Alexa wasn't so certain.

"Let me tell you something about Eve. She's never had any family—she grew up in the foster system in the United States. She's been with me so long that I think she views me as family. It's only natural, I think."

Or freakily possessive. But Alexa did not say this. After all, maybe Colin was right. He knew Eve better than she did. "I'll keep that in mind."

"Thank you. And I'll talk to my band." Colin opened the door for her. "Next week, I'll set up a meeting so you can chat with them. Interview Eve, too. She can give you a great deal of insight into my crazy life."

"I will," Alexa said.

In fact, maybe the sooner, the better. A bizarre thought crossed her mind as she moved into the empty hall. What if Eve had sent the threatening notes? She certainly disliked Alexa enough, and knew where she lived, too. And she could have easily discovered that Alexa had gone sightseeing yesterday. Of course, Colin's life had been threatened, too. And she couldn't imagine Eve hurting Colin.

But what if the threats against Colin were only a ruse to throw the authorities off the true trail?

The idea of Eve being behind the threats made an odd sort of sense. Could it be true?

If so, Alexa didn't like the idea of being threatened, frightened, and her life constricted just because of a churlish, possessive secretary. Alexa wouldn't say anything yet, but if she found proof to bolster her theory, Eve's house of cards would come crashing down.

She would make an appointment to talk to Eve as soon as possible.

Like a shadow, Jamison joined her in the hall. A fanciful thought flitted through her brain. Like a stalking shadow. Silent and black.

How would it feel to walk alone again, with no fear? It was becoming hard to imagine. She would find out soon if Eve was the stalker. Then she could get rid of her shadow.

❋ ❋ ❋ ❋ ❋

Eve agreed to meet with Alexa on Saturday morning. The phone conversation had been abrupt, and Alexa didn't look forward to the meeting.

Alexa spent the remainder of Thursday struggling to work on the book, but the words flowed like molasses...slow, slow, slow, and she wasn't sure why. Maybe thinking about the stalker had upset her subconscious. She felt like a prisoner in the apartment.

Alexa microwaved a meal for dinner and ate it in her room. She felt grouchy. When she skulked out to deposit the container in the trash, Jamison said from the couch, "Avoiding me?"

"I'm working," she snapped.

He actually turned around. "What's wrong?"

"Nothing." She scrubbed her dirty fork. To her dismay, he joined her in the kitchen and leaned his hip against the counter.

"Talk to me."

"I can't talk to you, or I'll scream," she informed him.

"Writing going rough?"

She turned on him, hands on her hips. "What do you care?"

"That note's got you upset."

"You have all the answers, don't you?" she accused rudely. "Maybe it's time for you to remember the rule. You leave me alone, and I'll leave you alone!"

Hurt, swiftly replaced by anger, darkened his gaze to black. "Fine," he said, and returned to the couch.

Alexa watched him, her eyes suddenly brimming with tears. She bit her lip and hurried to her room, slamming the door behind her.

Now she felt even worse. Why did he have to go and be nice to her? Why did she have to snarl at him?

After a moment, she opened the door again. Jamison glanced at her, and then returned his attention to the television. He didn't look angry, but then again, Alexa suspected he buried his emotions deep, behind that carefully controlled bodyguard wall.

She cleared her throat. "I'm really sorry. I was hateful and rude."

He looked at her again, and after a moment said, "Okay."

"Good night." Alexa closed the door and promptly readied for bed. She pulled the covers to her eyeballs and began to bawl. *God please help me. I don't want to be like this.*

What was wrong? Maybe Jamison was right about the note, but somehow it felt like it went a lot deeper than that.

CHAPTER SEVEN

JAMISON LEFT HER alone on Friday morning, evidently deciding to stick to the rule for his own self-preservation. Alexa hid out in her room. She felt no better today. Each paragraph in the book took half an hour to write. What was *wrong* with her?

Alexa felt increasingly edgy, and it all culminated in a knot in her stomach. She felt constricted, like she was under house arrest. In prison. Anger with the faceless note writer festered. The thought that it might be Eve made it all the more intolerable. So did Jamison's cool politeness. And his very presence. But why did it seem worse now, all of a sudden?

Maybe it was because she could never escape her bodyguard. The fact that they didn't get along was the least of her problems. She couldn't concentrate with him watching television...or breathing...in the next room. Or maybe the tension she felt was a result of everything steadily building up over the last week; their fights, the threats...

Alexa couldn't take it another moment. At eleven o'clock, she bolted from her self-imposed solitary confinement into the living area. She needed tea. No. She needed to escape.

Alexa stood in the tiny kitchen, stirring her tea bag and plotting. If only she could get an hour away by herself. Maybe a walk outside in the clear, brisk air would clear her head. She could explore a little more of the fabulous city of Paris. Maybe then she could think and the words would flow again.

Where was Jamison? She popped a quick glance over her shoulder. He was watching television and restlessly moving his shoulders. Sitting all day must be hard on him. Although he worked out in the morning, he spent the rest of the day caged up with her.

Alexa was beginning to feel like a hamster, too. She had to take action. The more she thought about it, the more likely it seemed that Eve must be behind the threatening notes. Eve wanted to frighten Alexa into going home so she could have Colin for herself.

Why should Alexa stay cooped up in the flat when the notes were probably fakes?

No reason at all.

A plan formulated. A slow smile tugged at Alexa's lips, and for the first time, the late afternoon Parisian sun streaming through the windows touched her soul, too.

Grinning, Alexa retreated to her room and shut the door. How good it felt to smile, and to anticipate freedom.

Quickly, she dialed her sister's number and waited for her to pick up.

"Hello?"

"It's me, Alexa. I need a favor." Quickly, she detailed her request.

"Alexa..." Her sister did not sound happy.

"I'll pay you back."

"It's not that."

"You care about my mental well-being, don't you?" she pleaded.

"Yes, but..."

"Please, Beth. Just this once."

Her sister reluctantly agreed. Alexa tucked her passport and money into her pockets. Then she returned to the kitchen under the ruse that she had forgotten her tea. Not that Jamison paid any attention.

The phone rang. "I'll get it!" Alexa pounced on it. "Hello? You want Jamison? Whom may I say is calling?" To her glee, Jamison turned toward her with a questioning look. She held out the phone. "It's for you. A woman. She wouldn't give her name."

He frowned. "A woman?" It deepened as he tried to figure out who it could be.

"Would you like to take it in private?" she asked helpfully, plopping onto a chair beside the phone. She sipped her tea, as if planning to stay awhile.

He still looked puzzled. "Yes." He disappeared into his room and shut the door.

Alexa sprinted for the front door. She slipped out, held her breath while the catch clicked shut, then dashed for the stairs. She took them fast and then was free, out the lobby door and into the sunshine.

Fresh, clean, free air! Alexa gulped it greedily, but continued her fast pace down the road. She didn't want Jamison to catch her. She turned several corners, and then slowed down. Good thing she had worn sneakers today. Excellent for running. She smiled to herself. It felt fantastic to be free. Like a great weight had rolled off of her spirit.

She took long strides, putting as much distance between her and the luxury apartment building as possible, and in moments found herself on Rue Cler. By accident or design? Perfect, either way. She had wanted to buy Swiss cheese. Now she could.

A man bumped her elbow. "Excuse me," she said. He didn't glance at her, just hurried on. She stopped and gazed in the window of a shop named Gourmand Chocolats Confiseries. A whiff of chocolate tantalized her nose, and she sighed with rapture. She loved chocolate.

An older woman stopped beside her. "Don't they look delicious?"

Alexa offered a smile. An American. Until now, she hadn't realized how homesick she had been feeling. "I'm trying to control myself," she admitted.

"With your figure you can afford to eat a few," the stranger said. "Me, I'm a little dumpy and dowdy."

"No. Of course you're not," Alexa rushed to reassure her.

The woman's eyes narrowed. "Hey, aren't you that woman who hooked up with that singer? Colin somebody."

Alexa flushed. "You must be mistaken."

"Margie's never mistaken." The man's voice came from behind her. An uncomfortable sensation wiggled down Alexa's spine. She froze.

"Who's Colin?" she improvised, edging left.

"We've been following you," the woman smiled. "We adore Colin. Since you're an American, we figure you'll introduce us to him. Since you're friends and all."

Alexa's heart beat faster. Colin did have a lot of fans. And the death threats had continued here. Were these two behind them? Obviously, they had been stalking Alexa from the apartment building. She had never even suspected.

Somehow, she had to escape.

"If you're fans, I'm sure he'd be delighted to meet you. Why don't you call his manager? Give him your names and number so he can set up an appointment."

The man grabbed a painful hunk of her hair. "*You* are our appointment."

Alexa gasped with fright and viciously kicked the man's knee. When he cried out, the woman rushed forward. A knife glinted in her hand. The blade arced toward Alexa, sparkling in the sunlight.

Alexa screamed and threw up her hands to cover her face. A sudden clatter hit the cobblestones. Just as fast, the man's grip released her. She opened her eyes.

A muscular man in black wrestled the woman to the ground. Swiftly, he snapped on handcuffs.

"Jamison!" Never had she been so glad to see someone. She glanced quickly about. "The man. He's gone!"

Jamison hoisted the woman to her feet by the armpit. His face looked pale beneath his tan, and black eyes bored into hers. "We are going to have a serious talk." He snapped open his cell phone and placed a call, apparently to the police, if her high school French was still accurate.

As they headed back to their building, he shoved the struggling prisoner along with them.

"My husband will find you!" the woman spat. "He'll kill you both!"

Jamison said nothing, and Alexa followed his lead. She had no experience whatsoever with criminal etiquette. One thing became clear, though. Eve couldn't possibly be behind the threats. Alexa didn't know if she was relieved or not. She had been foolish to leave the flat, and Jamison was rightly furious with her.

The police were at the building when they arrived. She gave her statement, and then Jamison quietly talked with them in fluent French before the gendarmes bore the woman, still spewing threats, away.

Alexa stood with her arms crossed, shaking now from reaction to the whole episode. When the remaining policemen left, Jamison turned to her. His expression looked forbidding.

He took her elbow and directed her to the elevator. She was cold now, and shivered. His fingers felt warm, and she didn't have the courage or will to pull away.

The ride to their floor elapsed in silence. In equal silence they entered their apartment. There, he let go and faced her.

"Proud of yourself? That was a stupid stunt."

"I wanted freedom. I wanted to be by myself."

"You act like a child!" His Italian accent was thick. "I can't believe you would pull a trick like that."

Alexa fought tears. "I didn't think it was a real threat. I thought..." Maybe it would be best not to mention her mistaken suspicions about Eve.

He stepped closer. "Then why do I waste my time with you? Staying here...letting you drive me crazy! When I came out of that room, and you were gone..." He thrust a hand through his hair. "At first, I thought you'd been kidnapped. And then I realized you'd run out!"

She hugged her arms tighter around herself. "I'm sorry." Her voice trembled.

"You're sorry. Great. That fixes everything." He headed for the kitchen.

Anger flared, fed by the fear that still shook her. "Sorry's not good enough for you? You're an impossible man to live with." She mumbled, "If I hadn't escaped, I was going to go loco."

Luckily, he didn't seem to hear. "I'm going to ask Colin to take me out and put Mart here."

Hurt stabbed deep. However irrational it might be, his words made her feel rejected and abandoned. Her mouth ran off faster than her brain. "Good! Then maybe this nightmare will end. It'll start feeling positive around here."

"Like your fairy tale," he sneered.

"The end of one Grimm fairy tale, anyway—the Princess and the..." Just in time, she stopped. She had gone much too far today. Calling him an elf would not help matters.

A terrible moment of silence elapsed. He turned back to her. "And the *what?*" he said through his teeth.

"Nothing."

"Whatever demeaning thing you're thinking, say it to my face, princess."

"I'm not. You're a perfectly adequate bodyguard."

He moved closer. Tightly leashed aggression simmered. "Is that a *thank you?*" he asked through thinned lips.

"No... I mean, yes." His threatening, hostile stance snapped something deep inside of her. Fear blossomed, chased by panic. She was going to lose it! Horrified, she struggled to blink back welling tears. One popped out anyway, and rolled down her cheek.

Immediately, his expression changed. "Don't cry." For once, he looked at a loss.

"I'm not!" she gasped. "And certainly not because of you!" She fled to her room, slamming the door behind her.

Alexa sat on her bed, pressing the heels of her hands to her eyes. She wept helplessly. Outside, a truck backfired and she jumped, for the sound shot straight through her soul. With a gasp, she sobbed harder.

The bed sagged down beside her. He had followed her into the room. She flinched away.

"Alexa." It was one of the few times he had ever said her name. And never like that. Quiet and gentle.

"Go away." She couldn't bear anyone to be close right now. She wanted to be alone, just like years ago, when she had hidden in the library in order to find peace in her world.

He touched her shoulder, and she jumped a foot. "Don't!" she flared. "Can't you hear? I said, 'go.'"

"Answer one question first."

"What?" She sniffed, and it sounded like a juicy snort. Embarrassment upon unbearable embarrassment.

"The attack scared you. I understand that. But so did that truck backfire. Why?"

More relentless tears seeped out. "It's nothing." Why wouldn't he go away?

He didn't move. The stubborn, tenacious man.

"It's nothing. I told you," she said, mopping up the tears. "That loud sound…and the violence, and the hatred spewing from that woman… It reminded me of when I was a kid."

The crazed attacks reminded her of her parents' endless fights. Most of them had escalated into irrational screaming fits. Even as she had grown into a teen, Alexa had hidden in her bedroom with her arms over her head, trying to block out the sounds.

Telling Jamison a little more of this truth would hurt. But maybe if she did, he'd leave her alone. She wanted to be alone.

"My parents fought," she whispered. "Sometimes they threw plates. They'd shatter against the wall." It had terrified her. Much like today's attack.

"They threw dishes at each other?"

"No, at the floor, or walls…or cupboards." At least, they had until the end. Alexa drew in a long, choking breath. It was all in the past. Over and forgotten, she had thought.

"I'm sorry," he said quietly.

Alexa wiped her slippery cheeks. "It's over. It shouldn't bother me anymore."

"It scared you," he murmured.

It felt strange to be having such an intimate conversation with the man she had fought with since the day they'd met. And yet, it felt unexpectedly comfortable and right, too. He cared. She sensed it. And yet, why? Lately, she had been nothing but a gigantic, prickly pain to him.

In a small voice, she admitted, "I didn't understand why they wanted to hurt each other. When I was very young, they loved each other."

"Do they still fight?"

"They're divorced. Their relationship is better now. But neither has remarried."

"Some wounds cut deep."

Pain lanced her heart. "Yes."

"Your parents' fights probably seemed unpredictable and violent to you. Just like the attack today. One reminded you of the other."

"Yes." She swiped at the still leaking tears. "I'm all right." She felt exposed now, after having revealed her vulnerable side to Jamison.

"You are not okay. A woman pulled a knife on you. You're scared. That's all right."

Unexpected, hot tears welled up. "I'm so *sorry*, Jamison. I'm sorry I ran off, and I'm sorry for how I've been treating you. I felt stifled...and scared, and I took it out on you. I wanted to escape."

"It's okay. I understand."

Alexa suddenly turned to him, but couldn't look into his face. "What would I have done if you hadn't come?" More fear choked her words, and her heart.

"You kicked the man well." She heard his faint amusement.

"But I froze when I saw that knife coming at me." Through watery eyes, she finally glanced at him. While sitting, his face was level with her own. And for once, his eyes actually looked brown—a lot softer than the hard black she usually elicited from him.

"That's why you need me."

What if she had succeeded in her escape like she had planned? What if Jamison hadn't found her? And how had he, anyway? He must have shot out of the building like a bullet in order to find her as quickly as he had.

If he hadn't been at the top of his game, she would probably be dead.

More tears wrenched out. She couldn't stop them.

His arms went around her and he pulled her close. For once, she wanted his comfort more than she needed to keep this man at arm's length. She cautiously leaned into him and wept into his black shirt. He felt solid and strong. Alexa gulped for breath, trying to find control. When he stroked her hair, she relaxed a little. Over her head, he murmured soft Italian words. They soothed her, even though she didn't know what they meant.

She sniffed, trying to stop crying. Why did she feel so secure in his arms? So comforted? Alexa decided she had been there long enough. She pulled away, snuffling.

"Here." He put a white, neatly folded handkerchief into her hand.

With surprise, she said, "You carry a handkerchief?"

"My mother impressed on me that I need to carry a clean hanky everywhere. They have many purposes."

"Like sopping up a stupid girl who ran off and almost got killed."

"That, too." She heard the smile in his voice.

She dabbed at her eyes. Her mascara left black marks on the snowy white linen. "Now look what I've done."

"You can wash it," he teased.

"Thanks so much!" Quickly, though, she said, "I'm joking. I'd be happy to."

He pulled it from her grasp and stood, stuffing it into his pocket as he crossed the room to her bath. He returned with a box full of tissues. "Here."

She accepted them. "Thanks. Did you think I was going to contaminate your hanky? Like radiation left over from nuclear waste?"

Jamison laughed. "You can be very funny."

"When it's not directed at you, you mean," she said dryly. Alexa swiped at her dripping nose. She didn't want to honk it in his presence.

Finally, she looked up. "Thank you," she said simply.

For the first time, his brown eyes actually looked gentle. "You're welcome, Alexa." And then he left, quietly closing the door behind him.

Alexa felt better after talking to Jamison, but she needed deeper comfort, too. Before starting work, she looked in her Bible for verses on fear.

Psalm 27:1 spoke to her heart. "The LORD is my light and my salvation—whom shall I fear? The LORD is the stronghold of my life—of whom shall I be afraid?" *Lord, please heal me...of all my fears.*

❈ ❈ ❈ ❈ ❈

The next morning, Jamison said, "The attack on you hit the papers."

"It did? How? I thought only the police knew." The truce between them felt strange today. Uncomfortable, too. Alexa wasn't sure how to handle it. Then again, maybe Jamison would switch with Mart, like he had threatened. Maybe this would be the last morning they'd spend together.

"Colin's a big star," Jamison said grimly. "Gossip is hot." He pushed the paper across the table. A wide-eyed picture of Alexa staring up at Colin, on stage, blazed across the front page.

"Great," she groaned. "I look like a love-struck groupie."

A faint smile curled Jamison's lips. "Aren't you?"

She elected to ignore that comment. "Will I need to stay inside now? Or wear a disguise when I go out?"

"It wouldn't hurt. You could wear sunglasses. It's not the best picture of you."

Alexa wondered if that was a backhanded compliment.

Jamison found a bag of peanuts and pulled it open. Would that be his breakfast, she wondered. Usually he fixed bacon and egg white omelettes, or something healthy. Maybe it was just a snack.

She broke the lengthening silence. Diffidently, she asked, "Have you asked Colin if Mart can take your place?"

Jamison put a nut between his teeth and leaned against the counter. "Not yet."

"Will you?"

"Should I?"

"Of course." But she said it with no heat.

Jamison popped another nut into his mouth. "Then I'll stay." He met her eyes. "That okay with you?"

Alexa shrugged. "Sure."

"Good."

With a small smile, Alexa returned to work.

❋ ❋ ❋ ❋ ❋

Mart let Alexa into the penthouse for her interview with Eve later that morning. The secretary stood with her back to Alexa, talking on her cell phone.

"Go ahead and sit down." Mart advised. "Eve will be right with you." The bodyguard disappeared into another room.

Alexa settled her notepad on her lap and tried not to eavesdrop on Eve's conversation. It was hard, for Eve's high voice sounded hysterical. "Is Mother okay?" Silence. "Yes, but..." and then, "Are you sure? What can I do?" More silence. "Okay. 'Bye." She flipped the cell phone shut. Anguish contorted her features.

"Is everything all right?" Alexa asked, concerned.

Eve blinked, as if seeing her for the first time. "My mother is in the hospital."

"I'm so sorry. Will she be okay?"

"Yes. She'll be out in a few days." Eve put away the phone, tidied her desk, and then sat opposite her, looking calmer.

Alexa didn't want to be nosy, but she said gently, "I'm glad. But I thought you didn't have parents. I heard you grew up in the foster system."

Eve frowned, obviously upset her personal life had been disclosed to Alexa. "Of course I have parents. They had problems, and the courts thought I'd be better off in the foster system. But I was talking about my *foster* mother."

"Oh."

Eve glared, as if finally remembering she disliked Alexa. "Why did you want to meet with me? I assume you have questions for the book."

Of course, Alexa couldn't tell Colin's secretary that she had been at the top of her suspect list. Good thing she had discovered Eve couldn't be involved, or she might have stuck her foot in her mouth and irreparably damaged their shaky working relationship.

"Yes. I asked Colin if I could interview you and a few others for the book. I'm guessing you have insights others don't have into Colin."

"You just want the inside scoop for yourself."

Would the secretary never let up on the pit bull mentality? Patiently, she said, "After reading the book, people will want to feel like they know Colin better. They like and admire him already. Your insights could increase goodwill for him."

"And increase your book sales," Eve finished with contempt. "What a mercenary you are."

Alexa wanted to roll her eyes. Could Eve even think logically? "It's Colin's book," she reminded her. "And it could increase sales of his CDs, too."

"Perfect. Manipulate me into helping you. If I don't, I'm betraying Colin."

Goodness gracious! "I'm not trying to guilt trip you. I want to interview you. And yes, I think it will help Colin. Don't you want to help him?"

Eve rolled her eyes to the ceiling. "Fine. I only have ten minutes. Colin needs me." She said this last with a note of triumph.

Alexa's patience felt sorely tried. "Fine. Tell me how you met him."

"I worked at his recording company. He noticed my hard work and asked me to become his secretary."

"It's a plum job."

"I've earned it. I do a good job." Antagonism rang through the words.

Insight dawned. Eve clearly felt defensive. Possibly even insecure. But why? Was she afraid of losing her job? Or afraid of losing Colin? "What does Colin mean to you?" The question popped out before her brain could censor it.

Eve's eyes rounded. "That is none of your business, hussy! I certainly know what he means to you."

Alexa did not bother to answer this. "I'm sorry. I meant to say, how does Colin treat you on a day-to-day basis? What kind of a boss is he?"

Eve settled back on the couch, but her narrowed eyes still flashed. "He's perfect. Always considerate. A gentleman. He remembers my birthday, and gives me flowers for Administrative Professionals' Day in the U.S. He even gives me chocolates for Valentine's Day."

"That's sweet." It sounded just like Colin.

"You can wipe that mooning smile off your face. You're just another flash in the pan for Colin. Another in a long line."

"Are you suggesting he plans to use me, then throw me away? That doesn't sound like the Colin you just described."

Eve clearly didn't know what to say to this, for a silent moment elapsed. Then she spurted, "He'll wine and dine you, then get tired of you, and that will be that. He'll send you a note from time to time, because that's the kind of man he is. But you'll get the kiss-off, just like everyone else."

"Then there's you, right? Colin always keeps you by his side."

"That's right. He knows I'll never leave him."

"Because he pays you," Alexa returned, before she could censor her tongue.

Eve stared, as if she could not believe her ears, and then jumped to her feet. "I tried to warn you. Go ahead and get hurt."

"You don't care if I'm hurt. You want to warn me off. Is it because you want Colin for yourself?"

Eve gasped. "That is utterly ridiculous!"

Alexa gathered up her things. Clearly, this interview would go nowhere constructive. "If you're interested in him, why not say so?"

"I would *never* jeopardize my working relationship with Colin! Only tramps like you manipulate him into spending time with you...for the *book*, of course. Just remember, if it wasn't for the *book,* you wouldn't be here. And when it's done, you'll be gone."

"Is that why he invited me to dinner tomorrow night? For work?" Alexa immediately regretted the taunt, but couldn't take it back.

Eve gasped, obviously shocked by this news. "So you *are* a liar. You say you don't want a fling with him, but here you are, coercing dates with him!"

"It wasn't my idea. He invited me."

Eve crossed her arms. "Fine. I don't care. Soon you'll be gone. He'd never fall for someone like you."

"Why not?"

Eve's lips trembled. "This interview is over."

Alexa felt sorry for the secretary. For all of her spiteful vinegar, Eve had deep feelings for Colin. Unfortunately, they also appeared to be unhealthy, possessive ones.

Alexa struggled to find conciliatory words. "Colin is a kind, wonderful man. There are too few in the world today."

"At least you understand that."

"I won't hurt him. I promise you that." Alexa headed for the door.

"So you say. But I don't trust you. I never will. If you know what's best for you, you'll steer clear of him."

With narrowed eyes, Alexa turned back. "Is that a threat?"

"Of course not. Just friendly advice." But Eve's cold eyes looked anything but friendly. After calling for Mart, Alexa left without another word.

If she wasn't absolutely certain that Eve couldn't be the note writer, Eve's last statement would have pushed her to the top of her suspect list. As it was, Alexa could only hope the police would soon find the man involved.

In the meantime, Alexa would try to steer clear of Eve as much as possible. Somehow, she had to make Colin see that she couldn't work with his secretary. She would need to come to him directly for help on the book.

Alexa found herself looking forward to the date with him tomorrow night. For the first time, she admitted it for what it was. Eve had helped her to realize it. Alexa did like Colin, but was it in a romantic way? The question itself was strange. Shouldn't the answer be "yes"? In any case, Sunday night would tell her.

CHAPTER EIGHT

AFTER DINNER THAT NIGHT—pasta with a homemade spaghetti sauce, which Jamison had unexpectedly cooked—Alexa stared out the window. The lights of Paris sparkled below, traffic moved, and people hurried along the sidewalks. How she wanted to go out and feel the energy of a Paris night. On Wednesday night, they had hurried back so fast that she had been unable to experience any of the Parisian magic.

On a whim, she addressed Jamison, who currently prowled the sitting room. He looked caged and restless, much like she felt. "I want to go out."

He looked up. "Now?"

"Yes." Alexa grabbed a light jacket, slipped on her new flats, and headed for the door. Since it was dark, she decided not to worry about a disguise.

Jamison disappeared into his room and then reappeared, tucking his wallet and key in his pockets. He held open the door for her. "After you."

On the street, Alexa took a great breath of the crisp air. All sorts of different people hurried to and fro. Some were her age, and probably on their way to dance clubs, Alexa imagined. And others were older, maybe going out to dinner.

"Let's walk toward Rue Cler again," she suggested. Alexa wanted to rub out the tarnished blot the attack had left on that enchanting place, and replace it with new, bright memories.

"Okay." Jamison walked close by her side down the busy sidewalks. Sometimes his black jacket brushed her sleeve. It felt strangely intimate to walk with him on a Saturday night. Would others think they were on a date?

She cast a quick, self-conscious glance at Jamison. It certainly could appear that way. This was one of the reasons she had never dated a shorter man. What would people think of the two of them together? She an Amazon, and him...an elf.

But no one seemed to notice, or care. She received no strange looks. In fact, a middle-aged woman actually smiled as she hurried by, clutching a grocery bag.

"What are you thinking, princess?"

Alexa started. "Umm..." As if she would confess to viewing him—even for a millisecond—as her date! Hastily, she improvised. Walking in Paris brought to mind vacations and time off, which she had rarely appropriated until lately. What about Jamison? "Don't you ever get a day off?"

"Trying to get rid of me?"

"Yes." She smiled. "But seriously."

"I'll ask for a day in Italy, to visit my family. Otherwise, I'll take time off after the tour."

Cautiously, Alexa said, "What do you do with your free time?"

"You want to learn something about me?"

This was exactly the impression Alexa had hoped to avoid. But at the same time, she couldn't escape her curiosity. Her bodyguard possessed deeper, more complex layers than she had initially imagined.

"Just wondering if you ever let your hair down."

"It's been a long time." To her surprise, he took the question seriously.

Alexa could not imagine Jamison ever being anything other than tightly coiled, watchful, and controlled at all times.

Ahead, a bicycle appeared on the sidewalk. A teen wearing a knitted cap rode it.

"What in the world?" she said, as it zoomed closer.

A flux of people exited a restaurant, and the bicycle careened toward Alexa. Before she could react, Jamison grabbed her hand and hauled her into the deserted street.

Alexa's heart beat fast as they regained the sidewalk. "That wasn't an attack. Was it?" Uncertainly, she glanced at Jamison.

"No."

Alexa realized then that he still held her hand. His felt strong and warm, and hers fit neatly inside of it. Her breath caught as she absorbed the intimate connection to this man. Tingles ran over her palm, electrifying her bloodstream. Why didn't he let go? An inexplicable part of her didn't want him to, but the saner bit of her brain said she had better end it, if he wouldn't.

She discretely tugged at her hand. "Umm. Jamison?"

Instantly, he released it, as though it were a hot potato. "Sorry," he said roughly. "I was thinking...about something else."

"Glad to know I'm so memorable," she said, absurdly offended.

His white teeth gleamed in the dim light. "Do you want my undivided attention?"

"Please!" she scoffed, glad the low lighting hid her blush. "I couldn't want anything less. And frankly, who wants their hand held like a forgotten dishrag?" Oops! That hadn't come out right at all.

His widening grin proved it. "Shall I redeem myself?" he suggested. "You know we Italians have a reputation to uphold."

Alexa didn't have to fill in the blanks—that Italian men were the greatest lovers in the world. A tremor went through her, but she struggled to frown. "Of course not! I don't think of you in that context. You don't need to prove anything to me."

A faint smile remained, but he shoved his hands into his pockets. "Where to next, princess?"

She shrugged. "I don't know. I just want to walk."

They strolled a few more blocks, and then a whiff of chocolate kissed her nose. Where had it come from? They hadn't reached Rue Cler yet.

Like a greedy little mouse, she followed her nose forward a few more steps, and then gazed in at heaven. Bright lights lit the shop, illuminating the beautifully painted fresco of a tree and trellis on the far wall, and directly ahead clear display cases tempted her with pyramids of chocolate confections.

Alexa inhaled deeply when a customer exited.

"You like chocolate?" Jamison asked, at her side. She had all but forgotten him in the ecstasy of the moment.

"I *love* it!" Alexa breathed. "I can't have it in the house."

"Do you have any euros?"

"A few." She had made a point of procuring them immediately following the last debacle. But she had only stuffed a few in her pocket tonight. "Would you like some chocolate? I'll treat—it's my turn, after all."

"Sure."

Alexa eagerly entered the cool, sweet smelling shop, and drifted over to gaze into the display cases. Dark chocolate, milk chocolate, cream filled chocolates, caramel chocolates, and white chocolate. She nudged the corner of her mouth to make sure she wasn't drooling.

Alexa calculated prices in her head. "I've got enough money for two pieces each. What do you want?"

Jamison wanted a coconut cream filled and a chewy, nutty one. Alexa went for the pure dark chocolate—her absolute favorite in the world—and white chocolate with almonds. The girl behind the counter packaged up the sweets.

They sat at a small table outside. Alexa nibbled on her dark chocolate. "Yum," she sighed and closed her eyes in pure bliss. When she opened them, she discovered Jamison watching her with a faint smile.

"How is the book coming?" he asked, finishing his first chocolate. Obviously not a connoisseur, Alexa determined.

"Okay," she replied. "Colin's hard to pin down, but we're having dinner tomorrow night. It'll be a good opportunity to record more material."

Jamison raised a black brow. "That's all it is to you—a business dinner?"

A blush warmed her cheeks, and she hoped he couldn't see. "Not exactly."

Jamison looked away for a second. "Have you ever been to Spain?" The subject change felt deliberate.

"Nope. I've never been to Europe, period."

"I worked in Barcelona for a while. Maybe I could show you around."

Alexa smiled. "Sure."

Jamison told her about Barcelona while she nibbled the white chocolate. He watched as she finished the last morsel.

"Done," she sighed. "Are you ready to go back?"

By way of an answer, Jamison stood, and even helped edge back her chair.

"Thank you." Alexa was thrown a little off kilter by this. "I'm not used to you continental men being so chivalrous," she said, to cover her confused flutters.

"You think I'm suave and debonair?"

Alexa rolled her eyes. "Hardly. ...Well, maybe sometimes."

"Another backhanded compliment. I must be growing in your opinion."

"Let's not get ahead of ourselves."

He chuckled quietly and Alexa grinned, too. Were they actually ending this evening on a cordial note? It was hard to believe, and unexpectedly pleasant.

❈ ❈ ❈ ❈ ❈

Jamison had agreed to come to church with her this morning. Alexa finished hooking in her earrings, grabbed up her purse, and met Jamison at the front door.

With a glance, he took in her crisp, white linen jacket with the pale peach camisole, and pencil slim skirt. He said nothing about how nice she looked, par for the course. Instead, his gaze fell to her white, strappy three and a half inch stilettos. They were her highest heels, and matched her outfit exactly.

He said, "You couldn't resist, could you?"

With them on, he officially matched her lip level.

"Whatever could you mean?" she inquired, not so innocently.

After their breakthrough last night—actually ending an evening on a positive note—part of Alexa wanted to keep the peace. The other half didn't. Peace with Jamison disturbed her. She didn't know how, or why, but there it was. The truth.

Suspicion lurked in the dark gaze. "You did it on purpose."

Alexa gave him a cheeky grin. "I've got to keep you on your toes."

"I can't figure you out, Alexa." He opened the door.

"Don't try," she advised. "You might hurt yourself." She was very aware of his light hand on her back, urging her into the hall. Thankfully, the disturbing pressure fell quickly away.

"I don't intend to do that." He sounded grim, like he meant it.

They descended in the elevator in silence. Outside, Alexa observed brightly, "What a beautiful day!"

Jamison did not bother to respond.

Alexa wasn't sure if she felt happy or sad that she had succeeded in pricking last night's bubble of camaraderie. But she felt more at ease. As she had suspected, high heels and light, prickly banter were the best ways to keep him at arm's length. She wouldn't think too closely on why this seemed so necessary.

They entered the ancient, beautiful church and found seats. Here, she noted, Jamison allowed only two feet between them, instead of the three feet in England. Good, or bad?

Good, she decided. Friendly, but the perfect amount of distance. She sent him a perky grin.

"Alexa..."

"Ready to translate for me?" she demanded.

His broad shoulders relaxed back against the pew. Amusement simmered in his gaze. "Absolutely. At your service."

"Glad to hear it," she approved. "I'll tell you when I need help."

The service began. Alexa had taken four years of French in high school, but that had been over ten years ago. It tested her to the limit to try to understand the sermon. Jamison, on the other hand, seemed to understand every word. A few times she whispered to him, asking what the pastor had said. She struggled through the hymns in the hymnal, and then it was over.

"I liked it," she said, descending the steps. Alexa suddenly had to know the answer to a question which had been burning in her brain ever since visiting his church in England. "Are you a Christian?"

"Yes." He glanced at her. "No need to look so surprised."

"It's just you don't seem..."

"You don't know much about me, princess."

Alexa believed this. He surprised and disturbed her more every day.

He said, "Are you a Christian?"

"Yes!" She was offended that he had to ask. "Is it really that hard to tell?"

"You never know until you ask."

What sort of an answer was that? Alexa frowned. "I'm trying to pray for you," she said primly. She quickly refreshed his memory. "The sermon in London was about loving your enemies."

"Thank you." He gave her an odd look. "I need all the prayer I can get."

"I'm sure you do."

He gave a short chuckle, and looked away. "Okay, princess. Let's get home before we start slinging mud at each other again."

"I'll be good if you will."

He did not reply, which was probably for the best.

❈ ❈ ❈ ❈ ❈

Alexa dressed with care for her date with Colin. With a critical eye, she scanned her image in the closet's full-length mirror. The pale green silk dress fell in classic, simple lines down her willowy frame. She wore gold heels for flash, gold earrings, and a gold cross necklace. What would Colin think?

She tucked her hair behind one ear, feeling self-conscious, and then tugged it back out. More hairspray. That's what she needed.

Finally prepared, she gathered up her digital recorder and the outline. She had sent Colin a copy, just like she had promised, but she wanted to be able to take notes on her own copy. She spun back. Her purse!

Finally, she emerged into the living room, where her bodyguard watched soccer. Jamison stood and flipped off the game. "Ready?" He looked at her, and went still. "You look nice."

Alexa grinned, feeling oddly pleased. Was that the first, true compliment Jamison had ever paid her? Yes, indeedy.

Jamison opened the door for her, but did not touch her back, as he had for church this morning. "You're wearing perfume," he said, walking beside her to the elevator. "Pretty serious about this date, aren't you?"

Alexa would not tell him that this was a tester date, to see if something existed between Colin and herself. Instead, she said, "I'm dining with a famous star. How else should I dress?"

He did not respond, and they ascended to the penthouse in silence.

At Colin's door, Alexa said to Jamison, "Why don't you take the evening off? Go kick up your heels with the locals."

He sent her an unreadable, faintly amused look. "Have fun, Alexa."

With a grin, she knocked on Colin's door. "Good night."

Jamison waited until Colin opened the door, and then disappeared in the direction of the stairs. Briefly, Alexa wondered where he was going, but then Colin grabbed her whole attention. He wore a steel blue suit tonight, without a tie, and the top buttons of his shirt were undone, as if he hated the restriction around his neck. The blue suit amplified the color of Colin's eyes. He looked incredibly handsome.

He took her hand and pressed a kiss to the back. "You look gorgeous," he said with warm approval, and urged her into his penthouse.

Alexa caught her breath. The lights were low, and candles burned on every available surface. Across the room, velvet dusk enveloped Paris. Lights twinkled as far as her eyes could see. A table draped in white linen had been set beside one of the floor-to-ceiling windows, with a chair on either side. A low candle in a cut crystal holder was set between the two place settings, complete with crystal wine glasses and silver.

"It's beautiful," she breathed. "You shouldn't have. Not for me."

"Of course for you," he said. "What will you have? Sparkling cider, or cola?"

He had paid attention. Colin knew she didn't drink alcohol, and that her favorite drink was cola. Alexa felt flattered. "How about cola for now, and the cider with dinner?"

"Perfect," he agreed. After delivering their drinks, he sat beside her on the sofa. His arm slid along the back, behind her shoulders. He lifted his glass. "Cheers. Here's to getting to know you better."

"Cheers." Alexa touched his glass. As she sipped her drink, a note of caution slipped through her. The romantic mood of the penthouse, Colin's arm behind her... She placed her drink on the coffee table, and scooted back at the same time she turned toward him. "Colin, I'm flattered by all you've done. But...are you trying to put a move on me?"

Colin gave a startled laugh. "You are too clever by half, Alexa."

"Don't get me wrong," she said, gesturing to the room. "I love the candles and the opportunity to spend time with you. But I'm not going to be swept away...or whatever it is you might intend."

Colin laughed out loud. He withdrew the arm he'd placed on the sofa back. "Okay, Alexa, you're safe," he chuckled. "I won't use my charming wiles on you. If you do think I'm charming?"

Alexa sent him a tiny smile. "Of course. But I'd rather get to know the real you. Not some act you put on."

He leaned toward her, his gaze serious. "You mean that."

"Of course I do. I've already seen a little of who you are, Colin. You don't need to pretend to be anyone else."

"All right, then." He lifted his glass again. "To truth and honesty."

"Amen," she agreed.

"Your faith means a lot to you, doesn't it? Tell me about it."

A little surprised, Alexa told him how she had become a Christian a few years after her parents had divorced. "It was a hard time," she said. "I felt lost and alone, and then I met Christ, and I knew I'd never be alone again."

He nodded. "You're serious, aren't you?"

"Yes. I know I probably sound like one of those Jesus freaks. But God is real. I don't know what else to say, except you can find that out for yourself, too, if you want to."

Colin twirled his wine glass. "I'll think about it. I was brought up in Sunday school. My mum insisted on it."

Alexa nodded, and changed the subject. "Tell me more about your childhood. What were your parents like?"

"And there goes the recorder," Colin said ruefully.

"Please?" she said. "Just one story. I'm running out of material, Colin, and I need to finish this book. You're my only source, so far."

"I've talked to my band, and they'll meet with you next week. Maybe Sunday."

"Terrific."

"And what about Eve? Have you interviewed her?"

"I've been meaning to talk to you about Eve." Alexa hesitated. "She seems to dislike me. Every time I try to talk to her, she attacks me and accuses that I want to hurt you."

Colin frowned. "That's not right."

"I'm not angry with her. I think she feels insecure for some reason. I don't know why, Colin, so please be kind to her. But I just can't work with her."

"I'm sorry to hear that," he said slowly. "I'll speak to her, but I'll be careful about it."

"I know her mother just went into the hospital. Maybe that's why she was so upset yesterday."

Colin looked confused. "She has a mother? And she's in the hospital?"

"Her foster mother."

A knock came at the door, and Colin stood to open it.

A porter appeared, pushing a cart with silver-domed dishes on it.

Colin took her hand. "Dinner, my lady, ordered from the finest restaurant."

Alexa grabbed her outline and recorder and followed him to the table. She settled the white linen napkin across her lap while the waiter served their salads. "Merci," she told him.

And then they were left alone. The outline didn't fit on the table, so Alexa shoved it under her napkin.

Colin poured sparkling cider, and lifted his own glass, "To a wonderful evening."

Her stapled pages slipped to the floor between their feet. "Cheers," Alexa hastily agreed, and bent to retrieve the errant pages.

Colin watched her flushed attempts to get herself to rights again. "No one's ever brought an outline on a date before," he said with a grin.

"You're a hard man to get alone," she explained. "I have to take advantage of every opportunity.

"As I intend to make the most of this opportunity," Colin said. "Tell me about *your* childhood."

Alexa smiled at Colin's deft conversation switch. Obligingly, she told him about her home life. How her parents had loved Beth and her, but couldn't get along, especially as she entered junior high. How she had been a brainiac in school, and had entered the National Spelling Bee as a child. "But I never made it past the state level," she said modestly.

"Fascinating," Colin said. "A beautiful girl, and a good speller, too."

"Perfect combination for your book, right?" Alexa grinned.

After this, she managed to steer the conversation to Colin, and her recorder silently documented each word. Colin brimmed with anecdotes, and even slyly slipped in a few questions for her, too. By the time dessert—a delicate pecan and brown sugar torte—was finished, Alexa estimated she had accumulated thirty pages worth of material on her recorder. She clicked it off, and with a sigh gazed out at the sparkling lights of Paris. What a delightful evening. Good company, fun conversation...

"More cider?" Colin asked.

"No. Thank you. I think I'm about to turn into a pumpkin."

"What?"

Alexa laughed. "From *Cinderella*, remember? I'm getting tired."

Colin smiled across the table, and his unconscious charm warmed her. "I've enjoyed the evening."

"I have, too."

"I tried not to put on any pretences."

"I know." Alexa smiled.

Colin took her hand and intently gazed at her. "I want you to see the real me."

Alexa was flattered, and gently squeezed his hand. Flutters went through her heart at his obvious meaning. However, something cautioned her to be careful. "You're an incredible man, Colin. One day, you'll make a lucky woman very happy."

His intent, questioning gaze searched hers for a moment longer. Then he said, "I can live with that."

Alexa gathered up her things, and Colin called Mart to walk her downstairs. Mart edged into the hall, waiting, as Colin told Alexa goodnight.

"Call me if you need anything. Are you ready to travel to Barcelona tomorrow?"

"I still need to pack, but it won't take long."

He took her hand again. "Good. I intend to spend more time with you there."

"I hope so. We've got a lot more book to write."

"You're a funny girl, Alexa. I don't mean for the book."

It was impossible to ignore his meaning this time. "Thank you," she said softly, and Colin leaned toward her. He meant to kiss her! Flustered, Alexa turned her head at the last moment, so his kiss landed on her cheek.

Now, why had she done that? What would he think of her?

She pulled away. "I'm sorry, Colin. I think I'm a little... confused." But about what? That was the question.

He nodded, blue eyes surprisingly understanding. "You want to go slow. You told me that before. I understand."

Alexa smiled weakly. At least someone did. Impulsively, she hugged him. "Good night, Colin."

"Good night, love."

And then she was in the hall, walking beside Mart. Why had she withdrawn from Colin? Why didn't she want him to kiss her?

Had she lost her mind?

Colin was the most handsome, charming, genuinely nice man she had met in a long time. And she liked him. How could she *not* want him to kiss her? What in the world was her problem?

Nothing made sense, so Alexa decided to latch onto Colin's explanation for her behavior. She wanted to go slow, and be careful. Well, that much was true. She would not cheaply or easily throw her heart away again. In college, she had been lonely and starving for love. Now she knew that she could survive on her own. The man to whom she gave her heart would have to earn her trust, first. She would have to know him well, and long. Frankly, she still didn't know Colin that well.

She definitely liked him, but her sister's cautionary words flitted through her mind yet again. "Be careful." She would continue to take the warning to heart.

CHAPTER NINE

THE NEXT MORNING, Alexa grabbed breakfast and quickly packed up. She had come to actually like her Paris prison, she reflected, zipping her suitcase closed. She cast one last, fond glance around her room. Someday she would come back and sightsee everything she had missed this time.

But she was eager to see Barcelona, Spain, too. Of course, she had watched the Barcelona summer Olympics on television when she was younger, but what would it be like to visit in person?

She dragged her suitcases into the living room. Jamison's gigantic black case already waited beside the door. He sat on the couch, finishing a muffin for breakfast. It was the first time she had seen him since he had dropped her off at Colin's last night.

"Good morning!" she said.

"You're in a good mood. How was your date?"

"Terrific. Colin is a sweet man." It was true. It was also true she still didn't know what she felt for Colin. Why hadn't she let him kiss her last night? The question kept circling through her brain.

"You're falling for him." Jamison crumpled his napkin. His knuckles flashed briefly white.

Alexa didn't know what to say. "He seems to like me, too," she said at last.

"What's not to like?" He stood up.

Alexa's eyebrows shot up. Was that an actual compliment—for her?

But before she could speak, Jamison continued, "Colin likes beautiful women. Keep using that card to your best advantage, Alexa."

She gasped. "You rude man! How dare you accuse me of manipulating Colin? As if that's the only thing he could like about me."

Jamison moved to the sink to wash out his cup. "I never said it was."

"What kind of a remark is that?" she accused. "It's not even a backhanded compliment! Are you reverting back to your obnoxious self?"

His dark eyes flashed. "Don't you like me best this way?"

Better than too chummy. Sadly, this was true. Part of her missed the comfortable camaraderie of their walk on Saturday night, and even the time at church yesterday, but this prickliness was best.

"I know 'beautiful' is a dirty word in your books," she said. "Why?"

"It's a conversation that wouldn't interest you, princess."

He was wrong. She did want to know, but refused to admit it. She pressed on with her attack. "Well, I prefer to take 'beautiful' as a compliment. So be careful how you throw it around. I might start to think you have inappropriate feelings for me."

His white teeth flashed in a smile. "You don't like peace, do you?"

"Do you?"

Whatever snit had attacked him relaxed out of his stiff shoulders. His black gaze burned into hers, and her heart thumped uncomfortably fast. "About as much as you do, Alexa."

Apparently, he preferred the walls between them, too. She wondered why.

He asked then, "Packed up? Colin's meeting us downstairs."

※ ※ ※ ※ ※

Barcelona was a bustling city, Alexa noted through her new apartment window. The flat was similar in layout to the one in Paris, but the walls looked whitewashed, the floors were of red tile, and the heavy furniture was made of dark wood and leather. Dusk descended over the city, five stories below.

"Pizza's ready," Jamison announced. He dropped the hot pan with a clatter onto the stove top.

"Yum." She scooped two slices onto a plate and followed him into the living room. Alexa let him take the couch, while she took the chair. The coffee table served as the dining table.

"Meeting with Colin soon?" he asked unexpectedly.

"Nothing's scheduled. I've got enough to work on for now."

"No date planned, then."

She shot him a narrow-eyed look. "Why do you care?"

He shrugged. "I'd think if you were falling in love, you'd be champing at the bit to see him again."

"My feelings for Colin are exactly none of your business." Whatever they were, she finished silently. She still felt confused, but had decided to take it one day at a time with Colin. If it was right, it would work out in time.

"Prickly, aren't you, princess?"

"You've got to stop calling me princess."

"I call them as I see them, princess." Before she could gather her wits to launch another verbal assault, he changed direction. "What does your family call you?"

"Alexa." An evil imp danced into her mind. "How about you, Jethro?"

An unknown emotion simmered in him. Alexa hoped it was embarrassed mortification. But he only said, "Colin can have a big mouth."

She pressed harder. "Does anyone ever call you JJ?"

Jamison just looked at her. "Don't you dare."

"I'll call it as I see it," she returned, swallowing her bite of pizza with relish. "Or I could call you Jethro. It's amazing how all those names fit you. They're providential, don't you think—names? How we grow to look just like them."

"Alexa fits you."

"What is that supposed to mean?" Nothing good, she suspected.

"Upper crust. Snobby..."

"I am not snobby!"

"Beautiful..."

She flinched. "Please! As if that's a compliment, coming from you."

"I never said it was. Know what I thought the first time I saw you?"

Alexa did not respond, but viewed him through narrowed eyes.

"I said, 'There's a woman too beautiful for her own good.'"

His comment did not stroke her ego in the least. "That's fine," she said, raising her eyebrows, as if she couldn't care less. And she did not! "The first time I saw you, you reminded me of an elf." She bit off more pizza.

"An elf?" he yelped. Suddenly, he was standing. "An elf!" Anger shook through his voice. The black eyes blazed.

Unease tripped Alexa's heart faster. What had she just done? "I don't mean to say you look like an elf. You just reminded me of one...in an old fairy tale movie."

Jamison's face darkened to a ruddy color. She decided now wasn't the time to tell him that he'd also reminded her of a germophobe on cable. He probably wouldn't take it well, if this outburst was any indication.

His body trembled now, and she watched, amazed. It was a little like watching a train about to smash into something. Hopefully not her, she thought uneasily.

Alexa said, "Please don't have a conniption fit." She tried to placate him. "Elves are cute."

"Cute? You think I'm *cute?*" he roared. It was the first time he had ever raised his voice to her.

"Well, no. Not exactly..."

"You are demeaning me!"

"No..."

"Yes, you are! You just called me an elf! I'm an average-sized man..." His Italian accent definitely thickened when he was angry, she noted.

"Well, no, you're not. Average is about five foot ten."

He clenched his fists. "I can't stay here and talk to you. I'm afraid I'll say something I regret. But I won't. I'm a bigger man than you are woman."

"That doesn't even make sense," she pointed out.

He raised a hand, bit off an exclamation, and stalked out, slamming the front door behind him.

Great. Now she was alone. Exactly what she had wanted for over a week. She didn't need a bodyguard. At least not in an apartment, five floors up!

Grabbing more pizza on a napkin, she hurried to her room and shut the door. Finally, she could work in peace and quiet. No television murmured in the next room. It was silent.

Too silent.

Biting her lip, she pulled out her recorder and turned on the computer. Time to start transcribing notes from her date last night.

❋ ❋ ❋ ❋ ❋

Guilt prickled at Alexa soon after Jamison left. Unfortunately, he stayed out late that night. Alexa never heard him return, but Mart took his place in the meantime.

As soon as Jamison returned from the gym the next morning, Alexa slipped into their mutual living area.

He wore black shorts, which revealed the thick, corded muscles in his legs, and a formfitting black T-shirt, which did the same for his upper body. Perspiration dampened his dark hair and glistened on his deeply tanned arms.

The black gaze rested on her, but he kept moving toward his room.

"Uh, Jamison," she said. "I need to talk to you."

"More derogatory comments you forgot to mention last night? Like how I resemble a dwarf, or a gnome, maybe?"

"I want to apologize. I'm really sorry. I didn't mean to hurt your feelings."

"You meant to pay me a compliment?"

"No. We were joking around. I didn't think you'd take it so seriously."

He flexed his shoulders and gave her an unfriendly look. "How did you expect me to take it, Alexa? From the first minute I met you, you've degraded short men. You called us munchkins. Now you say I reminded you of an elf."

"Jamison." Alexa bit her lip. "Sometimes my mouth runs off before I can stop it. You know that about me."

"I do."

"I don't think of you as an elf. Or a munchkin. Please forgive me."

"My opinion matters to you?"

"Of course it does." Alexa looked at him with pleading in her eyes. She didn't mind sparring and spatting with him, but she didn't want to hurt his feelings, and she didn't like him angry with her, either. His respect meant too much to her.

"You want me to forgive you?" The hard look softened.

"Yes. Please," she added.

"Enough to cook me dinner tonight?"

She smiled. "Done. But I can't promise it'll be gourmet." Or even edible, but she felt it wise not to mention this.

"Okay, princess. You're forgiven. But I expect a five course meal."

"Do chips count as a course?" she called after him. His chuckle restored peace within her soul.

❈ ❈ ❈ ❈ ❈

"You're in for a tasty treat," Alexa informed Jamison as soon as he arrived on the scene for dinner.

Words for the book had flowed all day, but still Alexa had stopped early so she could try her hand at a full five course meal. At home, she was lucky to survive one course. She figured she would type late into the night to make up for it. As she knew, while the words flowed, she had to take full advantage—and also while the night with Colin was still fresh in her mind, including the nuances and laughter he brought to each of the stories. It should be enough material to keep her busy for another day or two.

Jamison pulled up a stool to the kitchen bar counter. "Interesting smells."

"Don't wrinkle your nose," she admonished. So what if she had burned the bottom of the tomato soup? She had saved most of it, and even strained out the black bits. Waste not, want not, right?

With flourish, she scooted a white platter before him. "Cheese and crackers," she said proudly. Not even a sliced finger to show for it.

"Number one," he said. Was that a small smile? Surely not. He ducked his head to take a bite before she could see.

Alexa nibbled on a cracker too, but kept a worried eye on the oven. No smoke billowed out yet. Good sign.

She slipped back to the counter to check the tomato soup in their white bowls. She stuck her finger in one—hers, of course. Cold. Oops.

"Round two will be up in a flash," she promised, and popped the bowls in the microwave. She pressed buttons to set it for two minutes.

After a minute, a juicy explosion sounded in the microwave. Dismayed, she rushed to open the door. Tomato soup spattered every surface.

"Rrr," she growled. Grabbing one bowl, she ferried the piping hot dish to Jamison. "Ow, ow, *ow!*" Her fingers burned, and she dropped it the last inch. Thankfully, little sloshed out. She blew on her fingers and retreated to clean up the mess.

Jamison ate silently. Too silently. She now sipped her own soup from the other side of the counter, and fixed a suspicious gaze upon him. He didn't bother to hide his smile any longer.

"What?" she demanded. "Aren't my cooking skills up to snuff?"

"Can't wait to see what you're cooking up next, princess."

"You'll love it," she promised. The timer on the stove dinged, and she flipped off the oven and grabbed the oven mitts. Heat billowed out as she opened the door, but she was pleased to discover the contents looked brown and crispy. Well, maybe a little burnt around the edges, but definitely edible.

Pleased, Alexa flipped the oven shut and prepared their plates.

"Voilà."

Jamison stared at his plate. "Fish sticks and French fries."

"Don't you like them? I even have ketchup." She squirted a big dollop on her plate and passed the bottle to him. "I believe this counts as two courses. Meat and potatoes."

Jamison shoved a fry in his mouth and chewed rapidly, but he couldn't stop a grin, or his chuckle from erupting when he swallowed. "Meat and potatoes. Right."

Alexa fixed him with a glare. "What did you expect? I'll bet your mother is a fabulous Italian cook."

"She is."

"Well, I'm sorry I don't make the grade." She sounded huffy to her own ears, and rapidly chewed ketchup soaked fries to assuage her hurt feelings.

Jamison finished. "It's delicious," he told her with a straight face. "Thank you." His gaze fell to her mouth.

"Thank you." Alexa delicately finished the last of her portion. "I especially love the mixture of grease and batter and fish. It's especially yummy with ketchup, don't you think? In fact, maybe this is a six course meal. Ketchup is our vegetable."

"Ketchup is not a course, princess."

"Fine, then." She looked up with a frown. "I hope dessert pleases your majesty." She noticed him staring at her mouth again. "What?"

"You've got ketchup on your lip."

"Oh!" Hastily, she wiped her mouth. "I wondered why you kept staring at me."

He smiled a little, as if at some private joke.

"What? Is it gone?"

"Not quite." He leaned forward, napkin in hand, and gently dabbed under her lip. His smiling dark eyes held hers for a long moment. "All gone." Alexa stared at him, her heart beating uncomfortably fast. With a faint smile he leaned back, which thankfully broke the bizarre spell.

"Well. Thank you," she said, feeling flustered. "I don't know what I'd do without you." Quickly, she cleared their places and set to work assembling dessert.

First, chocolate chip cookies warmed in the microwave. Thankfully, they couldn't explode. Then vanilla ice cream on top. She presented it to her irksome bodyguard.

"I hope you're pleased." She handed him a spoon. "I've never made a five course meal for anyone before."

"I'm honored."

"No, you aren't. You think my cooking is pitiful." She felt oddly upset that she had disappointed him, and couldn't hide the hurt from her expression.

His dark eyes gentled to brown. "Alexa, you made a wonderful meal." He kissed his fingertips and flicked them open. "It was marvelous—meraviglioso, mia bella." His accent lilted, sounding classically Italian.

Although Alexa wasn't exactly sure what he had said, the context promised it was good. "Thank you. But I'm certainly not one to bring home to mama."

He glanced down for a second. "I wouldn't say that. Actually, I wanted to ask you a favor."

"Really? What?"

"Next week we go to Italy. Instead of taking a day off, I'd like you to come with me to visit my family."

"You want *me* to visit your family?" She was stunned.

"It would be a favor. A business arrangement," he clarified.

"A business arrangement. Oh. Of course." Why had she felt so honored and ridiculously pleased when she'd thought Jamison wanted her to meet his family? It made no sense at all. She forced a smile. "I'd be happy to come...and help you out." She spooned up a big bite of ice cream.

Jamison watched her. Not much eluded her observant bodyguard, and that troubled her for the first time. "We'll have fun," he said quietly.

"Of course. I can't wait," she mumbled.

Thankfully, the telephone rang then. "I'll get it." Alexa rushed to answer it, swallowing the last of her ice cream. "Hello?"

"Alexa, love."

"Colin!" She turned away from Jamison. "How nice to hear from you."

"You're working too hard. Jamison said you didn't leave the building all day."

"The book is flowing. I wanted to take full advantage."

"Take time off tomorrow. That's an order—understand, young lady?"

Alexa giggled. "Okay. Your wish is my command."

"Good. Sightsee. Have Jamison take you. He knows the lay of the land. I won't let you work yourself to death."

Alexa smiled. "Thank you. You're the sweetest guy, Colin."

She heard his soft chuckle. "How about tickets for the concert tomorrow tonight? Or are you bored with concerts already?"

"I've only been to one. Of course I'd like to come!"

"Great. Also, I've hired a photographer for the show. Can you work that into the book?"

"Absolutely. Just have him e-mail me pictures."

"See you tomorrow, Alexa."

"See you then." She hung up with a smile.

"Another date?" Jamison inquired.

She would not let him spoil her mood. "Sort of. I'm going to the concert tomorrow night."

"That means I am, too. Just as well. Colin could use the extra security."

Alexa frowned. "I've told you not to waste time guarding me in this apartment."

The dark eyes rested on her face. "You're important, too, princess."

She blinked. "Stop calling me that."

"Why? You can't stand terms of affection?"

"Hah! Like you feel any affection for me."

"Don't I?"

She stared at him, her mouth slightly agape. Why in the world had he said that? "More like you feel sorry for me," she retorted. "Because I can't cook."

He did not deny it. Or confirm it, either, for that matter.

"I'm going to my room," she informed him. "I have work to do."

"What about the dishes?"

"Cooks don't clean." And she needed to be alone. How could Jamison's innocuous comment disturb her so deeply? Did he really feel affection for her? Probably after tonight's debacle he felt pity for her. Like a child, or a dog. That was what he had meant.

"Cleaning's not part of the apology?"

"Are you saying my debt isn't paid in full?" She frowned immediately.

He smiled then, and she knew he'd only said it to rile her. "Good night, princess."

"Good night, Jethro."

❈ ❈ ❈ ❈ ❈

Alexa rubbed her temples four hours later. It was late. She was afraid to look at her watch. She had transcribed without stopping for several hours, and for the last hour she had gone back to weave her impressions of Colin throughout the segments, trying to impart a flavor of his personality.

She yawned. It was late, but the words kept coming. Maybe she should make tea and stay up for another hour, writing. She glanced down at herself. Could she risk sashaying out in this? She had put on a silky, thigh-length nighty, intending to go to bed an hour ago. Since she had grown a little cool, she had slipped on the short, matching peach wrap, too. She wore bunny slippers on her feet.

Surely Jamison had retreated to his room by now. And who cared if he was in the living room? She was decent. It's not like he ever took notice of her in that way, anyway. Thank goodness for small favors.

Getting up, she opened her bedroom door and strode into the sitting area. Her heart thunked to her pink slippers when she spied Jamison sitting on the couch, watching television. When he looked over his shoulder, his eyes narrowed.

Alexa beat him to the punch. "Why are you still up?" She yanked at the loose sash around her waist, tightening it.

"Trying on nighties?" he queried. "Need help choosing the best one for Colin?"

Alexa gasped in outrage. "Kindly get your mind out of the gutter! Colin and I are just friends."

"Men and women can't be just friends," he returned.

"I'd expect a sexist remark like that from you. And what are we, then?"

"Are we friends, princess?"

Alexa scowled. "No. You're right. We're adversaries."

He threw popcorn into his mouth. "You can call it that if it makes you feel more comfortable."

Alexa didn't like the turn of the conversation, and walked over so she blocked his view of the television. "Excuse me?" she demanded, hands on her hips. Unfortunately, her sash failed her and the robe gaped open, showing her lacy-edged silk nighty.

When they had first met at the airport and her blouse was soaked, he had paid no attention. This time, he did look. Her face burned and her blood heated. She wanted to snatch her robe together, but didn't. She wasn't intimidated by him.

His eyes raised to hers after an interminable moment. "Princess, I'm a red-blooded man. You shouldn't be standing in front of me like that." She blinked at the quiet force in his voice. "Unless, of course, you want some TLC."

Alexa's face flamed, and she snatched her robe closed. "You pervert!" she hissed.

"You're the one exposing yourself to me."

"I was not! And...and," she fished about for the most cutting remark she could make. "As far as TLC goes—in your dreams! You can't even reach my radar screen."

Something flashed in his eyes. Anger...or hurt? The thought that it might be hurt bothered her until he spoke.

"That's just the way I like it."

Now that hurt her. She curled her lip at him. "At least we can agree on something." She spun on her heel and retreated to her room, slamming the door behind her. All thoughts of tea had disappeared. She felt agitated enough to burn through two more hours of work. No caffeine required.

CHAPTER TEN

THE NEXT MORNING, Alexa decided to follow Colin's advice. She would sightsee this morning, and attend the concert tonight. It was sweet of Colin to be concerned about her working too hard, she reflected. After all, he was the busy one. So many people wanted a piece of him. What must it be like to live in a fish bowl, where everyone recognized you?

That reminded her of the incident in Paris. What if that deranged husband of the woman arrested in Paris had followed them here? Maybe today when they went sightseeing she should wear sunglasses, and maybe a scarf over her head. Or maybe a hat of some kind... Yes. She had just the thing.

Alexa pulled her hair into a ponytail, threaded on a pink baseball cap, and slid her sunglasses onto her nose. Grabbing up her purse, she headed out.

"We're sightseeing, I assume." Jamison appeared at her side.

"Why, yes. How good of you to accompany me."

"Don't have much choice, do I, princess?"

She smiled. "I enjoy your company too, Jethro."

Alexa thought she heard a mock growl come from his throat, but couldn't be sure. She smiled. All was right with the world. "Where should we go? You're the expert."

"How about Montjuïc?" he suggested.

"Perfect, and after that I'd like to shop on Las Ramblas," she agreed.

They took the Metro to the Plaça d'Espanya, and then climbed the steps to Montjuïc. Alexa loved the view of Barcelona. They spent the morning exploring the beautifully landscaped Jardi Botanic, and the Museu Nacional d'Art de Catalunya.

Afterward, they enjoyed a delicious lunch of paella in one of the cafés in the Poble Espanyol. Alexa learned the enchanting Spanish village was built for the 1929 World Fair. Varying types of architecture from different regions of Spain were depicted in the beautiful village. Alexa loved it, and she also enjoyed perusing the crafts made by local artists.

After descending again from Montjuïc, she wanted to inspect the Magic Fountain. In her internet wanderings before her trip to Europe, Alexa had read about how spectacular its light and water show was. Of course, now it was daytime, and nothing spectacular was going on.

"They'll have shows on Friday night. We'll come back then," Jamison promised.

Alexa was tired, and was glad to take the underground Metro back to the Plaça Catalunya, near their flat. The rest rejuvenated her.

"Where are some good shops?" she asked, when they disembarked. "I want to buy souvenirs for my family."

Jamison led the way to the wide, main street, called Las Ramblas. It was like no street Alexa had ever seen before. The wide, center portion was a tree-lined, pedestrian walkway, while a narrow car lane bordered each side. She followed him through the throngs of people filling the middle section. Mimes caught her eye, and so did colorful stalls selling riots of blooming flowers, newspapers, and even pets, such as rabbits, tortoises, and birds.

Alexa found several toys for her niece and nephew, but couldn't find anything for her sister. Maybe a tablecloth—then she could give it to both Beth and Ted. She fingered a lacy, embroidered one. It cost the earth, but she knew her sister would love it. Capitulating, she bought it.

Jamison stood nearby, testing yo-yos, while she finished up.

Together, they walked away from the stand. "Why don't you ever buy anything for yourself?" he asked.

They had shopped together once at the Louvre in Paris. Funny he would remember that detail.

"I don't need anything. Maybe I'll get a magnet later for my refrigerator."

He smiled. "Is that how you keep track of your travels?"

"And pictures." She lifted her digital camera. A thought struck her. "Stand over there, so I can snap a panoramic of Las Ramblas."

"You don't want a picture of me," he objected.

"Yes, I do. I have to capture the source of my greatest irritation. And contrast you with the bright, colorful local scenery."

His reluctant capitulation came through in the picture she snapped. "You're pouting," she complained. "Buck up."

He lifted the dark slash of his eyebrows and bared all his teeth in a mock smile. She snapped the shutter, but frowned. "Now it looks like you're the big bad wolf and you're going to eat me."

"Not *exactly* what I want to do," he muttered.

"You big baby. Pretend I'm someone you like. Or we're somewhere fun, like Disneyland. And here comes Snow White and the seven..."

She snapped a scowl that time. "What?" she complained.

"You won't give it a rest, will you?"

"What?" She pretended ignorance.

He abandoned his post. "You work to push me away."

"Isn't that what our relationship is about?"

"Yes. Push...and pull." His dark eyes met hers. "But you don't like the pull part, do you, princess?"

Warm agitation stirred in her. "I don't know what you're talking about."

"Keep the walls up," he advised. "That's probably best for both of us."

They walked side by side as Alexa perused more open-air stalls. However, at several points the crowds were so thick that he fell in behind her as they snaked through the mass of people. During one of these times, Alexa wondered about the excitement in the air. What could be going on, on a Wednesday afternoon?

Would Jamison know? Just as she turned to ask him, a hard hand grabbed her arm and something sharp poked into her kidney area. Terror electrified her mind. "Jamison." Her voice sounded thin and whispery.

"Don't shout," snarled a voice in her ear. "Or I'll kill you." The man smelled bad. He dragged her fast sideways, between two market stalls, and then toward the street. When she realized he was about to yank her into traffic, Alexa remembered basic self-defense and buckled her knees, collapsing to the ground. Now the man would be forced to drag her full weight.

She hadn't counted upon him sticking the knife under her ear. "Up! Or you'll join Van Gogh's fan club. Or..." he chuckled, and a nasty stench assailed her nostrils, "...I can stun you, like I did your friend. But I'd prefer you to walk."

The man had stunned Jamison? Horrified, she teetered back up on her high heels. How? When? Why wasn't anyone noticing? But she was behind the stalls now, bordering the street, and the drivers looked straight ahead, paying no attention. Her abductor unexpectedly jerked her through traffic, and gained the sidewalk on the other side. He was surprisingly strong, and moved fast.

"Let go!" Terror trembled inside of her. She dug in her heels, not that it accomplished much. Everything was happening so fast. "What do you want with me?"

"Revenge. And leverage. Now shut up!" He yanked her onto a narrow side street. Tall buildings cast the lane into shadows. At this unfortunate moment in time, it was deserted, except for a car parked down the road.

If she got in that car she would never go free again. She would die at this crazed man's hands. Wouldn't it be better to risk injury now, rather than certain death later?

It seemed logical, so she screamed, long and loud. Although she knew little Spanish, she did know one word for sure. *Dangerous.* "Peligroso! Peligroso!" she cried out. Then other words—a phrase her father had teased her with once—blurted out, "El hombre es loco en la cabasa!" The man is crazy in the head!

He had already managed to drag her at least fifteen yards from Las Ramblas. Cars continued to roll down that road. No one slowed down. No pedestrians were on this side street. Did anyone hear her?

The knife twisted under her skin, and she screamed in earnest, then. Alexa kicked his knee, then his instep, and pumped her elbows backwards. She made one good contact, and the air *oomphed* out of him. His grip loosened. Lunging free, she ran for her life toward the busy street. And slammed straight into Jamison. It felt like hitting a brick wall.

His eyes looked faintly dazed, but his arms closed securely around her. "What happened?"

"That man," she cried out. "He tried to kidnap me!"

A motor roared. Her captor's tires screeched, and he pealed away from the curb. Jamison took off running, pulling out his cell phone, but by the time he reached the end of the block, the car was long gone. She caught up, heart pumping. "Did you get a license plate?"

"A partial." He turned away and spoke rapid Spanish into his phone.

Did he have the police on speed dial in every country, she wondered. And apparently he spoke fluent English, French, now Spanish, and certainly Italian, too. What other unlikely depths lurked in this unassuming man?

Jamison flipped his phone shut. "The police will do what they can."

"Are you all right?" Alexa blurted. "Did he stun you?"

Grim lines etched Jamison's mouth. "I saw him coming out the corner of my eye, so he only got a piece of me. I woke up lying between two stalls. I'm fine."

Alexa found this hard to believe. She certainly did not feel fine, and she hadn't been shocked unconscious. "Jamison, are you sure?"

"I've got thick skin."

Somehow, Alexa doubted this. It must have showed in her expression, for he offered a small smile. "I'm fine. Don't worry. Let's get you back to the flat." He retrieved her purse and shopping bag from the sidewalk, where she had dropped it.

"We don't have to go. I'm probably safer now than I was before," she objected, taking both from him. Although she felt shaken up, she didn't want to break down like last time. "Let's walk around a little more, if that's all right with you." Maybe that would firm up the jelly in her limbs.

He looked at her closely, concern in his eyes. "Are you okay?"

"Not exactly, but I don't want to dwell on it." She crossed back to the center, pedestrian aisle of Las Ramblas.

"You have blood on your neck."

"What?" Her fingers flew to the spot where the knife had poked her. Blood came away on her fingers. Unwanted tears burned then. It was too much.

"Sit down." Jamison directed her to nearby chairs.

Her lips wobbled. "I think I've got a bandage in my purse. Maybe that sanitizing gel, too." With trembling hands, she dug through her purse, finding the items. The bandage was one of those round, useless ones.

"That ought to work." Jamison took them from her.

"What are you doing?"

"Patching you up. Sit still." He dragged a chair to face her.

Alexa shivered, teeth chattering gently. She thought about saying she could do it herself, but didn't. It felt good to have him care for her. She felt vulnerable right now, and Jamison's touch soothed her soul.

He took his handkerchief and wiped off the extra blood at the point under her chin, and then dabbed on the alcohol sanitizer. Alexa flinched at the sharp burn.

"Sorry," he murmured, and gently affixed the bandage.

"Is it bad?" she wanted to know. "Will I have a scar?"

"No. It's a pin prick."

Alexa shivered harder now. Jamison's large, warm hands took hers, calming her, stilling the shakes. More tears burned in her eyes. She didn't *want* to be afraid. She didn't want that horrible man to ruin her day.

"Did you get a good look at him?" he asked quietly.

"No. He was behind me the whole time. But he was tall, and he stank. I remember that." She gave a choked laugh.

"Did he say anything to you?"

"He wanted revenge...and leverage. I think he was the man from Paris. He probably wanted to take me hostage so they'd let his wife out of prison."

Jamison nodded. "Makes sense. I'll tell the police later."

Teeth still chattering a bit, Alexa said in a small voice, "I'd like to go home now."

"All right." He helped her up. "Let me carry that." He reached for the shopping bag.

She did not protest. Silently, he walked her home. Alexa felt fragile, like she was about to shatter into pieces, but refused to break down. She was all right. The man was gone.

But when would he be back? That was what really scared her.

❈ ❈ ❈ ❈ ❈

That evening, Alexa sat in the front row of the concert. Her nerves had finally settled from the incident that afternoon. When she had returned to the flat, Colin had called, clearly upset, and asked if she was all right. His concern touched her, but she had assured him that she was fine.

Physically, anyway. After she hung up, she had holed up in her room and prayed for peace and deliverance from the suffocating fear.

The verse from Isaiah 41:10 had helped soothe her soul. "So do not fear, for I am with you; do not be dismayed, for I am your God. I will strengthen you and help you; I will uphold you with my righteous right hand."

The verse comforted her. God was with her. And Jamison had been on the scene within seconds. He would never have allowed the man to drag her into his car. She believed this, deep in her soul.

Afterward, she worked on the book.

Now she felt safer, and glad to be out. Colin had ordered extra security for the concert tonight, so she had no reason to fear.

If only she had gotten a glimpse of the man who had attacked her. For the hundredth time, Alexa struggled to remember details about her captor who had stayed hidden behind her. But all she had glimpsed was a tall, thin man with stringy gray hair. He must be the husband of the woman who had attacked her in Paris, she reasoned. Surely by now Interpol would have tracked down his name and maybe even his passport photo.

Unless he had worn a disguise. Alexa put this disturbing thought from her. At least she had escaped. Again, she thanked God that Jamison had been close. He would have rescued her in any case. She was certain of this.

Jamison. Her gaze strayed to him as the concert began. He stood at stage right, in the wings, near the curtain. He was hidden from most people, but her position close to the stage afforded her a good view of him standing with his shoulders straight, and hands clasped in front of him. Clad in his inimitable black, as usual. She knew he carried a gun, but didn't know where.

Colin kicked off the concert with one of her favorite love songs, and her gaze riveted upon him. The invigorating music revived her spirits. Again, she marveled at how easily his charisma spilled off the stage. He held the audience in the palm of his hand.

Colin threw her a wink. Alexa's heart swelled like an adolescent schoolgirl's. She couldn't control her silly smile. It was as if the homecoming king flirted with the lowly brainiac.

That's what she had been in high school. Tall and gawky, and unsure of her place in the world—especially with boys. It was nice how maturity and confidence had smoothed out most of those problems. And Colin liked the woman that she had become.

Unlike Jamison. Her gaze strayed to him, who still stood, unmoving, in his corner. What had he been like in high school? He was smart, obviously, if his gift with languages was any indication. Had he been involved in sports? It was hard to imagine. He struck her as more of a loner than a team playing, backslapping sort of a guy.

Colin sang one heart-melting song after another, and her gaze kept drifting between him and Jamison. Colin was obviously a huge success in life, but she admired Jamison, too. He had an important job, to be trusted as the best in the world to keep a famous star safe. Even more impressive, he was the chief of Colin's security team.

Speaking of bodyguards, Mart strolled by, patrolling the stage. He gave her a finger wave, and she grinned, feeling ridiculously giddy and important. Again, she felt like a teenager with access to her favorite star's world—actually, dead center in that world! It was a heady feeling.

She scanned the huge hall, noting the extra security that Colin had hired. A few men would remain with them throughout the tour because of the continuing threats that Colin had received, coupled with the attacks on her. Alexa had noticed two extra bodyguards shadowing Colin ever since Paris. Since Jamison was sidelined, protecting her, the new ones were obviously necessary. She wondered if everyone would be glad when she left, so things could go back to normal. Jamison would, no doubt.

She felt a prickling awareness and glanced sideways. Jamison's gaze was upon her. No finger waves from him. Just an impassive face.

Of course, she knew very well the fire that simmered in him. She sent him a bright grin.

He looked away, as if uncomfortable. That made her smile wider. She enjoyed getting under his skin.

The little imp in her danced to life. What could she do to disturb him more? She should behave herself, of course. But the temptation to irk her bodyguard overwhelmed her more sensible inclinations.

Her brain buzzed, watching Colin. She loved these songs! Unconsciously, she swayed to the music. Meanwhile, she cast quick glances at Jamison, waiting for him to seek her out again. If he would.

Colin moved across the stage, heading for the exit, when finally Jamison's gaze flickered her way.

Grinning, she puckered up and blew him a juicy kiss.

Jamison stared at her, and then actually looked over his shoulder. Seeing no one, he shifted his shoulders and looked away, obviously uncomfortable.

Alexa giggled, feeling an unholy glee. Maybe she was acting like a silly adolescent, but it felt good—especially after feeling so fearful for most of the afternoon. Why should she have to bury every ounce of fun under a load of adult guilt? Over nothing, in her opinion. It was harmless fun.

Jamison did not look her way again, to her extreme disappointment.

At the end of the show, she went backstage and congratulated Colin on a terrific performance—along with a glob of other people. Jamison and Mart were in full bodyguard mode, so she melted toward one of the couches to wait for everything to settle down.

Finally, the high spirits and possibly high people disappeared, leaving the crew and basic staff.

"'Night, all," Colin said to his band. He headed straight for Alexa. "Ready, love?" Taking her hand, he escorted her to the limousine.

Cameras flashed. Screaming fans shouted from behind concrete barriers. Alexa's heart pounded with excitement as she walked beside Colin. He waved his free hand and smiled, but said nothing. He slid into the limousine after Alexa. Mart and Jamison squeezed into the front seat, next to the driver.

Colin hugged an arm around her shoulders. "How was it? Be honest."

"Terrific! Incredible," Alexa sparkled.

Colin sighed in satisfaction. "How about a nightcap when we get back?"

"Sure." Just for a little while, she promised herself. Colin always behaved like a perfect gentleman, but tonight he was high from the show. Frankly, she was, too.

At the luxury apartment building, they left Jamison and Mart and slipped alone into Colin's flat, where she accepted a cold soda.

"You're a good girl, did you know that?" His eyes gleamed, still glowing from the excitement and adulation of the evening. He joined her on the couch.

"I try."

Colin rested his arm along the top of the couch. This time, she didn't pull away. "Where do you see yourself in five years?" he unexpectedly asked.

Alexa blinked at the serious topic. "I don't know. Married. With a family, maybe."

"Anyone special?" His blue gaze was intent.

Alexa felt flustered. "No."

"Good. Just wanted to make certain. How about we spend tomorrow evening together? No notes or tape recorders. Just fun."

Alexa smiled. "I'd love to."

"Good. Be ready at seven o'clock. And bring a jacket. It might be windy."

Alexa knew he had an early afternoon concert on Thursday, instead of an evening one. "Where are we going?"

"It's a surprise."

She grinned back. "I love surprises."

After a little more small talk, Alexa finished her drink and headed back to her room, accompanied by Mart. A surprise!

What could Colin mean? Her mind spun with exciting possibilities as she bid Mart goodnight and let herself into her flat.

Jamison prowled the kitchen.

"Isn't it a lovely evening?" she sang out, floating toward her room.

He came closer. "Is it?"

Alexa halted, sensing unknown, suppressed emotion in him. She frowned. "Are you a sourpuss?"

"No. Enjoy yourself with Colin?"

Her ebullient feeling soared again. "Of course. And tomorrow..." she twirled, "we're going somewhere special."

"Are you drunk?"

Her mouth gaped open. "No! How dare you? You know I don't drink."

"You've been acting tipsy all night," he growled.

So that's what this was about. With a grin, she asked sweetly, "Did I disturb you at the concert?"

He swiped a hand through his black hair. Alexa wondered what it felt like. Wiry or soft? And then she blinked. What did she care what Jamison's hair felt like?

"You're acting like a child again, princess."

"Please!" she scoffed. "I was having fun. You looked so ultra-serious that I decided to blow a little sunshine your way."

His brows wrenched together. "You like this, don't you?"

"What?"

"Twisting men around your fingers. Then you can satisfy your lust for power and control over them."

Alexa laughed out loud. "That is absurd!"

"You blow me a kiss, just to get under my skin. Who knows what line you're feeding Colin."

"I am not feeding Colin a line!" she said indignantly.

"But it's okay to feed me one."

Alexa stared at him. "You knew I was playing with you."

"Why?" He paced closer now, making her feel uncomfortable.

"Because I like to yank your chain. You know that."

"Am I entitled to yank yours?"

"Don't be ridiculous. You do it all the time. Why ask permission now?"

His strong hands closed around her arms, just above her elbows. His eyes looked impossibly dark and dangerous. "You blew me a kiss. Does that mean I can return the favor?"

Alexa stared at his mouth—a well-shaped mouth it was, too—coming inexorably closer.

"No," she squeaked.

"Why?"

"Because it isn't done! You're my bodyguard." Why she wasn't slapping him and running away, she couldn't figure out.

"You mean I'm not a real man with real feelings. You can play games with me, then blow me off, and I can't respond?"

"Yes," she agreed, heart pumping too fast.

"Bull," he said quietly. "If you play with me, you get the consequences."

"No," she gasped, but it was too late. His mouth touched hers, and the shock of it rocketed to her toes. His lips roughly caressed hers, and the flaming friction made her tremble. A sizzle began to burn, low in her tummy.

He broke contact and stepped back. The dark eyes burned, but quickly hardened.

"Unless you want more, I advise you to direct your game playing to one man."

Her lips throbbed. "You mean Colin?" she forced out. "I don't play games with him."

"Then ask yourself why you do with me." With that, he turned on his heel and shut himself in his room.

Alexa stared at his closed door, trembling. Why hadn't she tried to escape? Why had she let that happen?

Because she had wanted to know what his kiss would feel like.

Now she knew, and it disturbed her. It was just an experiment, she told herself. Like seeing if her tongue would stick to a frozen flagpole in the dead of winter. A dare she had unfortunately accepted as a child. Neither, she determined now, was an experience she intended to repeat.

CHAPTER ELEVEN

ALEXA RECEIVED A CALL from Beth the next morning.

Her sister said, "I got your message. So, you're in Barcelona now. Lucky chicky!"

"You shouldn't be calling me," Alexa said. "This will cost you a fortune."

"Even though I don't have a *bestseller,* I don't think it will break me."

"Bestseller?" Alexa squealed. "No. You're pulling my leg."

"Number five for nonfiction this week."

Alexa had to sit down. "I can't believe it."

"Believe it. I'm cutting out the *New York Times* list as we speak."

Alexa whispered a silent prayer of thanks to God. She had been thrilled to be published—but to be in the top ten of the *New York Times* list! She couldn't believe it.

Beth said, "And with this next book you're writing, you're going to be hot property, Alexa. You can write your own ticket. Maybe even sell some of that fiction you've been writing."

"This is a dream come true."

"Soon the royalties will start pouring in," Beth predicted. "So, how has it been going there?"

"Oh." Alexa pulled her mind back to reality. "Fine. I went to a concert last night. It was fun."

"Colin's, I assume."

"Yes. He asked me out tonight."

"Again? Where's he taking you?"

"It's a surprise."

"I expect you to tell me all about it."

"I will."

"Your book's coming okay?"

"It's almost half done. I'll try to get more anecdotes from Colin tonight, even though he probably won't want to talk business. He's got so little free time that I've got to take advantage of every moment I can."

"Are you falling for him?" Caution laced her sister's tone.

"Colin? No." It was true. She liked him a lot, but falling in love with him? Not yet.

"What about your bodyguard?"

Alexa stiffened. "What about him?"

"Have you called a truce?"

"Not exactly." The memory of last night's kiss seared her mind again, as it had ever since she had woken up. She had repeatedly ordered herself to forget it.

"What happened?"

Alexa remained silent.

"Alexa. This is me, your sister. Give me the dirt."

Reluctantly, she admitted, "He kissed me last night. But it didn't mean anything," she rushed to make clear. "He was just mad and wanted me to pay...a consequence."

Her sister pealed with laughter. "This ought to be good. What'd you do?"

"Nothing much. At the concert he looked so stoic and vigilant. I wanted to have a little fun with him, that's all. I smiled at him, and he didn't like that, so I blew him a kiss. It was all in fun," she said, as her sister snorted in her ear. "But he got really hot under the collar about it."

"So right after the concert he grabbed you and kissed you?"

"Well, first I went up to Colin's for a nightcap."

"I see. And how long did this nightcap last?"

"What does that matter? Maybe an hour. Maybe more. That's when Colin asked me out."

"So after this nightcap you went back to your apartment and found Jamison hot under the collar."

"Yes. Pretty much that's what happened."

"I see." Laughter still bubbled in Beth's voice.

Alexa frowned. "What do you see?"

"Apparently more than you do, sis."

"This morning I'm going to tell him to back off. He behaved very unprofessionally last night."

"You do that. Let me know how that turns out."

Alexa frowned again. "I wish you'd stop laughing at me!"

"I'm sorry, Alexa, but your life sounds like a soap opera. How was it, by the way?"

"What?"

"The kiss!"

Alexa rolled her eyes, but unfortunately, her sister couldn't see. "Average."

Her sister snorted again.

"Okay! Slightly above average." She refused to admit to more than that.

Beth's laughter quieted. "Slightly above average, hmm?"

"Don't make something out of it," Alexa warned.

"I think the question is; why aren't you? Knowing your powers of understatement, I wonder if the kiss was more like an A plus."

"Beth, stop it! It means nothing. The man irritates me at every turn. I can barely breathe without him in my face. I told you, I'm going to tell him to back off."

"Uh huh. Tell me something. Why are you so determined to push him away?"

Alexa gaped soundlessly. "I am not."

"Right. Does this have something to do with your *long* dating criteria list?"

"It's not like that with Jamison! Colin is the man I'm interested in."

"Really?" Her sister sounded dubious. "Then why are sparks flying between you and Jamison?"

"I won't answer that ridiculous question, because you're not listening to me. Colin is civilized, refined...everything I want in a man."

A pause elapsed. "You've finally found the perfect man, and it's Colin, the rock star?"

"Well, I can't tell if he's absolutely perfect yet. I'm still getting to know him."

"You mean you're looking for excuses to push him away, like you've done every man since Paul."

"That's not fair."

"Isn't it? Tell me again why you have that long list?"

Stiffly, she returned, "I don't want a man like Paul."

"Paul had blond hair, too. And he appeared to be civilized—until he dumped you."

Tears threatened. "You're not being fair, Beth."

More kindly, her sister said, "I think you need to be honest with yourself. Otherwise, when you do find the right man, you'll chase him away."

"Now you're being cruel."

"I don't mean to be. But I want you to be happy, Alexa. And until you face whatever's got you running scared from connecting with another man... I'm afraid you'll never find that happily-ever-after you want." Another pause elapsed. "Do you still love Paul? Is that it?"

"No. That was a gigantic mistake."

"I want you to be happy, Alexa," her sister repeated gently. "I love you."

Alexa wiped away a tear, and wondered why it was even there. "I know you do, and I love you, too."

"Everything will work out," Beth said with strengthening confidence. "You'll see. I'll be praying for you."

Alexa heard a faint wail in the background.

"Uh oh," Beth said. "Annie's crying. I've got to go. Call me the next time he kisses you. Smooches!" Her sister hung up.

Alexa stared at the phone. Next time? There would be no next time! In fact, she would make sure of it right now.

Unfortunately, when she entered the living area, she found Mart. Her gaze swept the room. "Where's Jamison?"

A smile lurked in his green eyes. "He's helping train security for the concert. He'll be back this evening."

"Oh. Well, good." Alexa felt unsettled, but relieved, too. Maybe Jamison would decide to forget the whole incident. A day apart would certainly do them both good.

She smiled at Mart. "Well then. I'd better get to work."

He tipped his fingers to her. "Later."

But Alexa found it hard to concentrate on the book. Her mind kept returning to her sister's words. Was Beth right? Was she running scared? Or maybe even hiding behind an emotional wall? Surely not. Her list of dating criteria was logical. It encompassed every virtue she admired most in a man. No. She was on the right track. Being careful was only wise. She simply hadn't found the right man yet.

One thing was for sure. It was not Jamison.

❋ ❋ ❋ ❋ ❋

That night, when Jamison ushered Alexa down to the limousine to meet Colin, he was all cool and professional. Distant. She had only been alone with him for one moment today in the flat, and it was clear from his attitude that he didn't want to discuss last night. In fact, it appeared he wanted to forget it had ever happened. Which was fine by her.

Tonight, Jamison wore a dark maroon tie and a black suit jacket to complement his unending black wardrobe. The cut accentuated the breadth of his shoulders, but with no extra fluff, unlike Colin's suit jackets—she had noticed they were cut a little larger than his frame. Now, comparing the two as Jamison stood beside Colin, waiting for her to enter the limousine, she was surprised to see that the bodyguard's frame, even though he was shorter, easily eclipsed Colin's. Of course, he did work out all the time.

She dismissed these inconsequential thoughts as Colin slid in beside her. She grinned. "Give me a hint. Where are we going?"

He smiled. "You'll see soon enough."

The limousine wound through the busy streets of Barcelona until they reached the harbor. Alexa breathlessly turned to Colin. "We're going out on the water?"

"Yes. Do you like cruises?"

"I love anything to do with the water. Colin, this is perfect!" Impulsively, she hugged him, just as Jamison opened the door. His face remained expressionless, but the dark eyes looked cold. Or maybe she was imagining it.

Alexa followed Colin to the huge powerboat waiting at the dock.

"I've asked them to tour the harbor while we eat dinner," Colin said as they walked up the gangplank.

Alexa sighed. "Fabulous."

The small ship was beautiful. Clean, shining white decks, plush interior. And on the aft deck a table had been set up with sparkling crystal and red damask napkins.

"Colin," Alexa said. "You shouldn't have! This is too much."

"How can it be too much? You love it and I love it. Now we can enjoy it."

Alexa followed Colin into a tiny sitting room with deep red couches.

He said, "The wine steward is sick today, but Jamison has agreed to fill in."

Apparently, Mart got to stand guard on deck—the cushy job, by all accounts. In fact, as the engines rumbled to life, Alexa wanted to be on deck, too. She loved the feel of the wind in her hair.

"What would you like to drink?" Colin was asking. Jamison stood nearby, waiting patiently, his body language unassuming and deferential. However, she wasn't fooled. She struggled to ignore him. "A cola, please."

"And I'll take a scotch on the rocks, to start," Colin said. He settled back on the couch, his arm behind her shoulders. Jamison returned soon with their drinks. His fingers brushed hers as he handed her the cold glass. Why did she get the feeling it wasn't accidental? She frowned up at him and found his eyes gleaming at her. The troublemaker! Her skin prickled, and she was relieved when he left them alone. It wouldn't do to be more aware of Jamison's presence than Colin's.

"I brought my digital recorder in my purse," she confessed. "I know you don't want to talk business tonight, but maybe you could tell me a few stories about your early career. I know your fans will love your personal anecdotes."

Colin laughed. "Maybe later. Let's enjoy our time for now."

"Could we go out on deck? I love looking at the ocean."

"Of course." He stood immediately.

On deck, she led the way to the bow of the boat, and stood, wind whipping through her hair as they cut through the waves. She smiled at Colin. "I love it out here, don't you?"

"I didn't realize you had such an adventurous side to you."

"I don't know about adventurous. But it's exhilarating. It makes me feel alive. And God feels so close."

"Your faith means a lot to you."

"Yes. What about you? Do you think about God much?"

"I have been lately. My mum would be pleased. She's been praying for my lost soul for years." He frowned down into his drink. "I do know I've made wrong decisions. Someday, I need to make things right with God."

She felt compassion for him. "Don't wait. Ask Him for forgiveness soon."

"Yeah. I need to." He fell silent.

"I'll be praying for you, too."

He touched her arm. "Thanks, Alexa."

"Dinner is served." Jamison's deep voice called Alexa's attention away from the dancing waves. Pink sparkles shone on them as the sun neared the rosy horizon.

Alexa and Colin watched the sun set as they ate on the back deck. The night settled into dusk. The cool breeze was getting chilly by the time she finished her main course, so Alexa pulled on her jacket.

"How are your drinks?" Jamison appeared again. "More wine, Colin?"

"Sure."

"Alexa, how is yours?"

Alexa eyed her lemon-lime drink. "A fine vintage," she told him.

His lips curved slightly. "I aim to please," he said in a low voice, and melted into the night.

Alexa took a quick sip to settle the flutter in her stomach. How could she possibly be more aware of her exasperating bodyguard than Colin, one of the most famous, charming men in the world? She must be losing her marbles.

"Alexa." She looked up quickly into Colin's sharp gaze.

"Yes?"

"Are you and Jamison getting on better?"

Alexa remembered Beth's theory that Colin had assigned Jamison as her bodyguard because he'd be no threat to Colin romantically. Uneasiness shifted in her, and she hedged, "Um, a little."

The intent look in his eyes quieted, and Alexa relaxed. She wondered what Colin would think if he knew Jamison had kissed her last night. Not that it meant anything. But still, she was glad he didn't know. She wanted to keep that memory private.

Alexa changed the subject. "Was the concert sold out last night? I didn't see any empty seats."

Colin smiled. "The crowds last night and today were unbelievable. We're sold out now in both Barcelona and Rome."

"That's wonderful! But what happened? Has something changed?"

"Didn't you see the paper today?"

"No. Why?"

"The attack on you made the first page."

"Oh no!"

Ruefully, Colin said, "Both attacks have made the world news, too. I think the ghoulish want to see what happens next."

Shocked, Alexa said, "Are you saying the attacks have been good for the tour?"

"Unfortunately, yes. In fact, if you hadn't been hurt, I would wonder if Paddy had rigged them as publicity stunts."

"Publicity stunts!" This thought had never entered her head. At first she had thought Eve had sent the threatening notes, and then it appeared a crazed older couple was behind the stalker attacks. Now Colin's manager flashed through her mind. She remembered his brash, bulldog personality and hard eyes. The man was all about profit. And hadn't Colin said Paddy's percentage of the profits would go up if the tour sold out? What was more, it did seem odd that while Colin had been threatened, he had never actually been attacked. Maybe the note writer had never intended to hurt Colin. Maybe Colin's threatening notes were a smokescreen for the stalker's real plan; to attack her—a pawn—to increase publicity for Colin's tour.

The assaults were accomplishing this goal. What if Paddy had hired the older couple to accost her? Maybe he hadn't meant for her to get hurt, but what if the crazed couple had gone further than he had intended? On the other hand, how could he have found a couple like that? Did crazed, stalker fans cross his path often?

It all seemed very confusing. Certainly, no evidence linked Paddy to the crimes, and Colin didn't believe he was involved. All the same, Colin's manager jumped onto her suspect list.

"To change the subject," Colin said, "I'm thinking about a new album. What sorts of songs do you like best?"

She smiled. "Love ballads. If you made an album just of those, I would buy it."

"Do you think others feel the same way?"

"Absolutely."

"I love those songs best, too," he admitted quietly, fingering his glass.

She looked at him more closely. "What's wrong?"

He gulped the last of his wine, and his silver watch flashed in the moonlight. "I've put out eleven albums, did you know it? Four went platinum. I'm starting to wonder how much is enough. Maybe it's strange, but I feel like life is passing me by."

Alexa waited for him to continue.

"I've been a bit wild and crazy, and I've got a million friends, but I'm lonely." Shadows cut his features into sharp lines. His mouth was straight, unsmiling. "I want to find the one, now. Someone who loves me, and not my money."

"Colin." Impulsively, Alexa covered his hand, touched by his honesty. "You'll find the right person. I know you will."

He turned his hand, so it held hers now. "How will I know if I've found her?"

"Your heart will tell you. I think it's important to become friends, first, though. You need to develop trust, and that comes from knowing someone well."

He laughed a little. "I've never had a woman friend. Not a real friend, anyway. Just business associates."

"I hope you'll think of me as your friend. I do care about you, Colin, and I want you to be happy."

"I know you do."

Alexa gently extricated her hand. "I'll bet you have more friends than you think."

He gave her a quizzical look. "Maybe." A pause elapsed. "Don't you ever get lonely, Alexa?"

"Yes."

"Why haven't you found anyone? You're a beautiful girl."

She looked down. "I'm picky, I guess."

Colin laughed. "I haven't been. But I've never let anyone into my heart, either."

"It's scary—at least, I'd think it would be after years of pushing people away."

"Opening up my heart might invite pain," Colin admitted. "But I'm ready to feel. I want to truly live. All of this," he gestured to the opulent boat, "doesn't take away the loneliness."

His words struck deep into her heart. "I know what you mean," she said softly.

Jamison served their dessert course, and Alexa watched his neat, broad-shouldered figure pause on the way indoors to speak to Mart. Now there was a man who was very sure of himself. Nothing seemed to scare him, and yet he had walls, too, just like she did. Just like Colin did. What had caused Jamison's? Because it took two people to clash, and they had been sparking from the first day they'd met.

"Alexa?" Colin's cultured voice drew her attention back to her debonair escort. "Are you all right?"

She smiled. "Just thinking you and I aren't so different, after all."

His smile looked pleased.

After they finished dessert, the boat's engines roared to life. She said, "Can we go to the bow again before we get back?"

"Absolutely. Come on." He caught her hand and they left the sheltering enclave at the back of the boat and walked into the stiff, cold breeze. Alexa shivered, and wished she had brought a heavier jacket.

"It's cold, isn't it?" Colin laughed. He released her hand when they reached the bow, and Alexa grasped the wooden railing. The bow pointed toward the lighted quay, still a good distance away. The boat rose and dipped, surging forward on the waves. It felt wild and free out here, with the chill wind in her teeth. Alexa shivered again, and crossed her arms. She loved it, and didn't want to return to the cocooned area in the back. This was how she wanted to live life; at the front, meeting every challenge head on. She didn't want to be afraid anymore.

Spray misted her cheek as they cut through a wave. "This is the life, isn't it?" she laughed to Colin.

"It's certainly cold."

"Go on back if you want. I'll be fine."

"Are you sure?" His face looked white. Probably hers did, too, but how could she leave? This was an adventure she would never live again—on a ship in Barcelona's harbor.

"Yes. Go."

"Don't freeze," he told her.

And then Alexa was alone at the bow of the ship. She didn't mind. In fact, she liked it. Shivering, she fantasized about being on the only ship in the raging ocean, and they were about to make port after months at sea. Her teeth chattered sharply, and she crossed her arms against the cold. Her writer's imagination painted more romantic pictures in her head. She had just been swept into port by an artic gale. Only a few had survived the savage journey. The captain, Colin, and the first mate, Jamison. And, of course, herself.

Alexa giggled at the silliness of her imagination.

"What are you laughing at, princess?" Jamison appeared.

"Oh," she gasped. "Nothing. It was silly. I was imagining we'd been swept here by an arctic gale after months at sea."

Now, why had she gone and told him that? Now he'd think she was bonkers, for sure.

His teeth flashed white in the gloom. "Spending too much time writing?"

"What's wrong with a little fantasy?" she scoffed. "Keeps life exciting."

"You need your life to be more exciting?"

"A girl always wants a little romance."

"What's romantic about standing in a freezing gale?"

Alexa rolled her eyes. "You have no romance in your soul, Jamison." She gave a mighty shudder, and her teeth clicked uncontrollably.

"You're going to catch pneumonia." Before she realized what he was doing, Jamison shrugged out of his suit jacket and tucked it around her shoulders. It felt warm from his body heat, and smelled like him. Alexa gripped the lapels and tucked the jacket tightly to her, relishing the warmth and the scent.

At least for a few seconds, anyway.

"I can't take your jacket. You'll freeze to death," she said, about to take it off.

"Stop." His hands closed over hers. In the night, his eyes looked impossibly dark, and his hands felt warm over hers. "Take it. I'm going back inside, anyway."

"Do you have..." she cut the words off, aghast at what she had almost said.

"Want me to stay?" He smiled. "I don't think Colin would appreciate that."

"Of course I don't want you to stay," she retorted. Jamison turned to leave. "But thank you for the jacket."

"You're welcome," he said softly, and his black form disappeared down the deck. Alexa watched him go, and wondered why she had wanted so much for him to stay.

Alexa stayed on deck until they reached the dock, and then joined Colin in the back of the boat. Colin noted the jacket around her shoulders. "Jamison's a chivalrous guy." His gaze scanned hers.

"Yes," Alexa agreed, and pulled it off.

Jamison strolled by and plucked it from her fingers. "Thank you," he said, and kept moving.

Alexa sat silently beside Colin in the limo until they pulled up in front of their building. Then she turned to him. "Thank you, Colin, for a wonderful evening. I'll never forget it."

"Nor will I." He helped her out of the limousine. "Can you meet with me for breakfast on Sunday? I feel I've cheated you out of quotes for the book tonight."

"Please don't apologize. I couldn't have had a better evening. And yes, Sunday sounds great."

"Terrific." He pressed a kiss to her cheek, and she smiled at him, then headed into the building after Jamison. They got off on their floor, and left Colin and Mart in the elevator on the way to the penthouse.

Jamison keyed open their door. "Have a nice evening?"

"Of course. And thank you again for the jacket."

He locked the door behind them, and shrugged off that same jacket. For a moment, Alexa realized how domestic this felt. Like they were coming home after a night out together; Jamison loosening his tie with his fingers, and she about to get ready for bed.

It disturbed her deeply, because it felt so natural...so *right*.

No. It wasn't natural, and it wasn't right. She had been living with Jamison for too long, that was all.

"Goodnight," she said, moving quickly toward her own room.

"'Night." She felt his gaze follow her. Alexa shut the door and leaned against it. What was wrong with her? How could she feel so intensely aware of Jamison's gaze and of his every move tonight? Why had his dark presence continually distracted her from Colin? Colin was a famous pop star, for heaven's sake. And a wonderful, sweet, charming man.

And yet Jamison could be surprisingly sweet and charming, too.

Alexa swiftly closed her eyes, feeling even more disturbed. What was she *thinking?* Jamison was nothing like Colin. She needed water. Maybe she was coming down with something.

❋ ❋ ❋ ❋ ❋

On Friday morning Alexa continued to work on the book, and tried to forget the disturbing closeness she had felt with Jamison the previous night. She had transcribed all of the recordings, and now flipped through the scrapbooks, looking for more material that she could discuss with Colin. The book was over halfway done, and she was pleased by the progress. She'd also read through everything she had written so far, smoothing items, and writing down questions she needed to ask Colin on Sunday. He had promised she would meet with his band on Sunday, too. That material should keep her going for most of their stay in Italy. They would travel there on Monday.

At lunchtime, Alexa made a tuna sandwich. When Jamison emerged from his room, she turned her full attention to adding a pile of chips to her plate. It was the first time she had seen him since yesterday, as Mart still took over for Jamison during breakfast. She still felt acutely aware of her bodyguard, uncomfortably so, much like last night.

"Hello," she said, pouring a glass of milk. Her hand trembled a little.

He joined her at the counter, only a few disturbing feet away. She found herself edging backward.

Knock it off! she told herself. *What is wrong with you?* "Tuna?" she offered, shoving the bowl his way.

"Thanks."

Alexa snatched up her lunch and deposited it on the table. To her consternation, Jamison soon took the chair opposite.

She eyed him uncomfortably. "Why are you sitting there? You never sit here."

"Enjoy my company that much, princess?" He took a bite of sandwich.

"I didn't realize you wanted to be so chummy." She took a big bite and chewed rapidly.

"Am I disturbing you?" Was that a gleam in his eyes?

"Of course not. I just wondered why you're changing your routine. Isn't a soccer game on?"

"Maybe I like your company."

Alexa gaped. "Since when do you *like* anything about me?"

He smiled. "Don't you like my company?"

What was his purpose in this conversation? To annoy her? Or to push closer? Flutters multiplied in her stomach.

"Of course not. We get along much better when you're across the room."

Jamison sipped water. "Are you sure? You might actually like me if you tried to get to know me."

"Hmph," she snorted. "I know you plenty well. And it doesn't entice me to know you any better." Did she actually mean these flippant words? Or was she pushing him away, and hard, like her sister had suggested?

"How about a game of chess?"

She blinked. "You want to play a game with me?"

"Put me out of my misery. I'm bored."

Alexa realized that she hadn't given enough thought to what he could be feeling, cooped up with her. Boredom must be the least of it. "I'm no good at chess," she said. "I don't think that far ahead."

"Checkers?"

"Set it up," she agreed. He set up the game, and they engaged in an intense, quiet game of checkers. Jamison won, not that she was surprised.

"Same time tomorrow?" he asked.

"I suppose. At least it's one thing we can do without fighting."

"I could think up more." His brown eyes smiled. Was he flirting with her? Certainly not!

"Don't strain your brain," she advised, and hastily retreated to her room. Inside, she leaned against the door, trembling. What was wrong with her? She had shot off scads of prickly retorts at Jamison, like flaming arrows. She *had* been pushing him away. Why?

Her eyes closed. After a moment, she crossed to look out at the bustling city of Barcelona. *Why* had she just behaved like that? It deeply disturbed her. Hadn't their relationship begun to evolve past that sort of behavior? Or maybe that was the problem.

The easy banter with Jamison felt safe. Familiar, too. Just like with Ben. This quiet truth settled gently into her soul.

In elementary school, her friend Ben had teased her unmercifully, and she had given as good as she had received. Their light, teasing relationship reminded her a little of Jamison and herself. It also reminded her of the happy days of her early childhood, before all the problems, and before her parents' vicious fights and ultimate divorce.

She had thought about Ben twice now, in two weeks. Why?

They had lost touch in seventh grade, for Ben had gone to a different school. As a junior, he had returned to her high school, but by then he had become a stranger to Alexa. He was a football jock, highly popular, and a confident, rowdy, partying type.

A memory slammed in. One she had tried to forget. Alexa had been sixteen. It was just before her parents had separated. At that time, their loud, violent fights were horrible, and she had often stayed as late as possible in the school library, reluctant to go home, since both of her parents' work shifts ended in the early afternoon. Finally, the librarian had shooed her into the hall.

Football practice had just let out, and a group of uniformed boys, looking big in their shoulder pads, advanced down the hall. Blond-haired Ben, their quarterback, led the pack.

"Alexa," he called out.

Her steps faltered, surprised that he had acknowledged her. They hadn't spoken a word since sixth grade.

The loud, tromping footsteps of the pack of young men made her feel uneasy. The halls were deserted. Only Mrs. Page, the librarian, was still there. She cast a quick glance at the closed library door.

Ben wouldn't hurt or embarrass her, would he? Of course not.

"Hey," she said, striving to sound casual.

Ben chuckled at something one of his buddies said, and directed his attention back to her. His jaw worked, chewing gum. "You going to the Homecoming Dance?"

"I hadn't thought about it." Why was he asking her? Her gaze flickered from him to his husky cronies. Their expressions ranged from disinterest to bold appraisal. Alexa clutched her book bag tighter to her stomach.

Ben popped his gum. "So. You wanna go?"

"With you?" Alexa's brows shot up.

"Yeah, with me." Ben grinned at his buddies, chomping louder on his gum. "Who else?"

He didn't mean it. He couldn't possibly. In fact, was this some sort of a joke to him? His smile looked goofy, and his face was slack now as he waited for her response. *Was* this a joke to him? Did he intend to make fun of her if she—the school brainiac—said 'yes' to the golden boy jock? Hurt twisted. At least it was a spur of the moment joke. He hadn't deliberately set out to hurt her, because this meeting in the hall couldn't have been planned. Not that it mattered.

"Thanks. But no."

An odd expression registered, quickly covered by a hearty, "Why not, Red? Got a better offer?"

Alexa flushed. Of course she hadn't. He had to know that. She was too quiet and shy for boys to bother with. "I'm not in the mood for jokes, Ben."

He flushed, and shrugged his shoulders. "Suit yourself. Come on, guys."

The boys sneered as they passed, and a few uncomplimentary remarks burned Alexa's ears. Tears swam in her eyes. She felt small, like a worm squished beneath their monstrous, cleated shoes. And then she had gone home and hidden in her room while her parents screamed at each other and threw breakables against the walls. And then her mother had shrieked in pain.

Both Alexa and Beth flew to peek out the door.

Her burly father bent over her mother, who lay sprawled on the floor. "Anne. *Anne!*" he cried out, shaking her.

Beth slipped out and Alexa followed close behind.

"What's wrong?" she whispered.

Her father looked up. Tears streamed down his cheeks. "She's hurt. I didn't mean for the vase to hit her."

Her mother stirred, and Alexa's father carefully carried her to the couch. That night was the beginning of the end. The next day, her parents had finally separated.

Now Alexa pressed her forehead to the glass, wondering why those memories had surfaced now. She hadn't thought about Ben in ages. He had never spoken to her after the homecoming invitation, which had been fine with her, for she had taken great pains to avoid him. The whole episode had left her feeling confused and hurt. It was only now, looking back from a detached perspective, that she finally recognized the odd expression that had crossed Ben's face when she had rejected him. It had been hurt.

Like a kaleidoscope, the events of that day shifted. *Had he truly meant his invitation to the dance?* Why had she assumed he had wanted to make fun of her—that it had been a joke? A deeper insight came. Or had she jumped to that conclusion in order to push him away, for fear of getting hurt?

She had pushed Ben away then, just like she pushed Jamison away now.

She had been wrong about Ben. How many other men had she rejected? Three or more, perhaps. Particularly, she realized now, strong, physically self-assured men. Men like her father. Until she had met quiet, calm Paul. The man who had broken her heart. After him, she had allowed no one to get close at all.

Tears blurred her eyes. *What's wrong with me, Lord? Please help me.*

❈ ❈ ❈ ❈ ❈

That night, after a long day of writing and an early dinner, Alexa desperately wanted to get out. She felt stifled and wanted to break free. Here she was, visiting all of these fabulous countries, but she spent most of her time cooped up in her room, working.

Jamison paced the living area. "Want to see the Magic Fountain?" he asked abruptly.

She turned to him with a smile of relief. "Would I ever. I'd forgotten all about it." Alexa grabbed a jacket from her room and followed him out the door. It was still light out, but the sun dipped closer to the horizon.

The streets of Barcelona bustled. It was a Friday night, after all.

They made it to Montjuïc just before eight o'clock and joined the crowds gathered around the fountain. Opera music played. Alexa gasped when yellow and red water shot several stories high. The water soared up in varying formations, in yellows and whites and blues and reds...it was stunning. Majestic.

"I love it!" she whispered. She would never forget this moment.

"Want to see another one? It'll have different music," Jamison told her.

"Sure," she agreed, and waited in the gathering dusk for the next show at 8:30 P.M.—this time to classical music. When the water finally died down, she reluctantly stepped back. "Let's go down to the harbor again," she suggested. Seeing the fountain show had pulled her heart toward the restless sea. "Then I'd like to window-shop."

After descending to the Plaça d'Espanya, Jamison hailed a cab with its green light glowing on top, indicating it was available, and they arrived at the waterfront in short order. It was fully dark now, but thankfully the breeze didn't feel quite as arctic as last night. Alexa buttoned her jacket and followed Jamison to the walkway bordering the water. She wondered why she had felt drawn to come here.

It was quiet and peaceful. Restful to her soul. Maybe that was why.

Alexa gazed out at the wrinkled, undulating water, and then further out to sea. "Wouldn't it be cool to take a ship and just go over the horizon... To see what's there. Explore new lands."

"You want to discover a new continent, princess?"

"Don't be silly." She lightly punched his well-muscled arm. "I just mean it would be neat to travel and see all kinds of new places."

"Like we're doing now."

"Yes. But without the work. I mean, I'm happy to write the book, but I wish I could spend more time exploring the places we're visiting."

"You'll have to come back later."

"I'd like to. Maybe I will. But I'll need to save up a lot of money, first."

"Maybe your future husband will bring you here on your honeymoon."

Alexa laughed, feeling a bit uncomfortable. "He'd have to be rich."

"Or know people here."

"That's not likely." Depression slivered through her soul.

A moment elapsed. Jamison said, "You and Colin are getting closer."

"I guess so. He's not at all what I had expected."

"What do you mean?"

Alexa hesitated, trying to find the right words. "He's genuine, and I like that. But he's also lonely, and I think he's hurting, too."

"You feel sorry for him?"

"No. I want him to be happy. He's a great guy, and he deserves it."

"Most people don't see beyond the fame and the charm."

"I feel honored, because he's opened up and been honest with me. It makes me feel responsible."

"For what?"

"Being careful not to hurt him. You know, with the book— or in any other way."

"I can't see you hurting him on purpose."

"No. Never," Alexa agreed.

She felt Jamison's gaze on her. "He's taken with you," he said abruptly.

"I know... But so far we're just friends."

"Why?"

Alexa searched her heart. Why *was* she dragging her feet with Colin?

Jamison's broad shoulders shifted. "He hasn't made a move on you, has he?"

"Not exactly." Alexa remembered the time he had almost kissed her. "I told him before I signed on that I wasn't interested in a fling."

"You did."

"Yes. I'm very careful...about relationships."

"I've noticed. Have you been hurt?"

"Who hasn't?" Alexa shrugged, in an effort to make light of it. She added, "I think I'm a little confused. That's the problem."

"Confused about what?"

Alexa looked at him, at the breeze rifling his wavy hair and the serious expression on his face. He listened to her intently, as if what she said was important to him. She realized then that they were having another real conversation; just like that night in Paris. The dark seemed to lower her guard to him. But how could she tell Jamison that *he* was the source of her confusion? Especially when she could barely admit it to herself.

"I want to be careful," she said at last. "I don't want to make any mistakes."

"To make a mistake, first you have to get your feet wet."

Alexa laughed. "I hope not in this water! It looks awfully cold."

Jamison said quietly, "Sometimes you have to take a chance, Alexa, to see if something is there."

She looked out to sea. "You mean like a shark?"

Jamison exhaled. "You're good at the jokes when things get too personal."

She smiled. "It's my wall. A good one, don't you think? I get to make people laugh, too."

"Walk with me." He held out his hand.

Alexa stared. "You want me to hold your hand?"

"Yes."

Her heart beat faster. "Why?"

"To prove a point."

"What point?" She felt wary.

"That I don't bite. And your world won't crash if you hold my hand for longer than a second."

"I'd rather pass on that experiment, thank you."

"Why?"

"Because it's silly. I don't need to prove anything to you. Plus," she said primly, "it's inappropriate."

"You're scared."

"Of what?" she scoffed.

"Me."

"I most certainly am not!"

"One block," he said. "I dare you." A smile gleamed through the dim light.

Unfortunately, Alexa had a bad track record with dares. She knew this. All the ones she had taken had ended in disaster.

"Fine," she said. "One block."

She slipped her hand into his warm one, and his fingers closed around hers, strong and secure. His palm felt a little rough with calluses—probably from lifting weights—but it was a pleasant sensation. In fact, the whole experience felt entirely too pleasant. A warm, electric tingle sizzled up her arm and fizzed along the nerves throughout her body. At the same time, she felt a strange peace walking with him like this. And safety.

"Look." Jamison stopped in front of a shop window. Inside, a miniature train chugged around the track of snow covered mountains. Tiny white and silver snowflakes billowed in the air, pushed airborne by invisible gusts of wind.

"Cool." Alexa smiled at him. "Timmy would love it."

His fingers tightened around hers, and then he led her on.

Alexa was content to gaze in the store windows. Most shops were closed, which was no surprise. But maybe she would come back tomorrow if she saw something especially wonderful.

They had reached the end of the block, but Jamison made no move to release her hand. He must have forgotten he was holding it. Alexa didn't attempt to pull free, either, as they started the second block. Glittering jewels sparkled in one window, and she paused to look. Diamond engagement rings, jewel encrusted necklaces, and outrageously huge diamond drop earrings were displayed.

"What do you like?" Jamison asked.

Alexa was embarrassed to be caught staring at the costly baubles. "I'm not much of a jewelry girl. But the rings are pretty. They're classic and simple. The others are too gaudy for me."

"If you could have any of them, which would it be?"

Alexa laughed. "Now you're being silly."

"You're the one with romance in your soul. Pick one."

"Well," Alexa bit her lip, scanning the display. "I like the princess cut diamond. I've always thought it's beautiful."

"Fitting." Jamison's mouth curved, and he tugged her on. They reached the corner and crossed when it was safe.

Alexa spied a chocolate shop—unfortunately closed—and gazed in the window. Reluctantly, she turned away.

Jamison said, "Shall we go another two blocks?"

Alexa looked down at their interlinked hands, and then to Jamison's face. He watched her intently.

Slowly, she said, "Are you putting a move on me, Jamison?"

He smiled a little, and released her hand. "Can't have that, can we?"

"No," she mumbled, not certain at all that that was true. She missed the warmth of his hand. It was cold out, she reasoned, and stuffed them in her pockets. But she continued to enjoy walking with Jamison and gazing in the shop windows.

"Look at this." Alexa stopped before a toy store. "Annie would love that baby doll. Or maybe that tea set."

"You still have room in your suitcase?"

"It is getting full," she admitted with a sigh. "Let's come here tomorrow. Maybe I can find something smaller."

"It's a date," he told her.

She glanced at him uncertainly, but could read nothing in his gaze. She smiled, then. "If you call these outings dates, then we're going on a lot more dates than Colin and I are."

"And the jokes start again."

Softly, she said, "You know what you're getting into with me."

"I do, princess." His dark gaze held hers, warming her insides. "I sure do."

"Can we go back now? I'm cold." Actually, she felt too warm and jumpy inside.

"Walk, or cab?"

"Cab."

Jamison hailed one of the black cabs with bright yellow doors, and she sat beside him in silence. She was very aware of his presence the entire way back, and up into their flat.

"Thank you," she said. "I had a wonderful time."

"I did, too." His gaze flickered briefly to her mouth. "Good night."

"Good night." Quickly, she entered the sanctuary of her room. What in the world had gone on tonight?

She sank onto the bed. He had dared her to hold his hand, and had held it for two blocks. Had he actually decided to lower his guard to her—at least a little? Had Jamison truly made a move on her?

No. He couldn't possibly have feelings for her. Just like Alexa did not have feelings for him. As her bodyguard, he simply made her feel safe and protected. That was all. She couldn't possibly be developing real feelings for Jamison.

What had her sister said? People fell in love with their bodyguards all of the time. Even a movie had been made about it. No. It was trite and ridiculous. Alexa was spending too much time with him. That was the trouble. Their forced togetherness faked the feeling of true intimacy.

CHAPTER TWELVE

Early the next morning, Alexa wanted to call Beth. But when she tried, her sister wasn't home. What would Alexa say, anyway? "Things are getting stickier with my bodyguard"? Beth already found the situation hilarious enough as it was. She might latch onto the wrong idea about Alexa's feelings for Jamison. That would not do at all.

Alexa finished with the last of the scrapbooks. Now she could do no more until her breakfast with Colin tomorrow morning. Maybe she should grab a quick lunch before going shopping with Jamison. Ridiculously, her heart fluttered at the thought of spending more time with him today. She needed to get a grip.

She hurried out to the kitchen and discovered that Jamison had just made an omelette. Cheese melted over it, and she smelled peppers and onions.

"Yum." She noticed red pepper slivers and onion scraps on the cutting board. "Are you going to eat those?"

"You want an omelette?"

"It smells delicious."

"Have you ever made one before?" Jamison raised an eyebrow.

"I can scramble eggs," Alexa said with pride. "How much harder can an omelette be?"

Jamison pulled half a pepper and an onion from the refrigerator. "I'll make it."

"I can."

"You grate the cheese." He pulled a wicked looking knife from the sink and chopped the vegetables.

"I could do that," she informed him, and nicked her finger on the grater. "Ow!" She sucked it, and then examined the wound. Only a tiny smidge of blood.

"You're not touching this knife, princess."

Alexa frowned, but put her full concentration into completing her task. "There," she announced. Jamison had already set the vegetables to sizzling in the pan. "What are you doing?" she wanted to know. "Where are the eggs?"

"I cook the vegetables first, to make them tender."

She did not care for his amused look. "I like my vegetables cold and hard," she told him. "Just like you."

His eyebrows winged upward.

"I *mean*," she said, blushing, "just like your cold, hard heart."

"Your mouth's going to get you in trouble one of these days."

"Trouble makes life exciting," she asserted, and stood at his shoulder, watching him cook. He slid the cooked vegetables onto a plate, whisked the eggs, and then added them to the pan. When the eggs were almost done, he added the vegetables and folded it in half. Then he added cheese, and when it had melted, slipped it onto her plate.

"Thank you," she told him. "I think I've learned something. I'll try it next time."

"Warn me, so I can cover the smoke detector." He headed for the couch.

Alexa frowned at his shaking shoulders. "Think you're funny? I can do plenty of things you can't."

"Can't wait for you to show me."

She rolled her eyes as the phone rang. A quick step reached the receiver. "Hello?"

"Love, it's Colin."

"Colin! How marvelous to hear from you."

He chuckled quietly. "Thank you. I'm calling to see if ten o'clock will work for breakfast tomorrow."

No church, then, but Alexa didn't understand Spanish anyway. "Perfect. I can't wait. I've just finished all my material, so be ready to give me a lot of stories."

"Will do." He hesitated. "I enjoyed our dinner the other night."

"Me, too." She sighed dramatically. "It was fabulous."

He chuckled again. "You're in a funny mood, aren't you, Alexa?"

How could she say that Jamison brought out her outrageous side? "I can't wait until breakfast tomorrow," she said, instead.

"Come hungry. I'm ordering brunch."

"Even better!"

"Cheers, love." Alexa hung up, too.

"Another date?" Jamison asked from the couch.

"As a matter of fact, yes. And a working session." She collapsed into a chair catty-corner to him and forked up the delicious omelette.

"Is our date still on for today?"

She gave him a look. "It's hardly a date, Jamison."

"I thought we agreed that's exactly what it is."

Alexa struggled to keep her mouth shut so the food wouldn't fall out. "I don't know what dream world you're living in. But we are not dating."

"I didn't say we were. But we agreed this would be a date."

Alexa's jaw did drop this time. Luckily, she had already swallowed. "*No,*" she retorted. "Hardly. It's an outing we're forced to enjoy together."

Oh, her running mouth! When would her brain engage?

He grinned. "Glad you're looking forward to it."

Alexa rolled her eyes heavenward and decided to stay silent, before she stuck her foot further into her mouth.

"Are you interested in architecture?" Jamison asked.

"Yes. Oh! I forgot all about Gaudi's buildings. What are they called again?"

"La Sagrada Família, Casa Batlló, and La Pedrera, which is also known as Casa Milà. Would you like to visit them first, then shop?"

"Absolutely. Thanks for reminding me." She saw his small smile, obviously surprised by her positive comments.

After she finished lunch, they took a cab to La Sagrada Família. Alexa gazed up at the magnificent spires of the unfinished church. She was so glad Jamison had reminded her to visit it before she left. "Wow," was all she could find to say. "Why didn't they finish it after Gaudi died?"

"Architects can't agree on how it should be finished."

Alexa discovered that both the inside and the outside of the massive structure still needed to be completed. Still, it was majestic and inspiring. She especially loved the stained glass windows in one area inside—they were shaped like the letter "I" in groups of three up the wall, and depicted different scenes. At the top was a blue cluster that looked like a starburst. She snapped pictures with her camera.

When they finally decided to leave, Jamison said, "I thought we could drive by Casa Batlló, and then take the time to see La Pedrera. What do you think?"

"Fine."

He gave another small smile. "You're so agreeable, princess. And you were quiet exploring Montjuïc, too."

"Historical masterpieces make me forget about sniping with you," she said loftily.

His smile edged higher. "Now there's the girl I know."

"Do you want to fight?"

"No. Just amazed you can keep quiet for so long."

Unable to help herself, Alexa stuck out her tongue. Jamison chuckled as their cab rolled to a stop outside La Pedrera.

However, true to form, Alexa fell silent as she gazed up at the curved, unusual lines of the stone building, and noted the wrought iron fences that decorated odd outcroppings of balconies. It looked like a surreal painting. Inside, they viewed the soaring, curved atrium, and then traveled to the attic space, where they toured the exhibition area. Photos, drawings, models, and videos explained how Gaudi had come up with his unique, ingenious designs.

Finally, they toured the roof, which Alexa liked best of all. It supplied a wonderful view of Barcelona, but more amazing were the warm, sand colored, curved arches and bizarrely shaped chimneys—the tops of which looked like helmeted soldiers. She gazed down through the atrium to the court below.

Alexa and Jamison spent a leisurely time wandering around the roof with the other tourists. At times it felt crowded, and at others, while passing through one of the archways, she felt like they were completely on their own. It was at one of those times that an odd sensation prickled down the back of her neck.

Alexa turned quickly, but saw no one but a giant, blond-haired man. Clearly, he wasn't the middle-aged man who had attacked her twice before.

The man peered down into the atrium.

"What?" Jamison's sharp eyes missed nothing.

"I thought I felt someone staring at me. All this strange architecture must be warping my imagination."

"Want to go?"

She couldn't dismiss the unease still sliding through her spirit. "If you're done."

"I'm ready when you are, princess." An odd note colored the serious words.

Alexa glanced at him. What had he meant by that?

His dark gaze steadily met hers. Had she imagined a double meaning when he had meant none? She must be feeling jumpy.

They descended to Passeig de Gràcia.

"If you want to shop, you might like to try this street," Jamison suggested. "Later, we could go into Old Town."

"Okay," she agreed. Now the prickly feeling was gone. Maybe she had only imagined it, after all.

Passeig de Gràcia was a beautiful street, faced by architecturally unique buildings. Alexa quickly discovered that it was home to a number of smart shops, too. She hoped she could find something for each of her parents here.

"Isn't shopping boring for you?" she asked as they wove through the throngs of people.

"Nothing's boring with you, princess."

Alexa supposed she should take that as a compliment. A crowd of people surged by, momentarily forcing Alexa ahead of Jamison. Unease slid through her—just like she had felt at La Pedrera. She cast a quick glance over her shoulder, looking for Jamison; certain he was right behind her, protecting her. But he wasn't.

Panic rose as two people elbowed by. One was a woman, and the other a man with a derby hat and a long black trench coat.

Swallowing back fear, Alexa turned and followed the crowd, looking for her bodyguard. Someone yanked her hair backward, and pain pricked into her neck. And then, for the briefest second, she glimpsed Jamison in a shadowed doorway. He struggled with the enormous, blond-haired man.

"Jamison!" she gasped.

"Shut up!" snarled the man in her ear. "You're more trouble than you're worth." The knife poked harder and he gripped her close, the weapon camouflaged by a chiffon scarf he held to her neck. An awful stink drifted to her nose. It had to be the same man as last time. "Walk, or I'll kill you now."

He must be crazy.

It felt like déjà vu. Fear choked her.

He must have followed her from La Pedrera. So had the giant. Had they followed her all day, waiting for the perfect opportunity to strike? And who was that enormous man? Hired muscle?

Suddenly, the knife left her skin and she heard the awful sound of fist hitting flesh. The grip on her hair vanished.

She spun, clutching her neck. Jamison stood over the prone man's body. He appeared none the worse for wear. And then, out of the corner of her eye... "Jamison! Look out!"

Before Jamison could turn, the blond man kicked him in the kidney. Features convulsed with pain, Jamison twisted to face his attacker. His fist walloped into the man's stomach. The blond man grunted, but kicked him again; managing a hook to the other kidney. Jamison sank to his knees, his face wreathed in agony. A few people stopped, exclaiming in concern.

At that moment, the older man struggled to his feet. "Come on!" he cried to his accomplice, and both men darted into the crowd.

Horror-struck, Alexa flew to Jamison and sank to her knees. "Jamison! Are you all right?"

More people gathered around, and a few English speaking tourists asked if he was hurt.

Although his smile looked like a grimace, Jamison made it to his feet. "I'm fine," he said, and limped down the sidewalk. When it was obvious he could move on his own, the crowd dispersed.

Alexa clutched his arm. "You're not all right," she whispered. "That horrible man hurt you."

"It isn't the first time. I'll live."

"But Jamison..."

"I'm fine. Don't worry." The hard set to his jaw gradually relaxed. Jamison pulled out his phone and spent a few minutes talking—to the police, Alexa surmised.

With trembling fingers, she pulled out her compact and rubbed sanitizer on the red mark on her neck. Who knew where that knife had been? The last thing she needed was an infection. The gel stung.

Jamison snapped his phone shut. He walked more easily now, Alexa was thankful to see. "The police think they know the accomplice. He's a local with a record."

But he wasn't the true threat. Both of them realized this. Alexa hated that her hands shook as she zipped her purse closed again. "I'm sick of that horrible man!" she snapped. "Because of him, you've been hurt twice. And he wants to kill me..." Her lips quivered. "I won't live in fear. I will not!" She said this more to convince herself than anyone else.

"Alexa..."

She fought tears. "Do you need to sit down? Are you sure you're all right?"

"I'm fine. I told you. But..."

"Then I'd like to keep shopping. I am not going back to the flat."

"Alexa." Jamison's hand curled around her arm.

She shook it off. "Please. I don't want to think about it. Let's go to Old Town." Although she wanted to shop, Alexa also wanted to leave this place, and fast.

A cab drove them to Old Town, and Jamison silently walked beside Alexa as she hurried from store to store, not slowing a moment to enjoy the new scenery. She couldn't find a single item she wanted—although she did find a black T-shirt Jamison might like. It said "Peligroso" on the front, and sported the orange head of a tiger on the back. She guessed he wore an extra-large, and slapped it on the counter and paid for it.

Jamison followed as she snatched up the pink plastic bag and sped for the door.

"Are you tired yet?" he asked. "You've been running from shop to shop for an hour."

Alexa spied a bench shaded by a tree. "If you're tired, we can sit."

Jamison exhaled and patiently followed her to the bench. He sat silently while she clutched her purse and bag in her lap. After a while he said, "You all right?"

"Of course I'm all right. Why wouldn't I be all right?" she snapped.

"You're tearing holes in the bag."

Alexa glanced down. Indeed, her fingernails had already worked holes in the pink plastic. The black T-shirt showed through. She stilled her fingers.

"I hate being afraid," she said. "I hate worrying if that man's behind me right now, plotting to throw a knife at me...or hurt you. What's wrong with him? Why does he want to hurt me?" To her dismay, tears rolled down her cheeks.

Jamison shifted closer and his arm hugged securely around her shoulders. "I don't know. He must be insane. It's the only explanation." His muscled thigh brushed her own. She wanted to rest her head on his shoulder, and so she did. It felt hard, yet comfortable.

"I don't want to be scared," she said in a small voice. Jamison was right. The stalker must be insane. Even so, her suspicions about Paddy returned to mind. Surely Colin's manager wouldn't try to kill her, just for a profit, would he? Certainly he wouldn't try to hurt Jamison, either. Alexa considered mentioning her suspicions to Jamison, but just as quickly rejected the idea. With no shred of proof, it would sound ridiculous.

"I know you don't want to be afraid," Jamison murmured. "But I'm here. I'll protect you."

"I saw you fighting that huge man. I thought..." More tears burned her eyes.

"It was tough. I'll admit I shot up a prayer for help."

It had been close. Even Jamison admitted it.

A sob wrenched from her throat. She didn't want to be afraid, and yet she was. She couldn't help it. "I'm so scared, Jamison," she whispered. "I'm so *scared*." Strangled sobs escaped.

Jamison's arms tightened around her. "I'm here. I will always protect you. Trust me."

And Alexa did trust him. Within his strong arms, the fear slunk away. She let him hold her, soaking in his strength and his calm self-assurance. In another man, the raw, leashed power of his body might scare her, but she didn't feel that way with Jamison. His strong embrace comforted her. Everything would be all right when she was with Jamison. He had always protected her, and he always would.

"God is here, too," he murmured. "Do you know what I pray when I'm scared?"

She shook her head.

"A verse from Psalm ninety-one. '"Because he loves me," says the LORD, "I will rescue him; I will protect him, for he acknowledges my name."' He's the one who keeps us both safe."

Alexa nodded, and breathed a silent prayer of thanks to God. And she thanked Him for Jamison, too. She sniffed. "Thank you for taking care of me."

"It's my pleasure, Alexa."

She fell silent, trying to stem the useless tears. Alexa wanted to stay this way forever. Close to Jamison. She didn't want to be anywhere else.

After a while, the tears stopped leaking out of her eyes, and she brushed at them with the back of her hand. Jamison pulled his white hanky from his back pocket. "Here."

She took it and reluctantly straightened up to wipe away the damage to her make-up. To her relief, his arm remained around her. "I must look like a raccoon."

"Let me do it." He tugged the hanky from her fingers and tilted her chin up. His dark gaze looked compassionate, warm...and tender?

Alexa allowed him to dab her face, fully aware that his fingers were only a breath from her lips, and of the five o'clock shadow on his jaw. She wondered what it felt like. And his mouth. She knew what that felt like.

"Alexa." Unknown emotion roughened his voice. His eyes had darkened to black again, and appeared conflicted. She wouldn't look away.

"Alexa," he said more softly. His mouth brushed hers and lingered. Sweetness flowed from his gentle caress.

Alexa couldn't help herself; for so long she had wanted to know. She threaded her fingers into the thick hair at his nape. It felt crisp and soft. Jamison went very still, and then his arm around her shoulders tightened. His kiss deepened, urging a response from her, and Alexa willingly gave it.

He broke away first and sucked in a deep breath. He muttered softly in Italian, then, "What am I doing? You're upset."

"Not anymore."

His eyes searched hers. "Alexa, this is not a good idea."

She pulled away. "I'm sorry."

"Let's go for a walk." His hand closed around hers. "I need to clear my head."

"Are you sure you want to hold my hand?" she asked in a small voice.

"No. I'm not." He sounded frustrated, and not sure of himself, like he usually was. Abruptly, he stood. "Come on. Let's find a coffee shop. We need to talk."

In the small café, Jamison bought black coffee for himself and tea for Alexa, and then sat across the small round table from her. His intense black gaze held hers.

"Why are you going on dates with Colin, Alexa?"

Why was she? She cast about for a reason, but it took longer than she had expected to find one. "Because he's the perfect guy? He's everything I've ever looked for in a man. He meets all of my criteria—except I don't know if he's a Christian."

Jamison's eyes narrowed. "What are these criteria?"

Alexa felt embarrassed to tell him. Especially since he clearly matched few of them! "Well, ever since I can remember, I've looked for a guy who's got blond hair, blue eyes, and is over six foot one. Of course, he has to have high integrity and be a Christian, too. And..." her voice faltered, "if he was refined and sophisticated, that would be a plus."

"Really?" That one word sounded incredulous. Jamison expelled a harsh breath. "You've made it perfectly clear, then." His expression hardened.

"Jamison..." What could she say? What did she feel for him? She felt so confused. Wasn't he all wrong for her?

Then why did she enjoy his company so much? She even enjoyed their verbal sparring. She said, "We get along better when we fight, don't you think?"

"Fighting is easy."

"Are you implying I want to take the easy way out?"

"I don't think you know what you want, princess."

Relief flooded her then. He had called her princess. Maybe things could go back to normal.

"You're right about that."

"Colin's your dream man. Go for it."

Alexa said nothing. From a logical standpoint, Jamison's statement made sense. From her confused heart's perspective, not so much.

"Maybe you're right."

Jamison curled his fingers around the coffee cup. His knuckles showed white. "Fine," he said. "Just keep it straight with me."

"I wouldn't lie to you, Jamison."

His gaze scanned her features. "I know," he said quietly.

They fell silent and sipped their drinks.

After they had finished, Alexa decided it was time to lighten things up again. "Can I treat you to dinner?" she said. "My sister said my book has made the *Times* bestseller list. I can afford it."

"You want to celebrate."

"Absolutely." She grinned, but inside she was serious. Yes, she did want to celebrate. And she wanted to do it with Jamison. But telling him might upset their new, fragile understanding, so she thought it best to strive for a light, fluffy demeanor.

He piled change on the table for the waitress. "Okay. But it'll be hard for me to let you pay."

She grinned. "Because you're a chivalrous, old-fashioned kind of a guy?"

"Because my mama taught me manners. And one rule is to never let a lady pay."

She hooked her arm through his. "Jamison, this is the twenty-first century. We'll catch you up yet."

His arm felt stiff, and she quickly released it. What was she thinking? "Lead me to a fabulous restaurant," she instructed.

He finally smiled. "I know a place…meraviglioso…over a few blocks."

"Lead on."

The marvelous place was a tiny bistro with a line out the door. While they waited, Jamison found a Spanish paper and glanced through it while Alexa took in the sparkling white lights on a nearby tree, and watched the sky turn rose, then deepen into dusk. A fascinating array of people walked by—some were dressed to the nines, while others wore casual dress with cameras slung around their necks.

Their wait time flew by, and soon they sat with gold napkins on their laps and bread on the table, with a candle in a bottle in the center. They sat near a window overlooking the street, and Alexa watched more people gather outside to wait their turn to dine. Luckily, the menu was in French, so she knew enough to order chicken *cordon bleu* and a caesar salad. Jamison ordered fish, listed as fresh caught that day.

Their drinks arrived—both sparkling cider—and Jamison raised his glass. "To your book's success, and for the new one you're writing." His gaze darkened. "And may every one of your dreams come true."

Something inside Alexa melted. He cared for her. He truly wanted her to be happy. "Thank you." Softly, she clicked her glass against his.

"Tell me about your childhood," she said, when their salads arrived.

"I was a hell-raiser."

"No! I can't imagine that."

He smiled and popped a bite in his mouth. "I was always in trouble."

"Doing what?" Alexa could not imagine straight-laced Jamison ever running wild and free, like a young hellion.

"I rode the freight trains to play hooky from school. Sometimes I wouldn't get back until dark. My friends came with me. Sometimes we stole food for lunch." Jamison shrugged. "It grew worse as I got older. I tried alcohol, and started to drink regularly. I never got into other drugs, though."

Alexa listened with her mouth slightly agape. It sounded absolutely nothing like the Jamison she knew now. "How did you finish school, then? Or did you?"

"My father found out. Over and over again he'd wallop me with his belt. It worked for a while. And then I'd go off again. I got smarter as I grew older, and it took him a long time to find out about the amount of alcohol I was drinking." Jamison fell silent for a moment. "When he did, he put me to work in the fields. He owns a huge vineyard in Italy," he told her. "I worked from the minute school let out each day, until sundown. Then I had to do homework. He wouldn't let me out of his sight, except for approved activities, until I graduated from five tough years of *liceo*. Then he sent me to college in the United States. I think he'd had enough of me."

Jamison leaned back so the waiter could clear their places.

Alexa sipped water, trying to digest it all. "Why did you behave like that?"

"I wanted adventure. I liked danger, and I liked to travel. I still do."

"I can't believe it."

"Tell me about your childhood. Were you the perfect child?"

Alexa snorted. "Hardly." She waited while their food was delivered. The glistening chicken with julienned vegetables smelled and looked delicious. She eagerly forked up a bite.

"And?" he prompted.

She swallowed. "I took too many dares in elementary school."

"For instance?"

"I ate worms once." She wrinkled her nose, remembering the grittiness and the terrible taste. "And I sprained my ankle jumping off a shed roof. And once, when we lived in North Dakota, I stuck my tongue to a flagpole."

"Ow." Jamison flinched. "How did you get it unstuck?"

"A lot of hot air. Mine and my friends'. I knew kids who had ripped their skin off, and I didn't want that to happen to me."

He shook his head. "Tell me more."

"As a teenager, I had a rebellious attitude. I didn't like anyone telling me what to do or how to think, but I didn't do drugs or anything like that. I was mostly quiet, and ignored my parents as much as I could. I was mouthy at times."

Jamison chuckled.

"I know—surprise, surprise. But not to my dad. He's got a temper." Alexa fell silent.

Quietly, he said, "Tell me more about your home life."

"My parents fought constantly. It got worse when I was in junior high." Alexa bit her lip. "Their anger scared me. And so did the shouting...and the other things. I was terrified they'd get divorced. Then I wished they would."

"When did they separate?"

"When I was sixteen. Beth was eighteen. I think they stayed together for us." She released a short, humorless laugh. "The divorce was worse than all the fighting. It felt like my whole world exploded."

"I'm sorry."

"I started hanging out more with my friends, including Priscilla—you know, the one I wrote the book about? She encouraged me to get into trouble, but I didn't. As a senior, I became editor of the yearbook, and I was in the French Club. Other than that, I buried myself in books."

"Like you do in your writing now?"

"It's my own world," she admitted. "And it's safe." She had never told anyone that before.

"Is that why you're so careful with relationships?"

"Partly." Alexa fell silent and finished the last delicious morsels.

The waiter appeared and whisked away their plates. "Dessert?" he inquired in heavily accented English. He must have realized that they—or at least *she* was an American.

Alexa looked at Jamison. "I'll share one with you. Or I'll just take a bite, if you want a whole one for yourself."

The waiter grabbed this opportunity to rattle off a long list of desserts, most of which Alexa did not understand. She did, however, understand *soufflé* and *chocolat*.

Jamison smiled a little. "Chocolate soufflé?"

She nodded eagerly, and he said to the waiter, "We'll share a chocolate soufflé."

"Bien," he said, and bustled toward the kitchen. The waiter soon reappeared with the dessert in a dish with cream dolloped on top, and two spoons.

"Gracias," Alexa said, and poked through the cream to the tender insides. The warm chocolate melted in her mouth. "Yum. I've never had a soufflé before. This trip is very educational."

"You're easy to please, princess."

She grinned. "You know my Achilles heel. I'd better be careful."

"Afraid I'll use it against you?"

"Would you be so dastardly?"

A smile gleamed. "I might. If the stakes were high enough."

A tiny shiver slipped through her. What could make stakes that high for him?

Their spoons slid into the soufflé at the same time, dipping up bites. It felt intimate, sharing a dessert like this. Alexa tried not to think about it. Weren't they trying to keep things light and fluffy?

"You can finish it," Jamison told her.

She realized that she had already eaten half. "You think I'm a pig, don't you?"

"No." His lips twitched. "I think you're a chocoholic."

"And right you are." Gleefully, she savored the last tidbits, then sighed with regret and laid down her spoon. "Now *that* was meraviglioso!" She tried to flick her fingers like Jamison had done, but ended up snapping them instead.

He snorted out a chuckle. "No. Like this." He kissed his fingers, then flicked them outward.

"I forgot the kiss. Wait. I can do it." Alexa smooched her fingers and flung her hand out. Her nail caught the tall candle and it fell toward Jamison. With a swift hand he stopped it.

Alexa didn't know whether to laugh or feel horrified. "I'm sorry! I almost set you on fire."

"I think it's time for the check."

"I'm paying. Remember?" She snatched it from the waiter's hand when he arrived.

Jamison let her pay, but she could tell by his faint frown and averted gaze that it was hard for him to do.

Outside, it was dark, but the shop windows and the street lamps cast warm glows onto the sidewalk.

"Okay," she said. "Show me that Italian thingy again. I've got to prove I'm not totally incompetent."

"All right. Hold your fingers like this." He demonstrated, pressing his fingertips together.

"Like this?" Were his fingers that splayed out and flat?

"No." Sounding faintly amused, he stopped at the corner of a building. Shadows enveloped them. "Like this." He cupped the back of her hand and his fingers urged hers into the proper position.

"Oh." Her heart beat very fast at his nearness. "And then what?" Why did she feel so breathless? She had better stop talking—she might sound like a ninny.

"And then—" He leaned close and kissed her fingertips. Alexa drew startled, quick breath. A sweet song strummed through her blood. "Flick them out, like you're releasing a butterfly." His fingers flew outward and hers followed.

"Perfect." To her regret, he released her. "Now, do it on your own."

Alexa thought she could do it now. With flourish, she kissed her fingers and flicked them out, as though releasing pixie dust. "To my teacher, who is meraviglioso!"

He smiled and she giggled, feeling high on life. "Come on!" She grabbed his hand. "I'll race you to that craft store. I want to buy one more thing."

She didn't hold his hand for long. Mostly because he wasn't running, like she was. Well, it was more of a jog. Good thing she had worn flats. And good thing the store was only half a block away. She held the door open. "Come on, slowpoke."

Alexa knew exactly what she wanted. She went straight to the wooden yo-yo bin. "What color do you like?" she asked. "Besides black, please!"

He looked at her. "Red."

"Red it is." She plucked one out and paid for it, then tugged him outside and dropped it into his hand.

"What's this for?"

"I saw you playing with one the other day. You need a toy to keep you occupied, don't you think?"

He gave her a strange look. "I do?"

"All that soccer will turn your brain to mush. You need to practice hand-eye coordination. So when the bad guys come, you can zap them."

"With the yo-yo?"

"Sure. Why not?" Alexa knew she was being silly, and grinned at him.

He smiled back and tried out the yo-yo. It zinged perfectly back into his palm.

"See?" she said. "You're an expert already." Alexa thought about the T-shirt she had bought him. He'd like that, too. But she would wait until they got back home. She gave a not so fake yawn. "Let's head back. Are you ready?"

"Sure." Jamison gave the yo-yo a few more experimental throws and they took a cab home.

Inside, Alexa pulled off her jacket and ran to her room. "I've got one more surprise for you," she called over her shoulder. "So don't disappear." She ditched her purse and pulled the shirt from the pink bag. The pink package would tip him off. She cast about for potential wrapping paper, and then spied the towels. Perfect! Carefully, she rolled the gift inside the towel and trotted out to her bodyguard. He'd pulled off his jacket, and now waited for her with a faint smile.

"Close your eyes and put out your hands."

"Does it bite?" he wanted to know.

"Don't be silly!" She pushed the wrapped bundle into his hands. "Now look."

He opened his eyes. "A towel."

She gave an exasperated sigh. "Open it."

Slowly, he unrolled the towel to reveal the shirt. He smiled. "You bought it for me."

"Of course for you. See what it says? 'Dangerous.' And on the back, a tiger."

The dark gaze met hers. "Are you saying I'm dangerous?"

A blush warmed her cheeks. Actually, that is exactly what she had thought. Only she hadn't thought it through so clearly then. "Um. I guess."

He shook it open. "Dangerous to whom?"

"Um...bad guys?"

"Bad guys?"

Warm confusion swirled through her heart. Dare she tell him the truth? She swallowed. "To me," she said softly.

"Alexa." She heard the warning in his voice, and his gaze darkened. He dropped the shirt to the couch. "I thought we weren't going to do this."

She bit her lip. "I know."

He moved toward her, as if unable to help himself, and cupped her jaw. She gazed at him as soft and tender feelings tangled inside, and waited for him.

"Alexa." That single word sounded tormented. Alexa stepped toward him. Only a few inches separated them now. His breath warmed her chin. It was all she could do not to lean in and kiss him.

He wasn't moving toward her. Why?

And then, slowly, he did. Alexa's lids closed halfway, anticipating the contact. Wanting it more than she could ever have thought possible.

Why hadn't he kissed her? Her eyes flickered to his. Need burned in his black eyes. Also an unexpected plea. He wanted her to kiss him. She knew it, instinctively. To prove that she wanted *him*, too.

Alexa took a quick breath. Somehow it felt like a bold step; actually declaring her attraction to him. But she was attracted to him. No denying that. Tenderness swelled, overflowing her heart, and she felt joy that she could meet his heart-deep need.

Softly, with only a faint whisper of trepidation still in her heart, her mouth touched his. The sweet contact jolted through her.

He shuddered, and his hands closed around her waist, pulling her closer. Jamison commandeered the kiss from that moment on. The sweetness slowly intensified to flame and then bloomed into need...and hunger. Heat leaped in Alexa, and fire. He kissed her deeper, and a swift urgency blossomed within her. Her heart pounded too fast, and her world became only him. Only this moment. Then Alexa felt his tongue flick against her lips, urging her to open to him.

It wasn't a good idea.

What were they doing?

But searing need overrode her better sense, and willingly she surrendered to him. Slowly, he invaded her mouth, intimately branding her with the essence that was him. The shock of it ricocheted through her nervous system. The flame burned hotter, brighter. Her knees felt like jelly. The force and virility of the man surged through her, making her tremble. He was always so unassuming to the rest of the world, but not now. No more leashing himself into the invisible background. Now she felt the whole man, and her head spun with the potency that was him.

Jamison broke the contact, chest heaving rapidly against her. Feeling lost, she gazed at him, confused. His gaze looked tortured, but he stepped back, putting distance between them. "Better stop now, princess. Before you do something you regret."

At that moment, Alexa couldn't imagine what she could regret. She felt disoriented. Why had he kissed her like that, if only to pull away? "What do you mean?"

"I don't meet your criteria. Remember?"

For a second, she couldn't think what he was talking about. Then she remembered. Because of his height?

He pressed on relentlessly, "Isn't Colin your perfect man?"

She took a step back, feeling confused. "I wasn't thinking about Colin right now. I was thinking about you." How could she think about anyone else?

He waited, his face hard, shoulders stiff. "Tell me the truth, Alexa!"

"Why did you *kiss* me like that?" She begged for understanding. She felt like she had been through a car wreck.

"Because I couldn't help myself!" He slammed a hand through his hair. "I wanted you to respond to *me*. But it is not enough," he said through his teeth. "Tell me the truth—who do you want? Colin, or me?"

She stared at him, struggling to think clearly. Her heart wanted Jamison. Her head said she was insane. All they did was fight. Not to mention, they lived an ocean and a continent apart. One would be an unbreachable gulf, but two...

Didn't pursuing Colin make the most sense? Wasn't he her perfect man, like Jamison accused?

"You're right. That was...pleasant, but I..." She felt like a fool. What was she saying? She wanted to kiss him some more! Impulsively, before she could think, she touched his arm. It felt like steel under his ubiquitous black shirt. He tensed when she touched him. "Jamison..."

"Don't, Alexa." His deep voice sounded slightly strangled. "I never know if I'm coming or going with you. All I know is this has got to stop." He twisted his arm free.

"What do you mean?"

"Don't play *games* with me, Alexa! I can't take it."

"I'm n..." She cut her denial short, because truly, she didn't know what she was doing. She was attracted to Jamison in some twisted sort of a way. He was all wrong for her, wasn't he? They squabbled all the time. Colin was the perfect man— the man she had dreamed of her entire life. He met almost every single one of her criteria, and he was actually interested in her. And they had an adult, civilized relationship. Wouldn't she be a fool not to pursue him? "I'm sorry."

A muscle clenched in his jaw. "At least you're honest." He sounded bitter. "But I knew the score from the beginning, didn't I?"

"Jamison..."

"Don't try to placate me. You'll insult me by trying."

"I don't intend to placate you!" Her temper sparked. "Mr. Know-it-all!"

"I don't know anything when it comes to you." He took a harsh breath. "I think I need to pull myself out of this situation."

Her heart fell like a rock. "What are you saying?"

"I'm going to ask to switch with Mart."

"You coward," she accused in whisper. She didn't want him to go.

"You want me to stay so you can play more cat and mouse with me?" Frustration tightened his tone.

"I am not playing cat and mouse! You're as much a game player as I am—from the beginning, you've baited me. We do it to each other. Don't make out like I'm the one responsible for this mess!"

"So you admit it's a mess."

"I'll admit I don't know what to think about you. But I don't want you to leave." At last, she bared her heart in that honest plea.

He stared at her for a long moment. "Tell me, Alexa. What do you want from me?"

"I want things to stay the same. I want us to be friends."

He laughed shortly. "Are we friends?"

"We are when you call me 'princess.'"

"It's part of the game...Alexa." He sounded grim.

Tears burned her eyes. "Jamison." She couldn't form the words burgeoning in her heart. She was afraid. And truly, how could they possibly be right for each other? "Can we forget we ever kissed?"

"You want to live in denial? Because I can't."

"No. But I don't want to lose you."

His tormented gaze searched hers. "You mean that."

"Yes! I do." Tears swam in her eyes.

He exhaled and briefly clenched his fist. "All right. I'll stay. But no more games. If we kiss again, I want Colin out of the picture. Forever."

"I won't kiss you again." Her voice sounded thin to her own ears.

"Good night, Alexa." He abruptly left and shut himself in his room.

Tears finally slipped down her cheeks. What was she going to do? How could she have such intense feelings for that man? Weren't they totally wrong for each other?

Maybe it would be best if he switched with Mart, and she never saw him again. Just cut this thing off at the knees, before he wrapped around her heart anymore than he already had. She would be leaving soon, anyway. Soon it would be time to say goodbye. Pain cut through her like a knife, and Alexa ran to her room to cry.

CHAPTER THIRTEEN

MART BROUGHT ALEXA to the penthouse the next morning. Colin had already called Alexa earlier that morning, his voice sharp with worry, for Jamison had reported yesterday's attack. Alexa assured him that she had only received a scratch. "I'm fine. Please don't worry."

"I blame myself. If it wasn't for me, you wouldn't be in danger."

"Colin, Jamison is doing a wonderful job protecting me. Everything will be fine."

"I'll post another guard on you, if you'd like."

"No!" That was the last thing she needed—two bodyguards. She could barely manage one. "I'm fine, Colin, really. Please. I'd rather just forget about it, if you don't mind."

After another few minutes, he'd rung off, finally agreeing to leave things as they were, and that he looked forward to seeing her soon. Thank goodness. Colin didn't know the attack wasn't the biggest problem in her life right now.

Alexa hadn't seen Jamison since last night, and frankly, maybe that was a good thing. Her heart felt like it had been through the shredder.

It was time to make up her mind about Colin. Last night's drama had made this fact abundantly clear. She had dragged her feet for long enough.

Mart keyed open the door to the penthouse and ushered her inside. A man in a white chef's hat loitered in the kitchen. Across the room, Colin and Eve worked at the desk, their blond heads almost touching. Alexa didn't know what she felt about that. Concern? For Colin?

"Alexa's here," Mart said, and disappeared into another room.

Startled, the two looked up. Colin looked momentarily disconcerted, but a feline smile curled Eve's lips. She touched Colin's shoulder. "I'll be back later," she said in a low, throaty voice.

Alexa managed not to roll her eyes. She set the scrapbooks and recorder on the coffee table while Eve took her sweet time gathering up her purse and jacket. The secretary sent Alexa a narrow look before finally exiting.

"Eve is certainly dedicated to you," Alexa told Colin. "Working on a Sunday."

He kissed her cheek, then scanned the scratch on her neck. However, he said nothing, for which she was grateful. "That she is. She's my right arm. I couldn't get on without her."

Alexa still didn't understand what Colin saw in the other woman, but decided it was none of her business. "Before breakfast, I'd like to go through these last scrapbooks and note the stories you want in the book."

"Righto." Colin grinned and relaxed on the couch, his arms along the back. "I like you, Alexa. I can relax around you."

"You can?" She was surprised. "But I'm always pressing your nose to the grindstone. How can that possibly be relaxing?"

His fingers touched her arm. "It's you, Alexa. You're relaxing. Honest, open... No pretenses with you."

"That's me. Tactless and blunt to a fault."

He chuckled. "Show me the scrapbooks. I'm hungry for breakfast."

An hour passed before Alexa was satisfied. Colin made decisions about all of the stories he wanted in the last half of the book. Even better, after she had incorporated the stories, she would be finished with the scrapbooks for good.

They sampled fresh fruit while the unobtrusive chef took their omelette orders. When the steaming omelettes arrived,

Alexa compared hers to the one Jamison had made. The bodyguard's won.

"Tell me more about your first album," she urged Colin, while nibbling toast. "How did you feel when it went platinum?" Her recorder had been on for some time. In fact, she had switched the memory card once already.

"Later," he promised. "Right now, I want to talk about us."

"Us?" Alexa's heart beat faster.

"Alexa, I think you know I have feelings for you."

"You do? Are you sure?" What words were these, babbling from her lips? "I mean... Oh."

Colin covered her hand with his. She eyed it uncertainly.

"Alexa, I realize you don't want to have a fling, but..." From somewhere, Colin's famous song, "Runaway Love," began to play.

Alexa's gaze darted around the penthouse, trying to locate the source. Colin stood. "It's my cell phone. I'd better get it. But we're not finished," he warned.

"Of course," she said, and took a nervous gulp of orange juice.

Colin flipped open his phone and paced the room. Suddenly, he turned his back to Alexa. "What?" His voice dropped an octave. "No! When? ...How can that be? ...But I just saw him. He was fine. ...He is? ...No! ...They've got to be able to do... Yes, Mum.... Of course I'll come. I'll call you later. 'Bye."

Alexa stood. "Colin? What is it?" When she touched his arm, he swung around, as if startled by her presence. He looked lost, and utterly anguished. "What is it?"

His palm went to his temple. "It's me da." His voice broke. "He's had a heart attack. He's in intensive care. Mum's not certain if he'll make it." Shock and disbelief etched deep lines into his face.

"Oh, Colin!" she whispered. "I'm so sorry." She hugged him, offering comfort in the only way she knew how. Slowly, his arms came around her and he crushed her tight. Harsh breaths shuddered through his body.

His breath warmed her hair, and long moments passed by. When his arms loosened she stepped back, but gripped his hands. "Surely they can do something, Colin. They do so many wonders these days."

He pulled free. "I'm going to find the best specialist in the world. I need to call Eve."

"Of course. Can I do anything? Anything at all?"

"Um, no. You know the band's meeting you this afternoon at three? Here. At the penthouse." He turned away, phone to his ear. "Eve..."

Alexa gathered up her things. She felt useless and unsure what to do. As soon as he hung up, she said, "I'll leave. I know you've got a lot to do. But my prayers will be with your father, Colin. Please let me know what happens."

He smiled. It was tight and worried, but a smile all the same. "You're terrific, Alexa. If I could, I'd ask you to come with me. But you'd probably feel as useless as I will, and it'd only be selfishness on my part to have you come."

Alexa didn't know what to say. He wanted her to come with him? "Colin..."

"Here's Jamison, come to fetch you."

She whirled to see her black-eyed bodyguard, and then returned her attention to Colin. Softly, she said, "I wish only the best for your dad. Let me know if I can do anything."

"What happened?" Jamison asked.

Eve burst into the room. "Colin! I'm so sorry!" She rushed to him, and then stopped a few feet away and stiffened her shoulders, heaving breaths. She glanced at Alexa and Jamison, clearly uncomfortable with their presence. Then Colin reached for her, and she flew into his arms. "I'm so sorry, Colin." She looked up at him. "I called your pilot. He'll be ready to fly you home in two hours."

"And you. You're coming with me."

"I am?" Eve looked wonderstruck.

"Of course. Everything's a mess. You'll need to straighten it out for me." Gently, he put her from him. "As it is, I hope he's well enough so I can do the Rome concerts next week."

"Of course he'll be fine," Eve said. "He has to be." Were those tears in Eve's eyes?

"I'll need help packing," Colin said. "Can you start?"

"Of course!" Eve hurried toward Colin's bedroom.

"Alexa, love." Colin moved toward her. She hugged him again, and offered her cheek to kiss. "I'll call you when I know something. Thank you for being here."

"I'm not sure what I did. But you're welcome."

Colin disappeared into his bedroom, and Mart joined Alexa and Jamison in the sitting area. "What happened?" he asked.

Quickly, Alexa explained, and while she did, Colin came back out.

He said, "Mart, you'll stay here and help Jamison. Jamison, old boy, I expect you to keep things rolling with the move to Italy. Call Paddy. Between the two of you, we'll keep this concert on track."

"Right."

And then it was over. Alexa went back to her flat. She still felt stunned. She couldn't believe what had happened. At least Colin's father was still alive. He had a fighting chance to live. She winged a prayer heavenward for his health, and for safe travel for Colin and Eve. She wondered again what the secretary felt for Colin. A rabid devotion to her boss, or a more genuine, deeper emotion? And Colin—he had hugged Eve, and it had seemed so natural. Could he possibly have deeper feelings for his secretary than he thought?

❋ ❋ ❋ ❋ ❋

Alexa interviewed the band that afternoon. As a whole, they were a loud, high-energy group, and it was apparent they got along well. They talked over each other, laughed hard, and zinged jokes on their comrades during the entire interview. They also remembered a bunch of funny stories from their early road tours, which allowed her a glimpse inside the lighter side of Colin's personality. All in all, Alexa was very pleased with the material she could add to the book.

She spent the remainder of the afternoon working on the book, but found it hard to concentrate. How was Colin's father doing? At seven o'clock, she fixed a solitary meal of scrambled eggs. Jamison had already eaten, and sat reading his thick tome. When the phone rang, she snatched it up. "Hello?"

"Alexa, it's Colin."

"Colin! How's your father?" She gripped the phone tightly.

"He's still critical, but it's looking better. The doctor says he's almost out of the woods, but he may need a heart bypass. I plan to stay here through Tuesday, if all goes well."

"I'm glad. I'll keep praying for him."

"You do that." He hesitated. "I know it's doing some good. We almost lost him this afternoon. The doctor says it's a miracle he's still with us. I've said a few prayers myself."

Alexa smiled. "Talking to God is a good start."

"It's time for a change for me, Alexa. I know making things right with God is part of it."

"I'll be praying for you, too, Colin," she said softly.

"Thank you, love. Would you put Jamison on?"

"Of course." She put the phone on the table and picked up her plate. "Jamison, Colin wants to talk to you." It was the first time she had spoken to him today.

Jamison leaped to his feet. While he headed for the phone, Alexa retreated to her room with her dinner. She left the door ajar. Maybe it was wrong to eavesdrop, but she wanted to know what else might be going on with Colin's dad, or with the move to Italy tomorrow.

She didn't hear much. Only Jamison's low voice asking questions. She finished the eggs and pressed 'play' on her recorder. Earlier, she had listened to the first chip's worth, and this was the second one. She wanted to review it all in her mind before she transcribed it. Truthfully, she felt edgy, and didn't want to write at all.

She listened to Colin tell another story, and then heard the last bit of their conversation before that terrible phone call came.

Colin said, "Alexa, I think you know I have feelings for you."

"You do? Are you sure? I mean... Oh."

She heard the barely concealed edge of panic in her voice.

"Alexa, I realize you don't want to have a fling, but..." And then Colin's cell phone rang.

Alexa pressed 'rewind,' and then played it again. Had she really sounded that horrified? That terrified? Yes, she had. She listened with embarrassed confusion.

What must Colin think of her? What was wrong with her? A wonderful man had just told her that he had feelings for her.

"I knew it. It's not Colin *or* me, is it?" Jamison spoke from the doorway.

With a tiny gasp, Alexa looked up. "What are you doing—spying on me?"

"Why did you leave your door open?"

She did not reply, but clicked off the recorder. She would provide no further ammunition for her bodyguard. "I don't recall inviting you in."

Ignoring her not so subtle hint for him to vamoose, Jamison stepped fully into the room. The black gaze held hers. "You're afraid of having feelings for either of us. Colin or me."

"You don't know what you're talking about."

To her dismay, he plucked up the recorder and rewound it. "Listen to yourself. You're scared to death."

Alexa punched the 'stop' button. "Get out." She stood, but rued the fact her heels were kicked halfway across the room. Still, she could look down on him. Unfortunately, even that didn't give her the advantage she craved.

Jamison didn't move, which was just like him. "Colin was about to ask what you feel for him, and you panicked."

"I most certainly did not! I just..." Alexa suddenly wasn't sure what to say. She glared, to cover her loss of words. "I'm not sure what I felt—feel for him."

"You'd have run out if you could."

"What do you know?"

"You've beaten me off with a stick ever since you first laid eyes on me."

Alexa wrinkled her lip. "And that couldn't be because of your oh, so sweet personality? Oh—and let's not forget how obnoxious you are. So what's your problem?"

"We're talking about you, princess."

"We are *not*." Alexa marched to the door and swung it wide. She pointed to the living room. A clear order for him to leave.

Jamison didn't budge. That irksome man! He watched her. The black gaze bored into her soul, as if trying to hunt out her deepest secrets.

Alexa looked away. "I was confused, okay?"

"Maybe so. But underneath it all, you're scared."

"Who made *you* my psychiatrist?"

"You say you want a man who fits in your box. That's Colin. But you won't let him get close." Jamison stepped toward her, and she backed up against the door. "And you're scared of me."

Jamison did scare her. In a flash, she admitted this to herself. He possessed a raw virility that unnerved her—much like the confident, partying men had back in college. He was fully aware of who he was, and comfortable in his own skin. And she was still that scared girl who had hidden behind her textbooks.

"I am not!" Alexa cast a quick, longing glance at her heels. So near, and yet so far. She needed every psychological advantage to combat this alarming interrogation.

To her dismay, Jamison followed her gaze. His eyes narrowed. "That's why you wear those heels, isn't it? So you can look down at people. It's your way to have power and control over your environment."

"That is rubbish!"

"Is it? Why do you need to be six feet tall, Alexa? Why do you eliminate every man shorter than you, in heels? Is it because you're afraid to have a man—any man—so you eliminate all the possibilities?"

"I don't! Colin fits all my criteria perfectly!" Except, she didn't think he was a Christian. Not yet, anyway.

Jamison twisted his line of questioning. "Has he kissed you yet—on the lips?"

She flushed. "How can that be any of your business?"

"He hasn't, has he? You warn him off with your body language."

Alexa's mouth sagged open. "Excuse me! What do you know?"

"You're afraid to let yourself go," he told her. "You're afraid to lose control of your heart to another human being. I want to know why."

"I am not!" Her heart beat uncomfortably fast.

He stepped closer. To her chagrin she backed up, proving his point. "Sure you are. Your words tell me to back off, but your kisses tell me a different story."

"You're conceited! You think every woman should swoon for you."

His eyes gleamed. "Don't lie to yourself, princess. I'm no Don Juan, and you know it. But you're afraid of me because you respond to me, and that scares you to death."

"Bull," she said crudely. "I wasn't the one who pulled away from that kiss."

"No. Because for one minute you stopped thinking."

Outrage scorched her. "You don't know what you're talking about!"

"Do yourself a favor, Alexa. Tell yourself the truth. And until you do, stop playing games with Colin and me. We deserve better."

"I am *not* playing games, you horrible man!" Tears blurred her eyes. "I'm trying to be careful. I'm trying to make the right decisions, but I don't know what they are!"

"What happened to you?"

She stared at him, furious, and at a loss for words.

"You said last night that you were hurt." He spoke in a gentler tone, but Alexa wasn't fooled. He wanted answers, and he was playing for keeps. "Who hurt you? How did it happen?"

She bit her lip. "It's none of your business."

"I want to understand. Tell me, Alexa."

She heaved a breath. Maybe if she told him, he'd leave her alone. "I met a guy when I was a sophomore in college." And then she decided to go for the whole truth—for herself, more than for Jamison. "Actually, I'll go back." These memories were old. In fact, until this minute, they had been shut away and almost forgotten.

"I walled myself off when I was a kid," Alexa said quietly. "All the fighting in the house scared me. I felt alone. I knew my parents loved me, but I didn't feel it. In fact, although it sounds strange, I didn't *want* to feel it and I was afraid to give it back. In my mind, love hurt. They hurt each other, and I didn't trust them not to hurt me, too. So my heart closed off— self protection, I guess—and I basically ended up bottling up all of the love inside of me. I wanted to hide it and protect it. I didn't realize until later that a wall built up inside me, thicker and thicker over the years." She stared into space. "My parents were clueless."

"You bottled up all the love in your heart."

"Yes." She licked her lips. "I said someday I'd give it to someone. Someday I'd find someone I could truly love and trust, and then I'd be whole again." Alexa had never told anyone this before.

Concern drew Jamison's brows together. "And so you met this guy."

"Yes. Paul. I thought he was the one." Tears blurred her eyes. "I loved him. And he said he loved me, too. He said and did all the right things. He thought I was beautiful, and he told me how lucky he was that he'd found me. I believed him, and I gave my whole heart to him, thinking everything would work out like a fairy tale."

Jamison waited patiently. Sadness lurked in his bleak gaze, and that encouraged her to go on. She whispered, "He said if I truly loved him, I would...you know, be intimate with him." She bit her lip. "So I was. This was before I became a Christian. Things with Paul stayed okay for a few weeks, but then I felt him drawing away from me. He said he only felt friendship for me. Two days later, he went out with another pretty girl. It hurt." Her voice broke. "It took a long time to put the pieces back together."

She breathed slowly. "Since then, other men have been attracted to me, but they never wanted to know the real me. I'm like an object, or a trophy they can show their friends... But I never trusted any of them."

Alexa turned away. Of course, she had never shown her true heart to any of those men, either, she realized now. So maybe that was why those relationships had stayed superficial.

Whatever the case, she had refused to open up her heart to them. That was the real problem, she realized for the first time. She was afraid of exposing her heart and soul because she was afraid of getting hurt. Alexa believed Colin liked her, but she didn't trust him completely—not yet. Besides that, she didn't know what she felt for Colin. Jamison's fire and vitality, on the other hand, scared her. She felt the strong, terrifying attraction between them. Here was a man who, if she allowed him, would possess the power to utterly devastate her.

Jamison's warm hand curled around her arm, forcing her to look at him. "I'm sorry he hurt you."

"Me, too."

"And so you have your criteria."

"Yes. They've worked well so far."

"Because they eliminate ninety-five percent of the male population."

Alexa frowned again. "You don't let up, do you? Don't sneer—they've worked. Every man I've dated in the last few years has been nice."

"Nice. Is that how you see Colin?"

"Yes. Unlike you!"

"Why haven't you married any of these acceptable, *nice* men?"

"You're awfully nosy, do you know that? Why haven't *you* married? Why are *you* so obnoxious?"

He smiled. "It's part of my charm, princess."

"You've got walls, too. Someday I'll see them come down," she threatened.

He moved toward the door. "If you can do that, I will be in serious trouble."

"Run scared, then," she accused. But she was relieved he was finally leaving. She wasn't sure if she should have revealed all of those secrets to him. But when Jamison wanted something, she had just learned he'd push until he got it. Best to put him on the defensive for awhile, in order to protect herself.

She said, "I know where you live. Confidences are a two-way street, you know."

"When you're ready to be serious, I'll give you everything you want." And then he was gone.

Alexa stared after him. What in the world had he meant by that? Then she told herself she didn't want to know.

Jamison was a dangerous man. Time to put back on her prickly armor, or *she* would be the one in serious trouble.

CHAPTER FOURTEEN

ALEXA WASN'T SURPRISED to find Mart in the living room the next morning. After all, Jamison was supposed to help Paddy get everything rolling for the move. Again, she wondered if Colin's manager might be behind the attacks in Barcelona. How would she ever know? Worse, would the deranged stalker strike again in Rome?

Alexa packed up, and soon boarded the Lear jet Colin had sent to fly them to Rome. She buckled her seatbelt and gazed out at the high, distant hills, and pieces of Barcelona's skyline. *Someday I'll come back,* she promised silently. *Someday I'll explore every one of your streets and tourist attractions.* Although, thanks to Jamison, she had already seen so much.

The object of her contemplation strolled by, checking on everyone. Jamison glanced at her. "You okay?"

She grinned. "Just peachy."

He frowned a little, but moved on.

Alexa had allowed him to get too close last night. He had burrowed under her skin, and she had given him a glimpse of her deepest fears. No man had the right to get that close. Certainly not Jamison. Today she planned to be pleasant and friendly to him. However, if he tried to push too close, she'd need to put up a prickly wall.

Alexa gazed out the window again, but saw nothing. Last night's conversation continued to replay through her mind.

She was afraid to love. For the first time, Alexa admitted this truth, and even understood why. Thanks to her pushy bodyguard. As a child, she had closed off her heart to love. She had tried to protect it from the verbal assaults her parents had unleashed upon each other. Now, for the first time, she understood how those harsh words had flayed into her own soul, too, and made her afraid to trust. To love.

And then there was Paul. By the time she had met him, she had been starved for love. She had given him her entire heart, soul, and body. How desperately she had wanted the happily-ever-after her parents had never had. And then he had quietly turned and rejected her. No screaming fights had heralded the end of their relationship. Just indifference.

Paul's rejection had devastated Alexa. She had missed him horribly, but worse, she had felt unworthy, and feared something must be terribly wrong with her. She had given him everything she was, and he had not wanted any of it. Later, she had realized that Paul had been physically attracted to her, but after she had surrendered her body to him, his interest had quickly waned. He hadn't cared about the real person she was inside. ...Or maybe he hadn't liked the person he had seen.

Blinking back tears, Alexa stared out the window. Although the old pain had dulled, it still hurt.

So, after all of these years, she was still petrified to love. As much as she hungered for it, she was afraid to try again.

A verse—one of her favorites, from 2 Timothy 1:7—whispered through her mind. "For God has not given us a spirit of fear, but of power and of love and of a sound mind." NKJV™

Lord, please heal me. Help me to trust and not be afraid. Help me to know who the right man is for me, and give me the courage to give him my heart.

❋ ❋ ❋ ❋ ❋

In Rome, Alexa rubbernecked all the way to the newest apartment building. She couldn't wait to explore. She had already decided to take all day Wednesday to sightsee. By then, Jamison should be finished with his set up duties. Much as it might be unwise to spend time with him, he was Italian, and doubtless could help her sightsee more efficiently than Mart could.

The layout of the flat was much the same as the other two luxury buildings. This one had thick carpets, and floor-to-ceiling windows along the back wall of the tiny kitchenette and the dining nook. Fresh flowers adorned most available surfaces, including her bedside table. It smelled heavenly, like a florist's shop.

A sliding door, covered by sea foam colored, filmy drapes led off her bedroom and afforded a fabulous view of Rome. Alexa leaned on the rail and gazed over the ancient, yet modern city. She saw dome-topped old buildings crowned with spires, and thought she spied the Colosseum in the distance, but wasn't sure. To her left, another balcony jutted out—Jamison's, she was sure—and to her right, another room's balcony adjoined hers, although with a partial wall barrier.

Alexa retreated inside and unpacked. It was already late afternoon, and she wanted to start transcribing the clips she had recorded. She would work hard all day tomorrow, too. That way she wouldn't feel guilty about taking a whole day off to sightsee. Of course, it might be nice if she asked Jamison first if he would be available.

Alexa was perusing the freezer for dinner choices when the lock clicked and Jamison made his first appearance in the apartment.

"Hey, bud," Mart said, standing. He flicked two fingers to Alexa. "Later."

"'Bye, Mart. Thanks," she said.

While Mart disappeared, Jamison rolled his giant black suitcase, still near the door, toward his room. He looked tired.

"Hard day?"

Jamison looked at her. "I'm not ready to fight yet, princess."

Alexa frowned. Fine. He could be irritable. She had plenty of things to occupy her attention.

She microwaved a meal and ate it at the glossy, hardwood dining table, enjoying the view. Jamison still hadn't emerged when she finished, so she retreated to her room to write.

By eight o'clock, she had had enough. Alexa was bored. She peeked into the sitting area, and then the kitchen. *Aha.* Jamison had just pulled a meal from the microwave.

She waited for him to sit, and then zoomed over to join him. Alexa felt a regrettable, swelling urge to make trouble, but struggled to control herself. "So, what does your day look like tomorrow?" She fixed a pleasant smile upon her face.

Jamison sent her a tired, suspicious look. "We'll set up most of the day."

"What about Wednesday?"

The black gaze rested on her. "Back to baby-sitting duty."

Alexa shoved aside a prickle of annoyance. "Good. If you're game, I'd like you to show me the town."

"Tour guide again?" He couldn't sound less enthusiastic.

Hurt jabbed. "Yes, please. If it won't strain you too terribly."

"Fine." He continued to eat his meal.

Long seconds of silence ticked by. "Awful chatty, aren't you?"

"You ready to talk? Somehow I doubt it."

"What exactly do you mean by that?"

He looked at her. "You want to play games. I don't."

"Aren't *you* in a sweet temper? What's your problem?"

He shoved aside his empty plate. Black eyes bored into hers. "Let's talk, then. Why haven't you married, Alexa?"

Alarm replaced her persistent, barely acknowledged longing to spend time with him. He intended to continue last night's conversation. *No.* She wasn't ready. Time to erect that wall again.

Flippantly, she said, "I told you. I've never found the perfect guy."

"Until Colin. Right?" His gaze was intent.

"He is perfect."

Colin *was* everything she had ever looked for in a man. She reminded herself again why. He was tall, not short. She cast a narrowed glance Jamison's way. Charming, instead of obnoxious. Considerate, instead of blunt and in-her-face. Blond hair and blue eyes, not black-haired, black-eyed and black-hearted.

"Does he rev your engine?"

She blinked. "What is that supposed to mean?" she delicately inquired.

"Come on, princess. Do you want him to take you places you've never been before?"

"I hope you mean in a traveling context," she returned frostily. "Otherwise, your comments are extremely inappropriate!"

He looked unrepentant. "I guess that means 'no.'" He stood and cleared his place.

She curled her lips. "Imagine what you will. But my love life is none of your business."

"You don't know what you want."

Glaring, she stood now, too. "I know I don't want anyone like *you*. And that's a good starting point, as far as I'm concerned."

The way his lips curled up did not pass for a smile. "You've made that clear from day one."

"So you did overhear my comment about dating short men."

Jamison flipped his black jacket off the chair back and thrust his arms into the sleeves. He zipped it with a jerk. "Yeah, I heard you. And the munchkin comment. Why do you think we started on such a positive note?"

"Because you're such a sweet, sweet man?" she inquired. "Don't blame your rude behavior on me. I, for one, had no intention of hurting anyone's fragile ego at the studio."

"What about sneering down your nose at the airport? What about treating me like a servant? Was that intentional?"

"You were rude first," she reminded him. "And I tried to apologize, remember? But you wouldn't accept it. No, you disparaged my character because I'm beautiful." She frowned at his soaring eyebrows. "You said it!"

"Things haven't changed much, have they?" He looked grim.

"You're still rude, if that's what you mean."

He fished in his pocket and pulled out his room key, then shoved it back and headed for the door.

"Where are you going?" she demanded.

"Out."

"Again?"

"Mart will baby-sit you for an hour. I need air." He slammed the door behind him.

Alexa felt angry and hurt. Why had he just spouted off like that? Sure, they fought all the time, but usually it was more good-natured. Less...personal.

He was angry with her.

Because she wouldn't have a serious conversation? Probably. He certainly hadn't appreciated it when she had reverted to her flip, charming self. In fact, Alexa already regretted pushing him away with her snappy words. So what if he had tried to dig under her skin again, and she wasn't ready? Did she have to act like a cavewoman?

No. Of course not. Alexa felt further remorse and chagrin. And yet she hadn't been the only one acting like a prickly porcupine. They had both done a good job of pushing each other away just now.

Unfortunately, one thing rang loud and clear. Jamison possessed the ability to reach deep down and grip her soul. It scared her, and she didn't know how to handle it. Or him. Not yet. And the original question remained—why had he been so prickly, too?

She greeted Mart, and then elected to watch television with him on the couch. Midway through the show, she turned to him. "Is something wrong with me?"

His amused gaze scanned her face. "Not outwardly."

"Don't turn into Jamison on me," she warned. "We're friends, right? Tell me the truth."

"The truth is, I don't know what's going on between you and Jamison. And I'd rather stay out of it." He flipped the channel to a sports broadcast. As always, Alexa was amazed that sports seemed to run at all hours of the day and night. She glanced away from the distracting television, and found Mart's gaze glued to it.

With a sigh, she stood. "Fine. I won't torture you with my presence, either."

Now it was his turn to sigh. He pointed to the couch cushion. "Sit, Alexa."

She complied, but sat on the edge. She eyed him with caution.

He grinned. "I don't bite. And if you want to know what Jamison's thinking, ask him."

Arms crossed, Alexa settled back on the couch. Like that would happen. They seemed incapable of completing one civil conversation. Especially since that earthshaking kiss the other night.

"Now," Mart said. "Do you want to watch sports, or an action flick?"

"The movie." Alexa pulled her knees to her chin and draped her arms around them. Men. Somehow, Jamison and she had to work through this knotty mess, or the next two weeks would prove intolerable.

Soon she found herself zoning off into the movie, too, and barely noticed when Jamison returned and sprawled into a nearby chair to watch the movie, too.

Alexa jumped up when the credits rolled. She had dealt with enough testosterone for one night. "Good night, you two."

"Sleep tight," Mart said.

"Don't let the bedbugs bite." Jamison's dark look indicated he might wish bedbugs *would* bite her.

"You are so sweet." She shut herself in her room. Tomorrow had to be better. She would make sure of it, one way or another.

※ ※ ※ ※ ※

"I've got you today, kid," Mart said the next morning, when she emerged for breakfast.

"Jamison's left already?"

"He's helping set up." He sent her a wary, contemplative look. "And he said he needs a break from you."

That hurt, like a stab through the heart. "Perfect," she sallied back. "I much prefer your company, anyway."

"Thanks. I think."

"I can make scrambled eggs. Do you want some?"

"Sure." The wary edge remained. "I thought you couldn't cook."

More hurt bubbled. "Is that what Jamison told you?" She growled softly behind her teeth.

Mart eyed her with amusement. "You're scary, Alexa."

She sent him a narrowed glance. "Don't worry. I'll stay on my best behavior with you."

Mart picked up a piece of toast. "What's going on with you and Jamison?" He lifted his hand. "I'm not asking for personal details. But you've got him riled up. I've never seen him like this before."

Alexa mixed eggs and poured them into the pan. "Jamison and I are like sandpaper and steel wool. All we do is irritate each other. We can't seem to get along."

"Why? He's the most laidback guy I know."

"Maybe to you, but not to me."

"I hate to see my buddy so rattled. You're not chewing him up, are you, Alexa?"

She heard the warning in his voice, and remembered their conversation in the kitchen in London. How long ago that seemed.

"More like we're chewing each other up. I appreciate your concern for him, but I don't want to hurt Jamison." She spooned at the eggs. "We had a huge fight, and I'm not sure we can get past it." In fact, they had had more than one, since the kiss. Tears threatened, but she blinked them back. "I like

Jamison...when he's nice." When he didn't push too close to her heart. That scared her. Still, that wasn't his fault. It was no excuse for her to be flippant and rude to him.

"You be nice, Alexa. Make the first step."

She scooped the eggs onto plates for each of them. Quietly, she said, "You're right. I'll try." And she would, she vowed, even if lowering her guard allowed him to get closer. Honestly, this thought scared her to death. She swallowed. *Lord, please give me courage.*

"Good. Maybe I'll get some time off this evening, then." He grinned, to show he wasn't serious. At least, not entirely.

"When's Colin getting back?"

"Tonight. The first concert is tomorrow."

"Jamison's taking me sightseeing tomorrow. I'll try to patch things up then."

"You do that. By the way, these eggs are good."

"Thanks." She grinned. "I guess it proves I'm not hopeless. I can learn from my mistakes."

"I don't think you're hopeless. And I doubt Jamison does, either."

Alexa hoped he was right.

❄ ❄ ❄ ❄ ❄

That evening, a knock came at the door, and Mart opened it.

"Colin!" he said. "Come on in."

Alexa finished rinsing off her plate and hurried into the sitting area, wiping her hands on her skirt. "Colin!" she said. "How's your father?"

Colin came straight over and pulled her into a hug. He pressed a kiss into her hair. "He's fine, love. It's wonderful to see you."

Alexa pulled back with a smile. "I'm so glad to hear that. Will he need the bypass you mentioned?"

"He will. The doctor wants to wait until Da's more stable, and then he'll schedule it as soon as possible." Colin didn't look upset, though. For the first time, Alexa detected peace in his blue eyes.

"Would you like tea? I just boiled water."

"I'd love a cup, thank you." He followed her into the dining area.

"Mart? Do you want some?" Alexa called.

"Don't touch the stuff." Mart settled back on the sofa to watch a rugby match.

She fixed the tea and joined Colin at the table. "You seem different. Did something happen?"

"Da's good. And I finally made peace with God."

"You asked Jesus to be your savior?" Joy leaped in her heart.

"I did, and I feel a whole lot better. Like a big load of muck is off my back."

Alexa grinned. "Colin, that's wonderful!"

In her head, a mental click sounded as the last piece fell into place. Now Colin was a Christian, and he officially met every single one of her criteria. He was absolutely the perfect man for her.

Then why didn't she feel like leaping into his arms?

She sipped tea to cover her confusion. "Your trip went well?"

"Yes. Eve was indispensable. I don't know how I'd have gotten on without her."

Alexa scanned Colin's face. He smiled to himself, apparently at a memory. "Really." She still didn't understand what Colin saw in his secretary. But admittedly, she didn't know Eve that well. And certainly Eve had never shown Alexa her good side.

Colin's sharp gaze focused on her again. He smiled. "But I came tonight to ask you a question. Would you like to go on a private tour of Rome tomorrow?"

"With you?" Alexa was stunned.

"Of course, with me."

"Oh! Well, that sounds wonderful. But I just asked Jamison if he..."

"Jamison can come, too. You too, Mart," Colin told his bodyguard.

"Really?" She couldn't believe it. "But won't you be mobbed?"

"I'll wear a disguise. No one will recognize me."

Alexa got the feeling this might be an adventure for him.

"Jamison, old chap," Colin called unexpectedly. "I've just stolen your date for tomorrow."

The door clicked shut, and Alexa watched her bodyguard cross the room. Why couldn't she tear her eyes from his face? Why did she want so desperately to read his expression right now? It proved impossible, however.

She said, to explain, "Colin's just offered to give me a tour of Rome."

"And you're coming, too," Colin said.

"Great." Jamison poured a cup for himself and sat at Alexa's elbow, across from Colin.

Alexa was very aware of his hand, only inches from her own. Why, when Jamison and Colin were in the same room, did she only notice Jamison? Vitality crackled from him; quiet and barely detectable, but it strummed along her nerve endings. She looked at him. "Do you mind?"

The black gaze met hers. "You make your choices, Alexa. I'm just along for the ride."

She frowned. Not an acceptable answer.

Colin stood. "I'd best go. I need to unpack. See you both tomorrow at nine?"

"We'll be ready," her bodyguard said.

Alexa made to get up, but Colin put a hand on her shoulder and pressed a quick kiss to her temple. "I'll see myself out, love. I'm looking forward to tomorrow."

"Me, too." She smiled and watched him and Mart go.

Alone again, with Jamison.

"You didn't have to be so rude," she told him. Oops. Not exactly the nice she had promised Mart to be.

"Did you want me to be jealous?" he asked, too quietly.

She gasped. "No." Then she gritted her teeth. "Why can't we get along?"

He watched her, but said nothing.

Frustration flooded her, and Alexa slapped hands to her face. "Please, Jamison," she whispered. "I hate the way things are between us. I'm sorry for the way I've been acting. Can we start again?"

"You mean it?"

"Yes!" She dropped her hands, exasperated. "When you're not pushing me..." she bit her lip. "*Please* stop pushing me. I can't take it. Can't we be friends again? Please!"

Tension slowly relaxed out of his shoulders. His hand covered hers and squeezed once, gently, before letting go. "I'm sorry, too."

Alexa blinked, but this time they were tears of relief. "Really?"

"I'll stop pushing you so hard."

"So we're friends again?"

"I never stopped being your friend, princess."

Alexa relaxed. Princess. Now they were back on familiar footing. "Good." Her mind turned to other matters. "You know what? Colin just told me something awesome."

Jamison smiled, and it made her heart bloom with joy. She said, "He's become a Christian."

"That's terrific." His smile faded. "Now he's perfect for you."

She looked at him uncertainly. "No one's perfect, Jamison. All I know is I'm happy for him."

"Fair enough. We'll have fun touring Rome." Faint, smiling promise warmed his eyes.

Alexa wasn't sure if Jamison meant him and her, or all of them, collectively. Her heart skipped a little faster. "I can't wait."

❋ ❋ ❋ ❋ ❋

The next morning, Alexa placed a quick call to her sister to update her on her travels. She mentioned the tour of Rome today, but carefully did not mention a word about Jamison. She didn't want to give her sister any further misconstrued ideas about her bodyguard.

Jamison waited in the living room. This morning he wore a black T-shirt and the usual black jeans. Not the T-shirt she had given him, she noticed. This one was pure black and molded his shoulders. Beneath the black sleeves, his biceps looked very large and muscular.

He looked good—no, he looked better than good. Jamison caught her stare and smiled a little. Hastily, she looked away.

"Ready?" she inquired, heading for the door.

"Never seen you in jeans and a T-shirt before, princess."

She turned, raising her brows. "Do I pass muster?" Today she wore faded jeans and a white T-shirt which advertised her brother-in-law's magazine.

"You know you look good in everything you wear."

Her cheeks warmed, and she threw a dramatic hand to her chest. "Be still my beating heart! Was that an actual compliment coming from your lips?"

His smile stretched wider, and as he opened the door, Alexa felt his warm hand on her back. She escaped his touch as quickly as possible.

Colin had asked them to meet him downstairs, so when Alexa reached the lobby, she snapped her gaze to and fro, trying to pick him out. Colin had said he'd be in disguise.

But the only reason she found him was because she spotted Eve, and then Mart a short distance away. Eve stood beside a tall man with dark hair, a moustache, and sunglasses. Alexa hurried over. To her chagrin, Jamison had already reached the superstar. So much for her powers of observation.

"I didn't recognize you!" She grinned up at Colin. A snort came from Eve's direction. That woman wore narrow, fashionable sunglasses, combined with equally thinned lips. Had Colin invited his secretary along, too?

"You like it?" Colin glanced down at his blue jeans and Oxford shirt.

"I wouldn't have known it was you, if I hadn't seen Eve first."

Colin glanced at his secretary. "Eve's never been to Rome before, either. So I invited her along, too."

"The more, the merrier," Alexa said.

Colin's attention turned to a point over her left shoulder. "Paddy!" He moved away.

The muscular manager cut through a loose group of people like a pit bull through a chain link fence. One woman, dressed in a silk pantsuit, frowned and lifted her nose before returning to her companions.

Paddy's hard green eyes impaled Alexa, then dismissed her. "Colin."

"Have you got the latest figures?"

"I'm working on Zurich," Paddy said brusquely. "Trust me. It'll sell out."

How could he be so certain? A sudden chill went through Alexa. *Was* he behind the attacks, after all? Had he plotted another assault, here in Rome, just so sales would spike in Zurich?

"You're doing a splendid job." Colin clapped him on the shoulder. "You're a miracle worker. Haven't I said so a million times?"

A faint smile worked Paddy's mouth, but his thick shoulders still looked bunched and aggressive—like a thug's. Alexa blinked, trying dislodge the fanciful thought. Colin trusted Paddy completely. Shouldn't she, too? And yet the hard glitter in the manager's eyes unsettled her.

Taking a step back, she tugged Jamison's arm so he would follow her.

His dark eyes sharpened into alert black. "What?"

"You don't think..." She cast Paddy a quick glance, and then leaned forward and whispered, "Could Paddy be behind the attacks? Colin said the news coverage is helping to sell out the concerts. He even mentioned that if I hadn't been hurt, he'd think Paddy was behind them."

The thought obviously gave Jamison pause. He glanced at the manager for a split second, and then his gaze returned to Alexa. "I've known Paddy for years. He's cutthroat, but not that much. I don't think." A frown marked his brow.

"I don't want to slander him. But I'm scared."

"I'll talk to a few contacts and see what they can dig up."

Alexa felt better, now that Jamison knew of her fearful suspicions. Even more encouraging, he hadn't dismissed them as being silly. He would take care of her. She trusted him completely.

Colin joined them, and Paddy strode for the bank of elevators. Alexa was relieved to see the last of him.

"I've hired a car," Colin said, leading the way to the entrance. Out front, a blue sedan awaited. "Jamison, I'm hoping you'll drive. You know this city like the back of your hand, right?"

"No problem."

Colin slipped into the back, and Eve instantly scooted in beside him. Mart joined Jamison in the front, which pretty much took up all the space there, so Alexa was forced to sit in the back, beside Eve. Not her first choice, to be sure. She buckled her seatbelt and then scooted as close to the window as she could.

Eve ignored her, choosing instead to focus entirely upon her boss. "Colin, tell me again. Where are we going first?"

Colin rested his arm along the back of the seat. Eve smiled. Alexa, however, wanted to roll her eyes.

"Jamison, I thought we'd go to the Colosseum first," Colin said. "We can walk to a few places from there. At lunchtime, I thought we'd have a picnic at Villa Celimontana. My chef whipped up a basket for us."

"Sounds great," Jamison said.

Alexa remained silent while Eve chattered nonstop to Colin. He didn't seem to mind.

Jamison dropped them off and went to find a parking space. While they waited for him to return, they stood in line for combination tickets at the Roman Forum's main entrance.

The next few hours passed quickly. First, they visited the Colosseum. Their tour guide told them all sorts of grisly details about the ancient amphitheater, and inside the massive structure, Alexa felt an awestruck sort of fascination. To think that thousands of years ago people had built this huge stadium.

She had seen photos before, but in person it was amazing to see that the floor of the Colosseum was gone, and little rooms were below. Prisoners about to be executed had stayed there. Her imagination went wild, thinking about what it must have been like. Less than two thousand years ago, people had been brutally killed here before cheering, screaming audiences. To her surprise, the guide said no proof existed that Christians were killed at the Colosseum. Some believed those executions took place at Circus Flaminius, instead. Still. Alexa shivered and quickly walked on, following the group. How petty her problems seemed by comparison.

Colin took her hand, pointing out details of the architecture. Behind his disguise, his familiar, sharp features were animated, and Alexa smiled as she listened. She felt self-conscious, however, with her hand in his. Why? Because Jamison and Eve watched? Or because she didn't want to hold Colin's hand? At the first opportunity, she gently disengaged it and wandered away on the pretense of examining the stone of the Colosseum. Colin took her hand a few more times, too, and Alexa repeatedly found excuses to pull away. On one of those occasions, Jamison watched with a faint smile. She struggled to ignore him.

They also explored the Roman Forum, Palatine Hill, and the Arch of Constantine. By then, it was after noon, and they headed up Via Claudia to Villa Celimontana. They entered the gorgeous park through the elegant, white stone and iron decorated archway. Colin led the way to the right, where the green grass sloped, studded with palms and many other types of trees, and Alexa saw families scattered here and there on the grass, eating their picnic lunches.

"I'll get the basket," Jamison said, and disappeared back the way they had come.

By now, Alexa felt warm and a little tired. "Want to sit down?" she asked Colin.

"Sure." They sat in the cool shade of a tree, not caring that they had no blanket. Mart lounged against the tree trunk, his gaze roaming the park.

Eve did not sit. "I'm off to find a loo," she said, and hurried off.

Colin smiled at Alexa. "Are you enjoying yourself?"

"I'm having a fabulous time. I feel like we've just touched the surface, though. Caelian Hill sounds interesting. Isn't it one of the seven hills of Rome?"

"It is. We can explore it after lunch, if you'd like. It's not far." Colin frowned, and Alexa followed his gaze. Eve stood partially hidden by the trunk of a palm tree, talking to a tall, thin man in a baseball cap. Eve sketched a hand through the air and the man shook his head. They talked for another full minute, and then Eve hurried away.

Colin said nothing, so Alexa decided not to comment either, but she wondered about it. Why would Eve share an animated conversation with a complete stranger?

If he was a stranger. Now, where had that thought come from?

Eve and Jamison returned at the same time.

"Great!" Colin leaped up and helped the bodyguard distribute the food.

Alexa gladly accepted a cold cola and a ham and cheese sandwich. Jamison claimed the spot next to her, and she smiled at the way he wolfed down his first sandwich. "Eat much?" she muttered.

His smile gleamed. "Should I be flattered you're watching me?"

"Please," she scoffed, and sipped more cola.

Colin spoke to Eve, beside him. "Who was your friend?"

Eve stilled, chip halfway to her mouth, and Alexa fancied the secretary paled a bit. "What?"

"The man in the baseball cap. Did you know him?"

"Oh." Eve laughed. It sounded uncomfortable. "He was a tourist. He wanted directions, but I told him I didn't know anything. He kept asking questions anyway. Finally, I said I had to go." Eve gobbled her chip and fell silent.

Jamison murmured, "Who are they talking about?"

Alexa told him, and when he asked for a description of the man, she gave that, too. Jamison fell silent.

After lunch, Colin, Eve, and Mart decided to relax back on the grass for a few minutes, but Jamison rose to his feet. "I'm taking a walk. I'll be back soon."

Alexa found herself popping up as well. "Me, too."

She wanted to be with him. Unfortunately, she had reacted before her brain had fully engaged. Now she had to endure Jamison's small smile.

"Can't get enough of me, princess?"

She huffed in indignation. "Please. I want to know what you're up to."

"Do you."

"Of course. Tell me."

"I want to check out that guy Eve was talking to."

"Then it's a good thing I'm coming, since I've seen him and you haven't."

They wandered around the lush, beautiful park, but didn't spot the man. In one area, they found an art exhibition in full swing.

"Look at that." Alexa pointed to a blue photo of the moon rising over the water. "Isn't it dramatic?"

"Look at this one." Jamison tugged at her fingers and indicated a photo of two children with their arms crossed, resting on a sandstone wall, impish faces grinning. A sand-colored building stood to the left, in the background.

"They're cute," she said with a smile. "They look full of mischief."

"It was taken in my village," he said. "See the building? It's near my old school."

Alexa glanced back at the photo, and imagined Jamison as a boy in that same place. "Those children remind you of yourself, don't they? Eyes gleaming, and full of mischief."

"You're starting to know me."

He stood very close right now, his arm only a breath from hers. Alexa contrasted it to earlier, when she had wanted to escape every time Colin had tried to hold her hand or walk close beside her. Now, only millimeters separated her from Jamison, but she not only didn't mind it—she *liked* being so close to him. A dangerous admission from any account. Luckily, she hadn't babbled that out loud.

"Are you still taking me to visit your family?" She wasn't sure if he'd changed his mind, after the drama of the last few days.

"Are you trying to back out?"

"No. Why would you think that?"

He did not answer directly, which was just like his incorrigible self. "Glad to know I'm back in your good graces, princess."

"You're like a foxtail. I can't get rid of you."

"You say I'm a fox?" He grinned.

She burst into a peal of laughter. "Don't flatter yourself. I just called you a burr. You know, the weeds that stick to your socks in the summertime?"

He chuckled and moved on, eyeing more photos.

Mart appeared. "We're ready to go, you two." He glanced from one to the other, taking in their lingering smiles. "Am I interrupting something?"

"A moment of truce," Alexa said.

Mart smiled. "I'm glad to see your weapons are holstered. And that you took my advice, Alexa."

"What advice?" Jamison wanted to know.

"To be nice." Alexa grinned. "Haven't I been nice to you? Say yes, or Mart will pound me."

Jamison chuckled, but shot Mart a faintly warning glance. "Thanks for looking out for me, bud. But I can handle things with Alexa just fine on my own."

Mart took no offense. "I can see that."

The five of them headed toward Caelian Hill. On the southeastern side, they walked for half a mile and explored the beautiful Basilica of St. John Lateran, and then wandered back in the direction of Via Claudia, exploring the vast expanse of still standing and crumbling buildings. Apparently, long ago the wealthy had lived on this hill, and lavish villas had been uncovered under the Baths of Caracalla. As the afternoon passed, Alexa grew pleasantly tired.

At one point, the men all walked together, discussing the sights, and Alexa found herself behind them, walking beside Eve. She cast about for something to say. Time to try to be nice again, she decided. At any rate, it seemed rude to walk and say nothing.

"How is your foster mother?" she inquired with a smile. "Is she out of the hospital yet?"

"Uh...no." Eve glanced to the side, as if searching for an answer. "She needs more tests, and observation."

"I'm so sorry." Alexa didn't press further. Clearly, Eve didn't want to divulge details.

"Thanks," the secretary muttered, and glanced left again, as if something had caught her attention. Suddenly, she flapped her hand, as if swatting at a mosquito. Then she did it again, more urgently.

What in the world? Alexa followed Eve's line of vision. A man in a ball cap was partially hidden by the corner of an old ruin.

Was that the man Eve had spoken to earlier? Suspicion surged. Eve hurried ahead, as if eager to leave the man behind.

"Who was that?" Alexa demanded, swiftly keeping up.

"Who?"

"You know. The man in the baseball cap. The one you spoke to in the park."

"How would I know? He's a stranger. I hope he's not following me."

Alexa frowned and glanced back. The man had disappeared. "Are you sure you don't know him?"

"Are you accusing me of lying?"

"You act like you know him."

Eve glared. "You just don't quit, do you?"

"What do you mean?"

"You want Colin all for yourself, so you try to start lies about me. I don't have a secret boyfriend, if that's what you're thinking."

"I didn't think that." Alexa had received the impression the man was middle-aged.

"Forget that weirdo." As Eve hurried after Colin, she spat, "You're enjoying yourself, aren't you?"

"What do you mean?"

"Colin's drooling all over you, and you're lapping it up!"

Alexa wasn't sure if she cared for that particular metaphor. "Colin's sweet and thoughtful, like always."

"He doesn't have real feelings for you," Eve asserted, but no conviction rang through her words.

Alexa again felt an odd compassion for the prickly, insecure secretary. "He likes you, too."

Eve's jaw dropped a little, and she stared back in suspicion. "Why would you say that?"

"Because it's obvious he feels affection for you. But I don't know what he'd think if he knew how you treat me, however."

Eve's lips pressed white. "Back off," she hissed. "Can't you please do that? You're making things so difficult!"

"What things?" Eve's plans to snare her boss?

Eve glanced over her shoulder. "Just *things*," she hissed. "I've warned you. That's all I can do." She sped ahead to reach Colin's side.

Warned her? About what? Alexa glanced over her shoulder again, but the man had vanished. She wasn't sure if she believed Eve's story about the man being a random odd bird. But how could Eve possibly know someone here in Rome?

Alexa couldn't figure it out, but to her relief, saw no sign of the man again.

For the remainder of the afternoon, Eve appeared glued to Colin's side, and pointedly excluded Alexa from all conversations. It was rude, but then again, Eve hadn't enjoyed much time alone with Colin today, which she obviously craved. For the moment, with Colin talking to Eve, Alexa felt like the third wheel.

Where was Jamison? A quick glance spotted him leaning against a stone wall. Glad urgency quickened her steps, and she hurried to join him.

"Hi," she said. Jamison's elbows rested on the wall, much like the children's in the photo, and he looked out over the old ruins. Alexa placed her arms next to his and gazed out, enjoying the view, too. Enjoying his presence. The stone felt warm to the touch.

"Why aren't you with Colin?"

"I'd rather be with you." Oops! Open mouth, insert foot. "I mean, Eve wants to spend time with him. I decided to give them some space."

"You prefer to be with me?" His black gaze held hers.

She looked away. "Maybe."

His arm brushed hers. Accidentally? Or on purpose? She suspected the latter.

He said, "I enjoy your company too, Alexa."

The admission hung heavily between them. Alexa glanced uncertainly at him, and he looked back, his body posture calm. "The world hasn't come to an end, has it?" he asked quietly.

"No," she admitted, and glanced away, her heart beating rapidly.

He straightened and his hand settled on her lower back. Its warmth lingered for a moment. "I think they're looking for us."

"Oh!" Quickly, she turned. Colin and the others had stopped and were looking back. "Let's go, then." She hurried to catch up.

The warm feeling stayed inside of her, though, even when Colin slipped an arm around her shoulders and pointed out the Aqua of Claudia and then the Temple of Claudius, which they would visit next. Eve didn't like Colin's gesture, if her scowl was any indication, but Alexa wouldn't let the secretary ruin her day. Soon after, Alexa edged away from Colin, and enjoyed wandering around the old ruins.

At last, Alexa admitted why she didn't want to be close to Colin. She liked him a lot. He was perfect and wonderful, and one of the nicest guys she had ever known, but she only felt affection and friendship for him. No romantic interest at all. What she felt for Jamison, however, was an entirely different story. A troubling story, and not one she knew how to handle yet.

But how to tell Colin what she felt? The next time they had a serious conversation, she would tell him, she decided.

CHAPTER FIFTEEN

THE NEXT TWO DAYS flew by, with no opportunity to talk to Colin. Alexa was pleased with the progression of the book, and Saturday morning arrived quickly. It was the day to visit Jamison's family. Alexa dressed with care in casual slacks and a gold silk top. She felt nervous, but tried to ignore the butterflies in her stomach.

She emerged from her room, purse in hand.

Jamison leaned against the kitchen counter, waiting for her. He straightened and slowly closed the distance. "You still want to visit my family?"

"Of course. I can't wait." She grinned.

"Why do I feel scared?"

She lightly punched his arm. "You're not scared of me. Not a strong bodyguard like you. You could probably bench press little ol' me."

"Two of you," he corrected, without conceit.

She grinned still more. "So, what are you scared of?"

"Embarrass me, and you'll pay," he warned.

She rubbed her hands. "Now that sounds like a challenge I'd like to take."

His hand warmed her lower back as they walked out the door. It closed with a click behind them. Jamison glanced at her feet.

"Where's your heels, princess?"

A blush warmed Alexa's cheeks. Sometime not long ago, she had stopped wearing heels when she was with him. It hadn't been a conscious decision, but there it was. Funny, but when she wasn't wearing heels, he didn't seem nearly so short.

"I can put some on, if you'd prefer. Maybe my white ones. You like those best, don't you?" Those were her three and a half inch stilettos. She withdrew her key, but his hand closed around hers, stilling the movement.

"Can't be you're showing consideration for me?" he asked quietly. His warm, black gaze snared hers.

"Don't flatter yourself," she managed to scoff. "You know how I need control over my environment. I couldn't possibly trust you enough to want to be close to you." Oops!

"Close to me?" He smiled, then. "And you trust me. We're making progress."

"Hmph," she sniffed, feeling too unsettled for her liking. "Time's awasting. Didn't you say we have to drive three hours?"

"Yes, ma'am."

❋ ❋ ❋ ❋ ❋

"Here we are." Jamison parked the car in front of a sprawling home built out of weathered golden stones and topped by a tile roof. Flowers in pots bloomed on either side of the front door, which now opened. A gaggle of people burst out.

"Jamison!" cried a young girl, and vaulted into his arms.

"Ciao, Ana, piccolina," he hugged her tight and planted a kiss on her head.

Alexa stood to the side as his family greeted him, and then Jamison introduced her. To her surprise, they greeted her with equally warm hugs. She tried to sort out everyone. His mother, who liked to be called Mamma Tia; his father, Stephano; his grandmother, and three sisters all milled about.

"I'm pleased to meet all of you." She smiled, hoping they understood English. Apparently, they did.

"Come in. You are just in time for lunch," Mamma Tia said. "I knew you couldn't stay long, and I want to make sure my Jamison is well fed. He doesn't eat right, does he, Alexa?"

Alexa was surprised to be asked such a personal question about Jamison. They must know he was living with her, as her bodyguard. Hopefully, they didn't have the wrong idea about their relationship.

His mother bustled into the charming house. Flowers in vases bloomed on every available mantle and table, and beside them were pictures of her children at various ages. Alexa wanted to slow down and search out the ones of Jamison.

"Here." With a pleased expression, his mother waved to a long oak dining table. It was loaded with antipasto, fresh baked bread, wine, and dishes of pasta.

"It looks fabulous!" Alexa breathed. Her stomach rumbled—thankfully, quietly. However, Jamison sent her an amused glance.

Mamma Tia smiled widely, pleased by her comment. "At last, Jamison, you have brought home a good girl." She glanced at them both, speculation clear in her eyes.

Although Alexa felt a bit embarrassed, she was delighted to see the tips of Jamison's ears grow red.

Her bodyguard pulled out a chair for her. Under his breath, he said, "Sit and don't say a word."

"But Jamison," she twinkled up at him, "why ever not?"

"Alexa," he growled.

Alexa turned her bright smile upon his family. His mother said, "So tell me, Alexa, how has my Jamison been treating you?"

"Mamma," Jamison interjected, "Remember? Alexa and I are not seeing each other. I'm her bodyguard. Today, she was nice enough to come so I didn't have to take time off work."

His mother didn't blink. "I see." She returned her attention to Alexa. "How *has* Jamison been behaving?"

Jamison sent Alexa a warning, speaking glance. Unfortunately, it also fueled the little imp that enjoyed stirring up trouble for him. She smiled at his mother. "He has exemplary manners, and treats me with unfailing courtesy."

Mamma Tia's eyes narrowed, and Jamison coughed suddenly. Apparently his sip of water had gone down the wrong way.

Alexa kindly patted his back. "There, there." His muscles rippled, strong and hard under her fingertips, and she hastily removed them. "Are you all choked up because I gave you a compliment?" she asked kindly.

His brows lowered.

"Jamison," Mamma Tia said. "Why are you frowning at our guest?"

Obviously, his mother was a sharp lady. Not much would get by her. Alexa grinned now, thinking of the different, subtle ways she could torture him. Although maybe that wouldn't be proper guest behavior.

"Don't," he warned under his breath. Unfortunately, it also sounded like a dare. He cleared his throat and said to his mother, "Water went down the wrong way."

"I see." Mamma Tia didn't appear to believe her son. She turned a wide smile upon Alexa. "Tell me about yourself, Alexa. Where do you live in the United States?"

"California. Just north of Los Angeles."

"Oh! Jamison's Aunt Pauline and his cousins live in Los Angeles. He's very close with them. He stayed with them while he went to USC. He graduated at the top of his class," she added with a mother's pride.

"A great school," Alexa said. Obviously, the bodyguard had it going on academically in order to graduate from USC with honors. "But I'm afraid we're rivals. I went to UCLA."

"Surprise, surprise," Jamison muttered.

Alexa tacked on, "But you must have graduated way before me. We probably weren't at the same football games, TP-ing each other's cars."

"If you want to know how old I am, just ask."

She sent him a gleaming smile. "Well yes, now that you mention it, how very old are you?"

His black brows zoomed together.

"Sensitive about your age, too?" she suggested with sympathy.

"*No.*"

"Then tell me."

He sipped water. "I'm thirty-five."

"Good! Not as old as I feared," she said with a mock sigh of relief.

"And what do you mean by that?" he inquired, too quietly.

"I'm concerned for your well-being. Don't frown like that," she told him. "I just don't want you to get hurt, protecting me. You know, age-related degeneration makes one more susceptible to injury." She sipped her fruity drink. "Don't you want to know how young I am?"

"Eat your food," he growled.

Meanwhile, his family had watched this byplay with much interest. His oldest sister hid a smile behind her napkin. His mother glanced at the two of them with a delighted, considering look in her eyes. And his father looked pleased, period.

Alexa engaged Stephano with a smile. "Tell me, what was Jamison like as a little boy?" Of course, she had heard Jamison's side. She wanted to hear his family's.

Jamison's knee pressed in warning against hers under the table. Alexa threw him a sunny smile and patted his thigh in a comforting manner. It felt hard and muscular, and she snatched her hand free at the same time he jerked his leg clear of hers. A faint flush darkened his tan.

"Jamison was a troublemaker as a boy," Stephano said in thickly accented English. "But you would never believe it now. He turned his life around in college. He used to be a big partier. A drinker of much alcohol."

"Really?" Although Jamison had told her about his excesses in high school, Alexa still found it hard to believe. In fact, she had never seen Jamison touch any sort of liquor.

Mamma Tia shook her head at her husband. "Jamison has always been a good boy," she retorted. "He always had a lot of energy and curiosity. And a desire to explore the world. Sometimes it got him into trouble. But he has always treated his mama right."

"He'd better!" Stephano lifted his hand in mock warning. "Or he would know the consequence."

"I don't think Alexa is interested in my past."

"Of course she is," his father said. "How could she not, sitting beside you, so *bella*. Smiling at you. She asked me, did she not? I will tell her a story."

"Papa, no," Jamison groaned.

"*Sì*. Let me think." But whatever he'd been about to say was interrupted by the ringing phone. Stephano wiped his mouth and placed the napkin on the table. "That will be my manager. Please excuse me."

"Papa owns a vineyard near here," Jamison explained.

"I will tell you a story," Mamma Tia said. Her eyes were soft as she gazed at her son.

"Mamma," Jamison said, but Alexa heard the hopeless note in his voice. She grinned and turned to his mother, eager for every detail.

"Hush. When Jamison was six, I dropped him off at scuola primaria for the first time. I told him I would be back soon to pick him up. I was so proud of him. He didn't cry. But I did, as I walked the long block home. My baby was a big boy now, going to school. He didn't need me so much anymore.

"When I got home I settled into work. But I kept hearing a strange noise in the house. I looked," she glanced with love at Jamison, who now held his head in his hands, to Alexa's delight. "And there was Jamison Jethro's foot sticking out from under my bed. He was crying, my poor boy. I helped him out. He held his Pooh bear tight in his arms and sobbed that he couldn't go to a place that wouldn't allow his dear Pooh to go, too. 'Or you, Mamma,' he said." Her eyes misted now. "And then I knew I had not lost my son. And I still have not. I don't care what his papa says," she fluttered a dismissive hand at Stephano's empty chair. "He is the best boy in the world. With a heart of gold."

Though Jamison looked embarrassed, he stood and pressed a quick kiss to his mother's cheek. "I love you, Mamma. Even though you embarrass me in front of our guest." He sat again.

"Oh, pooh," Mamma Tia said with a smile. "Alexa needs to know these things about you. If I know you at all, son, you won't let your guard down enough to let her see the real you. The son I love."

"Thank you, Mamma," Jamison murmured. He cast a glance at Alexa. "I think."

"That was a beautiful story," Alexa said. "Thank you for telling me, Mamma Tia." It was another piece to the complex man she was beginning to know. It fascinated her, hearing this story of his childhood, and trying to mesh it with the man he was today.

He had walls. Not a surprise, to be honest. She had sensed them from the start. This impression had intensified when he'd unflatteringly labeled her beautiful, and therefore trouble. What was that all about? But inside, did he have that heart of gold everyone kept telling her about? She was beginning to suspect it was the truth. Then why and where had the walls come from? Were they a product of getting older and protecting himself from the cold, cruel world? Or had something happened to him, as it had to her?

Alexa enjoyed the rest of the meal, as well as more stories about Jamison. To her delight, Mamma Tia also brought out a photo album of Jamison as a boy. A devilish glint sparkled in his eyes, matched by a wide grin. When it came time to leave, Alexa received warm hugs and invitations to return soon. She promised she would—if she was ever in Italy again. She glanced at her bodyguard. Not likely.

The thought formed an uncomfortable ache inside of her.

Mamma Tia took Jamison aside just before they left and spoke in his ear.

"Your family is wonderful," Alexa told Jamison softly as they drove home. "I love them."

"They loved you, too. My mother was especially taken with you."

"What did she say to you, there at the end?" Not that it was any of her business. She truly didn't expect him to tell her.

Jamison remained silent for a long moment. "She said you're a keeper," he said quietly. "But mothers only see what they want to see."

"I liked her, too. And it was quite educational, learning more about you."

A faint smile curved his lips. "More ammunition against me, you mean."

"Of course. Isn't that what you expect?"

"I never know what to expect from you, princess."

"Isn't that what keeps our relationship interesting?" she suggested with a grin.

"Interesting." He glanced at her, and for just a second, his pensive black gaze rested on her mouth. "That's one way to put it."

❋ ❋ ❋ ❋ ❋

"Your father said you partied hard in college." Curiosity had been nipping at Alexa ever since Stephano had made those cryptic remarks yesterday. They now strolled along a bridge near their apartment building. "So, you didn't settle down when you left home for college. I still find it hard to believe."

"That's a good thing, I guess."

She glanced at his profile as he walked beside her. The sun set in the west, outlining his face in shadows. "What happened in college?" she asked softly. She wanted to know more of this complex man's secrets.

After a moment, he said, "I was foolish. I drank and partied through my freshman and half of my sophomore years."

"And you still graduated with honors?"

"I was lucky. I skated the first two years."

Alexa doubted that. "Why did you stop partying? Your father said you turned your life around, and I can see you have."

"Thank you." He stopped and put his elbows on the bridge, and gazed off toward the setting sun. Alexa did the same, resting her chin in her hands. In this position, he actually appeared taller and bigger than she was. He'd rolled his shirtsleeves to the elbow. Black hairs sprinkled his muscular forearms. Not too many, to be a turnoff to her.

"What happened?" she encouraged, tearing her eyes away. What was she doing, staring at his arms? What did she care if he had a truckload of Neanderthal fur, or not?

"I drank myself stupid at a party one night. And I drove—even stupider. The next thing I knew my car was wrapped around a tree, and the horn was blaring. That's what saved me. People came running and pulled me out before the car exploded. Otherwise I would be dead." Grimness settled into his voice.

Horror hit Alexa. She couldn't imagine the world without this man in it. "I'm glad you're not," she whispered.

"Yeah. Me, too. Anyway, I was lucky. I wasn't hurt, and I hadn't hurt anyone else. It scared me, though, and I decided to reassess my life. My father helped." He laughed shortly. "He threatened to cut off my college money if I didn't straighten up. So I went to AA. That was the beginning."

"That's when you became a Christian."

"Yes. I haven't touched liquor since."

Her respect and pride in him grew. He had completely turned his life around. Look at the man he was today. One of the best in his field. Colin Radcliffe trusted him with his life. She trusted him with hers, without question.

"How did you get into bodyguarding?" she wanted to know. "I mean, you don't exactly look like the bodyguard type."

"Because I'm short?" His half-smile said he didn't take offense—this time.

"Yes. But you're tough, aren't you?" How did she know this?

"I used to play rugby—I still do, sometimes. It's a brutal sport."

"You played rugby?"

"Yes. And soccer. They were the approved activities my father allowed in high school."

"That's funny. I don't see you as the team type."

"Again, you don't know much about me, princess."

"I'm realizing that more every day." She kept learning fascinating depths to this man. She threw him a grin. "Were you any good?"

Jamison shrugged. "My opponents seemed to think so."

Alexa laughed. That was so like him. Unwilling to accept praise or stand in the limelight. "So you were a jock *and* a brain."

He glanced at her, and he was very near. Dark stubble darkened his jaw, and the faint, spicy scent that was just him filled her senses. Memories of the kisses they had shared flitted through her brain. Several long heartbeats thumped by. How could his eyes be so impossibly dark?

He said, "You're staring at me."

"So? You're like two inches away. How can I ignore you?" Flustered, she looked away. What would it feel like if his lips grazed her cheek—just by accident, of course? Or not. Agitation churned faster. Sugar flakes. What was she thinking? Hadn't they agreed to avoid this kind of craziness? Look at last time. They'd fought, and she had feared she had lost his friendship. Now, more than ever, she couldn't bear the thought of losing Jamison.

When his arm brushed hers, she nearly jumped out of her skin. "What are you doing?" she exclaimed, and quickly shifted away.

"Touchy, aren't you?"

"I don't want *you* touching me," she asserted. What a big fat liar she was!

He smiled, but said nothing.

Alexa glanced down at their hands, separated now only by inches. His larger one looked sculpted and incredibly tan next to her own, which looked slim and golden brown from their excursions in the sun, touring Europe. He had beautiful hands.

Her heart fluttered alarmingly. What was wrong with her? She was losing it!

Alexa swallowed. "We should go back. Doesn't Colin need you at the concert tonight?"

"Not for another hour."

"Who's going to baby-sit me, then? Or have you decided I'm mature now, and don't need a bodyguard in my own room?"

"A new guy will be with you. Colin has received threats directed at this concert. He needs experience there tonight."

Alexa nodded. Of course Jamison had to be there. "Be careful."

His shoulder shifted slightly nearer. "You care, princess?"

"Of course I don't want you hurt. Then who would cook me pizza?"

He chuckled, low in his chest, and his hand slid over hers. Her heart jerked out of rhythm, and the breath left her lungs when his fingers curled around hers. He lifted her hand to his lips. His black gaze held hers as he pressed a warm kiss to her skin. "Thanks, Alexa." Slowly, he turned her fingers, and his lips grazed her pulse point.

Alexa stared at him, unblinking, lips parted. "What are you doing?" she squeaked.

"If I have to tell you, I must not be doing it right." His gaze held her disturbed one. "But I think I might be," he added softly.

She tugged her hand free. "That is quite enough. Thank you." She trembled inside, but couldn't let him see that. "I'm heading back."

They walked in silence back to the building, but Alexa was very aware of his presence beside her—and the proximity of his arm when he pulled open the door for her. Good thing he was going out tonight. Her hormones were surely whacked out. Hopefully by tomorrow they'd be back under control. She would do well to curl up in front of the television and watch a mindless show. In Italian—which she couldn't understand, and which would give her mind ample opportunity to wander.

Maybe she had better read a book. A mystery, though. Not a ridiculous love story.

❈ ❈ ❈ ❈ ❈

Alexa fell asleep in bed reading the murder mystery. She awoke sometime in the middle of the night, discombobulated. Her room was dark. But hadn't she fallen asleep with the lamp on? In her peripheral vision, the sheer curtains of the sliding door billowed. A breeze puffed into the room.

Her slider was open. Why? Alarm, like a spark of electricity, jolted her. But before she could move, claw-like hands appeared in her peripheral vision.

The talons strangled her scream.

Choking for air, Alexa grabbed the skeletal arms and writhed to free herself. The grip loosened, allowing her a shallow gulp of oxygen. "Ja..." But the maniacally strong fingers tightened again. *Where was Jamison?* Was he back? He would hear her, she knew it, if he was here.

But Alexa heard and saw nothing but the dark room and the ghostly figure over her, his stringy hair tangled around his contorted face. An awful stink came from him. She clawed at her neck, trying to loosen the fingers squeezing away her life. She couldn't die. She didn't want to die!

Frantic and desperate, she kneed the man, twisting her body to try to make solid contact. But the man turned, taking the brunt of the kicks on his side.

He was too strong. She couldn't budge his steely hands. Her world went gray, with popping white lights. Was this how it would end? With her life stolen...to never see Jamison again. To have no future?

Despairing fury ripped through her. *No!* She wanted to scream, but the air in her lungs was long gone. She clawed at the man's face, viciously ripping skin, tearing at his ears.

He cried out, and his grip loosened enough so she could gasp in another tiny breath, but then he bore down on her even harder, his white face twisted in grotesque wrath.

A black hulk hurtled into her attacker. With a hiss, the ghostly man jerked sideways and crumpled to the floor. Alexa gasped for oxygen. Her throat felt raw and painful. Although it hurt to breathe, the air tasted sweet and delicious.

On the floor, a silent struggle took place. Alexa watched, horrified, while she dragged in ragged breaths. She recognized her bodyguard's bulk, struggling to subdue the ghostly figure. Jamison! Fear cramped through her. What if the attacker had a knife, or a gun? But if so, why hadn't he used them on her?

The struggle was over within seconds. Jamison's knee dug into the ghost's back, and he wrenched the man's wrists backwards.

"Alexa. Get the lights and my cuffs. On my dresser."

She quickly switched on the lamp and gasped with relief. Jamison appeared to be unharmed. Only faint muscle flickers indicated the effort he made, pinning the "ghost" to the floor. He wore no shirt. Only black, silky boxers.

Jamison's eyes gleamed at her. "Cuffs," he repeated.

"Yes!" Alexa leaped to her feet. "I'll get them."

She ran across the empty sitting area to Jamison's room. The covers had been thrown to one side, but the rest of the room looked as neat as a pin. His cuffs lay on the dresser, along with his cell phone and wallet. She grabbed the phone, too, and sprinted to deliver them to Jamison.

He quickly snapped the cuffs on the stringy, gray-haired man. Her attacker wore a long, dirty white shirt and gray sweats. This lovely specimen twisted his neck to look at Alexa. The dark eyes looked demonic. He hissed. "You'll both die! My daughter will see to it."

His voice was familiar, as was the stink. "It's the guy who attacked me in Barcelona!" Alexa exclaimed.

Jamison looked grim. "Good. Thanks." He accepted the phone and dialed a number.

The stalker's last words finally registered. Alexa stared at the man. What daughter? Was there a third person involved in this stalker plot? Or four, if perhaps Paddy was the mastermind.

In her thin scrap of a nighty, Alexa suddenly felt vulnerable to her attacker's baleful eyes. Not to mention Jamison, who hadn't yet paid much attention to her. And the police would be coming. Grabbing a T-shirt and sweats, she hurried into the bathroom.

When she reentered the room, Jamison was still talking on the phone, torso tilted away from her, apparently to look at the clock. She realized anew that he wore nothing but the black silk boxers. Her eyes greedily scanned him, taking advantage of his momentary distraction.

Thick muscles rippled across his broad back. He slowly turned, still talking in rapid Italian, so his side faced her. She moved closer. His torso was deeply tanned, and a faint 'v' of dark hair matted his chest. Sculpted, hard muscles outlined his chest and arms.

Belatedly, she realized that he had snapped the phone shut and now watched her ogle him. A flush burned her cheeks. She blurted, "When are the police coming?"

"Soon." He dragged the man to his feet and shoved him into the living room.

The next two hours passed in a blur. Jamison grilled the attacker for information on his briefly mentioned daughter, but the man clammed up. Alexa made coffee for the officers, and even drank some herself, although she hated the bitter stuff. She was exhausted after the adrenaline wore off. But she had to stay awake in order to answer the police officers' endless questions. Jamison helped her, of course, but she was so tired she wished they would leave. Finally, they exited, and the prisoner spat more warnings as the police marched him away. It was three o'clock in the morning.

Alexa yawned. "Do you think that'll be the end of the threats?"

"Maybe," Jamison said. "But it sounds like he's got a daughter out there."

"Could she be as loony as her parents?"

"We have to be prepared for that possibility."

Alexa's old suspicions returned. "And what about Paddy? What have you found out about him?"

"He's clean. But a few years back he was in deep debt to two bookies."

"Gambling?"

Jamison nodded. "Horseracing. He rarely goes to the track anymore."

So, either Paddy had quit betting on horses, or he had secretly gone deeper into debt. Maybe he desperately needed Colin's bonus money to pay off his hidden vice.

"I see that suspicion in your eyes, princess. Don't worry. I asked my contact to keep digging."

"Good." Alexa suddenly remembered the heightened security that evening. "Was there an attack at the concert?"

"No. I think they meant to target you here. I'd only been home a few minutes when I heard a sound come from your room."

Tears burned her eyes. "I knew you'd come." She blinked them back. "I guess I owe you another thanks for saving my life."

"It's my job."

"Why do you do that?"

"Do what?"

"Refuse to accept praise."

"I should accept praise for doing my job?"

"For doing it well."

"Thank you," he said, and offered a faint smile. Alexa smiled, too.

Another thought crossed her mind. "Don't you think it's strange that I'm the only one who's been attacked? I mean, I'm glad Colin is safe, but..." She trailed off.

"It is strange," he agreed grimly. "We need to find out why you're the only one being targeted."

"When we know that, we'll probably solve the case."

"Hopefully, my contacts will turn up leads soon."

Before it was too late. He didn't have to say this, but a shiver went down Alexa's spine anyway.

Jamison moved to the sink to wash out his coffee cup. He wore a white T-shirt now that advertised his home town in Italy, and black jeans. The T-shirt looked soft and well-washed. It hugged his torso and clung to the muscles of his upper arms. The white accented his deep tan.

Alexa's mouth ran before she could stop it. "I've never seen you in white before."

"Should I be flattered you notice every detail of my state of dress—or undress?"

Alexa's face burned, remembering how she had been caught staring earlier. "Excuse me for being observant," she said stiffly.

He apparently decided to cut her some slack. "This shirt is fifteen years old. My sister Sophia gave it to me for my birthday."

"I thought it looked old…and soft. Is it?"

Jamison stared at her, and then paced closer. "Would you like to find out?"

Alexa's breath caught in her throat. "Back off, Jethro. I'm not asking to feel you up." She yawned hugely. "Sorry to disappoint you."

"Go to bed, princess."

Alexa thought about returning to her room. The slider lock was broken. And the memories of the man's hands choking the life from her…

She shuddered. "I think I'll stay up for awhile. Maybe watch some TV." Not likely. Alexa was so tired that she stumbled on the way to the couch. With a sigh, she slid down on the soft leather and tucked a pillow under her head. The remote rested on the coffee table. Jamison's hand scooped it up at the same instant she reached for it. He deposited it in the chair across the room.

"Hey." She frowned.

A soft blanket fell across her shoulders, and Jamison appeared, very near, now. *He's sitting on the coffee table, that's why,* her foggy brain computed.

"Sleep, princess."

"I'm not tired," she yawned.

She felt, rather than heard his chuckle. His lips brushed her brow and he stood. "I'll leave my door open. Call if you need me."

Alexa lifted her heavy head. "Will you stay until I fall asleep?" The words sounded childish and pitiful, but she was afraid.

Jamison sat down on the coffee table again. His hand closed around hers, warm and strong. "Of course I will."

"Thank you," she mumbled, and slowly drifted toward sleep, feeling his warm hand holding her secure.

He murmured soft Italian words, then more familiar English ones, from Psalm 56:3. "Whenever I am afraid, I will trust in you." NKJV™ The quiet verse comforted her soul.

In this crazy ship of stalkers and an international star's limelight, God was her anchor. And Jamison was His right-hand man. She would be safe, as long as he stayed with her.

CHAPTER SIXTEEN

THEY TRAVELED TO ZURICH, Switzerland the next morning, and the next few days passed quickly. The book was nearing completion, and Alexa met with Colin to flesh out the last segments. When Colin spotted the make-up muted bruises on her throat, left from the attack, he was appalled. However, Alexa assured him that she was fine and healing rapidly. The stalker had been caught, and that was the most important thing to her.

Unfortunately, during this meeting frosty Eve was also present, which didn't give Alexa the opportunity to tell Colin about her feelings—or lack of romantic feelings—for him. If the chance presented itself, she would tell him. In fact, the sooner the better.

Alexa loved Switzerland. She loved the precise symmetry of Zurich, the clean streets, and the clocks. Charming buildings on narrow streets sported windows framed by dark shutters, and red flags with the Swiss cross fluttered above shop doorways in Old Town.

Alexa took all of Wednesday afternoon off in order to sightsee with Jamison—after first changing travelers checks into Swiss francs. They toured the Swiss National Museum first, which reminded Alexa of a fairy castle. She enjoyed seeing the paintings, toys, clocks, flags, and other objects of Swiss culture collected over the years.

Then they took a walking tour of the Bahnhofstrasse, a beautiful, tree-lined street with world banks and pricey shops selling luxury merchandise. It reminded her of Fifth Avenue in New York.

Jamison patiently waited while Alexa wandered through several shops, fingering linens and embroidered napkins. She finally bought a set for her mother, and bought Swiss Army knives for Ted and her father. And in the Schweizer Heimatwerk, she found wooden folk toys for Annie and Timmy. One thing Alexa repeatedly noticed while shopping was the marked difference between some of the noisy tourists and the softer spoken Swiss sales clerks. Not that Alexa was noisy, but it made her want to speak quietly, too.

As the afternoon slowly waned, Alexa couldn't resist stopping at the Confiserie Sprüngli, which, according to her guidebook, was famous for its chocolates. She bought a box of chocolates for Beth and a bag for Jamison and herself to enjoy later, and then hurried on to the Fraumünster church. It looked Gothic to Alexa, with its majestic spire. In the choir, Marc Chagall's tall, narrow stained glass windows, each of a different predominant color, were stunning.

After that, they visited the Grossmünster, the two-towered cathedral across the River Limmat from the Fraumünster. Augusto Giacometti's three soaring panels of stained glass in this choir were breathtaking, too. Alexa and Jamison elected to pay a small fee and climbed up into the southern tower. At the top, they enjoyed a breathtaking view of Old Town and Lake Zurich.

Afterward, Alexa sat with relief on a bench overlooking Lake Zurich. She plopped the bags at her feet. "I'm tired," she sighed.

Jamison smiled, and for a peaceful while they watched motor boats and sailboats glide by in the clear blue, early May evening. Until Alexa's stomach growled, and she remembered her bag of chocolates.

"Want some?" She offered the open bag to Jamison.

"Sure." He took two.

"Do you do this all the time?" she asked. "I mean, travel to all of these neat countries and sightsee?"

"Most of the time I work with Colin. I don't get much time to sightsee."

"So baby-sitting me has its perks."

He shot her a small smile. "Perks. That's one way to put it."

She elbowed him. "You're not very appreciative of the benefits I provide you."

"And what benefits would those be?"

Alexa fluttered her hand, encompassing the beautiful scenery. "You get to sample all this, along with me."

His lips pressed together, obviously trying to suppress a grin.

"What?" she demanded.

"You choose unusual word combinations, Alexa. Are they deliberate?"

"Huh?"

"I get to sample all this, and you, too?"

With a gasp, she swatted his leg. The black denim felt warm from the sun, and the muscles beneath, hard. She hastily retracted her hand. "No, you do not get to sample me, you lascivious man!"

"Now there's a mouthful."

Sweetly, she inquired, "Do you know what it means?"

"Yes. Shall I prove it?"

Her face felt warm. "This conversation is inappropriate. And I'll thank you not to make a move on me."

"I hadn't thought of it. But at your suggestion..." His arm slid behind her on the bench top. His fingers lightly curled around her shoulder. A few inches still separated them, but his smiling, testing black gaze seemed too close.

Alexa stiffened, and then told herself not to be a ninny. Forcing herself to relax, she smiled. "You make a good escort, Jamison."

He chuckled, deep in his chest. "Good thing you're not paying for my services, or I might take offense."

Alexa fidgeted. That man always had a comeback for every mouthy comment with which she slapped him.

"Uncomfortable, princess?"

She gave him a look. "It's time to head back, don't you think?" The sun now edged lower on the western horizon, casting a muted, golden haze over the lake. A small breeze had kicked up too, and Alexa felt chilly. She zipped her jacket to her chin.

"Cold?" her bodyguard asked. "Scoot closer to me."

Alexa gaped. "In your dreams, Jethro." Although she did remember how warm his leg had felt, and imagined snuggling up close to him, under his arm.

She struggled to dismiss her idiotic fantasies. Arms crossed tight, Alexa stared out at the lake.

"I don't bite." His low Italian voice lilted, suspiciously close to her ear. "I promise."

Alexa glanced at him in complete astonishment. "Jamison Jethro Constanzo, you *are* making a move on me!"

He smiled. "What do you think about that?"

She didn't know what to think. Or say. Except a little imp insanely urged her to lean over and kiss him. Of course, she didn't.

"Last chance," he told her.

"What?" For a flabbergasted second, Alexa wondered if he had read her mind.

He urged her closer. Against her better judgment, she did scoot nearer, until his warm thigh touched hers and she was tucked close under his arm, by his side.

"It's just because I'm cold," she told him. A whiff of his unique, spicy scent teased her nose. What cologne did he use? Forever from now, when she smelled it, she would think of Jamison.

Sadness poked her at the thought of a future without him in it. She pressed nearer to him, wanting this moment to last forever.

"What?" he said.

"Nothing." She swallowed back the ache in her throat.

"It's not nothing." His free, warm hand closed over hers. "Your hands are like ice."

"I get cold easily."

The hand on her shoulder lifted, and his fingers threaded through her hair.

"Jamison," she said. His quiet, intent gaze caught hers, and his fingers stroked the back of her neck. "I thought we weren't going to do this."

"Do what?" Amusement glimmered.

"You're trying to seduce me."

"How am I doing?" Point blank. A deliberate admission. He *was* pursuing her. Both excitement and anxiety churned in her, but mostly his declaration thrilled her to the core.

Jumping nerves inspired her next words. "Maybe we'd better go—before we do something we regret. Again."

When he leaned forward, it was clear he intended to kiss her. Weak-willed as she was, she met him halfway. Gentle purpose warmed his kiss, edged by carefully controlled passion. When he pulled back, Alexa followed him. And then she realized he had meant to end the kiss.

"Oh," she gasped, embarrassed, and pulled back.

He grinned, obviously pleased by her response. Luckily, he didn't know how hard her heart pounded, but no flip words could deny her obvious desire to kiss him.

"Why?" she asked, trying to understand.

"Because I wanted to kiss you."

She pulled away. "Jamison, I'm leaving next week. We need to be careful."

"Isn't it too late to be careful, princess?"

Alexa was afraid he was right. "Let's go," she begged. "I want to write more tonight."

When he stood, he held out his hand.

"Jamison."

He just looked at her, and she put her hand into his. It felt good and right to hold his hand. She felt secure in his clasp and never wanted to let go.

It scared her to death.

Back at the flat, Alexa closeted herself in her room, both to write and to put distance between herself and Jamison. They had crossed the line again, and part of her desperately wanted to jump back to the safe side. What had she been thinking? It couldn't be too late, could it? She couldn't be losing her heart to Jamison. She just couldn't.

❈ ❈ ❈ ❈ ❈

"The threats have stopped," Jamison told Alexa the next morning.

"Great!" Or was it? If she was no longer in danger, would she need a bodyguard? The thought of Jamison moving out caused a tight, uncomfortable feeling in her chest. Of course, she would be flying home next week, no matter what. That didn't rest any easier in her heart. "But what about the daughter the man mentioned?"

"Apparently he doesn't have a daughter."

"He doesn't? Did he make that up?"

"We don't know. Interpol is working with the FBI to unlock court documents."

Alexa pondered this bizarre turn of events. "Maybe he's lost his mind," she suggested.

"Not likely. I have a gut feeling there's more to the story."

"So until they find out, you'll stay my bodyguard?"

"Afraid you'd lose me?"

Alexa scoffed at his knowing smile. "Please." She struggled, as she had since last night, to find a barrier to protect herself. She couldn't lose her heart to a man she'd say goodbye to in a week. She just couldn't. Unfortunately, the old, porcupine repartee came to her rescue. "I'm counting the days until I can be rid of you."

"When do you fly home?"

As if he didn't know. "Next week. I suppose you're saying you can't wait to get rid of me."

"Did I say that?"

"No." She turned away, fiddling with her tea cup.

"How's your book coming?" His voice was quiet.

"Good." She turned back. "I think one more session with Colin should finish it."

"How will you feel about leaving him?"

The black gaze didn't leave hers. For the first time, she could tell he wanted—no, that intense gaze *demanded*—to know what she felt for the famous pop star. "I'll be sad. I always hate to say goodbye to friends."

"Not heartbroken?" His voice sounded rough.

"Do you think I'm in love with him, Jamison?"

"Are you?"

Alexa rethought what she felt for Colin. She liked him. Colin was a wonderful, vulnerable man. She felt oddly protective of him, and knew he liked her. In fact, she hoped he didn't like her too much. "No. I'm not in love with Colin."

A smile tugged at his lips. "So you can leave without looking back?"

Could she? She would miss Colin and Mart. But the person she couldn't face leaving was this complicated man, beside her. "Not exactly. I've gotten used to having my own, personal chef."

He chuckled. "You'll miss me?" Despite the light words, his dark eyes held hers.

This conversation was heading in a disturbing direction. Alexa didn't want to say goodbye to him at all, but could barely admit this truth to herself. She retreated to the couch. "I'll miss sharpening wits with you."

He followed, which disturbed Alexa still more, and perched on the armrest. "You don't want to talk to me, princess?"

"Will you please stop calling me that?" But she said it with no heat.

He moved down to the couch, beside her. She narrowed her eyes. "Don't come any closer."

"You're still afraid of me?"

"Of course not," she scoffed. Ungrammatically, she finished, "What do I have to be scared of?"

"You tell me, Alexa. We never seem to finish this conversation."

She looked away. Why did she keep running from him?

The terrifying answer came, hard and fast. Jamison already had a grip on her heart. If she allowed him any closer, he'd steal it, irrevocably and forever. Leaving him then just might destroy her.

She couldn't handle that kind of hurt again. Shouldn't she keep the distance between them? How could she willingly step into heartbreak?

Her throat ached. Time for a subject change. "How did you become a bodyguard, anyway? You never told me."

A small moment of silence ticked by. Then, to her relief, he followed her change of topic. "I stepped into it backwards."

"What does that mean?"

"It means I graduated with a degree in Comparative Literature, which is basically useless, and I didn't know what I wanted to do with my life."

"Literature? You?" Alexa found this hard to believe.

"I like poetry. What can I say? I also majored in Business, with a Kinesiology minor. I was interested in exercise and nutrition."

Alexa blinked. "You double majored? With a minor? How long did it take you to graduate?"

"Five years. But I didn't want to get a master's or a Ph.D., and I didn't want to go into business yet. I wanted to travel the world."

"So how did the bodyguard angle come about?"

"I worked out a lot, and got to know guys in the field. One recommended a bodyguard school, so I took courses and graduated from that. Afterward, I got my first job. I liked it, and took more courses from the International Bodyguard Association in London in order to improve my skills. I met Colin when I was guarding a female star. He visited her often, and we became friends. Things cooled off between them, and when he lost a guard later, he asked me to join him. I decided it was time for a change." Harshness twisted the last words.

Alexa pounced on this. "Change? Why?"

"The woman liked to wrap men around her finger. When Colin left, so she went after me. Desperate, I know."

"I'm sure she wasn't desperate."

"I had a thing for her, even before I started working for her. I let her attention go to my head. Before I knew it, I was in way too deep. Soon, she got bored with me. She started dating another star at the same time she strung me along."

"Jamison." Alexa put her hand over his. "I'm sorry."

He looked at their hands, and then pulled his away. "She was the most beautiful woman I'd ever seen. I was a fool to think she had real feelings for me."

"Jamison. Not everyone is like her. She was the foolish one."

"Really, Alexa?" His hard gaze bored into her, and she remembered how he had been prejudiced against her from the beginning, because he'd labeled her a beautiful woman. Now she understood why.

"I'm not her, Jamison."

"You're similar. You play games, too. You are right now."

"How can you say that?" she said, appalled. "We *both* play games. And I'd appreciate it if you'd stop judging me based on my appearance!"

"You judge me."

Because he was shorter than she was—it was funny, but lately she had stopped noticing. He was a wonderful man. Even if it meant opening up her heart to a truth that scared her, Alexa had to make Jamison understand a little of what she saw in him.

"You're..." she heaved a fortifying breath, "...nice looking."

"Don't choke on it."

She glared. "I'm not. I don't want you to get a big head."

"You think that's a problem?" He regarded her, his eyes still hard. Why? To hide his anger—or his hurt?

"It's difficult for me to say positive things to you."

"Why?"

"Because I'm afraid."

"That I'll take it the wrong way?"

No. She was more afraid he'd take it the right way. Which was that she was too drawn to him for her own good, and that terrified her.

He said, "So you think I'm nice looking."

"*Very* nice looking." She bit her lip and glanced away.

He remained silent, so she looked back at him.

"You mean that." He smiled a little, searching her gaze.

"Yes. I do." She stared at him, daring him to make something of it.

He leaned forward. "Is this progress, princess?"

"I'm just trying to tell you the truth."

"Come out with me tonight," he said quietly, unexpectedly.

"Why?" Trepidation edged the word.

His smile edged higher. "A restaurant I know serves the best chocolates in the world."

"That's not fair. You know I have a weakness for chocolate." As she had a weakness for him.

"Will you come?"

"For the chocolate, of course."

"Of course...only for the chocolate. Six o'clock work for you?"

"Fine. I'd better get to work, then." She left the sitting area with undo haste, and closed her bedroom door. What had she just done? Agreed to a real date with Jamison? Had she lost all of her marbles?

What a foolish girl she was. This date would only bring them closer together. Or was that what she wanted?

Yes. Alexa closed her eyes, unable to ignore this relentless truth. But she had made it clear it was only about the chocolate. Surely he would take her at her word.

But when had words ever been simple between them? As always, they hummed with double meanings, flirting with the truth of the attraction between them.

She crossed the room to stare into the mirror. Her blue-green eyes, looking disturbed and serious, confronted her. What was she doing? Was she truly leading him on, with no intention of anything else, like that hussy of a star had done? After all, where could their relationship possibly lead? Nowhere. She would go home soon. And Alexa wouldn't hurt Jamison for anything. She cared about him too much.

But she did want to go...and taste the chocolates.

❊ ❊ ❊ ❊ ❊

They drove from Zurich to a small town nestled near the base of the Swiss Alps. The scenery on the way was breathtaking, especially the gray, craggy mountains which grew closer and larger with each kilometer they drove. Pristine white snow clung to the peaks.

The restaurant was beautiful. Wooden beams arched overhead, and on the tables were candles in cut crystal glasses. A wall of windows offered Alexa a breathtaking view of the Swiss Alps. Even though it was well past 7:30 P.M., the sun had yet to reach the far horizon. A terrace edged the back of the restaurant, but it was too chilly for anyone to eat outside tonight.

Jamison settled across the table from her, his eyes gleaming. "Like it?"

"How could I not? It's beautiful." And disconcertingly romantic, too, for the dim lighting cast his face into shadows. In fact, those same shadows cut his nose and mouth into chiseled planes. Discomfort prickled. She should be staring at the menu, not admiring him. Wouldn't that be for the best?

Unfortunately, she recognized few words on the page. "I suppose you speak German, too?"

"Not much. But I can try to interpret. What do you want?"

"A chicken something would be good."

"Living dangerously, are you?"

Alexa sent him a look. "And what are you going to eat?" she inquired sweetly. "A bloody steak? Seems like that would be right up your alley. In fact, I could see you as the type to hunt it down and rip into it fresh."

"Are you disparaging my character again?"

"Never." She raised her eyebrows. "I never said you were a Neanderthal."

He laughed. "Sheathe the claws, princess, or you can pay for dinner."

She smiled. "You want me to be nice to you?"

"Until dessert. Then you can sharpen your tongue again."

Feeling a bit uncomfortable with her cutting wisecracks, she studied her indecipherable menu. Why did she always resort to flippancy whenever her heart threatened to open up to him?

It was simple. She was afraid.

Jamison leaned over and quietly pointed out a few items she might enjoy. She decided on meatloaf and mashed potatoes.

Once the waiter took their order and departed, she said, "Thank you."

A black brow raised. "Can't let you starve."

"I'm sorry," she blurted, and then bit her lip. "I mean about calling you a Neanderthal. I don't know why I say things like that."

His hand closed around hers, impelling her to meet his dark gaze. "Don't you?"

Wasn't it time to be honest? Even if it did make her vulnerable. "You're right. I'm afraid of this whole date thing with you. Remember, last time didn't end so well."

"Why do you want to live in denial, Alexa?" His hand felt warm and gentle around hers. His thumb stroked the back, disturbing her.

"I want it to be about the chocolate. And seeing if we can be civil to each other for one whole evening." And she did. In fact, she very much wanted to enjoy a warm, intimate dinner with him. Could she do it without pushing him away, and still not irrevocably lose her heart to him? Maybe she was a coward, but the threat of falling in love with him terrified her. Then leaving him next week would rip her soul apart.

He exhaled softly. "All right. I'm game to try if you are." She felt loss when he released her hand.

"Okay."

"I'll start us out." His Italian accent had thickened, and the dark gaze held hers. "You are beautiful as always tonight, Alexa."

She glanced away. "No need to go overboard."

"Accept a compliment, princess."

His compliment fizzed in her stomach. It was dangerous, because she liked it. "Thank you." Her gaze skittered from his. "How did you find this restaurant?"

"A friend told me about it. I needed a place to bring a date."

"A date?"

"I'm a man, Alexa. I date. And sometimes groupies latch onto bodyguards. I could go out as often as I'd like."

Colin had said as much in Paris. Jealousy squeezed Alexa's heart.

"I'm sure you could." She fiddled with her glass. The thought of some vapid hussy fawning over Jamison bothered her. More than she wanted to admit.

"Some women actually find me attractive." He grinned.

"I'm sure more than a few." Now, what had she done, stroking his ego like that? She would create a monster, if she wasn't careful.

Then she mentally rolled her eyes. Porcupine mentality again. Jamison deserved far more than one praise. He was a wonderful man.

Jamison's grin widened. "Another compliment? In one night? Careful. It might go to my head."

Alexa liked seeing him smile like that, in pleasure. With a return smile, she softly teased, "As long as you realize that's your full quota for tonight."

Dinner arrived, and the meatloaf and potatoes melted in her mouth. "Much better than frozen," she told Jamison. Conversation during the meal remained warm and civil. No double meanings—well, some, but they were subtly teasing. Alexa enjoyed her time with Jamison. All over again, she realized how smart and funny he was. And he could converse on any number of topics in depth and with ease.

As the waiter cleared their dishes, she said, "You're obviously very smart, Jamison. Do you plan to stay a bodyguard?" Hastily, she added, "Not that it isn't a perfectly good career."

"No, I don't. I want to form a security service—the best in Europe."

"You do? Really?" Alexa was amazed by this latest insight into this complex man. "That's terrific."

"Thanks. We'd do background checks, contract out the best guards, and offer top-of-the-line training. We'd specialize in personalized service to top athletes and stars. I've got a bunch of contacts already."

"Not to mention your reputation as being the best in the business."

Jamison dipped his head. "Eventually, I want to tie in personal training, too. Mostly for the guards, but also for any top athlete who wants to train. Security and a professional environment will be one of the foundations of my business."

"What great ideas. You've done the market research, I assume? Found your competition?" She wanted him to succeed, even now, in the fledgling idea stage.

"Yes. It's viable. I even have clients lined up—Colin being one. I've saved up half the capital I need to start, and I'm lining up backing for the rest."

Alexa was even more amazed. She had never guessed Jamison was contemplating—no, *planning*—to go into business on his own. "That's awesome. When do you plan to start?"

"Within a year, most likely. I enjoy what I'm doing for the moment."

"You like to travel."

He grinned. "Yes."

"No doubt you'll need to travel to attract the best clients from all over Europe. Or maybe you could set up facilities in several different countries."

"You've got vision, princess. I like that."

She lifted her glass. "To your future, and continuing success."

His glass softly clinked hers. "Thank you."

The waiter appeared with dessert menus in hand.

Jamison told Alexa, "I know what I'd like to order for dessert. I'd like to surprise you."

"Okay," she smiled, and realized that she had been doing a lot of that this evening. Should she be concerned about their deepening intimacy? Or continue to enjoy it? It wasn't hard to decide, although her choice was probably foolish.

Jamison spoke quickly to the waiter, and the man melted in the direction of the kitchen.

"When he comes back, humor me and close your eyes," he told her.

"I'm supposed to trust you?" Alexa raised her brows. "You aren't going to smash cake on my face, are you?"

His dark eyes gleamed. "Trust me, princess. Will you?"

"Okay," she agreed dubiously.

When the waiter returned, she obediently closed her eyes.

"Okay," Jamison said. "Open." He'd arranged his napkin to hide whatever was on his plate.

"Those aren't chocolate-covered frog legs, are they?"

"No frog legs."

"Or squid parts?"

He chuckled. "Just chocolate, Alexa, relax. Now close your eyes again, and open your mouth."

Anxiety mixed with sparkles of anticipation. Logic warned she shouldn't agree to this. It seemed too...intimate.

However, she fixed a saucy smile upon her face. "Okay. Here goes. But if you feed me toad gizzards, you'll pay."

He chuckled and a hard, square morsel entered her mouth. She savored it. "Mmm," she sighed. Pure ambrosia. Chocolate heaven.

"You can open now." The dark eyes laughed with her, enjoying her pleasure. "What kind was it?"

"This is a test?" she demanded, outraged.

"If you want the next piece, give me your best guess."

Alexa frowned. "Black-heart." She rolled her tongue around the inside of her mouth, trying to recapture the last bits of flavor. "I'd say pure dark chocolate. Seventy percent or higher."

"Correct. Close your eyes again."

"What's my prize if I guess them all right?" she wanted to know.

She heard his faint laugh. "I'll work on that later." Another morsel entered her mouth. His fingers gently brushed her lips as he retreated. Her lips tingled where he'd touched them, but she tried to forget that and focus on the chocolate in her mouth. It tasted creamier. Milkier.

"Easy," she proclaimed. "Milk chocolate."

"Two for two. I'm impressed. But it's going to get harder."

"Lead on," Alexa commanded feistily. "You won't stump me. I am the chocolate queen...princess."

"Okay, princess. Open wide."

A larger piece entered this time. Alexa felt very aware of one finger touching her lip, while two others deposited the confection on her tongue. Warm heat pumped through her blood as he withdrew. She tasted, slowly. The outside of the morsel tasted milky and bland, but as that layer melted in her mouth, another layer emerged. That one was more milk chocolatey. And then that layer melted, leaving the sharp, pure core of the chocolate she loved best.

She opened her eyes and favored him with a pitying grin. "You can't fool me, Jethro. White chocolate on the outside, with milk chocolate next, and a dark chocolate core. Pretty tricky, but not tricky enough for the master chocolate connoisseur."

"Okay, Miss Connoisseur. One left. It's a little more tricky. Be patient."

Tricky? Patient? Whatever could he mean by that? And why was her heart suddenly pumping faster?

"Don't mind my finger. It's clean. Pretty much, anyway."

Why would he warn her about his finger? Like a trusting little bird, she opened her mouth. A sweet, pasty substance touched her tongue. It had the texture of nougat, and it stuck to his finger.

"Lick it off, princess," he said roughly.

She gave his finger a tentative swab. The creamy paste was delicious. She wanted more, but the bulk of it still clung to his index finger. Why hadn't he presented it to her on a spoon, she wondered inconsequentially. She gave it a bolder swipe, and more melted into her mouth. Alarmingly, Alexa wanted to suck the last of the sweet goodness off his finger. And not just for the chocolate. Heat burned her face, just thinking about it.

"Done?"

"Yes." He withdrew, leaving her alone with the sweet taste still in her mouth. But she couldn't seem to think about anything but his warm finger in her mouth, and her reaction to it. Her heart bumped and thundered in alarm. This would not do. This would not do at all!

She blinked her eyes open, and found him watching her with an intensely black, hooded gaze.

"I...I didn't get enough of that one to make a guess," she gulped.

"Would you like more?"

"Not...not like that," she squeaked.

"A spoon?"

"Yes. Please."

"Guess first."

"But I can't!"

His gaze touched her lips. "Sure you can. And then I'll give you a spoon, and all the chocolate you want."

"I don't want any more chocolate."

"Why?"

Why couldn't she look away from him, would be a better question. She couldn't find a comfortable answer for that, either.

"It's too rich," she said.

"Intoxicating?"

She swallowed hard, and nodded. "Intoxicating."

She sensed, rather than saw him reach out to cup her chin. He leaned toward her, urging her closer. "Jamison..."

"Shh," and his lips burned into hers. They tasted sweet, like he'd been sampling the chocolates, too.

"Yum," she whispered. Tentatively, she tasted him with her tongue.

"Alexa!" he growled harshly.

"Can't I cheat?" she whispered. "I needed another taste."

He pulled away, but his black gaze held hers. "Make your guess, then."

"Chocolate nougat," she murmured, "mixed with caramel. And cherry."

His thumb slowly grazed her lips. "Yes. What prize do you want?"

Alexa wanted to kiss him again. But that would be purely stupid. And dangerous. Right?

She pulled away. "Take me for a walk on the terrace. The mountains look so close. Like I could touch them."

"Like your fairy tale you keep chasing?"

"Maybe." She had never seen the similarity before. Both beautiful, both untouchable, at least from where she stood now.

Jamison laid several bills on the table. "What would you do if your fairy tale came true? Would you keep it, or run away?"

"I'm not a coward," she protested.

His hand cupped her elbow and he led her onto the empty, chilly terrace. They leaned against the far rail, looking up at the immense, snowcapped Alps, bathed in moonlight. The late evening twilight had finally deepened into night.

"I'd like to climb them," she said suddenly. "Imagine the view from the top."

"It must be incredible," he agreed. Silence elapsed. "But at some point you'd have to come back to earth. To us mortals."

"It would be lonely up there," she admitted, and shivered. "Cold, too, probably." All she could think was that she would like to come back to this man and be warmed in his arms. Forever.

"Alexa..."

"Jamison. I think I want to go home now." Maybe she was a coward. But how could Jamison possibly be the right man for her? Didn't they squabble all the time? And next week she would fly back home and never see him again. Right?

"Are you running now, princess?"

"I'm cold. Please take me home."

"Okay." He ushered her back inside, made sure all was square with the waiter, and then drove back to the apartment building.

Inside their living room, Alexa peeled off her coat and draped it over her arm. She hugged it to her stomach, like a shield. "Thank you, Jamison. I had a lovely time."

His intent gaze held hers. "And the chocolates?"

"Delicious." She bit her lip.

Gently, he said, "Good night, Alexa."

"Good night." She closed her bedroom door and leaned against it. What had she just done?

They had overstepped the boundaries, yet again. She had known a date would be a bad idea. She had warned herself. But she was as helpless to resist Jamison as she was her favorite chocolates. It scared her.

Wasn't he all wrong for her? He met almost none of the physical attributes she had desired in a man since she was fourteen. As far as character qualities; well, he aced those. He was a Christian, a man of impeccable integrity, and she respected him. Did she look up to him?

A few weeks ago, that question would have made her giggle hysterically. The answer wasn't so funny anymore.

CHAPTER SEVENTEEN

ALEXA WOKE WITH LAST night's memories still warm in her mind. The chocolates. Jamison's kiss. The relaxation of sleep had lowered her defenses, and the truth of her feelings swamped her. Her heart ached for him and useless tears burned. Was it too late?

More truths unrolled in this moment of clarity. From the beginning, she had pushed Jamison away, for he brought out her fiery, spicy side—her true self. As a teen, she had alternately tried to bury it, or had used it as a weapon to protect herself. Lately, she had fervently wielded it to push Jamison away. It hadn't worked. Alarmingly, he had dug deeper into her heart.

He had made her face the fear that strangled her.

Jamison wasn't her father. He would never hurt her, as her father had inadvertently hurt her mother. Although both were physically strong men, that was where the similarity ended. Even during his violent struggle with the stalker in Rome, Jamison had remained in complete, tightly leashed control. Never would he succumb to a hysterical screaming fit, like her parents had done. Never would he allow his emotions to get the better of him. Never.

Alexa trusted Jamison completely, with her whole heart and her life. She had never met a man with such bone-deep integrity. On top of that, he was generous, honorable, and unselfish, just like the gallant knights of old. A faint smile curved her mouth. Had she wanted a knight all along, instead of a prince? He made her feel like a princess—like the most beautiful woman in the world.

She wanted more with Jamison. So much more. It both elated and terrified her.

Today's verse from her daily devotional seemed heaven-sent.

"There is no fear in love. But perfect love drives out fear, because fear has to do with punishment. The one who fears is not made perfect in love." 1 John 4:18

Please take away my fear to love, Lord, and to be loved. She didn't want to be afraid any longer.

Alexa jumped out of bed and quickly dressed, unable and unwilling to deny her eagerness to see Jamison this morning. Was he back yet from working out? She popped her head out the door.

He was. Jamison stood in the kitchen buttering toast. Her heart gave a glad leap. "Good morning!"

He turned, and his smile warmed her from her toes up. "Morning, princess." His grin edged higher. "Did you brush your hair?"

Alexa's hand flew to her head. No. She had forgotten, in her rush to see Jamison. "I just came out for tea," she said loftily. "I'm not up yet."

He closed the distance between them. "I like it." His fingers slid a few strands of hair behind her ear. A quick breath caught in her throat. "There. Now you're presentable."

Her heart swelled, and she offered a small smile. "Thanks for taking care of me."

"Always." Seriousness darkened his eyes.

Agitation stirred, and she pulled away. Questioning her sanity, she trotted for the kitchen. What was wrong with her? Why was she already running from him? Didn't she want his attention?

"Have you made me breakfast?" Alexa put her hands on her hips, surveying the solitary omelette in evidence. "I see not. I guess I'll have to fend for myself."

Quietly, he chuckled. "I thought you just wanted tea."

"You discombobulated me." Oops. Now, why had she gone and admitted that?

He grinned. "So you admit it."

"I admit nothing," she told him, and filled her mug with water.

"Okay. Play that game for now." He carried his plate to the table. "I've got news."

"What news?"

"The woman escaped from the Paris police."

"What? *How?*" Horror gripped Alexa.

"While they were transferring her to another prison, she somehow escaped. They're looking to see if she had help. Maybe from the mysterious daughter."

"She's on the loose again?" Dread built in Alexa. Three days remained on the tour, plus three more in London. Would she be safe when she went home? Surely the authorities would catch the malicious woman before then.

But only if the woman came out of hiding. Which meant, only if she tried to attack Alexa again.

She drew a shaky breath. "I'll stick close to the flat for the next few days. I'm almost done with the first draft, anyway."

"Really."

"Don't sound so amazed, Jethro. I'm good at what I do."

"A book is a long assignment. I'm impressed you're finishing so quickly."

She smiled. "Thank you."

"When will you finish?"

"Today, for the most part. Colin said we can meet late tomorrow morning to iron out the last details. Then, in London, I'll finish polishing the rough draft and print it out before I go."

He nodded and unexpectedly said, "Will you come to breakfast with me tomorrow?"

"Another date?" Both pleasure and anxiety flared.

His brown gaze met hers. "Yes."

Despite all logic, and all the fear warning her to run while she still could, Alexa softly agreed. "All right."

"Eight o'clock okay?"

She wanted to say "perfect," but what about their ill-fated relationship was perfect? By accepting this date with Jamison, wasn't she sticking her head in the sand? Sure, she could enjoy their last days together—and how she did want to do that. But the end game would remain the same. Heartbreak. And wouldn't the pain grow more awful with every minute she spent with him, loving him more?

Love.

"Alexa?" Jamison frowned. "Are you all right?"

No, she most certainly was not! "Umm," she stammered. "I felt a sharp pain." In her heart! The stab of cupid's arrow slicing through her last, flimsy defense.

She struggled to redirect the conversation. "Um, eight o'clock sounds terrific. I'd better get to work, then." With haste, she retreated to her room. Unfortunately, she felt Jamison's puzzled gaze following her.

Alexa crumpled at the desk and clamped her arms over her head. No. She could not be in love with Jamison! *No.* Her mouth contorted into a soundless cry. Tears gathered, balling up into an ache in her throat.

No. *No, no, no, no, no!*

But it was too late. The feeble denials wouldn't change the truth. Helpless sobs wrenched her. Tears slicked her face and soaked her sleeves. She loved Jamison. She loved him with her whole heart.

When had it happened?

Did it matter? Another truth punctured her soul. From now on, every moment she spent with him would painfully deepen that love more and more.

Leaving him next week just might kill her.

❆ ❆ ❆ ❆ ❆

The next morning, Jamison waited for Alexa in the living area. She had dressed with care in nice linen slacks and a muted gold top. She wore flats, of course. Just for him.

He smiled when he saw her. "You look beautiful, as always."

"Thank you." He had dressed up in black jeans and a black shirt of a smooth, silky texture. She grinned. "I guess silk does go with cotton, after all."

"Like you and me, princess."

Alexa didn't know what to say to this, and followed him into the hall. "Where are we going?"

"A restaurant a block from here."

When Jamison pushed open the building's heavy glass door to the street, he reached for her hand, his gaze questioning but intent. It would be silly to deny her feelings for him now. What would be the purpose? She loved him. She wanted to hold his hand.

With a smile, she reached for him. He smiled, too, and they walked close together to a tiny restaurant. Lace curtains edged the bottom half of the windows, and inside, a blast of warmth and sweet smells enveloped them.

"Breakfast?" A waitress asked in accented English. "Come with me."

Soon they were seated across from each other at a small wooden table. Alexa slipped her paper napkin onto her lap and glanced about the room. An assortment of people populated the tiny café. Some were obviously tourists, if their camera bags were any indication, but others, possibly locals, conversed in quiet voices.

"What's a typical Swiss breakfast?" Alexa asked.

"Bread, butter, marmalade, cereal, cheese. Or anything you want."

Alexa perused the menu and spied something called Birchermuesli. It sounded like cereal. She tilted the menu toward Jamison. "What's in this?"

He read swiftly. "Looks like rolled oats, nuts, dried fruit, apples and honey."

"I'll get that," Alexa decided, "and milk."

Soon the waitress appeared and took their orders. Jamison chose a different cereal, with scrambled eggs on the side.

Alexa sipped water and said, "I love it here. I'd like to come back when I don't have to worry about being attacked."

"It's a nice place to honeymoon."

Alexa shot him a startled look. A warm sensation curled in her stomach. What had he meant by that? Certainly nothing concerning her. She couldn't read his gaze. "Probably," she agreed artlessly.

After the waitress delivered their drinks, Alexa said, "I've never asked you, Jamison, but what's your idea of the perfect woman? Italian, maybe? Or a fabulous cook?"

"I don't have set ideas like you do, Alexa."

"Oh, come, now. Surely you know what type of woman you're attracted to."

He smiled slowly. "You're ready to stop playing games?"

"I think so," she replied softly.

"All right. I said I'd tell you everything when you were ready. So here goes." His hands closed over hers. "I'm looking for a woman who is warm, funny, and sweet."

"Then you can't possibly be talking about me." Alexa couldn't stop the flip reply.

His hand tightened. "Don't mouth off to me, princess. Let me finish."

"Fine." But apprehension coiled in her middle. What if he wanted a dark-haired, voluptuous Italian woman? Someone of normal height, and possibly even a gourmet cook! None of those descriptions remotely applied to her.

Jamison stroked her thumb. "I see that wild look in your eyes, princess. Focus, here." She blinked and he continued, "I'm looking for a woman who will make me laugh. Even better, one who gets my blood pumping every time I see her."

Well, that might describe her. "And?" she raised her brow. "Is that it, Jethro?"

His dark eyes smiled. "You can't help yourself, can you?"

"I'm trying."

He lifted her hand and pressed a kiss onto the knuckles. Her heart melted into a warm, soft puddle.

He watched her. "Do I have your attention now?"

"Yes," she whispered, unable to look away.

"In case I haven't made myself perfectly clear, I'm attracted to *you*, Alexa."

She sighed, unable to help herself. Tender love bloomed like a bright, swiftly unfurling sunflower. "You're not so bad yourself, Jamison."

"Even though I don't meet your criteria?" His gaze searched hers.

She smiled. "God broke the mold when He made you. I never could have thought you up, all on my own."

He grinned, then. "I'll take that as a compliment."

"You should," she said softly.

He leaned over the small table and gently kissed her. Instant flame sizzled between them, but Jamison pulled back with a small smile. "Here's not the place. Later."

It was just in time, too, for the waitress arrived with plates of food.

"Yum," Alexa said. The smile she flashed Jamison suggested she meant more than the food.

Appreciation gleamed in his eyes, and they dug into breakfast in companionable silence. During the meal, they talked about Colin's tour; everything, except the fact she would fly home next week. Just as well. Alexa wanted to enjoy the fairy tale for a little longer.

After breakfast, she was pleasantly surprised when the waitress left them each with a piece of chocolate.

"Do they have chocolate with every meal?" Alexa wanted to know.

"Many times, at least in restaurants, that's true."

"I could definitely live here," Alexa approved, savoring the sweet morsel.

Holding hands, they slowly strolled back to the apartment building. He held open the door for her. Before she could help herself, she blurted, "Have you forgotten your promise, Jamison?"

"No." To her surprise, he tugged her into a secluded corner. "I haven't forgotten anything."

Her heart beat rapidly. "I didn't mean *here*," she hissed.

His hands curled around her waist and he gently drew her to him. "Now seems like a good time to me."

Alexa slid her hands over his hard, muscular shoulders, and Jamison kissed her. She felt breathless with the swell of love and need she felt for this man.

"What are you doing?" she whispered. "Everyone can see us."

"I won't kiss you in our flat. I won't touch you there, either."

Alexa understood. Temptation burned bright now. In their rooms, it might prove impossible to resist. She nodded.

His gaze held hers. "Have we reached an understanding?"

"Understanding?" Warmth, and the familiar anxiety churned through her. She pulled back.

Jamison exhaled softly. "Alexa..." He sounded warning. "It's time to stop running."

How could she admit her love for him? How could it ever work out? Surely, if she denied it, it would go away.

No, it wouldn't.

Helplessly, she said, "Jamison, I care about you so much." What weak, namby pamby words! "But..."

"But?" Grimness stiffened his features.

"I'm leaving in six days!" Someone had to be practical, here. "Don't you think *we* are not the best of ideas?"

"It's not the game plan I would choose. But I can't help what I feel for you, Alexa."

And she couldn't help what she felt for him. What was she going to do? "How did we get into this mess?" she whispered.

"We sparked from the first day we met."

So true. She had ignored his warning to back off the set, and had called him—and all short men—munchkins. And implied they were unacceptable dating material. He had radiated antagonism toward her from the get-go.

"You must be pleased with yourself," she told him.

He smiled. "Why?"

"Because you made me eat my words. I've been on two dates with you."

"More than that."

She looked away for a second. "Yes, more than that," she admitted.

"Alexa."

"What?"

"Can't we make it past this? I'd like to try."

Hope made her heart beat faster. "You would?"

"Do *you* want to make it work?"

She floundered. "But I live six thousand miles away!"

Pain etched lines into his features. "Yes. But I don't want to lose you."

And she didn't want to lose him. "How?" she asked simply.

"I have time off coming. I could fly to L.A. and stay with my aunt. We could date like normal people for a few weeks."

It sounded oh, so terribly wonderful and tempting to Alexa. "But then what?" she said, still trying to be logical. "I can't afford to fly to London and visit you more than once or twice a year. And you wouldn't be able to visit me much, either. And I've got my job. And probably another book tour. The publisher wants to put Colin's book on the fast track."

His fists briefly clenched. "You're saying no." He sounded bleak.

"No! I'm saying I *don't* know. I mean, I want to, but I don't see how it could possibly work."

"Try with me, Alexa."

She stared at him while hope and logic warred within her. Wanting to try. But petrified of loving him more and more deeply—and what if he didn't feel the same for her? Or what if he changed his mind and broke her heart? It would completely and utterly devastate her.

Did he truly love her? Or was he only attracted to her? She knew from painful past experience that physical attraction would soon fizzle out if nothing else was there. Now she was older, wiser. She desperately wanted Jamison to be the one. But she had to be careful.

"I'm scared," she whispered.

"Why? I'm serious about you, Alexa. Otherwise, I wouldn't even try." His black gaze held hers, intense, passionate, and pleading—something she had never, ever expected to see from him.

She drew a fortifying breath, "I..."

"Alexa, love!" She jumped, startled, when Colin appeared out of nowhere and slung an arm across her shoulders. "I've got a spot of time now. Why don't you come up and we'll hash out the last of the book?"

"Um." She glanced at Jamison.

"Go," he said. "But we're not finished."

Jamison was right, she admitted at last. They weren't finished. Wasn't it high time for her to gather up her courage? To face her fear, even if it ultimately meant unimaginable heartbreak? She loved him, and so she had to try. Otherwise, she would regret it forever.

She stood close beside Jamison in the elevator, hoping with her body language to convey a little of what she had decided. She felt his warm hand on her lower back as they crossed the hall to Colin's door. Inside, she smiled at him before he disappeared into the television room with Mart.

Eve appeared suddenly. She paled when she saw Alexa. "Colin," she said. "I need to speak to you."

"Later. Would you be good enough to leave Alexa and me alone for a few minutes? I need to speak with her privately."

Eve frowned, but disappeared into another room.

Puzzled, Alexa looked up at Colin. "What is it? Is it about the book? Because we're almost finished."

He shook his head, blue eyes serious. "Your time here is running out, Alexa."

"I know." How she knew that!

"I feel we've barely reached first base."

Alexa's brows twitched into a puzzled frown. "Colin..."

"We've passed the time for talk, don't you think?" His hands curled around her arms, he leaned toward her.

Alexa barely managed to squeak out a horrified, "Colin!" before he kissed her. He was an expert. She could tell this at once, by the way his mouth moved against hers. But she felt nothing, except for a flicker of affection. She put her hands on his chest, but before she could push him away, he pulled back.

His eyes looked quizzical. "And how was that?"

Black flashed out of the corner of Alexa's eye, and she turned.

Jamison. He stared at her, his face white beneath the tan. Hurt, disbelief...and then sudden fury blazed in his black eyes.

"Jamison." She stepped toward him.

He shook his head. Body movements stiff, he yanked open the penthouse door. It slammed behind him, ricocheting like a gunshot. Alexa gasped in a breath. *No.* She bolted for the door.

"Alexa." Colin caught her arm. "What is it?"

"Let *go*. Please!"

Frowning, Colin did so, and Alexa rushed into the hall. Jamison was gone. Tears burned her eyes.

What must he think of her? She had to make things right!

"What's his cell phone number?" she cried to Colin, running back into the penthouse.

He gave it to her, and she hastily punched it into her cell phone. Jamison had his cell with him at all times. She knew that. But now it rang and rang, without an answer. She hung up without leaving a message.

She would see him later. She had to make things right with him.

Colin's phone rang and he turned away, speaking in a low voice. Finally, he said, "Okay. I'll be right down."

"What is it?"

He frowned, looking puzzled. "The concierge says Paddy wants to speak to me downstairs. Don't go. I'll be back in a flash," he promised. "Mart! We're going out."

The two men disappeared out the door.

Alexa felt like a whirlwind had just whisked through her heart and her life, and so at first she didn't hear Eve's breathless, "Watch out."

She spun. "What?"

"Watch out!" Eve screamed, and from nowhere, a gray-haired woman hurtled toward Alexa. A knife glinted in her hand.

CHAPTER EIGHTEEN

Alexa barely had time to lift her hands in self-defense before the woman was upon her. Luckily, Alexa deflected the knife with her wrist. She felt dull pain, but that discomfort was forgotten as she fought for her life.

The woman thrashed at her, crazily stabbing the air. She grunted unintelligible words. Alexa looked wildly about for a weapon, a shield...something!

She spied a vase and lunged toward it. The knife caught at her blouse, ripping it, as she grabbed the vase and whirled, swinging the glazed orb. It glanced off the woman's shoulder, and the woman's frantic flailing paused; she shrieked—a high, warbling note of fury. Spit flew as she lunged for Alexa.

Alexa twisted and jerked back. Her calves hit the coffee table and she fell backward, arms flailing, onto the table. The knife arched toward her, but Alexa rolled in the nick of time. She landed on her back on the floor. The air *oomphed* out of her.

Somewhere nearby, Eve was still screaming.

Alexa swiftly sat up, knowing her position was completely vulnerable. The crazed woman pounced upon her, knife arcing toward her throat. Alexa caught her wrists in midair and struggled, fighting against the woman's maniacal strength. A fury of her own fortified her. This woman and her husband had made life a living hell for over a month, and she would not let this stalker kill her!

Alexa kneed the woman. She twisted her body, forcing the woman to the floor, and then, with both hands grabbed her knife-wielding arm and slammed it to the floor. Alexa slammed it again and again, blind with a fury of her own. When the woman tried to claw her, Alexa elbowed her sharply, with no mercy. And then the knife skittered free.

The woman screamed, long and piercingly, and yanked Alexa's hair.

"Stop it!" Alexa cried out. The old woman fought like a tiger, and suddenly Alexa toppled backwards again, off balance. A wicked light entered the woman's eyes. She loomed over Alexa, and pulled a tiny blade from nowhere. Holding it tight in her fist, she breathed, "Now."

"No!" This gulping sob came from Eve.

Distracted, the woman turned. Face horribly scrunched up, Eve clobbered the woman with a skillet. A dazed expression dulled the woman's eyes, and Alexa took the opportunity to wrench the knife free. She threw it across the floor.

"I'm sorry," Eve whispered.

The woman shrieked, "*No*. Eve!" Then, with a crazed look, she lunged for Alexa's neck and squeezed tight.

Alexa choked for air. Why didn't Eve help? But then a black body hurtled through the air, knocking the woman off Alexa.

Jamison.

Alexa gasped for oxygen, and Mart rushed to help subdue the woman. It was over within moments.

Jamison spun on his knees and moved beside Alexa, still on the floor.

"Are you okay?"

"Yes." She gulped in another cool draft of air.

His expressive dark eyes warred with multiple emotions—betrayal, pain...and then helpless capitulation as he leaned forward and kissed her. Bleakness simmered in his gaze. "Then that's all that matters."

Alexa gripped his shoulder. "Jamison," she said urgently, anxious to explain what had happened before.

He flinched, and closed his eyes. "Don't." A harsh note of self-disgust sounded in his voice. "Just don't. No more, Alexa."

He quickly rose and left her alone.

Colin and Eve looked on, each with varying degrees of horror on their faces. Paddy stood in the background, his arms crossed.

Paddy! All of Alexa's suspicions rushed to the forefront.

Her meeting with Colin this morning hadn't been a secret. Had Paddy called Colin downstairs so Alexa would be alone in the penthouse? Except for Eve, of course. Alexa struggled to sit up. The danger wasn't over yet.

Jamison marched the woman into the next room.

"Are you okay, Alexa?" Colin rushed to help her to her feet.

"I'm fine." She turned to Paddy. "Luckily Eve hit that woman with the frying pan. It didn't turn out quite like you thought it would, did it?"

Paddy frowned. "What?"

Alexa trembled now from reaction, and from fury. "Did you plan this? Has all of this been a publicity stunt? If so, it's gone too far!"

Paddy's hard gaze flicked to Colin. "What is she talking about?"

"I don't know. Alexa?"

Alexa trembled harder now. He meant to play innocent? Did he think he could get away scot-free? Voice shaking, she said, "How far did you plan to go? Did you actually pay her to kill me?"

Red darkened Paddy's bulldog face.

"Stop, Alexa." In a small voice, Eve spoke up. "It wasn't Paddy. This is all my fault."

The manager's mottled skin toned down a notch, while Alexa turned in surprise.

Eve turned to Colin. "I should have told you. But I just couldn't! I tried to make them stop." She burst into tears.

Colin slid an arm around her shoulders. Confusion wrinkled his brow. "What, love? What did you know?"

Eve looked helplessly at Alexa.

Comprehension finally dawned. "That woman is your mother, isn't she, Eve?"

The secretary nodded, sniffling. "And my father attacked you in Barcelona and in Rome."

Colin pulled away, his face paling. "You knew? They're your parents?"

"Yes," Eve wept. "I'm sorry, Colin. I told them to stop, but they wouldn't."

"Why would they do such a thing?" Alexa demanded.

"They're mentally unstable. That's why I was in foster care. When they take their medication they're fine. But they've stopped, and they got it in their heads that Colin should be with me." She sent Colin an apologetic look. "I wanted to tell you, but I didn't know how that would help. I didn't know where they were. I didn't know any more than you."

"But your father called you, when your mother was jailed in Paris." Alexa remembered the phone call. "You said your mother was in the hospital. Later you said it was your *foster* mother."

"Wait a minute," Colin said. "You mean to say you knew all along that your parents were threatening Alexa and me?"

Eve seemed to shrivel up within herself, but met his gaze. "Yes."

In the background, Paddy swore.

Anger flushed Colin's sharp features. "If we had known, the police would have had their descriptions sooner! We could have protected Alexa better. Your parents almost killed her four times!"

Alexa's heart pounded, staring from one to the other. "When did you know, Eve? From the beginning?"

"No! No, I didn't. I guessed first in Paris, when my father called and asked me to help get my mother out of jail. I wouldn't. And in Rome, I told him to stop, to go away."

"He was the man in the park. How did your mother get in here today?"

"I don't know."

"That message from Paddy was a fake. Eve's mother set it up to get Mart and me out of here," Colin said through his teeth. "You should have told us, Eve. Frankly, I feel I can't trust you anymore."

So Paddy hadn't asked the concierge to give Colin that message after all. Now Alexa felt terrible about her accusations.

"I understand," Eve whispered. "I'll pack my things."

"Wait," Alexa said. She had to know something. "You've hated me from the beginning. Did you want your parents to hurt me? To take me out of the picture with Colin?"

Eve's eyes narrowed. "Yes, I hated you. And I was wrong. I was scared, and I wanted to warn you off, but I never wanted you hurt. You've got to believe me. I'm sorry for all of the hateful, horrible things I've said to you."

"Why didn't you tell me about your parents?" Colin asked.

"I kept hoping they'd go away. I told them to stop, every time they called."

"And how often was that?" Colin sounded grim.

"Twice. Once in Paris. Once in Rome."

Colin ran a hand through his hair and turned away. "What a mess." The words sounded harsh.

Eve said, "They're my parents. I love them. I didn't want them to get into trouble. I wanted them to quit and go home. I tried so hard to make them see reason! I see now I should have done things differently."

Colin spun back. "Yes, you should have done things differently! I trusted you. When Alexa mentioned how you were treating her, I took your side. How could you do this to me?"

Tears slid down the secretary's face. "I never wanted to hurt you, Colin. I wanted to protect you. I thought Alexa was another one of those...those floozies. I'm so sick of them. They use you, and you use them!" She choked on a sob. "You deserve so much better."

"You mean that?"

"Of course I do!"

The two stared at each other, and Alexa suddenly felt like the third wheel. But she had one more thing to say. "Colin, Eve saved my life just now. She hit her mother with that pan. Yes, she was wrong not to tell us her suspicions about her parents. But their actions are not her fault. She tried to stop them. We all tried to stop them. The police knew their identities and descriptions. Her father wore disguises. Her mother escaped and made it all the way to Switzerland, undetected. How could we stop that?"

Eve cast her a surprised, grateful glance.

Colin shook his head. "Even so. You were wrong, Eve. *Wrong!*"

Eve jumped at the harsh lash of his voice. "You're right. I'm sorry. I'll leave immediately."

Alexa had once wondered about Eve's mental stability, but now everything made complete sense. Maybe Eve's hatred of her was over the top, but probably that was because she had loved Colin for so long, and had suffered through his many disastrous affairs. She had reached the snapping point with Alexa. And Alexa believed Eve's account concerning her parents. She believed they had acted on their own, without Eve's consent.

What a mess everything was. And that reminded Alexa of Colin's kiss, and of all the havoc she had caused by simply not telling him the truth about her feelings the moment she had realized what they were, back on that seventh hill of Rome.

"Colin," she said. "We need to talk about what happened before the attack."

He sighed, and tore his glance from Eve. "Dinner tonight?"

"Okay."

"I need to make some calls." Colin disappeared into his room, and Alexa was left alone with Eve and Paddy.

The manager headed for the door.

"Paddy, wait," Alexa said. "I owe you an apology. I'm sorry."

Paddy shrugged one thick shoulder. "Would've been a good publicity stunt, if I'd thought of it." With a hard click, the door closed behind him.

What had that meant? Would he have pursued the plan, if he'd thought of it? With a frown, Alexa turned to Eve.

The other woman wiped her tears. "So you get him, after all."

It took a moment for Alexa to realign her thoughts. "No. Colin's not the man for me."

"He's not?" Comprehension swiftly replaced incredulity. "Jamison."

Alexa looked away. "I don't see how he can be right for me, either. I forgive you, Eve. And I believe you. I hope things work out between you and Colin. Just treat him right."

"I will."

Colin reappeared, heading for his desk, and Alexa said to Eve on her way to the door, "He's all yours."

❈ ❈ ❈ ❈ ❈

Alexa realized after she got back to her room that her wrist was bleeding. In all of the excitement, she hadn't noticed. She bandaged it up and then tried to work, but that was useless. She kept listening for Jamison to return.

Finally, an hour later, a door click indicated that he had entered the flat. She hurried out, just in time to see his bedroom door shut. Fine. She plopped onto the couch, crossed her arms, and waited for him to come out. It didn't take long.

He exited his room, hauling his gigantic suitcase behind him. The stalkers were in custody. Clearly, she didn't need a bodyguard anymore, so he was moving out.

"Jamison!" She leaped to her feet. "Wait."

"You've made it perfectly clear whom you prefer." He headed for the door.

"Jamison."

He lifted his hand. "No more games, Alexa." He sounded weary. "No more games."

"I am not playing games!" In a flash, she knew what he was thinking. And why he was so angry. "I'm not like that starlet woman. I am not stringing you along!"

"Aren't you?"

"No!" she cried out, horrified.

"You wouldn't commit to me, even though I almost went on my knees, begging you. Instead, you kissed Colin." Fury burned in his black gaze. "You want him. You have all along. Don't deny it."

"No! It's not what you think. *He* kissed me. I'm going to dinner with him..."

"Stop!" He raised his hand. His harsh voice bit out, "I can't *take anymore*." He opened the door and shoved his suitcase into the hall.

"Jamison, stop!" She ran and grabbed the door.

Anger, tempered by resignation flashed in his eyes. His gaze fell to her bandaged arm and he went very still. "I'm sorry I wasn't there to protect you."

"It's okay."

He looked away, clearly unwilling to accept that. If she knew him at all, he was angry with himself for his failure. Finally, he looked back. A muscle clenched in his jaw. "I'm leaving, Alexa. Don't call me. I can't handle seeing you anymore."

She drew in a quick, dismayed breath. "Where are you going?"

"Goodbye, Alexa." The finality of that cold dismissal chilled her soul. And then he stalked down the hall and turned the corner, out of sight.

Alexa crossed her arms tight and choked on a sob. That stubborn man! Why wouldn't he listen to reason? And where was he going?

She ran to her room and cried until she ached.

✹ ✹ ✹ ✹ ✹

As soon as she had calmed down a little, Alexa called her sister. She needed a shoulder to cry on. Now she felt as angry with Jamison for not hearing her explanation as she did with herself for not handling things right.

"I hate him, Beth! And I hate myself," Alexa's voice broke. "I've messed everything up."

"What happened?" Her sister didn't even ask which man she was talking about.

"Jamison hates me. He saw Colin kiss me, and thinks I was kissing him back."

"Were you?" She heard curiosity in her sister's voice.

"Of course not! I don't love Colin. I told Jamison that, and I've told you that, too."

"So tell him again."

"He packed up and marched out of here. He doesn't want to speak to me. I think he's gone." Her voice caught.

"Gone where?"

"I don't know!"

"You've got to tell him the truth, Alexa. Call him, if you have to."

"Even if I did, how would it make any difference? I'm flying home in five days."

"Maybe you could work something out."

Alexa closed her eyes. "It's impossible, Beth."

"You can't leave without telling him the truth. It's not fair to either of you." Her sister sounded uncharacteristically stern. "Do the right thing, Alexa."

Beth was right. She couldn't leave with a misunderstanding between them. It would be stupid, and immature, too. "Okay. I'll tell him. I promise." If she ever saw him again. If he answered her phone calls.

"Good." Her sister sounded gentler now. "What can I do?"

"I think I'm going to be a mess when I come home." Alexa's voice wavered. "Can I stay with you for a few days?"

"You don't even need to ask. I'll make up the guest room for you. And I'll tell Ted you need another week off."

"Thank you, Beth. I don't know what I'd do without you."

Her sister laughed, but it sounded sad, too. "I told you not to leave your heart with a man in Europe."

Alexa didn't have the strength to deny it. All she wanted to do was cry.

❈ ❈ ❈ ❈ ❈

That night, she sat across from Colin in a small, intimate restaurant. A candle burned on the table, reminding her of the meals she had shared with Jamison.

"You're quiet tonight," Colin said. He had drunk none of the wine before him and sampled none of the bread. Much like Alexa.

She took a fortifying breath. "Colin, I need to tell you something."

"You have no romantic feelings for me."

Surprised, she said, "You know?"

"I guessed, after what happened today."

"I'm sorry, Colin. You're a wonderful man. In fact, I thought you might be the perfect one for me."

"And I thought you could be the woman for me."

"I'm so sorry. I should have told you sooner. I finally realized the truth in Rome."

"It's all right." He smiled, and his hand curled over hers and gave it a gentle squeeze. "We're still friends, though?"

She pressed his hand in return. "Always."

Colin's sharp eyes watched her. "When did you and Jamison stop fighting?"

"We haven't. Everything's such a mess." Alexa swallowed the lump in her throat, and picked up her water glass.

"I messed things up with you two, didn't I?"

"No. I did that. I wasn't honest with him, you, or myself about my feelings. And now it's too late. Where did he go?"

"Home."

"Italy?" Despair licked at her.

"Yes."

Would she see him again before she left for home? "Is he coming back to London?"

"Yes. Late Wednesday night."

She left on Thursday morning. Alexa bit her lip and held back tears. Nothing was turning out like she had hoped. And it was all her fault. Fear had stopped her from saying "yes" to Jamison.

On the other hand, why had he run off? Why hadn't he given her a chance to explain? She stared down into her water glass, eyes blurring.

Because she had never given him a reason to stay.

Their salads arrived. After a few bites, Colin said, "I have a question for you. This afternoon you told Eve, 'he's all yours.' Why did you say that?"

She looked at Colin's familiar features. He was a sharp, intelligent man. How couldn't he know? "She's in love with you."

Colin stopped chewing altogether. "What?"

"She loves you," she said gently.

Colin swallowed and took a breath. Slowly, the muscles in his jaw went tight and he put his head in his hands. "Why?" he said through his teeth. "Why did it have to happen like this?"

Concerned, Alexa said, "What do you mean?"

Colin raked his fingers down his face. "I don't want to lose Eve."

"Then don't."

"How can I trust her?"

"Remember, she did help save my life. Eve made a mistake, but she was in an intolerable position, Colin. You can choose to forgive her. I'm sure she'll never make the same mistake again."

"I don't know."

Alexa touched his hand. "Pray about it, Colin. And follow your heart. We all need forgiveness. Eve does, too."

He finally nodded. "I'll talk to her."

❄ ❄ ❄ ❄ ❄

The next few days passed in a fog of pain for Alexa. It was fitting that they landed to low, gray clouds and drizzle in London on Monday afternoon. Monday night she finished the book and printed a draft for Colin to read.

Although she didn't much feel like it, on Tuesday Alexa spent most of the day sightseeing more of London. It was a gray, drizzly day, which matched her mood exactly. She first toured the Tower of London, since her guidebook said to get there early, and she enjoyed seeing the Crown Jewels the most. Then she found the place where the River Thames tour started, and descended the steps to the dock to wait for the next boat to arrive. She especially loved seeing London Bridge, the Houses of Parliament, and the Clock Tower, which was nicknamed Big Ben. She was surprised to learn that Big Ben referred to the fourteen ton bell inside the tower. After that, she took the tube to Harrods, but she wasn't in a shopping mood, and soon decided to return home.

On Wednesday, she set to work incorporating all of the changes Colin had made to the manuscript the day before. Late that night, she printed two copies. One for Colin, and one for the publisher in New York.

Jamison was supposed to be back late that night. More than once, she had flipped open her cell phone and stared at his number that she had input after that horrible Saturday afternoon. But she didn't call. She still wanted to speak to him in person. Alexa missed Jamison desperately. Everything about him. His smile. Him calling her "princess." Life without him was empty and bleak.

Thursday morning, after she had packed up, Alexa brought the boxed manuscript for the publishers down to Colin's office. Still no Jamison. Had he come back? Would she ever see him again? Despair bit through her.

She found Eve in Colin's office. Colin had not fired his secretary, but Alexa knew little more than that. "This goes to the publisher. Will you see that it's sent?"

"Of course." Eve took it and then paused, about to turn away. "By the way, thank you." For the first time, the secretary looked hesitant and uncertain.

"For what?"

"For talking to Colin for me. If it wasn't for you, I'm sure I would be fired."

"He told you that?"

"Yes. I was so wrong about you. I'm sorry...for every horrible thing I said to you."

Alexa smiled. "I'm glad we can finally be friends."

Eve smiled, too. "I'm sure we'll see each other on the book tour."

Colin appeared and put a casual arm around Eve's shoulders. With a blush, the secretary looked up at him and offered a shy smile. He said, "I'm glad my best girls are getting along now."

"We've made peace," Alexa said. "And I see you two have, too."

Colin looked down at Eve. "We're working things out."

Eve blushed again, and tugged away. "I need to get to work."

Colin planted a kiss in her hair and let go. "Alexa." He turned to her. "It's been fun. I'll miss you."

Alexa hugged him. "I'll miss you, too. Thank you, Colin, for everything. I had an amazing time on your tour."

"I'll be in touch." Colin's eyes focused on a point behind her. "Your ride to the airport has arrived." The pleased, self-satisfied note in his voice made Alexa spin.

Jamison. Unsmiling, but there in the flesh. Hungrily, her eyes feasted upon him. He wore his inimitable black; black jeans and black zipped jacket. Expressionless black eyes met hers. "Are you ready?"

Alexa licked suddenly dry lips. She didn't know what to say to him, or how to say all the things she needed to say. He seemed like a remote stranger. "Um...my things are upstairs."

"I'll get them. The car is in the driveway."

"I'll get my purse and laptop."

He headed for the stairs as if he hadn't heard her. Upstairs, if she had hoped for a moment alone with him, she was disappointed. He gathered up her two suitcases and swiftly exited the room. Frustration and misery ached through her.

That ornery man. She would find a way to speak to him before she flew home. And she wouldn't allow him to escape until she did.

Outside, Jamison had already deposited her bags into the trunk. When she appeared, he opened the car door and let her into the backseat. His features still looked stiff. Only his actions were courteous. Reluctantly, Alexa slipped inside. This reminded her of when she had arrived in London—only then, she had chosen to sit in the back, and this time he had directed her to do so.

New hurt burned Alexa, and she looked quickly away, allowing him to shut the door. During the entire ride to the airport, she silently stared out the window, seeing nothing. But she rehearsed what she would say when they stopped.

Jamison made no effort to speak to her, either.

At the airport, he pulled her bags from the car and followed her inside. The long line to the check-in counter spilled outside the delineated walkways. He set down the bags and glanced at her, clearly about to tell her *arrivederci*. Before he could say a word, Alexa blurted, "You never let me tell you what happened."

Jamison's jaw tensed and he looked away, clearly wishing to be elsewhere.

"I am going to tell you," she asserted. "Whether you want to hear it or not, you obstinate man!"

Jamison's eyes flashed fire. "Tell me, then. Whatever's so important."

Alexa heaved a calming breath. "I am not in love with Colin. I *told* you that before. When he kissed me, it caught me by surprise. And then all those other things happened. I ate dinner with him that night so I could tell him the truth."

Unsmiling antagonism simmering in his dark gaze. "And he took it well."

"Colin's fine. I have a feeling Eve will comfort him. I also think he feels more for her than he realizes yet."

"And what does any of this mean to me?"

His antagonism was starting to rub on her nerves. Clearly, he didn't possess any feelings for her at all, except for anger. "I'm sorry, Jamison. But please know I never lied to you."

The line suddenly moved forward ten feet.

Unsmiling, he said, "Need help with your bags?"

"Yes, please." Alexa was about to say goodbye to him forever, and she couldn't stand it. She wanted to keep him with her one more second, and then another, and another.

Jamison moved her bags forward and unzipped his black jacket, obviously warm. He turned to her. "You can take it from here." He said it as a statement, but Alexa heard the faint question in his voice. Chivalrous to the end.

Her gaze dropped, and she noticed the white letters of the T-shirt he wore. "eligro" *Peligroso*. He wore the shirt she had given him. Today, of all days. It must mean something. She raised her eyes. "You're wearing the shirt."

The black gaze held hers for a fathomless minute.

"Why am I a danger to you, Alexa?"

He had been a danger to her heart from the beginning. And now it pulsed, raw and bleeding, inside of her. She bit her lip when the truth dawned on her.

He did not intend to stop her from leaving. Alexa had to accept that they would never have a future together. Deep, visceral pain ripped through her.

She whispered, "You still like it, then?"

He watched her, his dark eyes bleak. "I'll wear it until it's old and worn out, like the one my sister gave me."

"At least you'll remember me."

"I will never forget you, Alexa," he said, unsmiling. "Goodbye."

"Goodbye." Alexa couldn't help herself; she impulsively leaned forward and hugged him. His arms closed around her, fierce and hard, but swiftly released her. Tears seared her eyes, and she quickly stepped back.

She whispered, "Goodbye, Jamison." After the briefest pause, he turned and walked away. A strong, solid man, all in black. She watched his wavy head until it disappeared through the doors and he was outside, lost to her forever. She couldn't stop the tears then. Alexa didn't care who saw her. Pain burned like an unquenchable fire through her soul.

CHAPTER NINETEEN

"You've been moping around here for a week," Beth said, swiping dust off the coffee table.

Alexa sat curled in a fetal position in the recliner. After flying home from London, she had found refuge in her sister's house. Her heart still felt ripped in two bloody halves, but Alexa knew herself well enough to know that she couldn't be alone or she would wallow in misery. Not that she hadn't done the same here, but at least there were people here who loved her.

She looked down and realized she still held the pictures of Jamison that she had printed from her digital camera. The ones in Spain, with colorful Las Ramblas in the background. Hastily, she shoved them into the chair.

"What are you hiding?"

"You're too much a mom."

"Give them up." Beth wiggled her fingers.

Reluctantly, Alexa pulled out the three photos. Beth leaned over her shoulder. "That's Jamison?"

"Yes."

Beth snatched them out of her hand and looked them over carefully. "He's cute, Alexa," she said softly. "Even with all the scowling you made him do. I see you brought out the best in him."

Alexa's eyes filled with tears. With a compassionate look, Beth hugged her. "Call him, sis." She handed the pictures back.

Alexa gazed at the top photo. Jamison was scowling because she had just insinuated he was a dwarf, she remembered. A big fat tear plopped onto it. Hastily, she swiped it off, so it wouldn't be ruined.

"I can't. What would I say?"

"Tell him how you feel."

"I can't! I can't, Beth."

"Why not?"

"Because he doesn't want me!" Alexa choked on a sob and hugged her arms tightly against herself.

"Did he say that?"

"Not exactly. He didn't have to. He told me goodbye, and he didn't look back."

"I think you've got some crossed wires."

"No! We don't," Alexa said fiercely. "One thing that's always been clear between Jamison and me is that we are all wrong for each other."

"You had a fight before you left," Beth guessed.

"Of course! That's all we ever do."

"You mean like Mom and Dad?"

"No. Never like that," Alexa realized. "It was lighter...prickly. A way to protect my heart from him. He's a wonderful man, Beth. He's gentle and kind. He'd never hurt me on purpose." With anguish, she finished, "But it was all just a fairy tale, like I thought from the beginning. None of it was real."

"But I thought Colin was Prince Charming."

"No." Crazy as it was, Jamison had become her knight in shining armor. How had the man she had deemed an elf so long ago morph from being one of the most irritating, incorrigible men she had ever known, into the most irresistible?

She gazed at the picture again. Beth was right, and Alexa had admitted the partial truth to Jamison in Switzerland. He was nice looking. In fact, he was the most handsome man she had ever seen. Colin couldn't hold a candle to him. And how had she ever thought he looked like an elf? It was just self-protection, from the very beginning. He wasn't elf-like at all.

She studied his features, thirsty to memorize every detail. He had a straight nose, with that tiny bump, straight dark brows. Well-cut mouth. Thick, wavy hair—crisp and soft to the touch, she remembered. Straight, even white teeth. Not to mention his hard, muscular body, and his square, well-cut hands that could engulf her own, and hold her so gently.

But more than all the superficialities was the man inside. A man of integrity, honesty, faith, courage...and vulnerability, too. She had never met anyone like him before, and knew she never would again.

Alexa struggled to hold back the burning tears.

Beth said, "You love him, don't you?"

A tear slipped down her face. "Yes." For the first time, Alexa admitted it aloud. "He's not at all what I thought I was looking for in a man." Her thumb brushed his face in the picture. She remembered the texture of his skin. His smile. The heavy-lidded, smoky look in his eyes when he had fed her the chocolate. The burning fire when he kissed her.

"You'll regret it forever if you don't tell him. I'll leave you alone to think." Her sister retreated to the kitchen.

Alexa stared at the picture and thought about her cell phone, cravenly tucked into her pocket. Secretly, she had hoped he would call. He hadn't. She had known that he wouldn't.

Should she call him? Could he possibly want her still? He had been so remote at the airport. *Why,* if he loved her? Why had he let her go? And if he did love her, how could they ever make it work? They had made their forced cohabitation work, one rocky step at a time. Could it work for a lifetime?

She wanted to marry Jamison.

The realization hit her hard.

She gazed at the picture again and tears blurred her eyes. She curled up tighter and pressed the picture to her cheek. "Jamison," she whispered brokenly.

Oh God, please tell me what to do.

❋ ❋ ❋ ❋ ❋

Later that afternoon her cell phone rang, still in her sweat pants pocket. Blood zinged in her veins. Jamison!

Quickly, she flipped it open. "Hello?"

"Alexa, it's Mart." The bodyguard's voice sounded quiet. Ominous.

"Mart!" All sorts of horrible scenarios ran through her head. "What's wrong? Is someone hurt?" Fear cramped her heart, and her next word was only a whisper, "Jamison?"

"No one's injured."

"Thank goodness!" Relieved air whooshed back into her lungs. "Then what is it?"

"What have you done to my buddy, Alexa?"

"Me? To Jamison?"

"You chewed him up and spit him out, didn't you?" Anger hardened Mart's voice.

"I most certainly did not!"

"He's miserable. Does that make you happy?"

"No!"

"Call him. Straighten out whatever's going on between you two. Show some mercy, Alexa! He's no good to Colin or anyone else right now."

"You think *I'm* happy?" her voice broke.

"Fix it, Alexa." His voice gentled. "Fix it now." He cut the connection.

Jamison was miserable? Selfishly, her heart soared at the thought that he might be miserable because of her—because he loved her, and missed her?

And Mart blamed her. How could it be her fault? Jamison had stood there and told her goodbye! He hadn't asked her to stay.

Neither had she offered.

Two stubborn, hurting people, unwilling to admit to each other—or themselves—how they felt about one another.

Could he possibly love her? She loved him. So much so that she ached inside every day, knowing he was half a world away, and she would never see him again. *No.* She reassessed. She more than ached. Her soul felt like it had been sanded and twisted and hung up to dry in a scorching wasteland. Wasn't that what words were for? But even those words couldn't describe the desolate loneliness and grief she felt every minute of the day.

At last, the truth became clear. Once again, she had succumbed to fear. She had assumed, just like she had with Ben so long ago, that Jamison didn't truly want her. She had accepted his rejection of her love before he had been given the opportunity to know how she felt.

Never again. It was the last time she would allow fear to rule her life.

A beep from her phone indicated that she had received a text message. A glance discovered it was her daily Bible verse of the day. Beth had signed her up for the service when she had returned home. It was a gift meant to encourage and cheer her up.

The words seemed picture perfect for today.

"'For I know the plans I have for you,' declares the Lord, 'plans to prosper you and not to harm you, plans to give you hope and a future.'" Jeremiah 29:11

Yes. She had to see Jamison one last time. She had to tell him that she loved him. Afterwards, let the chips fall where they may. A phone conversation would not do. Alexa picked up her phone and booked a flight to London.

❄ ❄ ❄ ❄ ❄

Alexa hurriedly zipped her suitcase shut. Her flight left in three hours. She had to arrive at the airport in plenty of time to get through security. That meant she had to leave in five minutes if she wanted to have the full, two hour check-in period. She couldn't miss this flight. She wouldn't.

Her heart alternately soared and crashed, imaging seeing Jamison again. Would he be happy to see her? Or worse, indifferent, or still angry? Could he possibly want a future with her, or was she crazy for thinking it was a possibility? The logistics of any future with him seemed impossible to figure out. Like where they would live. Would he remain Colin's bodyguard? How could their lives possibly mesh together?

But she was getting ahead of herself. One step at a time. All Alexa knew was that she would go flat out for love. No more licking her wounds and crying her eyes out. It was well past time for action. She would force that stubborn man to hear how much she loved him. Then she would kiss him. Then...who knew what she would do next?

"Alexa," Beth called from the living room.

"I'm coming. Just a minute." Alexa slung her bag over her shoulder and then scooted out of the room, pulling her swaying, giant suitcase behind her. She hustled down the hall and veered left into the living room. The suitcase smashed to the floor.

"Rrrhhh!" she growled, whirling in frustration. She kicked it. "I've a good mind to get rid of you!"

"Taking out your frustration on inanimate objects, princess?" The familiar, deep Italian voice made her freeze. She spun.

"Jamison!" she gasped. Her shoulder bag dropped to the floor. She stared at him. As usual, he wore all black, and he stood next to her grinning sister. "What are you doing here? I was just... I have a plane to catch," she finished weakly.

His intense dark eyes scanned her, as if hungry for the sight of her.

"I'm hoping you'll miss that plane." His melodious voice filled her ears and her heart. She had missed the sound so much! She had missed *him* so much. Her gaze swept over him, thirsty for every detail, and for assurance that he really stood right in front of her, in her sister's house. He wore a black T-shirt, which revealed the corded muscles in his arms, and black jeans.

"What are you *doing* here?" she gasped again.

Beth said, "Aren't you going to greet him nicely, Alexa? He's come a long way to see you."

On rubbery legs, she moved toward him. She reached out and his warm, calloused hands wrapped around hers.

Beth cleared her throat. "I'll leave you two alone. Come on, kids, let's go get ice cream!" Her children whooped, and she herded them speedily out the door.

Alexa barely noticed. She stood where she was, staring into Jamison's intense dark eyes. A bit of uncertainty lurked in them. "Why are you here?" she whispered.

"I came to see you, Alexa."

"Why?"

"Why do you think?"

"But you hate me. Don't you?"

"Never."

Her heart thundered. "Mart told me..."

"Mart called you?" He glanced at the ceiling, as if exasperated.

"He said you were acting like a bear." Well, close enough.

He tugged her closer. She could not look away from the passion in his black gaze. He said, "I spent a lot of time thinking about what you said in London. I was a fool to let you go, Alexa. I need to tell you some things."

"I do, too." She gestured weakly at her bags. "I was on my way to London to talk to you."

"You were going to fly to London, just to see me?" A small smile lifted the corners of his mouth.

"Don't go getting a big head," she warned. Why, oh *why* did he always pull the incorrigible imp out of her?

"You were coming to see me. Why?"

She glanced away for a moment. "I wanted to tell you something." He waited patiently. She frowned. How like him to goad her into hanging her emotions out to dry first.

"You're frowning, princess. Did you plan to come and chew me out?"

"No!" she glared. "You really are an impossible man. I planned to *come*," she said with emphasis, "to tell you exactly what I think of you!"

The black gaze gentled to brown. "And what would that be?"

"You tell me why you're here," she sallied back. "To see your Aunt Pauline? Maybe to visit your alma mater. What reunion would that be? Almost twenty!"

He laughed, and it felt good to her soul to hear it. "You're as prickly as ever, aren't you, princess? Maybe that's why I love you so much." He looked momentarily startled by his admission, but his gaze held hers unwaveringly.

Alexa blinked, and felt like she was going to cry. She whispered, "You love me?"

"I love you, Alexa. You drive me crazy, but I can't live without you."

"I drive you crazy? I'm not sure that's a good thing."

"It means you keep my blood pumping. And under all your prickly thorns is a sweet, loving woman."

She blinked back her tears. "Jamison, when you left me at the airport, I felt like my heart ripped right in half. I have never felt such pain in my life."

"I'm sorry. I was hurting, and I was afraid to trust you... I was a complete and utter fool." His hands tightened around hers. "Why didn't you tell me how you felt?"

"Because you were mad at me! I thought you hated me, and you'd never trust me again. I didn't see how *we* could ever be possible." She brushed the tears from her eyes. She bit her lip hard, to stop the tears. "I thought I'd never see you again." She gave a mighty sniff.

"And that matters to you?" he asked quietly.

"Of course it matters to me, you exasperating, incorrigible, ...wonderful man! *I love you!*"

"You love me." He smiled then, a big one, flashing his white teeth. "Even though I don't fit your criteria?"

"I love you because *nothing* about you fits my criteria. I think my criteria were pretty boring, to be honest." Suddenly, she couldn't stand to be with him another minute without touching him still more. She pulled her hand free and touched his jaw. His stubble scratched into her sensitive fingertips. "I love you so much, Jamison." Her voice broke. "I felt like I was going to die from missing you."

"Alexa." His fingers plunged into her hair and he kissed her thoroughly. Alexa slipped her arms around his neck and kissed him back with all of the passion and love scorching inside her. He was here. She couldn't believe it. And he loved her.

After several more long, lingering kisses, he pulled back. Heat burned in his black gaze. "I think we'd better cool it."

She found his hands again and held them tight. "What's going to happen to us? Are you going to stay in Europe?"

"Yes. Will you move there and be with me?"

"I won't live in sin, if that's what you're asking."

He chuckled, deep in his chest. "No. That is not what I'm asking you."

"Then what are you proposing, Jamison Jethro?" She tried to look severe.

"I am proposing you marry me, and put me out of my misery. Or maybe that would be the beginning of it..."

"Jamison!" She made to punch him, but instead her fingers slid across his stomach, tickling him instead.

Sudden heat blazed in his eyes and he caught her hand. "Don't start that now, Alexa, because we can't finish it."

She leaned into him. "How long will it be before we can finish it?"

His gaze found her mouth. "As soon as my mother can put together a proper Italian wedding."

"Jamison..."

"She made me promise, that day we visited them."

Alexa gasped. "She knew? Even then?"

"Yes. Even when I didn't think there was a chance in the fiery furnace you'd ever fall for an elf like me."

"You are not an elf! And besides, he was kind of cute. But not as cute as you."

"Thanks, Alexa." To her shock, a black velvet box appeared in his hand. He opened it, and inside sparkled a diamond ring, reflecting all the brilliant colors of pure light. Princess cut, of course.

She gasped again, fingers pressed to her mouth.

His warm brown eyes smiled at her. "Marry me?"

"Oh, Jamison. Yes! I can't think of anything I want more." She flung her arms around his neck and held him tightly. "Just promise me one thing," she said, her voice muffled.

"What?"

"That our sons will have your looks and *my* height, and our daughters will have my looks and *your* height."

He grinned. "I promise you we'll work at it until we get it right."

"That sounds like a proposition I can agree to. And..."

Jamison kissed her, and whatever she had meant to say flew right out of her head.

He murmured against her lips, "I could get used to winning arguments this way."

She mumbled, "In your dreams, Jethro... I have plenty more to say." But she smiled in satisfaction when he kissed her again.

The End

"I sought the LORD, and He answered me;
He delivered me from all my fears."
Psalm 34:4

About the Author

Jennette Green has always had a passion for writing. She wrote her first story over thirty years ago, and her first romance novel, *The Commander's Desire*, was published in 2008. It was given the accolades of "Top Pick" novel and "Reader's Favorite Hero for 2009."

Jennette loves to travel with her husband and children, and particularly likes long walks along the ocean, dreaming up new stories.

She loves to hear from her readers.
You can write to Jennette at jennette@jennettegreen.com or visit her website at www.jennettegreen.com.

LaVergne, TN USA
13 August 2010
193236LV00001B/2/P